HUNTER

HUNTER

Kyle Michel Sullivan

KMSCB, Buffalo, NY
Published 2020 by KMSCB

Acknowledgements

Thanks to Vicki JH and Sue B for their help in keeping the formatting clean, the spelling and grammar correct, and assuring the story makes sense.

Other books by this author:

General:
The Alice '65
The Vanishing of Owen Taylor
David Martin
The Lyons' Den
Bobby Carapisi

Adult titles:
The Beast in the Nothing Room
Underground Guy
Rape in Holding Cell 6
Porno Manifesto
How To Rape A Straight Guy

Out of Print:
NYPD Blues

Table of Contents

HUNTER

Book One
"When I go Hunting..."

ONE

Call me Hunter.

And picture me giggling at myself as I write that. Not that I've ever actually read *Moby Dick*. It's just one of those little pop-culture touchstones that everybody knows about and is just too damn cute not to play with.

So Hunter it is, because that's who...and what...I am.

Oh, you might wonder, what is a *Hunter*? It's whoever finds and brings you whatever is needed, wanted or desired. And we're not talking about the mundane things soccer moms or breadwinners or anyone unimportant like them go shopping for; those creatures are too civilized and caught up in societal control. No, I am today's prowling beast, unchained by any constraints, hired to bring something specific home to my client.

And I love it. Love every bit of it. Love the name. The game. How the money came. Even love the fame...or in-fame.

Wait...is that a word? Is that how infamy formed? I should look it up, I guess. But truth is, I don't care; I'm having fun.

To clarify, I am not one of those numb-nuts who thinks taking a shot at a buck or bear from a hidden burrow makes him big-bad-butch and manly. Nor am I what you might call a *symbolic* one, who seeks to serve wealth, fortune and power with fresh employees for governments and societies and corporations to chew up and spit out like well-used wads of bubble gum. Nope, I'm just your typical, everyday capitalist who figured out he could make some serious cash by hunting, capturing and selling men to other men...and a few women.

Just in case you didn't notice, my specialty is men.

And not just any men. We're talking twenty to thirty-five years old, damn good-looking, and *nothing* underage. Period. Not because of moral objections; I learned long ago that morality is just a religious doctrine used to keep people in their place, even as those who claim to believe in it ignore it. Rather like the Catholic Church, when it protected its priests as they raped little boys and girls. That they were aided and abetted by so many different systems of justice, it's like the rules didn't exist, for them. It's almost funny, how blatant it was.

No, it's just that if an adult male vanishes, no matter what their age, it's halfway assumed they just walked away to another life and may eventually return home to their family. So long as no dead body is found. But when children disappear the media takes major notice, and that is dangerous to little hunters, like me. In fact, you even have to be careful about pretty blond women and young white males. The news makes sure that everyone cares about them and uses their disappearance to work up ratings and fear and panic. Especially if they're well-off and cute. But any other ethnic group or even hair color?

Meh, no ratings to be had, there.

Of course, the first thought that'll come to your mind is, *Hunting men? How awful! You're talking about slavery! EW!*

Well, duhh. That's why I've been so successful. I do what others don't. I've gotten away with a lot of shit considered immoral, illegal, inexcusable, and not even nice because I just plain do not care.

I do play it safe and never meet with my clients. I have a...well, let's just call him a *coordinator* who hands me their requisition and pays me a fee, plus expenses, to do the job. And we're not talking piddly amounts of money, here. Stealing a man is neither easy nor cheap. But the more cash you got, the better man you can get and the pricier lawyers and CPAs you can use to make it all nice and legit. And since I have a subterranean reputation as being one of the best at getting whoever you want when you want him, I'm the go-to guy for guys.

Like the job I'm currently on. One of my clients vacationed in Rio over the winter and got a real hard-on for a young man he saw on Copacabana Beach. He snapped a photo with his phone and sent his assistant down with an offer, which obviously was *not* one that could not be refused. Neither was the second, nor the third. Apparently, that made him so obsessed with having the lad, he offered a whole thirty thousand dollars for him to be taken.

Plus expenses, of course.

When the coordinator contacted me, I laughed at both the money offered and the client's stupidity. First off, his assistant knows about this obsession, and assistants are notorious as gossips. Second, it's almost guaranteed the object of his desire joked with friends and family about the fag who tried to buy him into bed, so if he just vanishes, that is going to come up. Third, while it was Brazil, which places a lower than average value on human life (and had recently proven to be a nice hunting ground), even if he was from one of the poorest favelas, the Rio cops might sense some extortion was possible and go looking too deep. Blackmail can be a greater motivator than merely being concerned about law-breaking or protecting for your fellow man.

Fourth and most important, the piddly-assed payment the client offered. My coordinator wouldn't even have bothered referring it to me except, as he put it, the guy had been a long-time client and never once argued about price, before. His suggestion was to do it as a goodwill gesture...and make up the cost through expense charges and on future orders the client would probably place.

I shrugged and agreed, even though it sounded wrong. No particular reason for my wariness; I just have this little warning bell that goes off in my gut when something's not quite right about a deal, and it's saved me more than a few times. But we'd grown to trust each other as much as someone can, in this business. He knew I was careful and quick and only would transport top quality merchandise, and he'd had my back a couple of times.

So I got the photo through a special service, on my phone; it's got the best encryption. It wasn't a great picture. Barely good enough to show the guy was tallish. Good form to his legs and an okay ass. A buff chest and flat belly.

Hair where hair should be and long on his head. Not much body-fat. What little I could see of his face hit me as sort of common, with deep-set eyes and a hawk-like nose, and a beard, which I tend to shy away from. I wouldn't have spent thirty bucks on him. But to each his own.

Now let me share a couple things about me before we go further. First off, I'm an Air Force brat, born thirty-two years ago in San Antonio, Texas. Second, I'm gay and was even before I was shown the meaning of life by an Airman First Class when dad was stationed in Spain. Third, I have no family thanks to point number two becoming a major bone of contention with both the dad and the mom and the church they worship. They and my siblings, of whom I have three, are ensconced somewhere in the Midwest, but there has been zero contact for the last fourteen years. Suits us both.

The last and most important point is, I love dick and I am not shy about it. I prefer them cut but it's not a deal-breaker. In fact, I don't care if the buy's black, white, brown, pink or purple polka-dotted, if his looks hit me right he gets a blow job like he's never had before...then I fuck him in ways he didn't know were possible. And if he's really good, he gets to fuck me.

Of course, I can't do that without being good-looking, myself. Floppy brown hair (the only part of me that's straight). Five-ten. One-ninety-five, all solid and formed just right, and kept that way with the oldie-but-goodie Air Force Workout. Did wrestling and Aikido up through high school, and I cannot tell you how many conquests those brought me. I'm told my face is nice and I'm not fool enough to disagree, and I know my own dick is above average.

The reason I'm mentioning this is because when I'm walking down the street, all you're going to see is just another guy. A little attitude, sure, and not bad-looking, but hardly a threat.

Which was my cover; hard to get scared around a guy who looks normal.

Anyway, my coordinator referred me to Vinicius, a man he knew in a Favela near the airport. I hopped on down to Rio to meet with him. Make plans. The usual shit. He had one of his men, a bulky character in loose black clothing that made him look bulkier, meet me at the airport with a placard that had my name on it. Like a livery driver...just in a Jaguar SUV.

Man, how cool was that?

He drove me up tight, twisty streets to a compound that was twice the size of the apartment block, next to it. Pink stucco walls encircled it and it was filled with the whisper of thick green trees instead of traffic noises. Guards were positioned at not only the gate but each corner, like a castle.

Proof money can buy peace if not happiness.

The house had whitewashed walls, black painted windows and doors, and stucco tiles on the roof. Before it was a courtyard that was the epitome of elegance and cool. Inside were flagstone floors topped by thick Persian carpets...and some of the most uncomfortable couches and chairs I'd ever sat in. Not a good place to have a business meeting.

Vinicius was a foul little toad, with eyes like a chimp and a jackal's

3

smile, who wore casual white everything and looked Dr. Evil in it. I didn't even like being in the same room with him. But he had the where-with-all to help me, so I laid out the deal and showed him the photo.

He recognized the guy! A musician and model named Thiago Belo. He was twenty-four and had a couple of records out. Acted in a Telenovela. Modeled Speedos and designer briefs. Hounded by men, women and media, alike. Hell, even dogs seemed to think he was cool, judging from some photos Google was kind enough to bring up. Hundreds of them, as many without the beard as with.

However, I finally got an idea as to why my client was so fixated. This guy...oh my god! The first image was of him crossing a beach in that male-model-strut, wearing a nice, tight Speedo of swirling colors, and was he ever built for it! Thighs and calves in perfect proportion. Hips at the perfect width. Soft hair swirling over perfectly formed pecs touched by golden nips. Arms to die for. He had a tattoo over one shoulder and above one ankle, both of which had looked like shadows in the original shot, and his crotch had obviously been airbrushed to minimize how nice and full it probably was, without really minimizing it. What was even better was his smile. I caught some headshots sans beard, and between hazel eyes surrounded by thick lashes and cheekbones that emphasized his perfect white teeth as he grinned into the camera, he'd have given the sun a run for its glory.

Now to anybody else, this sort of high-profile victim would send them scurrying back into their cubby hole crying *it's not worth the money*. But I'm a Hunter. Now all I saw in getting to Thiago was the challenge. The joy of capturing my prey as easily as I could.

Oh, and making sure I not only got away with it but was even better-paid.

So first thing I did was renegotiate the price. If the client wanted this guy so damn bad, he was gonna have to up the ante. I'd snagged the lead-singer of a fairly-famous boy band out of Azerbaijan for an oligarch, and the price for that had wound up a cool one-point-six million. Euros, not dollars. Thiago was only really big in Brazil...well, southern South America...so I quoted the same price, with a ten percent discount. Plus expenses.

The moment the client knew who he was getting, he agreed.

That set off my warning bell, again.

But the Coordinator was ecstatic. "He all but squealed," he said, when he called. He had this fey voice that was guaranteed to irritate so I tried to keep conversations to a minimum. "He's now gone impatient, so I've added twenty percent to the expected expenses."

"What you wanna bet he already knew who Thiago was?" I snarled. That was my first thought...that the cheap-assed bastard was trying to get us to do a premium job for a nothing price.

"I wouldn't put it past him. Some men will always try to buy a Rolls for the cost of a Chevy."

Man, I love the one-percent of the one-percent. They want you to think that numbers mean nothing to them, but DJT taught me they'll screw you for any money they can. So what you do is double the price you want, get half of it up front, and always have insurance, in case they try to fuck you over. Which is what I did. Then I strolled the Copacabana, enjoying the lovely lads in their Speedos, bringing a couple back to my room for some fun, waiting till the cash was in the bank before working up a plan.

Once I'd verified it and checked with my super-duper IT-guy the money could not be withdrawn, I had my second meeting with Vinicius. Truth is, I already had a plan worked out; I just needed his backup in it.

We spoke in English. While I knew Spanish, Portuguese was just different enough to where it could've made for miscommunication, and that is *not* something you want at this stage of the hunt. I gave him a song and dance about Thiago having knocked up a client's daughter and they wanted to make him marry her. I made sure to shake my head at the *selfishness and immorality of today's kids.* And I caught more than a hint of old-man jealousy against bright youth in the bastard's eyes. Which I never would have expected from him; he seemed so happy to be grabbing his maids' asses as they served us Brahma Maltzbiers and plates of Pastels de Queijo. Jesus, his hands went places that would've got him killed in the States, and the things he'd yell at his servants. Shit, I've have cut his throat.

"I will need two good strong young men," I told him, keeping my English good so he could understand every word. "They will act as bodyguards. Also a private jet and two pilots of my choosing. I prefer they speak English, but Spanish is okay."

"Where will they go?" Vinicius asked.

"Recife. There, he will be handed over to my client."

He nodded, eyeing me. "They don't handle this in Rio?"

"They are not as established in Rio as they are in Recife."

Meaning, no trustworthy contacts with the Rio cops.

Vinicius sneered. "I think I may know what family this is."

Okay, that was a stupid thing to say. All I did was take in a deep breath and murmur, "No, I do not believe you do."

The toad's brain finally caught up with his mouth and he said, "You are right; I am thinking of someone else."

"The jet must be in good condition and very comfortable, and the pilots need to be young and healthy," I said. "No drugs. No possibility of medical issues."

He shrugged. So far I hadn't asked for all that much. "What more do you need?"

"A nice new Suburban or Escalade. Expedition. Whatever. Big, black and gleaming."

"When?"

"Tuesday morning. Seven AM."

"That is in two days."

"I know. Have the men meet with me at my hotel, tonight, and we will go over my plan."

"On a Sunday?"

"Oh, are they Catholic?"

He snorted with full derision. "Who is not, in this country?" Then he nodded. "I will do this."

I paid him up front; that was understood. I didn't worry about him trying to screw me; word would get around and then no one would trust him.

Problem was, after this job he would never trust me, again, but that couldn't be helped. I always have to have insurance, and sometimes people just don't understand what it costs.

Anyway, last Friday, I'd called Thiago's modeling agency and pretended I was a reporter for *La Prensa Verdad* and could only speak Spanish. I'd managed to learn from a sweet little receptionist that he had a photo shoot coming up in Brasilia. He was flying there by private jet, Tuesday morning, and had a car arranged for 7:15. She thought I wanted to send photographers to snap pictures of him leaving for another of his glamorous jobs.

It was so cute.

So I met Reymon (*Rey* was okay) and William (*not* Bill or Guillermo, thank you) in my room. Rey was dark-haired, solid and sharp. He looked like he could bench three-fifty with no trouble, and he fit neatly into his black hoody and joggers. He seemed like a happy little bear cub. Didn't hurt that he had a lovely semi-bubble-butt I really wanted to dive into.

William was what the locals politely referred to as Misto, with light-coffee skin, sleek muscles made glorious by a form-fitting shirt and tight jeans, clean good looks, elegant eyes and thick lips that never once came close to smiling. My thought was, he'd be fucking gorgeous if he ever did. Of course, he also had a wedding band on one finger, so that may have been the reason for lack of smiles.

They caught on to my game plan real quick, both of them knowing Spanish as well as Portuguese, and going to Recife was like a joy ride for Rey; he had a cousin there. I suggested he invite the family for dinner.

What they didn't know was, I'd snuck a couple photos of them as they entered my room. After they left, I sent them off to the Coordinator. He came straight back a decent offer for William, so long as he was a virgin to men. I told him I'd check. As for Rey, he said he'd let me know before we reached Recife.

Never hurts to have a little more income on the side.

Vinicius found a Beechcraft turbo-prop job that just needed one pilot and sent me photos of three prospects to fly it. I wasn't crazy about this; I'd specified a jet because I wanted to get there faster, not whenever. But he insisted it was the only thing he could get on such short notice and without leaving a paper trail.

The youngest pilot offered looked to be about thirty, had a square face with cheekbones and a jaw to match, a bright smile and dark eyes that promised more than a little fun. He also had a light beard that suited him so well, I hoped he still had it.

There was a private airfield in Bara Da Tijuca, where Thiago's private jet was to leave from. Our plane would also be waiting behind a particular hanger, ready to take off.

Everything was falling into place, neatly enough, but almost like it was too neat. I still couldn't shake the nagging sense something was wrong about it. But...a deal's a deal, and it was too late to back out.

Thiago had a condominium overlooking the Copacabana, a big new building with a couple of doormen and reception that were probably armed and dangerous. Photographers were always camped around, waiting for that perfect shot, many of them with motorbikes parked nearby. He also would have a publicist and manager and his own bodyguards with him, so we needed to make sure they were separated from him and no press would follow.

Easy. Let his sense of safety do all the work.

Tuesday morning, William, Rey and I were parked in our Escalade just half a block from the condo entrance, watching a neat new minivan drive up. Five minutes later, Thiago's six-person entourage spilled out of the building, followed by him a minute behind them, a bag slung over one shoulder...and looking even hotter in person. Hair long and thick and flopping in his face. A touch of scruff around his chin. Form-fitting polo shirt tucked into tight jeans and wearing sneakers. Clean muscular arms. He was the epitome of a young male model.

And he was totally focused on his phone.

The photographers went crazy shooting him and shouting things to him, in Portuguese. He ignored them.

I was behind the wheel, Rey was in the front passenger seat and William was in the back, all of us in suits...and shit, did both men look good in them. It was damned hard to keep from grabbing Rey's promising crotch, so I had to distract myself by starting the car and asking what the photographers were saying.

William sneered, in Spanish, *"They call him names to make him angry. Get them better pictures to sell. Assholes."*

"Part of the deal," said Rey, not chuckling.

I shook my head. I also took note of a couple of the cuter paparazzi. Tight guys in tight jeans with tight hair and tight expressions. For fun, I calculated how much I could charge for them. Best I could come up with was twenty-two thousand; not enough to waste my time on.

Unless it was for fun; one of them did have a nice pair of legs topped off by a sweet ass and fat crotch, so...

So...Thiago's minivan started away, breaking the spell, and the photographers ran for their bikes. I drove the Escalade up onto the sidewalk where they had parked. Rey lowered his window and sprayed them with Mace. All of them. Then we zoomed after the minivan as they cursed us in words needing no translation. Now they'd think we were more of Thiago's guards.

The drive to Bara Da Tijuca was pretty easy, with traffic thick in the other direction. We passed the minivan, and even though its windows were frosted could we just see that Thiago was in the middle seat, to the left, still focused on his phone.

We reached the air field minutes ahead of the minivan. A man who could get us onto the tarmac was waiting to take the wheel. I stopped and got in the back, next to William, *accidentally* grabbing his thigh, just to test it. Oh, did my heart give a flip. I managed to say, *"Perdón,"* before he could get too angry, and I began to wonder how much he'd bring if he wasn't a virgin.

Sometimes I'm willing to take a price cut if the trade-off is right.

We drove on in and the minivan arrived a couple minutes later. It whipped past security and headed over to a Lear jet that was warming up. Its door was already open and a lovely woman was stepping out, in a blue uniform.

Now came the difficult part. You can't plan for how people get out of a car. Would Thiago get out on the right side? Use the door on the left to get out? Would his driver and bodyguards be out, first? Where would they congregate to guide him into the jet? Would they feel safe enough to let their guard down? There was no telling.

Vinicius had told me our plane would be hidden around the side of a hangar a couple hundred feet away; not far but not that close when you're kidnapping someone. So we had to play it by ear and hope we got lucky.

The van passed us and stopped...and Thiago slid his door back before the driver opened his! We were in luck!

"¡Vamos!" Rey snapped and our new driver gunned the engine. We zoomed up to block Thiago against the minivan and William popped the side door open. Before he could even think about what was happening, we'd yanked him inside to land face-down across William's and my laps. Then Rey sprayed Thiago's driver and bodyguards with Mace as we drove off.

Thiago howled and fought us. Little shit was strong and knew some kind of martial arts, but it's hard as hell to do Aikido in the back of an Escalade. I helped William bind his hands with packing tape, and that's all we had time for. We whipped around to the turbo-prop a second later.

I jumped out and wrapped my arm around Thiago's mouth then yanked him from the Escalade. William followed as Rey ran around to join us, then the car took off. We carried him into the plane, fighting and howling for help and spitting at us, and threw him on a long seat as I cried. *"¡Vamos la!"*

Rey closed the door as the plane started away. Through a window I could see Thiago's entourage racing for us, wiping at their eyes, but in moments we were heading down the runway. The pilot had been told to file a flight plan for São Paulo then fly low to the ground along the coast to a landing strip near Recife, so I wasn't worried about them tracking us. Not yet.

Even bound, Thiago nearly broke free of Reymon and William before I piled in, using my wrestling background to pin him down till they could wind tape around his ankles. Damn, he was solid, and his cursing and struggling and rubbing his crotch against mine got me harder than you can even imagine.

Then I let the guys manhandle him as I got out a kit with a syringe of Ketamine and slammed it into his bicep. I'd bought the vial from Vinicius and knew the right amount to inject into him. He shrieked and I'm fairly certain the words he used were meant to send me, my mother, my father, my aunts and uncles and brothers and sisters and cousins and friends all to hell, he was so angry. His shirt had been torn completely open and his jeans were halfway down his hips, revealing the loveliest pecs and sexiest little treasure trail ever as he squirmed and fought the effects of the drug...but soon he was just lying there. And we were en route to Recife.

Cool, we should be there in time for lunch.

*****

William and Rey took off their suit jackets and undid their ties. Their shirts were stuck to their skin, from sweat, revealing both wore those brutally sexy wife-beaters.

"*Who knew a boy like that could be such a fighter?*" Rey asked as he mopped his face with a bandana.

William just nodded and did the same.

I looked at Thiago, lying on the bench, softly moaning and muttering, his chest gently rising, the flow of his hair swirling around an oval pair of nicely tanned tits, his hips only half-surrounded by a pair of Unicos and those jeans, his legs elegantly formed. Fuck, at that moment I was so glad I'd worn tight briefs; no need to spook the natives with a very visible erection...and it would have been impossible to miss.

I opened and then handed Rey and William a couple of beers to relax...which they would; I'd snuck a roofie into each one. Then I slipped up to speak with the pilot, to give the drugs time to work.

Well...he wasn't the pilot I was expecting. His face was similar and he had the beard, but he was thinner and tighter, almost to the point of wiry. I mentioned it and he shrugged.

"That is my cousin, Carlos," he told me in lightly accented English. "He received another job with a regular client so asked me to take this."

"Did he check with Vinicius?" I asked, wary.

"Did he need to? I can fly this plane better than he. And I have been to the field you want to land at."

"Many times?"

He cast me a wary eye. "Why do you ask?"

I chuckled. If he had answered me, I'd have known he was full of shit. Besides, it was too late to do anything about it, now. We were flying about three-hundred feet over the ocean along a lovely coastline of sharp black rocks pounded by white-capped waves. Beyond them were rolling green hills. The sky was clear and the ride was smooth, so obviously this guy knew what he was doing. All I could do was shrug and say, "Okay."

I still managed to sneak a photo of him.

Then I asked, "What's your name?"

"Jose." And he said it in a way that let me know it wasn't.

"Okay, *Jose*, I'll need you to stay in the cockpit until I tell you it's clear."

He grinned and it softened his sharp features. "I know how this works."

I chuckled, thinking, *Wanna bet?*

I slipped back into the cabin to find William and Rey passed out. I took in the glorious view of three damn good-looking men lying everywhere, one with legs akimbo, and sighed. I sent the photo of Jose off to my Coordinator. He came back with an immediate, *Yes, two-fifty. May have someone for bear cub. Got full body photo?*

Rey was lying crawled up in his seat, so I carefully lowered his legs and crossed them at the ankle then bound them with packing tape. I wrapped his wrists, as well, and put his arms above his head. Next I unbuttoned his shirt and pulled his wife-beater up over his nips to reveal a spectacular set of hairy pecs before undoing his pants to show he was wearing a pair of cheap striped briefs. I played with his dick and balls, through the fabric, and soon he got hard.

I was damned close to losing control at the glorious feel of him. Form of him. Not a long dick but a fat one that begged to be sucked. Balls on the tight side, though I had a feeling with a little work they'd loosen up.

So I fondled and caressed and stroked and massaged him till he was fully erect, then I revealed his amazing dick, pulled the foreskin back and shot a photo of him, full body.

Then I slipped my hand into the briefs and between his legs to press my pinkie into his rectum. He squirmed and moaned, automatically. Damn, he was tight, meaning he was a virgin. I don't care one way or the other, but my clients? Shit, that could double his value. Dammit, now I was wishing we'd grabbed that cute photographer and brought him along for me to fuck.

I gave a long, tragic sigh and wrapped Rey back up in his clothes, washed my hands and sent the photos off, adding, *Virgin. No takers? He's mine.* Then I deleted it. Last of all, I wrapped tape around his mouth, as well. When he woke up, I knew he'd become very vocal.

I shifted my focus to William, who was already spoken for. Lying with his seat practically horizontal, hands folded across his belly, legs slightly akimbo, he was the epitome of smooth masculine perfection. In sleep his face took on a gentleness that added to his elegant beauty. I bound him like I had Rey, then undid his pants and slipped into his CK boxer-briefs to finger his rectum and my test turned out the same — too tight to have ever been fucked.

Of course the truth is, using your pinkie to check out a man's virginity is anything but foolproof, but it gave us cover to make the claim and oh, can it be fun. Especially if they're awake when you do it.

The thing was, looking at William...I couldn't believe he hadn't been propositioned at least a dozen times a week. This was fucking Rio, where pansexual is a way of life. For the right money any quy'll give it up, and William would have been worth the right money. Plus, if he'd been in prison he'd have lost it, early on, he was so pretty. No need to prove viability of his dick; the client hadn't even asked...though I did take a look. Not quite as nice as Rey's, but hardly without value.

Finally, there was Thiago. Virginity hadn't been discussed for him. Besides, I had a pretty good idea if I tried him out in any way, the client would make a fuss. Guys like him can tell if you've sampled their merchandise, and he could have used that to refuse the last of the payment. So I just caressed his face. And neck. Shoulders. Pecs. Nips. Arms. Abs. Hips. Crotch. Thighs. Calves. Back up to his nips...such lovely nips...and the hair gently swirling around his pecs and down his belly. I decided, *If they don't offer at least two for Rey, I'll keep him for myself.*

But halfway to Recife, I got notified Rey was bringing in three-seventy-five. Shit. Oh, well. Maybe I'd go back to Rio and find that cute photographer with the great ass and have my fun. Except that would take too long and be dangerous, considering what I was about to pull. So I just had myself a beer, watched the glorious Brazilian coast fly past, and relaxed till Jose called back, "Landing in twenty minutes."

Perfect timing, two of the three were just beginning to wake.

TWO

I suppose by now you're probably wondering how I got into this business. After all, aren't kidnapping and slavery illegal in the Twenty-first Century? Yes, they are, even in the post-Covid days. So are prostitution, gun running, drug smuggling, rape, murder, and the writing of fraudulent mortgages, yet those all still happen and people get away with them. So long as you have the right contacts and a nice bank account to back you up, all of which I now possess and none of which I had when I first got into the business.

The fact is, I could easily have wound up being taken like Rey, Thiago or William if I hadn't been paying attention.

And caught a little luck.

You see, I was mixed up with a guy named Trax, an ex-marine with a rock-hard-hotter-than-fuck Marine body, a dick built for porn and an ass built for breaking every one of the seven deadly sins. I was nineteen and he was twenty-six, and if he'd set out to kill the Pope I'd probably have gone along with him, I was so lost in lust and blind to reality.

Then he and I got busted for carting a few bricks of hash across the border in Nogales. In his car. Packed around the spare tire. Which I told him was stupid, but he'd sworn it wouldn't matter and said I was being dumb and paranoid, and horny little me was blind-idiot enough to go along with it. I sort of got lost in the idea that we were gonna smoke some hash and fuck all night. Hell, even in jail I was thinking, *Okay, once lights're out we can still have fun.*

Dumb. Just...dumb.

Because once we were booked and about to be carted off to our cells, he got to whispering with a Sheriff's deputy. Next thing I knew, he's gone and I'm left to take the rap. Nobody'd even heard of a guy named Trax getting busted with me, and it turned out the car was stolen from a poor little Mexican lady in Sáric. How the hell it got Arizona plates while in Mexico was never explained. So I wound up stuck in jail, unable to meet bond thanks to a nothing defense by the public defender assigned to my case.

That's where my education started. As noted, I was gay and I didn't fit the fem mold, so I was able to pick out a muscle-bound dude who was fairly attractive, quietly offer him my oral and anal services in exchange for protection, and spend my time listening and learning.

First thing I found out? My good-lovin' buddy'd been in, before, and bought his way out with yet another guy's ass. The motherfucker.

Well, *father*fucker, really, but you understand.

Seems the junkyard dog Sheriff of this county had a sideline going for men who liked to fuck guys on the down-low. Some good-looking kid gets into trouble? He could buy his way out of a record by letting that Sheriff introduce him to a high-roller and spend a night or two or five allowing the pervert do whatever he wanted. All depended on the severity of the crime. And all that got hurt was a little pride...and maybe some sexual identity.

Oh, and an STD or two.

Except word was, a couple of young, good-looking guys had vanished, completely. Both of them illegals. The feeling was someone got carried away and they were buried somewhere in the desert. But I learned a long time ago nobody in law enforcement really cared about a couple of Latino guys dying. Not in AZ.

After two weeks of info-gathering and sucking off my muscle queen and riding his dick, I let it slip to that same guard that *I was available*. I got taken to the Sheriff's office to be checked out, but I knew he'd go for it; as I said, I was young, hung, and in damn good shape.

So that Friday, my hands were cuffed behind me, I was blindfolded, thrown in the back of a van, and driven to a high class Phoenix penthouse; I could tell this by how quietly the elevator went straight up from the garage and how it opened straight into the place, because I wasn't taken through another door. They left the handcuffs on, and I was told to keep my back to the elevator and never remove the blindfold. I did as they said...and stood there for what seemed like hours before the elevator opened, behind me, and I was grabbed by a very strong man. Whose very strong hands groped me and mauled my ass and nips and bit at my neck and held me in a tight embrace as he shoved his still-clothed body against mine.

I struggled, at first, because I was startled. Thanks to the handcuffs and his tight hold on me, I couldn't get the wrestling moves I needed to break free, and I think he liked that. I heard what were probably grunts of pleasure from him as I tried to twist away...and I could feel he had a nice fat dick that was more than ready for me, tucked away in his pants.

He dragged me down a hall then threw onto a massive bed and tied my feet, then he groped and mauled me for several more minutes before tearing open my shirt and pinching my nips then yanking my pants down my legs and diving onto my dick to give me a...well, an okay blow job.

To be clear, I was enjoying the shit out of this. Trax and I had manhandled each other on many an occasion, adding to the heat. So when this guy ripped open my briefs, I had a woody like you wouldn't believe. Which he really seemed to like. Which may be why he spent ten minutes on my dick and balls, alone. Wasn't even trying to edge me; just felt like he was having fun. And like I said, he wasn't bad at it; he just wasn't the best I've had. That honor was still held by Trax, tho' that Airman in Spain had come in a close second, pun intended.

I still sort of fake-tried to get away from him and let out grunts and whimpers of "What you doin'?" Even though I knew exactly what he was up to. I also held back from firing, just to prolong the beauty of the moment. But finally I couldn't control it any longer and shot my wad all over him. In his mouth. On his face. Back on me. Shit, it was glorious, and I actually heard him chuckle.

Then he ripped every article of clothing off me and flipped me over and rammed himself into me with a minimum of grease, and pseudo-raped me. That was rougher than Trax had ever been, and he was slamming me harder than Trax ever had, but after I got over the initial shock and pain, I loved the feel of him slipping in and out and in and out, almost withdrawing but not quite, before shoving back in like a rutting pig.

Didn't even last five minutes before he slapped my ass and fired into me and all but howled like some fucking dog would howl at the moon. It was something of a let-down. Trax could go for an hour, no matter what kind of tricks I used on him. But this guy seemed happy. He caressed my ass...and I think he even kissed it.

Then he uncuffed me, whispering, "I'll call when I'm about to come up. Blindfold on. Cuffs not needed. I got you all weekend. Play along, and you'll be fine."

That's when he got off the bed and left. I don't think he'd even got undressed.

He took me seven times over the course of that weekend, and I loved it every time. I mean, granted, he wasn't the worst at fucking, and I had access to any food I wanted, any booze I wanted (even though I was not legal) and had video games and cable and a workout bench and bathroom as big as most hotel rooms, with a killer shower, and sheets made of thousand-thread-count cotton and a selection of clothes to wear to be ripped off me, each time.

His voice would come in over an intercom, tinny and growly, to let me know what game we were playing. I'd dress accordingly. One occasion was even in a CHiPs uniform with boots that fit! Bastard wouldn't let me keep them.

Man...I grew to appreciate what money could buy.

What was best? Even though I always had to wear that stupid blindfold so I could never actually *see* him (I wanted out so no fucking way was I not following the orders), and even though he kept his voice minimal and in a low register so I couldn't tell how he sounded, I found out who he was.

It was during our last little scenario. He told me to wear boxer-briefs, shorts and a wife-beater, thick socks and tennies, and be working out. So I did it, despite the fucking blindfold, as he snuck up and pounced on me and tied me to the bench then began ripping everything off in stages before sucking me into near oblivion. I got the feeling he wanted me to suck him, too, but didn't trust me, even though I swore to him I'd love to do it...and I really did want to.

As I said, I love dicks.

Instead, he flipped my legs in the air and shoved a butt plug into my ass. It was attached to electric wires, or something, because it sent jolts through me (which was an all-new experience and *not* something I took pleasure in). Then he applied a back massager to the head of my dick till I almost came before he took it away and smacked it around. Next he whipped my ass with a belt then fucked me longer and harder than he ever had. Same size dick as before, but he was ramming me harder and smacking my ass cruelly with each push into me. None of which I minded, because he finally came close to how Trax had been with me. I figured he wanted me to fight and cry out and beg, which I did...tho' I don't think I was very good at it. Too much pleasure in my voice and moans, I'm sure.

Still he covered my belly and chest with his cum and, after that, dropped my legs and gave me one of the longest, hardest, most intense blow jobs I'd ever had, bringing me up the brink four times before letting me explode in his face and all over myself, too. He mingled our cum together with his dick and I almost chuckled from the joy of it.

Then I felt him lick the cum off my shaft and belly, something Trax had never done, and I let out a sigh of the purest pleasure.

Once I was spent, he'd said, "You're done," and slapped me a few times before doing his usual vanishing act.

Well...those two words were said in a voice I recognized. Because late night hosts had made lots of fun at how he said it. *You're DONE.* He was a major action movie star! A guy I'd already figured was into guys. He was closing in on fifty, but had been keeping himself so trim and pumped up, I'd have been happy to fuck with him without the coercion.

If only his dick had been bigger. Shit.

So I unbound myself and took a nice long shower and dressed in neat new clothes and was taken back to the jail and set for release, after which I met with the Sheriff. He got all snarly and butch and growly, and warned me that I'd face death if I ever spoke of this.

It was so cute.

Now I wasn't dumb enough to tell him I knew who the actor was. We were alone in his office, and I could have wound up in a desert grave, myself. What I did tell him was how the gossip had been spreading around, regarding the guys who'd been *getting out early,* and mentioned I had a plan to make it go away. Something I'd been considering between *faux-rape* sessions with the actor. He wouldn't have listened to me except, since I'd cum in that actor's face every time while the previous guy couldn't get an erection except once, I'd really please the client. So I popped out with my little plan.

I knew the head of the cartel Trax had been buying the hash from, mainly because I was fluent in Spanish and had handled the transaction. His name? Hernandez. I'd also helped one of his sons keep from getting shot up in a nightclub attack by a rival gang, one night (long story to be told another time). Later, I'd learned one of guys who'd set his son up had been taken out into the desert. I'd met the guy and thought he'd been good-looking. I'd casually joked to Hernandez it seemed like a terrible waste of male flesh.

Now the man knew I was queer; his son told him. But what was also on my side was how I'd introduce said son to a really nice girl I'd met, and they were talking about getting married. Daddy was so very happy to see his hijo settling down, as well as going to university, for law, all because of how she wanted a legitimate life, when I'd said I was sorry he hadn't handed the now-dead guy off to me, he'd asked, in Spanish, *"What would you do with him?"*

16

He was smirking about it.

So just to be an ass, I'd smirked back and said, in Spanish, *"You do not want to know."* Then winked.

He roared with laughter at this barely nineteen-year-old brat acting like he's hot shit with him and said, *"Tell you what — next time I have a man like him who needs to be handled, I will give him to you. That would be a true punishment."*

I'd laughed with him and said, *"Only if he is pretty."*

But then I put it to the Sheriff, "What if I get some hot guys from across the border, bring 'em here, and you...oh, sell 'em?"

"Sell 'em?"

"You got a client base. See what they're up for. Let 'em know — no limits. See what they'll pay to own a man. A good-lookin' man."

He'd glared at me for a long time, his face unreadable and his eyes as cold as black ice.

"And after they're done with 'em?" he finally asked.

I shrugged. "You can always kick 'em back across the border. Who's gonna believe what they say?"

He went back to quiet for a good three minutes, then he asked, "How'll you get 'em to our side?"

Which made me hesitate. No discussion; just a question. Meaning his contacts went one hell of a lot deeper underground than I had thought, and gave me the feeling he might've already considered it but didn't have the Network south of the border.

"Money," I said, making my voice bright and happy. "My contact won't let me have 'em for free, but you could charge ten times more to your clients if they don't have to worry about gossip or any other repercussions. And these'd be guys they can do whatever they want to, so you'd have to be careful who you let in as a client. But if you keep usin' guys from the jail, word's gonna get out, especially if they keep vanishin'."

He eyed me and said, "Only one vanished, an' I think he *is* back in Mexico, now. Maybe your *contact* could find him for me."

"I can ask, but no guarantees."

"Askin' never hurt nothin'."

"Okay, but with the guys I bring? Who's gonna know where they came from or where they should go back to?"

He gave me the longest, coldest, scariest look I'd ever seen, and just as I was about to freak out and say I was only joking, he murmured, "Young men?"

I nodded.

"Good-lookin'?"

"You set the standard."

"You're a good base. Client you just got done with was real happy. Wants a repeat."

"Uh...thank you?" And hoped he wasn't talking about next weekend, because I was still sore from the butt plug.

"I told him nope. One time only. Safer that way."

Whew. "He got his money's worth..."

"Yeah. Some o' these fellas — we had performance issues, so you willin' to test 'em, first?"

"Test?"

"Get 'em up. Get 'em off. Nothin' more."

I chuckled and asked, "Can't I even use their mouths?"

"If'n you wanna risk it."

That made me laugh. "Point taken."

"An' they gotta be clean."

That got me huffy. "Hey, they take baths in Mexico, too."

"I ain't talkin' baths."

"Oh, you mean nothin' that can identify 'em. Right."

He just looked at me, unmoving. I nodded and said, "Got it. They'll be clean."

He nodded back, more slowly. "I might know some people interested."

That sent a glorious tingle right down to my balls.

So he backed me in getting a van to fix up and fronted me five-thousand, to start. He also gave me the name of a Border Patrol Agent working in Naco, for when I came back across. Since I knew Spanish but had a very WASP name and look, we decided I was visiting cousins on my half-Latina mother's side in Ignazio Zaragoza. (Oh, would mom have hated knowing I'd said she was anything but pure Anglo.) He even helped me get a US passport under the name of a kid who'd died in Utah. I'd been using my old dependents' Air Force ID to cross the border, but that was about to expire.

A couple months later everything was set and I contacted Hernandez. Asked if he had anyone good-looking he wanted to get rid of. He laughed for a good five minutes, then I mentioned I'd pay him three-thousand for the guy and he stopped cold.

"How do you have that kind of money?"

"You really want an answer to that?"

He'd thought about it then said, *"I have a sneaky little mule who thinks he will marry my daughter. I will never let that happen."*

"What does she think about that?" I did *not* want to get into the middle of a family squabble.

"She likes him, but she does not love him. This is what her mother tells me."

"Mothers know."

He laughed and had me come down to his estate near Cuitaca, a lovely spread overlooking green hills. Stucco walls painted tan. Tile roofs. Arches and verandas with huge screens and fans in the ceiling. Palm trees, grass and fountains, all lovely and rich and what I aspired to. I needed no directions on how to get there, but he was surprised by the old van I arrived in.

"You strike me as more the type interested in sports cars," he'd said

after greeting me.

"And be stopped by the Federales every five miles?" was my reply. *"Besides, this is better for work."*

He'd nodded and led me inside.

I was fed a massive lunch on the veranda, several big bad butch men in suit jackets and jeans standing guard. It was hot but lovely, and the food was magnificent. Not just guacamole and quesadillas but Pozole and Emoladas and Empanadas de Piña, with plenty of chilled beers and killer coffee. We talked about nothing for an hour, then after the last course was cleared away he rose and led me into a guest house by the pool.

Inside lying on a fold out couch bed was this lean, buff, swimmer-type dressed in a ragged t-shirt, distressed jeans, and boots. His caramel tan skin and smooth muscles were visible through the holes. His hair was longish, his face was Indio and his eyes were piercing, but I couldn't see what his mouth was like because he was gagged by duct tape. That stuff also bound his feet, and his hands were tied behind him.

"How do you want him?" Hernandez asked. *"Boxed or wrapped in a rug?"* He chuckled as he said it.

I also laughed. *"You have drugs that will work?"*

"Yes, keep him quiet for hours. Nando." He motioned to one of the guards. The man got a kit from the bathroom.

"First, I must inspect him," I said. *"I must see if he will be pleasing."*

"Inspect him how?" Hernandez asked.

I gave him my gentlest smile and asked, *"Do you really want to know?"*

Hernandez gave me a wary look. *"What is this? Am I selling him to a brothel in Juarez? What good will that do me?"*

"Do you really want to know?" This time my expression was more intense, and I did a *jacking off* motion with my hand.

He got the hint and said, *"Let us know when you are done."*

He and his guards left the guest house. I closed the door, drew the curtains, and turned to look at my new acquisition.

Damn...but him sitting on the bed like he was, his legs cocked up a little to show what great form they had, his body leaning forward as he struggled to free his hands, his hair flopping across his face, his chest pumping and his belly flat and his neck strained...I felt a hunger begin to gnaw at me in ways I'd never imagined.

Suddenly I understood why that actor got such pleasure out of his rape fantasies.

He scooted around on the bed to sit up and look at me with pleading eyes, trying to talk, but I think they had something stuffed in his mouth.

I returned to the foot of the bed and smiled. *"I am not going to hurt you,"* I said. *"I am not going to kill you. I am going to take you someplace where you will be safe, but you have to assist me in this. I have to know you will help me."*

He stopped struggling and looked at me, confused. I got on the bed to kneel by him and grabbed his thick hair to hold him in place then inspected his face. He did have the loveliest eyes, and his chin was sharp and well-shaped.

I nodded. *"I think you will be all right."*

Then I shoved him back...and tore open his shirt.

He howled and started to struggle, again, but by this time I was straddling his waist and had him pinned between my legs. There was no hair on his chest but his pecs were developed like a swimmer's and his nips were red and round. A wolverine's paw was tattooed over his left one, and it was pierced. I tore the shirt off him, completely, and checked his belly. Nice and flat with only a hint of a treasure trail. Noticeable if not super-taut abs. The barest of love-handles. So far, so good.

I got off him and flipped him onto his stomach. His hands were also held in place by Duct tape, so no way was he freeing himself. He didn't have much ass to him, but when I grabbed it I could feel that it was nice and solid enough.

Oh, but he did not like having his ass grabbed. He cursed me and wiggled and fought and howled and bucked and was working himself into a frenzy, so I flipped him onto his back and sat on his chest to say, *"If you keep this up, you will vomit or swallow your tongue and die. Is that what you want? I will not fuck you, but I am going to jack you off, and you will cum for me. I need this as proof. If you do not, I cannot help you."*

He forced himself to calm down and let me adjust myself to sit on his calves. And feel up his thighs. I could tell they were nice. Really, really sexy. So I undid his jeans and shifted them down to his knees. He shook his head and flinched but let me do it. And they met my expectations. No hair, with skin as smooth and golden as the rest of him. His 2xist briefs were off-kilter just enough to show his un-tanned skin was creamy.

It was his crotch that had me worried. I seriously hoped he was a grower and not a shower, because it didn't look like much. I groped him. Felt his little dick roll above a pair of fat, surprisingly heavy balls. I pulled his briefs down to reveal they actually were big, round and in desperate need of milking.

"Do you not jack yourself off?" I asked, surprised.

The hurt look on his face could have meant anything, so I let it go and kept rolling his balls in my hand. His dick was of the thimble type foreskin, which I do not find attractive, but it began to grow without me touching it...and that did catch my interest. He groaned and lay back to stare at the ceiling, shaking his head and flinching at my every touch.

And kept growing.

And growing.

Y'know, this was the first time I was, in effect, molesting another guy. Forcing him to do something he didn't want. I'd been the initiator and seducer, way more than once, and learned a long time ago there was no such thing as a man who couldn't be had, if I really wanted him. But this? This was, by any legal definition, rape.

And I fucking loved it.

Loved the power behind it. Loved the control. Loved knowing I could do anything I wanted to him and he could not stop me. What added even more to it was, I think he was a few years older than me, surer of his sexual identity, and I was fucking with it, totally.

Son-of-a-bitch, what a rush!

I reached up with my left hand and pinched his right nip. He jolted and glared at me, grunting in fear as he breathed. I just smiled and caressed it...and kept milking his balls.

And he kept growing.

His bush anchored his dick nicely, even after it was large enough and full enough to flop back on his groin. The head began to peek around the foreskin but seemed near the end of its length, until I reached down and ran my fingers up the length of it...and he gasped and it bounced up and suddenly only half the head was hidden.

I used my left hand to pull on his shaft, revealing the entire head...and with it pulled back like that, his head red and hard, his shaft beginning to pulse, I couldn't help but surround his dick with my mouth.

Oh, man, it fit me so nice.

I've worked bigger, sure, and one with a much fatter head, but this one just...I dunno, it just felt good. I truly hadn't intended to suck on it, but rolling his balls and just caressing the shaft with my tongue...I would up taking the full length of it down my throat. That was no trouble, even though he was getting bigger and harder and more needy.

Through it all he gave out little gasps and whimpers that told me I was making him feel things he'd never felt with a man, before. Within minutes, he was clenching and pumping against my mouth so I rose and used my hand to stroke him, hard, up and down and around and again...until with a near howl he let loose. Cum spurted from him, just onto his groin and into his pubes, but sufficient to show he was usable.

I continued to pull on him, even after he was done with firing off. Even as he squirmed from the overload of sensations. Right up to the point where his foreskin was beginning to reassert itself. Then I let go...and looked at him.

He was shocked as hell at how easily I'd gotten him off. It was obvious in his eyes. In his shallow breaths. In how perky his nips still were.

Then I rubbed my own dick up against his scrotum, my pubes caressing his balls and adding to his overwhelming sensations. I sucked on first his left tit and then the other, back and forth, pumping my dick between his legs and under his briefs, feeling almost like I was deep inside him until I was ready to fire so rose up to my knees and shot my wad all over his face and belly.

He screamed, at that.

I chuckled from the euphoria of it all, done without me removing one bit of my clothing, just like that actor. Then I grabbed his torn t-shirt and wiped him off with it. And cleaned myself. And tucked myself away. And played with his now little dick and now lighter balls, for a moment, before leaning down to whisper in his ear, *"Good dog."* Then I tucked him back inside his 2xist briefs and re-buttoned his jeans.

I called in Hernandez and gave him the three thousand, then the guy got a shot of Ketamine before we wrapped him in a blanket, and lay him in a little bed I'd had made under the van's floorboard. I put a mattress over it, then sent a special text to the Sheriff's contact in Naco and a couple hours later snuck him across the border, easy as pie.

By this time, the sun had set, so I met the Sheriff at an alley in Chandler. When I lifted off the covers, my cargo was semi-conscious. The Sheriff looked him over, silently, then had a couple of muscle men wearing balaclavas lift him out of the bed and let him inspect the guy's rear. He nodded and they carried him to the back of a minivan. I gave them a quick, easy instruction manual on his use and care...*Milk his balls*...and they took him away.

Thus was a very profitable partnership begun.

THREE

I took another forty-three trips over the border before the job blew up. I had made more connections, thanks to Hernandez, and was still taking the occasional guy from him, but some of these people had difficulty understanding that while I would accept all types of guys, from slim and pretty to buff bears to beefy and solid, from güeros to morenos, so long as they were in good shape, I'd accept no one over the age of thirty-five, nor anyone under the age of twenty. You do a lot of stupid shit up to that point, so it's crazy to dump on a guy that young. Meaning sometimes those trips wound up being a waste of time. Irritating but that's the biz.

Fortunately, my main source for merchandise had become the mayor of a town that was in a forest area. He was having trouble with lumber interests trying to take over the trees. But he had a little army that backed him up in keeping control, and when one of the bully-boys were deemed suitable enough to interest me, I'd get a text asking when I was *coming to visit grandma*. It was rarely more than one guy at a time, but they were all worth the money I'd pay.

Anyway, I'd gotten a text, and I knew the Sheriff had a client coming into Phoenix, looking for fun. So I zipped across the border at Nogales, in my van. I kept it in a special garage off the 19 near Rio Rico. It could be a bit of a hassle to get to and drop back off after delivering the merchandise, but it felt a lot safer than keeping it in Tucson or Phoenix.

I consistently made sure the vehicle was in top shape, because it's a long road, and not all of it was good. And even though it was late in the year, the AC was usually cranked on max.

I stayed on the highways till I got to the 16 and headed east. All of this was okay, since it led to a town that was big enough to have a new branch of the National University. On the outskirts, there was a little motel I always spent the night at, usually arriving about dusk. It was low-slung with blue-painted adobe walls and a bit skanky, but the bed was comfortable, the shower worked and its AC unit actually cooled the air. Plus a cantina around the corner made a Pollo Pozole that was to die for. A good place to stop, because I do not drive at night in Mexico.

The next morning I had a breakfast of amazing Chilaquiles then headed up a series of rough side roads into hills thick with trees until I reached an old cinder-block house surrounded by nothing but soft, still forest. The silence was punctuated only by the calls of the local fauna, and the lack of a breeze made even the cool air fell warm.

The protocol was simple — the Mayor would be waiting for me, alone. He'd see me and leave, his way of doing the hand-off. I'd test the quality of the merchandise, prepare him for a trip to the States and leave the cash in a hidden spot. He'd come back in the afternoon to collect.

Oh, by *prepare* them, I'd give the guy a shot of the same stuff Hernandez had told me about. I always made sure to use a bit under the recommended dosage, to be safe. It was a long trip and better if they were quiet the whole way, but I didn't want to chance an overdose. So I'd make sure the cargo was doing well before heading back across the border, and a booster shot was usually in order. Still, after hauling fifty-eight guys in the last six years, without issue, I was starting to feel like I knew what I was doing.

And feel like I was in a rut. Never a good place to be, in business.

This time, however, a nearly new pickup with a camper on its back was parked in front of the house. I didn't recognize it so almost turned around, but a good-looking man I *had* seen before appeared at the doorway and waved me in. I couldn't remember why he looked familiar, but he was pretty enough to shift my wariness into thinking about having some fun. Usually. He wore a neat button-down plain white shirt and form-fitting slacks that were tan and crease, with Oxfords on his feet. Broad shoulders. Full chest. Trim hips. Good legs. And a nice-enough face topped by shot black hair, but my inner alarm was screaming something about it wasn't right.

Problem is, once you've made the commitment you've got to follow through. Otherwise it's bad for business. So I parked, locked the truck and set the alarm passcode so no one could open it but me, then approached him, warily...and a bit hungry.

And finally remembered this guy had accompanied the mayor, once, when he'd handed two gorgeous men over to me. He'd been in boots, back then, with spiky dark hair. Hazel eyes that had a sloe feel to them had given me tingles, and he was right around thirty so workable. I also recalled he didn't have much ass, but he did have sloping legs that flowed so perfectly down to those boots they more than made up for it. He'd struck me, back then, as a bit of a weasel; now I knew he was.

Because there was no sign the Mayor's car had even been up there.

"Hi," I called, in Spanish, staying outside. *"Emilio?"*

He let a nice smile cross his face. *"You remember my name."*

"Why not? Is the Mayor here, too?"

"He had to go back. We expected you an hour ago."

Which was bullshit. The Mayor knew it was a ten hour drive from Nogales, in the best of times, and knew I didn't drive at night, so he always scheduled the transfers in the morning by eight. That way, he could make sure they didn't conflict with city business. But I played along.

"When will he return?"

"I do not think he will. It is a long meeting. He asked me to handle this."

"Too bad. I had questions for him." I pulled out a pocket knife and opened it to clean a fingernail in a way Emilio could not help but see. He grew tense.

I laughed. *"Do not worry. I always carry this, and I have a hangnail and forgot to bring my nail clippers."*

He nodded. *"That is good. We will leave you to it, then."*

We? There was someone else here? Uh, no way, motherfucker.

I held up a hand to stop him and said, *"Not so fast. I have to inspect the merchandise, first."*

"You do? You did not do this, last time."

I shook my head. *"This is every time; you just did not see it. I have to make sure he is up to my standards."*

"Oh. Sorry. I...I forgot." He backed inside.

The lying little shit.

I followed him into a room that was dank and empty, except for a box spring and mattress in the middle of a filthy floor. Lying on it, hands bound behind him, ankles crossed and tied together, gagged and blindfolded, was a guy who was maybe twenty, with close-cropped sandy-colored hair. His t-shirt was ripped open, revealing nicely pumped pecs and tight abs. More sandy hair whispered over them to swirl down behind the elastic band of a torn pair of CK Briefs. His jeans had been pulled down to his ankles, revealing his well-formed legs were also dusted with hair, and his left arm had a tattoo sleeve of a forest, adding to his sexiness.

But what really caught my attention was how his dick and balls were only half-hidden by the torn briefs...and while they did look lovely, I could tell he was most definitely cut.

None the guys I'd had to that point were. It's very rare in Mexico, and from what I could see of his face he looked very Northern European, but they also rarely circumcise their boys.

Meaning he was probably American. Maybe Canadian.

That was Emilio's stupid mistake number one.

Something I insisted on was absolutely no Americans or Canadians. You can do what you want with Latinos, but you mess with Anglos and everybody up north gets upset. That got proven a couple decades back when a WASP college boy on spring break in Matamoros was kidnapped, raped and murdered, and it turned out he was like their fifteenth or sixteenth victim. Then to top it off, it was discovered the all-male victims had been used for some ritual sacrifice by a crazy-cult. The locals had been complaining about them for years, so to have this explode so openly became an embarrassment to the police. They freaked out and most of the cult wound up dead after a siege. But reality is, if that last victim hadn't been Anglo they'd probably still be at it, because no one cares when Mexicans go missing. Look at how many women have been murdered in Juarez in what looks like a serial killer's work, with no one in law enforcement really doing anything to stop it.

Something else that bothered me about this situation was, there was another guy there to do the hand off. He was not at all familiar, though he and Emilio did look a bit like brothers. However, unknown guy was a lot more interesting. Sharp, strong face with cheekbones that could cut ice. Big dark eyes. Well-shaped lips. Obviously played a lot of soccer from his thick build. He wore a tight tennis shirt that revealed the likelihood of a nice hairy chest and slim-cut jeans that revealed he had a butt and bandy-legs on him to die for. I got the feeling he was there more to give Emilio back-up than anything else.

Fortunately, neither one came across as smart, just clever.

"Oh, a white boy," I said as I sat on the bed. *"It has been a long time since I've been offered one as pretty as him."*

They smirked at each other, the little bastards.

I knelt on the mattress and slipped the guy's dick free of the torn briefs. He squirmed and tried to yell at me, but the gag was too tight. Oh, yes; very nice. With rich, full balls.

"He worked for the lumber companies?" I asked, frowning.

"No," said Emilio. *"No, we are doing Señor Hernandez a favor. He was carrying drugs for him. A mule."*

That that was stupid mistake number two, but I held in my irritation. Not only would Hernandez never trust the Mayor to handle something like this for him, they were letting me know they knew all about a setup nobody was supposed to know about but the Mayor, Hernandez and me.

"Hernandez says he is stealing from him," said Soccer.

"He does not want this one to come back on him, at all."

"He asks for ten thousand. Dollars, not pesos."

Stupid mistake number three. They thought they were demanding for a lot of money in exchange for this guy, showing they were not privy to the Mayor's or Hernandez's business. I already had a set rate with them both, and it was now a lot higher than that. Once a supplier realizes how much money can be made, depending on the quality of the merchandise, then the quality goes up...but so does the price. That's business for you.

"That is so much money to give to a couple of guys I do not know," I said, still fondling the guy. He squirmed and twisted but couldn't get away.

"You know me," Emilio replied.

I just smiled. *"Roll him over; I want to see his ass."*

They looked at each other, hesitating.

"Come on," I snapped, *"I have a long drive ahead of me."*

They huffed and did so. The stupid little fucks. Part of the process had always included me inspecting all aspects of the merchandise, *alone*. After they were gone. And his clothing would never have been torn, like this.

Except I remembered, one of the guys Emilio had helped with had a torn shirt and his jeans were halfway down his hips. Looked like he had fought his captors. I smiled at the memory. He'd brought in my first six-figure sale.

I wasn't sure yet, but it was looking like the Mayor was not involved in this. When Emilio had been with him, that one time, everything was handled outside. And they had left as soon as I entered the house, so Emilio wasn't even remembering what he'd been part of.

Of course, since they had no idea what I normally did, that meant I could have all kinds of fun.

The sandy-haired guy had a gloriously adorable ass still covered by the cotton of the briefs, and another tattoo on the small of his back. I ran my hand over his butt, feeling how firm his cheeks were. How smooth. He was lovely, especially when he tried to wriggle away.

"Hold him down," I said.

They hesitated then one straddled his back as the other sat on his legs, neither of them comfortable at doing it.

Oh, this was going to be such fun.

I pulled the CKs down to reveal a softly-hairy butt and stuck my middle finger into his anus. He almost screamed from fear and anger. He was tight...but not tight enough. Not a virgin, and my bet was he'd been deflowered some time ago.

Still, I said, *"A virgin. Very good."* I pulled his CKs back up over his ass then said, *"Now roll him back."*

They did.

"I must now test him," I smiled. *"Make sure he will cum when he needs to. I will need your help. I do not have my assistant."*

"What?" Soccer cried.

"You did not have anyone with you, last time," Emilio said.

"You did not see him," I shot back. *"He was in the van."*

"We aren't queer!" said Soccer. A bit too emphatically.

"All you need to do," I said, *"is play with his tits while I work on his dick. Mainly suck on them, like you do a woman's, that is all. And if watching me masturbate him offends you, close your eyes."*

"But he's a man!" said Emilio.

"Do you want me to take him or not?" I shot back. *"If he does not cum, I do not want him. He will not be good for my use, no matter how pretty he is. And Hernandez will not like that."*

They exchanged wary glances then took in deep breaths and nodded.

I had to fight back a laugh. I'd never had an assistant with me. Too hard to keep mouths closed, and you did not want chit-chat about a job like this. In fact, that Emilio had been with the Mayor that one time had made me so damned angry I'd almost canceled the transaction, but he'd assured me all would be okay. Well, I now get to say *I told you so* and hope it translates well into Spanish.

But then I began thinking...and studying Emilio. I really liked how he flowed from his shoulders down his back to his little ass and along his legs into those shoes, and him kneeling on the bed as he held the guy down had made his thighs even more glorious. He'd bring a decent price if his dick was as pretty.

His buddy...or cousin or brother or whatever the fuck he was...was more common in his physical beauty, but still worth a lot on the open market, mainly thanks to his pumped up chest and nicely rounded ass.

Wow...guess I'd pretty much decided I was taking three back with me, not one.

So I straddled *Sandy's* legs and began fondling him as they knelt beside him and hesitantly started to finger his tits. His chest heaved and he tried to get away, but he was too well bound and they were flanking him too tightly. That didn't stop him from crying out and shaking his head and trying to buck me off him.

And look glorious as he did so.

Man, I loved the feel of his dick in my hand. He was going to be thick and nicely sloping, and I knew milking his round heavy balls would only add to the sense of perfection, they complimented each other so nicely. What was even better? Despite his struggles he was already beginning to get hard.

"Okay, I am going to work on him," I said, *"so I want you to suck on his tits."*

They rolled their eyes at each other then made themselves get off the mattress and kneel on each side. They breathed deep then put their lips on his nips and closed their eyes and got to work.

I snuck photos of them doing it, using my phone.

Then I tore the CKs off the guy, completely.

His dick flopped around, heavy and fat, as if it had woken from a long slumber. I kissed it. And slid my tongue along it and over his balls and through his pubes as my fingers caressed the hairs on his stomach and thighs. He quickly got harder...and harder. So quickly, I began to wonder if he knew Spanish and had heard my comment about not wanting him if he didn't cum. Maybe he thought it was better to get away from these two goons and be on his own with just me. That might afford him the opportunity to escape.

I began to suck on him, sliding my lips up and down his shaft, feeling him get fuller and fuller in my mouth. There is something almost mystical about a man's erection growing within you, knowing he'll soon be releasing the meaning of life into your throat. Damn...all of the times I'd had men do that as I worshiped them into near madness. Every blow job brought back glimmers of all the previous ones, and they combined to add to my intense love of having this much control of a man's dick. Hell, of him as I milked his balls and roamed all over his body, whether he wanted me to or not. It was the beginning, middle and end of existence, so far as I was concerned, and sometimes I did all I could to make it last for hours.

But not this time. Instead, I kept glancing at Emilio and Soccer, their eyes still closed as they worked *Sandy's* nips like a couple of pros.

That was the perfect time for video.

Ooohhh, was that lovely. I made sure to show the guy's dick in it, nice and hard as it flopped back on his belly. Aching to release. Throbbing in ways too beautiful for words to describe.

He started clenching his ass. He was close to finishing off. I had to prep my next action. I always carried zip-ties with me, but I only had three in my pocket. I'd have to be quick if this was going to work. It only had to hold them till I could get a roll of packing tape from the van to bind them tight.

I slipped the ties out. Readied them. Then I went hard on *Sandy's* dick. Used every trick I knew to increase the sensations as his shaft grew bigger and thicker and harder and his balls grew tighter and tighter. Soon he was grinding his hips into my mouth to make it all happen now, now, now. I pulled back just in time to see the first shot of cum fire out of him as he grunted. Then another and another.

Both of which I aimed at Emilio.

The stream hit him just below his eye. He howled and jumped up, and that's when I grabbed Soccer's left arm and twisted it around him then grabbed his right arm as he fought to stop me and strapped them together, at the wrist, tight as I could. He snarled in pain.

Next, I jumped across the bed to slam Emilio to the floor in a wrestling move and strapped his hands behind him so quickly, I don't think he even knew what had happened.

Both of them were cursing me and trying to get free. Soccer was even kicking at the box spring as he struggled to his feet, so I knocked him down and used the torn CKs to tie his ankles together. He tried to kick at me, but couldn't get a good angle before he was bound. Then I tore his shirt off and used half of that to gag him before using the rest to bind and gag Emilio. Now I had both guys hogtied.

Soccer's torso was nice. Not as firm as I'd thought, or as hairy as expected, but worth a decent price. I wanted to make a better comparison so ripped Emilio's shirt open to show he was built tighter and almost hairless, but had lovely nips and the beginning of a cute treasure trail. He'd do well.

That's when I called Hernandez. I wanted to be sure about them before I acted further.

Oh, was he pissed. *"I do not know who those little assholes are, and if I come get them, no one will ever see them, again."*

"No, no, no, no, no, no," I said. *"You know how much I hate waste. I will take them."*

"Good. I cannot have people thinking they can use my name to pull shit like this! What about the American?"

"I can handle him, but he now knows about this set-up."

"Too bad for him. Can you sell him, too?"

"You know better than that. But it means the end of this."

"That is the Mayor's problem." Then he ended the call.

I got the tape and bound Emilio and Soccer more securely, giving each one's ass a good feel. Oh, did they squeal and howl and fight. But what's funny is, they hated it even more when I pinched their tits. Even if I'd had to pay for them, they'd bring in a good profit. But I wasn't paying; I was taking them for free.

Or else.

I sat beside *Sandy* and raised him up to a sitting position and said, "Sorry about this. You American?"

He nodded.

"I'm gonna take off the gag and blindfold. I want to talk. Won't do you any good to yell or scream; we're in the middle of nowhere. So let's just talk. And don't worry; you'll be okay. I promise."

I removed the blindfold to reveal a very nice set of deep blue eyes, then off came the gag to show a lovely pair of lips. All in all, a very, very nice face. With a dash of freckles across his nose.

He croaked, "Water?" So I got a bottle from the van and held it to his mouth...and he drained it. "Thanks."

"What's your name?" I asked.

He gulped, thought and said, "Charlie Baker."

Bullshit, but I played along. "Where'd they grab you?"

He could barely speak. "El Paso. I'm stationed there."

"Army. Wow. How'd they get you?"

"Uh...I...I dunno. Last I remember I was at a...a bar on Montana..."

Okay, my patience vanished. "Cut the bullshit! I'll help you, but not if you lie to me, and I *will* know if you're lyin'." His big eyes looked at me, scared and wary and amazingly lovely. I gave him a lifeline. "I bet someone contacted you through one of the chat rooms. Hook up? Somethin' like that?"

"Sort of."

"Sort of? Were you tryin' to make a little extra cash?"

He shrank a little then nodded. "Couple thousand bucks."

"Shit, what'd they want to do?"

"Fuck me. I...I posted that I'm a virgin."

More bullshit, but still I acted offended. "Are you fuckin' kidding?! With somebody you don't even know?"

"I needed the money, and I was gonna get it up front. And I had condoms..."

Poor guy was shaking. I didn't really buy his story, but didn't want to spook him into lying more, so just asked, "What happened?"

"I...I went to a motel in Ysleta, parked, almost got to the door when I was grabbed. Then I'm here. All tied up."

"When was that?"

"Sunday night."

"It's now Tuesday."

"WHAT?! Aw, shit...I'm AWOL! My car's still there!"

"I think that's the least of your problems, right now. You really didn't know what day it is?"

He shook his head. "Been out of it. Starvin'. Kind of remember gettin' fed...pissin'...gettin' hosed down with really cold water...but it's blurry...and they...they..."

"They didn't fuck you; looks like you're still a virgin." Yeah, yeah, I was lying, but sometimes a good lie gets you more truth than truth does. "They cleaned you up 'fore I got here. Smells like Irish Spring."

He nodded then looked at me. "You gonna untie me?"

"Not yet." Because truth of the matter is, those torn CKs were too clean, there was a hint of cloves on his breath, and his wrists weren't raw from being bound for so long. I wanted to know what the hell was going on before I made any decisions.

I think he realized I was suspicious, because his voice cracked as he said, "Aw shit, man, what you gonna do?" He was close to tears.

"Nothin'. In fact, if you help me, I'll get you back 'cross the border."

That made him jolt. "We're in Mexico!?"

"Land of anything goes."

"But how'd they get me over here? How'll I get back? My ID's in my wallet and — "

"Don't worry about that; I'll take care of it. But I need you to play along a little longer. What's your name?"

"I told you!"

"Real name. C'mon."

He fought to keep control. "Verminsky. Frank."

"Mind if I call you Vermin?"

He huffed a laugh. "That's always been one of my names."

"Cool. I like it."

"Are you gonna fuck me?" He didn't look at me as he said it. "That why you're here? You gonna fuck me then kill me?"

"Oh, shut the fuck up. You're too pretty to kill."

Then I kissed him. And yep, cloves. And what's more, he almost kissed me back.

Oh, he was in on this. Question was, in what way?

*****

That seemed to soothe him enough to calm down, so I went outside and called the Mayor. I needed to let him know I was cancelling all future contracts, and while I had a feeling these little shits were not part of his group, I still faked like I didn't know what the hell was going on and asked him why he'd *sent such idiots to handle his business.*

As I suspected, he swore he knew nothing about it. He roared up to the house twenty minutes later, and when he saw the two guys tied up on the floor, he froze, then shook his head.

They saw him and started struggling and trying to speak, but I slapped them, hard and said, *"Shut the fuck up!"*

"You are right, they are idiots," the Mayor sighed. *"Was it just these two?"*

"What do you mean?"

"They run with a pack. Did the boy see others?"

"He did not say."

"Let me see him."

I took him into the next room. I'd moved Vermin onto a rickety chair, in just his torn t-shirt with his jeans still bunched around his ankles. I'd put the blindfold and gag back on him, as well. The shirt's tail draped down to barely cover his dick and balls. His naked legs were lovely, and with his hands tied behind him his pecs were even fuller and the hair on them richer. He looked so damned hot, like this, it hurt.

I began rethinking my wariness about using Americans.

But I kept my cool and told the mayor, *"This is how they offered him to me."*

"Not on the bed? Not in his clothing?"

"They did not even understand that I require virgins, as you know.

But this boy, I think he has been used by them."

The Mayor gave me a shocked glance. *"He told you this?"*

"He did not need to. You can smell them on him. You can taste them."

"Mother of God." He backed out of the room, shaken. *"You should not tell me these things in front of him."*

"It is okay. He doesn't speak Spanish."

"What will you do with him? You cannot let him go; he now knows about what we have done."

I knew that was coming. *"He is Anglo. His father is wealthy."*

"How do you know this?"

"Look at his skin; clean and clear. He is circumcised. His clothes were nice, not cheap. If he only disappears, people will search for him. They will have to find a body. If that happens, there will be an autopsy and they will find out what was done to him. It will not be pretty."

"Mother of God."

"There is another choice. I can feed him peyote and have him found while he is under its influence. No matter what he says, people will think he is not in his right mind. Even he will wonder if perhaps he dreamed it all. But as I told you, it means I cannot come back to Mexico. You will have to handle your problems in another way."

The mayor thought for a moment. *"What about the money you would pay?"*

"I will pay you for him, not the other two."

"Why? Are they worth nothing??" He seemed to be taking offense.

"Listen to me," I said. *"They told me one man, so I brought money for one man. Now they have brought you trouble beyond imaging. It is one thing to sell me the stupid scum who work with drug lords. With rich men to drive you off your land. Who work to make you their slaves. They vanish all the time, and I know you only offer me the best-looking of them. I do not ask what happens to the others. But these two who tried to make money off this boy — they know your secret. They took an Anglo boy and thought I would be stupid and accept him. They did not mean for you to know. And they know of your understanding with Hernandez. Know how to contact me. Hernandez is not happy. This worries me. Boys like this, you will need to do more than just punish them or they will do this, again and again."*

He looked at me, and I saw something odd in his eyes, a calculation he rarely had. He was already planning something.

"What do you want?" he asked.

"They run with a pack, you say. How many?"

"Four others."

"I will take them all, if they are attractive.

"You ask me to do something impossible." But his voice said he was seriously thinking about it.

"I ask you to be strong and accept reality, nothing more. I thought you already had. No coward can lead a city into refusing access to men who would poison your happiness. No fearful man could choose to turn those

jackals into money to use for the good of his people. That you cannot be as strong as you must, now, makes me sad. And sorry. But understand, I cannot return, no matter what you decide. Your city is now much too dangerous for me. Not just because of the drug lords who may learn of our arrangement, but the Federales and the Army..."

"They would not believe we do this!"

I let a smirk cross my face. *"Why not? Look at the evil that has spread within your borders."*

He looked at me, and I could see him silently adding up just how much cash I'd brought in. I could have told him; in the four years since he'd joined with Hernandez and myself, I'd made twenty-nine trips just to his town, and I'd left with forty-three men at thirty-thousand bucks a head. Considering how little money they got from Mexico City, that was an insane amount, and included was a growing reputation as a town nobody wanted to mess with. Their forest was left alone. Their crops undamaged by human hands. Of course, God only knew how much he'd probably siphoned off for himself. But now that would vanish and he'd have to handle the loggers and drug cartels in profitless ways. All because some spoiled brats had gotten stupid and greedy.

He finally said, *"It is my fault. I should not have asked Emilio to help me, that time, but no one else was around. But I know his wife...his children..."*

"That is not my problem."

"Yes, it is mine. This is not the first trouble he has caused. But they cannot just disappear. They are of our people."

Okay, time to bring out the asshole in me. *"What do your people think of homosexuals?"*

He looked at me, coldly. *"We do not think of such things. And do not tell me this is two-faced of us — that we sell you men to be used in unnatural ways so have no right to dislike how this is done. Those men are animals and deserve everything that happens to them. I hope this does not offend you."*

I shook my head. I learned a long time ago anybody can justify anything in their mind, if they want to, no matter how repugnant it might be to them. But his answer was exactly what I wanted to hear.

"I will make your town, even Emilio's wife, happy to be rid of them."

"How can you do that?" He was only vaguely interested. That set off a warning in my gut. I may need to deal with this, once I had everything else settled.

"As I told you, they raped this boy, anally and orally."

"I do not believe him when he says —"

"Stop it! You know I tell you only the truth. He was assaulted only hours before I arrived. He was still bleeding. His mouth tasted of their children."

"Do not say such things to me!"

"Those six are homosexuals masquerading as macho men. That is why they run together. I can prove this to you and any who ask. Will their parents still want them? Will your people refuse to let you handle this in the best way for everyone? Do you not wonder how many other boys they have

done this to?"

He looked at me. *"You can prove this?"*

"They helped me test this boy." I showed him the video of Emilio and Soccer sucking on Vermin's tits, his dick hard in the foreground.

He shuddered and damn near stopped breathing. I shut up to give him time to think about it. He wasn't a stupid man, and me using the inbred homophobia of his people as a way to make my argument was hardly subtle, or even politically correct, but I could see him contemplating the reality of the situation.

He wandered back to the room holding the two guys. I followed. They saw us and their eyes got big. I guess the Mayor's expression was *not* a welcoming one.

"What are their names?" I asked.

"Emilio you know," he said, then pointed to soccer. *"He is Reuben. The others are Oscar, Miguel, Theo, and Rene."*

"Are they as good to look at as these?"

"I suppose." Meaning *yes*.

Which would be very unusual. This big-assed snake was using me, in some way, and his next comment made me sure of it.

"Rene is the best of them. The leader. Even my daughter thinks he should be in the cinema, because of his looks. But girls are stupid about such things."

Rene and the mayor's daughter? Was that all that this was about? He just wanted to get a lothario away from her? Could he have set up Emilio and Reuben, knowing I would not accept Vermin from him? Was he tossing away his extra income to keep his daughter away from a guy he hated? Seemed a bit excessive.

Of course, if this Rene was the leader of this group, they would cause trouble were he the only one to vanish. So make all of them vanish? Again, just a bit much...

Yeah, but fathers and daughters, who knows what it's about?

Almost like he was reading my mind, the Mayor stopped and said, *"No, I have known these boys since babies. I know the girls they have been with. This is no good. No one will believe us. Emilio's wife is happy with him. Reuben is engaged."*

"That means nothing. Watch what happens with a man's hand."

I set my phone to record and handed it to the Mayor. Then I smiled at Emilio, and if his eyes could've killed me, they would have. No question he'd bring in some nice cash. Bound like he was — arms behind him, taped at the knees and ankles — it emphasized how full his pecs were and flat his stomach was. It also made his legs look better than they had when he was standing up. His big lashes gave him a nearly angelic look, and his crotch looked full enough to be more than acceptable. It would be so very interesting to see just how big he actually wound up being. What made it even better was, he knew what I was up to and he was going to fight me.

So let's have at it, you little fuck.

I strolled over to him, grabbed him in a wrestler hold and rolled him onto the mattress, then I sat up beside him, smiling. He tried to shift away from me, so I grabbed his neck and shoved him face down and wrapped tape around his hands. Now he could not maneuver his fingers.

He squirmed and tried to scream and fought to yell through his gag, *"I have done nothing! Let me go! Do not touch me, faggot! Mayor, please stop him! I have helped you!"*

I chuckled and yanked him into a sitting position, then wrapped the tape around his mouth, several times, so you couldn't make out his words. Finally, I positioned myself on the bed, behind him, my knees flanking his hips, my crotch pressed against his ass, all holding his body in place. He tried to grab at me, but the tape held tight. All he could do was grunt with anger and fear and confusion.

I glanced at Reuben. Truth is, he was looking less pumped up and more fleshy and round. Obviously, he'd been holding his gut in. Still he did have that nice light flow of hair over his pecs and around his nips and across his belly and along his forearms. He was watching with horror, his chest heaving from his sudden sharp breaths, giving him a bear-like sensuality. Well, bear cub. I knew we had one client who loved his type, the butcher the better.

The Mayor's eyes grew more and more narrow as he watched me get ready to prove Emilio could be used.

I cast a deliberate glance at Reuben's crotch, smirking. It hadn't gotten fuller or anything, but that made the Mayor think I believed he had.

It worked. The Mayor all but dropped the phone and said, *"Stop. I do not want to see this!"*

"But you want proof, do you not?"

"The video you shot will be enough to raise questions. I will add a story about catching them doing it." He gave me the phone and said, *"What do you want me to do?"*

I rose, smiling. *"Bring the others to me. I will drug them, no trouble."*

"You are very certain of yourself."

"Will they meet my conditions?" He hesitated. *"You know what I want. Emilio would be good for this. Reuben...I don't know; I will have to see what my sources are looking for."*

"Miguel and Rene will please you. Maybe Theo."

"Very good. I will wait here. And when I am home, I will let you know where to access this video."

The mayor sighed, nodded and left.

I went into the next room and untied Vermin. "I'm thirsty," he said. I gave him another water bottle and he gulped some down then said, "Shit, are you Mexican?"

I laughed. "No, why?"

"You speak Mexican."

"Spanish, dumbass. I just ain't some stupid-fuck Anglo who thinks English is the only language in the world."

He nodded, then remembered he was practically naked so pulled his jeans up to hide what I'd already seen plenty of. It made me smile.

"What happened?" he asked. "What'd you two decide?"

I looked at him, for a long moment. He was very attractive, but what was most interesting was, he wasn't all that scared. I now had a pretty good idea he wasn't an unwilling participant in this game being played, but I wasn't ready to confront him, yet. I felt like playing for a while.

"You wanna get back at those guys?" I asked.

He hesitated. "You gonna call the cops?"

"Mexican cops won't do jack shit for us. You're a gringo, and I'm on their shit list for not payin' them bribes. You wanna get even? Gotta do it, yourself."

That made him blink. "Uh...like how?"

"Like I take them instead of you."

"Take?"

"Yeah."

"Shit, what'd you and that old guy talk about?"

"You don't wanna know, trust me. But if you help me, I'll get you back in the US, nice and safe, again. What d'you say?"

He looked at me for a long, long moment...then shrugged. "I...I guess. See what happens." What made it truly interesting was, I caught zero wariness in his eyes.

To my surprise, that made me happy. Not that he was so easily open to helping me transport a couple of men across the border to the States, but that he didn't give off even a hint of moral judgement. I'd grown used to sensing that from Americans.

I got Vermin one of my shirts and a pair of fresh undies from the van, and he now pulled them on in front of me, without any hint of modesty, like it was just a changing room at the gym. Even though I let my eyes linger over him tucking himself in. He was just...well, just cool about it all.

At the same time, I prepped several injections for the guys. I always had extra syringes on me, so no problem there, but I was getting low on Ketamine. I had enough left for maybe two more shots, once everything was set, then that was it. I needed to contact Hernandez, quick...but now was not the time.

Then the Mayor called.

"I have thought about this, and I believe it is better if they simply vanish. Then I can blame the cartels. Maybe the loggers. The rich men behind them."

I get leery when people want to renegotiate the contract at the last minute. It's like they're just marking time till they can figure out a better way to go, and in the process fuck me over. But I also understood what he was getting at. His men were trustworthy enough to handle bad boys, but locals? Not so sure. Word might get around and even with a video, people would raise questions.

"All right," I said. *"What do you want to do?"*

"Can you get men to help you take them?"

"No. I will not do that. What I can do is take them one at a time, if I know where they are and when they will be alone."

The mayor sighed. *"Theo works at a pharmacy. He lives close to it and does not have a car so walks home."*

I turned to Vermin. "Did you see the guys who grabbed you?"

He shook his head.

I turned back to the phone. *"Give me his information. What about the others?"*

"Oscar will be at the college for his class. Miguel and Rene, I still have to learn where they will be during the day, but this night...I would say a cantina on San Sebastian. Miguel works there; Rene drinks there."

Night? I wasn't staying here all day, or keeping guys for that long. I had no way to control them, and driving at night on Mexico's back roads was begging for trouble.

"Find out where Miguel and Rene will be in the next two hours," I said. *"I must leave by then."*

"I don't know if I can."

"Then I cannot take them."

That made him hesitate. *"I will try, and will text you."*

So I got all Theo's and Oscar's specifics then turned to Vermin. "Can you drive a van?"

"Of course," he said. "What you doin'?"

"Don't ask that. You do not want to know."

He looked at me. "Those guys...you said they were gonna give me to you. What were you gonna do with me?"

"Oh, for fuck's sake, nothing," I said, and I meant it. "You're white! That's what clued me in there was somethin' wrong goin' on. It's stupid and racist and hypocritical, but the fact that you're white means I can *not* avoid gettin' into trouble over you. But some guy who's Latino? No problem."

"I don't understand. Who the fuck are you?"

I'd had enough. I gave Emilio a shot of Ketamine. He howled as I said, "So you don't wanna drive the van. Okay. Fine."

"I didn't say that."

"Then you can't ask me questions! I'm settin' it up so you can go back to your life, not because I'm a good guy but because it's better for business. But you can't know anything about me except what you've seen. You got that?"

He nodded.

"Then shut the fuck up about it and help me!"

I gave Reuben a shot and waited till they were both out, then we carried them to the van, tucked them both into my hiding slot and headed into town.

Time to rumble.

FOUR

The Mayor's city was medium-size for Mexico, with a central square and arched buildings surrounding it, and church bell towers the tallest buildings in town. Lots of cars. Lots of people wandering around over brick streets. Two festivals a year, a couple of archeological digs and a recent extension of the NUM adding to its sense of importance. I could see why he wanted to maintain his position here.

The *farmacia* was in a nice enough neighborhood on the older north side. A cinder-block building washed in a sort of sandy pink, it had a couple of windows and a noisy AC unit on the roof. Ads were painted on its walls and *Farmacia Miramin* was written in big letters across its front. A few cars were parked in the lot that was surrounded by trees, next to it. Curbs and fences lined the asphalt roads. Only a few buckled sidewalks. Not exactly high class but better than most other Mexican towns. There was the occasional passing car but nothing massive; the area was more residential than anything.

It wasn't quite ten am when we parked close by the *farmacia*, under a shady tree. The weather was still on the cool side, but it would soon get a lot warmer.

Fortunately, Theo walked out a few minutes later, a satchel hanging from his shoulder...and why the Mayor didn't think he'd suit my needs made zero sense. Granted, he was only about five-eight and probably weighed about one-fifty, but everything fit together oh-so-very neatly, from his back whipping down to his trim hips to his cute little ass rolling nicely under a tight pair of pants to his colt legs. Even his calves suggested there was decent form to them. His shirt clung to his torso and showed he wasn't so much built up as just nicely put together, with hints of hair on his forearms. He had the look of a sneaky puppy, with his big dark eyes, and brown hair, not black, There was even a hint of scruff around his chin. His nose was a little mashed in and his lips almost ready to sneer, but I was pretty sure they worked into a lovely smile. I'd have accepted him, no hesitation.

I started the van and turned to Vermin, saying, "Drive past him and park the second you find a space. Hopefully he won't turn down a side street, first. Then open the slidin' door and get back behind the wheel. Don't turn off the engine."

Vermin gave me his bigger-than-shit eyes but slipped behind the wheel as I hopped out. Then I followed Theo. Vermin slowly drove past us and parked at the corner of the first street. If all went well, no one would see or hear a thing.

Man, did I love watching Theo's perky little ass churn in those pants. Watching his legs strain against the fabric. He really was damn near beautiful, and would bring an excellent bit of cash...so long as he was a virgin in the right way.

I intended to have fun finding out.

We were closing in on the van, and I could see its side door was open, just like I'd asked, so I pulled out my knife. The second Theo was parallel to it, I grabbed him by the satchel's strap and yanked him into its back. He let out a yelp, but then I had my arm wrapped around his neck and the knife pressed to his throat.

"Be quiet or I will cut you!" I snarled. *"¡VAMOS!"*

Everybody knows what that word means.

Vermin hit the gas and we zoomed away. I used the sudden movement to twist Theo onto the floor and crush myself on top of him, saying to Vermin, "Third street down, take a left."

Theo started to wriggle but the sharpness of the knife kept him from doing too much...and I was almost sorry for that; I loved the feel of him squirming under me.

"Hands behind you, now!!"

He did as he was told. I took my arm away from his mouth and wrapped packing tape around his wrists.

"What are you doing?" he asked, his voice quivering. *"I have done nothing wrong! You have the wrong guy! Let me go! My father has no money! I'm a poor man, like you!"*

I then wrapped tape around his ankles so fast, I nearly caught myself in it then shifted around and taped his mouth closed.

It wasn't till then that I closed the sliding door.

"Anybody followin' us?" I asked Vermin. He shook his head, close to freaking out.

Theo was lying face down, struggling, and his lovely little butt was just begging to be smacked, so I did. Then I rolled him onto his side. He finally got a good look at me and his big eyes got bigger. He shook his head and tried to yell, *"No, I am not one of your guys! I am not! You got the wrong guy for this! You got it wrong! I live in this city!"*

His voice was muffled, but I understood every word, and him knowing who I was and what I look like did *not* sit well.

I got close to him and whispered, *"How do you know me?"*

"You are the man who takes men away," he managed to mutter. *"I am not one of the men you take."*

"Answer me — how do you know I do this? Who else knows?"

It finally sank in that he'd said the wrong thing. He stopped talking, but it was too late; he'd piqued my paranoia, bigtime.

How the hell could Theo, Emilio and Reuben know this much about me? When I picked up the men being offered, only the Mayor would be there. And he would leave the moment I arrived. Emilio might have suspected I was going to vanish the two guys he helped the Mayor bring, but he wasn't around to know what I was interested in...and yet, he had known. Except...he didn't know I'd test the ones I wanted, and leave behind the ones I didn't want. And that I'd leave the money in the house, tacitly letting the Mayor know it was up to him what happened to my rejects. So how did Theo know what I looked like? How?

"I don't know where we are," said Vermin, his voice near panic.

I rose and looked out the front. He'd missed the turn. I patted him on the shoulder. "Keep our guest company," I said. "I'll take over."

He pulled to a stop and we switched places. When Theo saw Vermin, he all but wailed, *"No, do not do this! You cannot do this to me!"*

"What...what's he sayin'?" asked Vermin.

"That he's innocent," I said. "Why not check his dick out?"

"What?! What're you gonna do with him?"

"We've been over that."

Vermin huffed then carefully settled down by Theo, cross-legged, looking at him like he was some experiment. I turned the van around and headed back to the turn, then set the rear-view mirror to where I could watch what Vermin was doing.

He rolled Theo back on his side...and this surprising mix of interest and uncertainty crossed his face. He was torn up about something, and I figured it was time to find out what.

I made the turn, drove down a few blocks, headed down an alley then stopped the van in a parking space behind a vacant building. There was no shade, so I left it running with the AC on low, got in the back and crouched between the two of them. I kept my face turned to Vermin but I was half watching Theo as I said, "You two know each other."

Vermin shook his head, shaken. "No!"

But what really mattered was Theo casting me a sudden sharp look of horror then focusing his eyes on Vermin. I was right, and what was more? The little shit knew English.

I shoved Vermin to the other end of the van and pulled my knife. "What the fuck kind of game're you two playin' at?" I snapped, my eyes sharp on Vermin.

He crouched by the rear doors, scared, his eyes locked on me.

Theo kicked at the back of the driver's seat and jammed against me, so I flipped him on his back and straddled his hips to keep him still, and man, him squirming under me was like heaven. I almost giggled from joy of it. So just to be a dick, I used the knife to slit his shirt open, showing him just how sharp it was. He still twisted and shifted under me and son-of-a-bitch, his body...so taut and tight, not muscular but trim, with a bit more hair around his little brown nips than I expected...it screamed to my inner animal and I pinched both tits. He howled.

"I know you speak English," I growled to Theo, "so don't fuck with me. You two get one chance to make this right. Tell me what the fuck you're up to, or somebody's gonna lose an ear. A nose. Finger. And if you think you can stop me, just try."

Theo looked back at Vermin, not even trying to hide it.

Vermin now kept glancing between me and Theo, confused.

I nodded. *"Okay, Theo, I am removing the gag. But if you yell, I will cut your left tit off. Got it?"*

He scrunched his eyes shut then opened them, looked away from me and nodded.

I sliced through the tape and pulled it away. He was scared and gasping for breath, so I added. "I mean it, I'm not gonna hurt you if you tell me the truth. I may even let you go. So be smart. Be cool. Lay it out. Let's start with Emilio and Reuben."

"You know their names," Theo said, his accent light.

"The Mayor told him," said Vermin.

I glared at him. "You *do* speak Spanish."

"Not really. I know some...and I heard the names."

Theo was horrified. *"The Mayor is behind this? Oh, shit, we are fucked. we are all fucked."*

"Not if you explain this to me!" I snapped.

"He is an evil man! He works with you to hurt us! To hurt others! The men he sold to you were decent! They were his opponents! He made them vanish to keep his power!"

"You're lying..."

"No, I swear to you —"

"Stop it!" And I let every ounce of fury I felt color my face as I snarled, *"You think I trust him? You think me stupid enough to believe what he said to me? I verified it through other sources. People who do not care about him keeping power. I do not go blind into a business deal. The men he gave to me worked with drug cartels and for rich men trying to steal your wealth. I checked every one."*

"No, no, that is not true!"

I sat back, irritated. He thought he could bullshit me, and oh, did that really piss me off. I grabbed the tape and wrapped it back around his mouth before he could scream, then I twisted him around to where he was seated against me, facing Vermin.

"You asked me what I was up to?" I snarled. "I'll show you." I kept the knife in my left hand and used my right to unbuckle Theo's belt, my eyes on Vermin as I continued, "And as I do, you tell me how they got you to be part of this."

"He...he was gonna tell you..."

"He don't know what's he's got himself into and thinks I'll believe his bullshit. But the Mayor of this town ain't the only man I deal with, in Mexico, and the others vouched for him. They wouldn't if they couldn't trust him. So how'd you get caught up in it?"

I caressed Theo's left nip with the knife, making him cringe, then unzipped his pants, my eyes locked on Vermin.

He gave in. "I...I needed money. I'm stuck in El Paso and it's a shit hole and I wanna go home."

"But the Army..."

"I'm not in the Army, anymore. They...they found out I'm gay and kicked me out. General discharge."

"But *Don't ask, don't tell...*"

He snorted. "They didn't ask and I didn't tell, but they still did it. Told me to make my own way. But I'm broke. Workin' thirty hours at a fuckin' Micky D's and can barely make rent and food...and...and I'm sick of it..."

I slipped my hand inside Theo's pants, to his horror, and fondled him through his briefs. He howled and tried to twist away.

"Where's home?" I asked.

"Manhattan Beach. I need the money to get set up, get a car, get my life back."

"What about your folks?"

"My fuckin' CO told 'em about me. They don't...they don't wanna see me, no more."

"Shit. I know how that goes." I slit Theo's pants open wider, with the knife, and gazed at a nice little bulge caught behind colorful Hugo Boss boxer briefs. "How much're they payin' you?"

"Ten thousand. Dollars. Got half up front."

I groped Theo some more, rolling his dick and balls inside the Hugos. "And what'd they tell you was gonna happen?"

"You'd been kidnappin' and rapin' guys. They wanted you to get caught. I thought you'd do a lot more'n you did."

"Get caught how?" By this point Theo wasn't fighting me, just letting me do what I wanted.

"They said you took guys back to the States," Vermin said, "but they'd get you busted at the border, with me in the car, and...and they were gonna tie it to the Mayor."

I nearly howled. "You went along with that? You gotta be fuckin' kiddin' me."

He shook his head. "They were gonna call in the Army, get you stopped. One of 'em has a contact."

"And they told you all of this? Seriously?"

He nodded his head and heaved a sigh, as if he was relieved not to have to keep up the pretense, anymore. "The guys I ran with were Latino. Reason I learned some Spanish was so I'd know if they were talkin' 'bout me. We all went in the Army, together and..."

"And..."

"He...Theo and Emilio argued over it," he said, nodding to Theo, "in Spanish."

I kissed Theo's neck and slipped my hand holding the knife inside his Hugos, slicing into them. He cringed.

"Theo wasn't all that sure about it," Vermin continued. "But they were gonna follow and keep watch. They hired me 'cause they needed a guy who didn't mind having sex with another guy, in case it went that far...so..."

I nodded and leaned back, letting the knife slice open the Hugos along one leg. Theo nearly started weeping.

Y'know, I liked Vermin. Liked the way he looked. I even liked how he was spooked by all of this, yet vaguely interested. Oh, I was still going to have the Sheriff check his story, but if he was acting, he should be in the movies.

"It's all fucked up now, ain't it?" he asked. "I'm not gonna get the rest. They may even want back what they paid me."

"Why? I did rape you."

Theo looked around at me, startled.

Vermin just frowned. "You gave me a blow job. And it was damn good, so it don't count. Besides, you were sayin' shit to me, to calm me down, and...and havin' Emilio and Reuben suckin' on my tits...that was weird..."

"That's 'cause they thought they were bein' clever, but didn't really know what was what." Then I looked at Theo and cooed, "Ain't that right, sweet cheeks," and pinched his right nip. He yelped.

"Yeah," said Vermin. "You said you don't deal in Anglo guys. That got me all confused."

"Yep, just guys like adorable little Theo, here. Shall I show much I like to take pretty little Mexicans like you?"

I kissed his ear then fondled him under the remains of the Hugos. He jolted and tried to twist away, but I had too good a grip on him. I let my fingers trail up and then down his little bit of a treasure trail to the top of his pants, slowly, lovingly. He slammed his feet against the floor and sides of the van, horrified, but it didn't do him any good. I pulled the sliced Hugos aside to reveal his pubes and then the base of his dick. And I seriously hoped he was a grower and not a shower, because he wasn't that big, but then I showed it all.

And froze.

He was circumcised.

Cut.

What the actual fuck?

Almost no men in Mexico are cut.

I shoved him face down on the van's floor and dug his wallet from his back pocket then found his ID for the local college. Theoden Miramin.

The same name as the pharmacy, and he had a thousand pesos on him, around fifty bucks. And Hugo Boss undies ain't cheap, either!

I rolled Theo to one side then jumped over to pull the mattress off the hideaway slot, making Vermin crush against the back doors, and opened it. "Help me get 'em out," I shot at him.

He did, confused.

Theo whined at seeing Emilio and Rueben. They were still unconscious. I dug in Emilio's jeans to find his wallet and searched through it. No student ID on him, but nearly three-thousand pesos and a photo of his wife and kids. Reuben did have an ID to the same college, showing he was twenty-one, with not quite five-hundred pesos in his wallet.

Holy fucking shit, Hunter, pay attention! They paid Vermin five-thousand dollars, up front, if his story was true, so these guys were part of Mexico's middle class. If they vanished, there would be hell to pay.

I returned to Theo. He tried to roll away from me but I jumped over to sit on his legs and asked, *"Are you Jewish?"*

He just glared at me.

"Muslim?"

At that, he just rolled his eyes.

I looked at his ID, again. He was nineteen. I dug into his satchel to find a couple books on politics and Mexican law.

Oh, I did not like the picture building in my head. Middle-class life. Youthful idealism. College educated. Plenty of time to think about something other than survival. That can be a scary combination to the powers that be, and easy to manipulate.

I grabbed Theo by the hair and made him look at Emilio, asking, "Does he work for the Mayor?"

Theo hesitated then nodded, growing angry.

"I could've told you that," said Vermin.

"Be quiet," I snapped then turned back to Theo. *"Was all of this his idea?"*

Theo seemed to surrender to reality, at that point, and nodded.

Which brought up a new possibility. Emilio was out to dethrone the mayor, and he thought he could use me to help him do it. He thought he'd trick me into handling the dirty work for him, and was using some college kids to help him with it. Maybe all of them pulled together the money to hire Vermin.

Okay...I needed time to think, but I noticed Vermin looking hard at me, confused.

"What is it?" I asked.

"I don't understand what's goin' on," he said, his voice quivering. "The whole thing's blown up, so why's it still goin' on? Why're these guys still tied up? You gonna rape 'em? Or...or kill 'em?"

I chuckled. "No, I don't waste men. I'm just tryin' to figure things out. And...I need to come up with a new business strategy. The old model's blown apart even worse than I thought it had."

"C'mon, man, that don't make sense!"

I looked straight at him then grinned and shifted to sit next to Theo. I showed his balls off to Vermin as I said, "I'm a hunter. I get somethin' some people want. Something they'll pay for. Pay well."

"Somethin'? You mean, guys? Like...like...like him. And me?" I nodded. "You thought they were gonna give me to you for...to be...a slave?"

"Not give. Sell. It's a business transaction." Then I looked at Theo, grinned and pulled at his dick. "Only now, you're the new package in this, sweet cheeks."

He grimaced and tensed...but what was better? He was starting to grow...and grow nicely.

"Shit," said Vermin. "How much were you gonna get? For me?"

Okay, that set my inner wildcat to purring. When they want to talk money, you know they're yours for the right price.

"I dunno. Theo's young. Cute. Circumcised. Nice tan line. Tight body. Fine legs and ass. He might bring in seventy-five, maybe a hundred thou. Normally, I'd pay thirty for him..."

"Dollars or pesos?"

I laughed. "Dollars, of course." I caressed Theo's chin. He didn't even think to flinch. "Guy like you, Vermin, you'd bring triple that."

"Because I'm white?"

I nodded. "And cut. And built nice and tight."

Theo began to whimper and lose his growing erection.

I kissed his ear, murmuring, *"Don't worry, sweet cheeks; I will never let anything happen to you. You're too pretty."*

"Shit, so you did take guys back to the States?" I nodded. "Like a coyote."

"Don't be insulting," I snapped.

"But how? Everything you're talkin' about's illegal."

"Lots of things're illegal, but they happen."

He ran his hands through his hair, horrified...and yet, I could see he was thinking. Considering. Trying to take it all in. That was a good sign. Inner wildcat began to purr.

"What happens when you turn 'em over?" he asked.

I shrugged. "My involvement ends." I held Theo closer and kissed his neck before saying, "Though with you, I'll exercise my droit morale." And pinched his nips, again.

"What's that?" Now Vermin was just plain interested.

I licked Theo's ear. "It means whoever takes him can't hurt him without my permission. Which I'll never give."

I continued playing with Theo's lovely dick and balls and pubes and hair and nips and pecs and hips and belly. He was finally proving to be a grower, not only in length but also girth. I could see, once full, he would be more than glorious. I halfway wondered if I wanted to let go of him. To get a good payout, I needed to keep him virginal, but a nice fucking would do a lot to sort out the chaos in my head.

So was it the mayor behind this shit? Or was Emilio pulling a fast one? Was it a group of college guys thinking they were doing a good thing? Seemed awfully elaborate and immoral for any of them...and the execution of it was so damn sloppy and amateurish. Made me wonder if something else was going on. Something I hadn't figured out yet.

I rolled Theo over, pushed his pants down and caressed what turned out to be a really amazingly adorable ass...and slowly talked myself out of fucking it. Dammit.

He wasn't struggling, anymore. He'd finally figured out he was caught so let me put my hands where I wanted. He whimpered a little when I became too intimate for him to deal with, and I loved the sound of it. He was such a beautiful boy.

Boy.

Just seven years younger than me and I'm calling him boy. Had I really aged that much since being nineteen? I'd made a lot of money, true. Had enjoyed myself without much worry. Had a nice rhythm going. Maybe too nice. I'd been thinking I was in a rut, but now that I could see it changing, I wanted it to stay the same. That's not smart. It's lazy and careless, and puts you behind the curve when it comes to growing your business. You have to look to the future to maintain momentum. And what had my lazy-kitty complacence brought about? I was now being used to do something I'd said I'd never do.

What made it awkward is, I loved having Theo lying against me. Caressing him from his dick along his belly to his nips. If he'd been one of the troublemakers out to harm the Mayor's city, I'd have had no problem taking him and providing him to someone else to make use of. But I had a growing suspicion he was just a dumb kid caught in a political fight that was way over his head.

I nestled my lips close to his ear and whispered, *"What have you done to the Mayor?"*

He looked at me, startled. Still squirming just a little under my gentle caresses.

"Do you threaten him, in some way?"

He almost tried to answered, and that said a lot.

"Did you try to drive him from office? You, others like you? Rene? Manuel? Oscar? Are you all students? Are there more young men and women in your group? Are you five the best-looking boys? Were you trying to use me so you could get to the Mayor?"

At the last sentence, he grew tense and turned to look straight up at the roof of the van.

Okay...that was a pretty strong indication I'd hit a nerve.

Which built up scenario number four — they were students in a democracy group trying to get rid of a corrupt Mayor. And Emilio had caught on and was working with the mayor to set them up. Have them vanish like a busload of guys in southern Mexico had, never to be seen, again. Mix in a government that didn't give a shit about them, and it's done.

So how could it have worked?

Well...hire a desperate gay man as bait. A guy who's had sex with guys. Maybe sold himself a few times. Promise him a shitload of cash to help them. Call me down. I give them the money for him, and get busted en route back to the States by the army. With a kidnapped American man in my van. That would be a lovely scandal. Emilio presents evident to tie it back to the college kids, and they're now neutralized.

But still, the whole question of Catholic morality factored into this, and there were no guarantees everything would go right. Hell, it might just bring their antagonism against the Mayor out in the open. Plus, the army would have to play along, and they were notorious for doing the exact opposite of what you expect. Granted, Hernandez was strong with them, as were a couple of other people I knew, but I seriously doubted the mayor had the same level of contact within that hierarchy.

Plus, if the mayor was behind this, he'd have known my prohibition against Anglo-Americans as merchandise, which could have killed the whole deal. So that idea got shot down.

Or...could that be another reason they chose Vermin? They knew I'd have taken him back, doped him up and released him. I had one idiot referred to me try to palm off an Anglo guy who'd dumped her. Hernandez had handled her after I dropped the kid in San Diego, hopped up on acid. But no one else knew of that.

No one...except the mayor. Stupid little Hunter had told him about it when emphasizing *no gringos*.

Shit. Teach me to open my big mouth.

Well...that was their fatal flaw. Not enough research and too many assumptions. That's a quick way to do a crash and burn. You always need to know all the angles...and they hadn't.

Anyway, whatever plan had been in motion, I'd reversed it. And I had a deep dark feeling the Mayor was behind the whole thing. That he and Emilio were working together to get rid of some democracy boys. He hadn't been all that shocked at finding Emilio there. And he had changed the backup plan without any input from me. He'd have had time to make sure he had an alibi not only for himself but his men. But that way the American would be saved, and five troublesome brats would be gone, as well as an associate who could prove to be a problem down the road, and people would focus on their disappearance and blame a dozen other groups while the Mayor kept his position and scam going.

Oh, this was lovely.

"What's goin' on?"

I jolted. I'd almost forgotten about Vermin.

"What're we waitin' for?"

I looked at Theo's dick and saw it was erect but not completely hard. I wouldn't have minded sucking on it for a couple hours, it was so pretty. Instead, I tucked him back into the remains of the Hugos and checked my phone. No message yet from the Mayor.

"Info on the guys," I said. "The mayor said, wait here."

I rolled Theo onto his belly, pulled out the shots and gave one to him in his shoulder. He nearly screamed in horror but quickly succumbed to the drug.

Ten minutes later, I was still trying to narrow down the likeliest possibilities when I got a text. *Oscar walking your way. Black jeans. Green hooded shirt. Backpack.*

Finally! The morning coolness was starting to burn away. I wanted this completed within the next hour so I could get on the road and crank up the AC to keep my cargo safe from heatstroke.

That also broke me out of my thoughts, so I asked Vermin, "Who'd you meet with, when settin' this all up?"

"Huh?" He looked at me, lost, then said, "Told you, Theo and Emilio."

"When?"

"Uh...Sunday. I came down with them. Stayed at a hotel not far away, that night."

"A hotel?"

"Yeah."

"On your own?"

"Yeah. It's real pretty. Quiet. I went walkin' in the woods. There's trails out back."

"Did you see anybody? Talk to anybody?"

"People that run the place. Restaurant next door."

"This hotel has blue walls and a tile roof?"

"Yeah. Been there?"

I nodded. That's where I'd stayed.

"You weren't there, last night," I said.

"No, we camped up at the house. They said you'd come up real early."

Things were finally getting sorted in my brain. Anglo guy shows up at a hotel and sees people then vanishes and is located, bound and gagged in the back of my van after being molested. Which led me to another issue. No matter how alive he was when the van was stopped, could Vermin could have wound up dead? Strangled? Leaving everything on me? That would really fire the American justice system into going nuts over an American raped and murdered by a fellow American male. The house wouldn't even be part of the revelation. Nor would any payoff. Just a corrupt Customs official, or two.

But why? There had to be a reason to mess with a successful operation. Had I done something to piss the Mayor off? Done enough to cancel a lucrative contract, for him? Was our deal close to being discovered and broadcast, so he set out to derail it? Had the people he was going up against finally got to him? Bought him off? Had he shifted the total blame to me to save himself?

Shit, I was back to having too damn many questions bouncing around my brain that I had no answers to, yet. I needed time to do my research and figure things out, time I didn't have.

"Vermin, did they sneak you out of the hotel?"

"No. Just said some guy they knew was there and they didn't wanna see him, so I met 'em down the road."

"And you still went with them to the house!?"

He looked at me, confused. "Yeah, it was just Emilio. Reuben was already there. But they'd paid me half the money, and I'd let a couple buddies know where I was going, so..."

I sighed. "So they tied you and tore your clothes there?"

He hesitated. "Yeah. Reuben jumped me while I was still asleep. That did spook me. I dunno...but I...well, I started thinkin' he *was* gonna do somethin'. He was havin' all kinds of fun. Kept grabbin' at me. Rollin' around with me. Gigglin' like some Steven King freak. Emilio kept tellin' him to calm down, but he wasn't...not till you showed up."

"Oh, fuck."

"Yeah. I was kind of relieved."

Things were starting to make sense. I'd been contacted two days before, the moment they knew Vermin would go along with it. So now I was ninety percent sure I was targeted to be caught, and one way or the other blamed, for some reason.

I doubted I'd ever get a truly straight answer as to why this was happening; I just knew it was over. Everything in Mexico was over. Even Hernandez. What I needed to do now was make sure I exited with a decent package so I could reframe my business strategy.

I did a quick calculation of income versus expenses taking into account risk factors and backup allowance needed to finance a shift in operations. So...I'd tested Emilio and knew he could bring in seventy-five thousand, easy. Maybe eighty. Reuben forty or fifty...though I'd have a better idea once I examined and tested him. But if he was into games with guys, that could mean no virginity and a more narrow focus on clientele...so figure on thirty to thirty-five.

Theo was a good hundred-K, now that I'd seen the size of his dick, virgin or not.

Keeping reserves at the low end of expectations, that made for just past two-hundred K when I needed at least twice that much.

I looked Vermin over, again. Tested. Works well. Not a virgin, but with a guy like him it's not as much of a deal-breaker. Even with his tattoos, he could bring in two-hundred, maybe two-fifty. And since he was at the lower end of the Anglo scale, with no one in his corner to fight for him, he might be doable. But I needed to know more about him before committing. Manhattan Beach has some high-end people, and if a rich kid goes missing, even if his folks weren't happy with him that raises too many issues. Plus he might have brothers or sisters or friends, oh my.

I put him in the emergency backup category.

Okay, so let's see what Oscar might bring.

I pulled out a shot of anesthetic.

"Keep watch on Theo," I said to Vermin.

"What're you gonna do?"

Shit, that fucking question, again. "Get verification," I snapped.

Vermin slipped over...and I snuck the second shot into his bicep. He jolted and spun around, crying, "What the...fuck..." He started to argue and grab at me, but then he was out of it.

I let him lie next to Theo then got out of the van, crept down the alley and looked up the road. It was a two-lane blacktop with buildings and walls along one side and a tree-shaded park along the other. Some cars were parked at the curb but overall it was quiet and very middle class.

And striding towards me was Oscar.

With a couple of guys.

Shit.

I got back in the van and sent the Mayor a text, *Has to wait; with friends.*

No time, was the response.

My reply was, *Then he's a No.*

I didn't mean it; I already had a plan. I got out three shots of the anesthetic, carefully held two in one hand and had the other ready to go, then slipped back down the alley.

Oscar and his buddies were just passing its entrance...and now that I got a good look at him, I nearly stopped breathing. Tight body. Glorious ass. Legs to die for. Arms of perfection. Hair dancing over tan skin in all the right places. Thick brunette mop on his head. Classic Latino features. Fuck...he was at least two-hundred-thousand.

His two buddies weren't all that bad, either. Obviously gym rats, the way they were pumped up and dressed, with nice faces and solid muscles. Not overdone but not natural build, either. The beefier one was dressed in clingy fleece shorts and a loose sleeveless tee, with hairless legs that gave him a serious strut and a face that looked like a growl; the taller, trimmer one was in cutoff jeans that had been rolled up to reveal wonderfully hairy legs, a dress shirt that was only half tucked in, and a form to his butt that promised heaven to whoever wanted it. His face was long and sharp.

Fifty-K each, no matter what.

I let them pass then ran up behind them, saying, *"Oscar, hi, got a message from Theo, for you."*

As he turned around, I slammed a shot into jeans guy's bicep, on his right, who yelped.

"Message from who?" he asked, confused, not realizing what I was doing before I slipped a shot into the back of his left bicep. *"Hey!"*

Shorts guy caught on and jumped me. The other two piled on and we tumbled to the ground.

Three on one? Oh, was it fun! Hardbodies slamming against hardbodies. Hands gripping and grabbing. Legs tangled with each other. I got hold of some good places they wouldn't have wanted me to grab...proving they had nice butts, nice balls, nice dicks...so yeah, I was enjoying the shit out of it. Hell, I almost shot my wad during the tussle.

I managed to jab Shorts in the thigh, with the shot, and within moments, all three were unconscious on the sidewalk. I picked Oscar up and carried him to the van to lay him next to Vermin and Theo.

I had to drag shorts guy; he weighed at least two-forty, every bit of it muscle. But oh, did it feel nice. Jeans was easier to carry and looked more solid than he really was, but I didn't care. He had the look.

Once all three were in the van, I quietly drove away. That's when I noticed a message from the Mayor. *End it. No good.*

Too late, buddy. I had already aimed the van straight for Agua Prieta. Rene and Miguel would have to be some other time. I wanted to get my cargo the hell out of Mexico before night fell, and that was my closest crossing point.

And safest.

FIVE

Once I was out of town, I bound and gagged Vermin. I needed consistency, here. Then I got Oscar's wallet to find he was twenty-one and at the college. His friends were Juan (shorts) and Tomás (jeans) both a year or two older and also at the college. A quick check showed none of them were Jewish or Muslim, though Oscar had been endowed not only with good looks but everything else.

Life is so fucking unfair.

I bound and gagged them all, and it was seeing the seven of them laid out together, in a line, that made me realize just how fucking insane I was for trying this.

And giggle from the rush of it.

I sent a text to the Sheriff: *7 items, Agua Prieta.*

His response was immediate. *Are you nuts?*

My answer? *Probably.*

I hit the gas and headed north.

The hardest part of the whole deal used to be getting my cargo back into the states without being caught. The van I had before this was an old 4-wheel drive job with a jacked up suspension. I knew a couple spots in the Rio Grande that were shallow enough to get across, if I was careful, especially during the drought. But border patrol had caught onto it, so I'd connected with a couple of guys who'd tied some boards to a trio of skiffs and could float me across a deeper spot. That was a bit too scary for me; no need to have your van wind up underwater and your cargo drowned. Still, it worked a couple of times.

But then I connected with Horace, in Douglas, Arizona, just across from Aqua Prieta.

In a Dairy Queen by a Walmart, swear to god.

I was finishing up a cheeseburger and fries and thinking seriously about a chocolate cone when he strutted in. One of those big, beefy, hair on his chest rednecks who manage to make shitkicker jeans held up by a thick leather belt with a brass buckle the size of my head and a cowboy shirt with mother-of-pearl snaps look too goddamned perfect, even over the hint of a beer belly. And he wore Dingo boots! He had a nose that went straight down from his forehead and those smallish cowboy eyes, and he all but rolled as he walked, he was so loose and fluid.

What made him especially worthy of my attention was, the second I saw him I knew he was open to possibilities.

Contrasting him was his near-twin, albeit with cafe-au-lait colored skin instead of sunburn and semi-freckles. One of those guys who aren't black or white or Latino, but some fine exotic mixture of the three made even more intense by sloe-eyes and clean-cut looks. It was obvious they were gym buddies, and just as obvious that was as far as it went. No pings off the twin. Dammit. I'd loved to have been the meat in their sandwich, every pun you can think of intended.

They got a couple of double burgers, fries and shakes and sat in a booth two down from me. Horace facing my way and so careful not to look at me, I knew I had to have some fun. I was going to do an overnight at a motel, close by, and head down to Hernandez the next morning, so I hopped back to the window and got a vanilla cone. Then returned to my booth and gave that cone the best damn licking in the history of DQ. And the whole time, my eyes were locked on Horace.

Oh, I was not in the mood to be subtle.

He noticed, holy shit did he notice. I caught the beginning of a smile as he and his buddy chatted. Then he stuck a perfect leg out of the booth and did a number on his shake's straw that brought a grin to my face. I put my own leg out, sucked in the rest of the cone, and wrote my motel info on a napkin. I waited till they were pretty much done with their meal, then I *casually* went to dump the crap on my tray and *let* the napkin float down to the floor, faked like I hadn't noticed, strolled out to my van and drove back to the motel, a long low ranch-style place that was new in the 40s, maybe, but hadn't been worked on since.

An hour later, just as the room was cool enough to be comfortable, guess who knocked at my door, in a nice, tight, amazingly perfect Border Patrol officer's uniform, holding the napkin.

"You really shouldn't litter," he said in a drawl that went clear to Texas. Then he slipped the napkin in my jeans pocket.

I wound a finger through a belt loop and pulled him into the room, whispering, "You gonna arrest me?"

"No time," he said. "I'm on duty in an hour."

He shoved me back on the bed. I bounced and wound up leaning on my elbows, looking up at him, my legs hanging over the side. He slipped between them, hands resting on hips and a bulge in his crotch.

"Just had a shower," he said. "I'm feelin' real good. You think of anything that'll send me to work with a real smile?"

It was so fucking goofy and porn-style, I laughed and sat up and ran my fingers over his fly. There was definitely something there ready for fun.

"Parade rest," I said.

He took in a deep breath, spread his legs a bit wider, and put his hands behind him. I put my hands on his hips, just below his belt.

"Keep 'em there," I whispered. "Like you're handcuffed."

He let the breath out and I felt his ass clench, then he did as he was told.

I unbuckled his belt and undid the pants and slid the zipper down...down...down. He wore boxers that were maybe a size too small for him, making for a nice bulge as his dick tried to escape through the narrow fly. I unbuttoned his shirt and opened it to reveal golden hair fanning up from his pubes and over his lovely waving belly. He still smelled of Dial soap. I ran my lips over those hairs as I slipped my fingers up to diddle his nips. They had hair around them, soft and elegant, and I was praising every god there was that he didn't shave.

He grunted when I pinched them, his ass clenching and his dick jolting.

I chuckled. "Don't move. I'm gonna take you to the edge so many times in the next forty-five minutes, you're gonna scream 'fore you cream. But for the full experience, don't move."

He didn't. Even as I slipped his dick out and felt the weight of it in my hand. Long and nice, not the prettiest or even the biggest I'd ever seen, but he was cut and the form was just plain lovely.

I ran my lips up and down and around. My tongue joined in, especially around the head and slit. I was so soft and easy and steady with it all, my hands holding his ass to keep in him place. His breath grew ragged and me even thinking of touching his tits made him groan and his dick stiffen just a little more.

Holy shit, did I love the way it looked once it was full on hard. Fat and round, slightly twisty, with a head that was damn near perfection. Veins curling around it in all the right places. No piercings or discoloration. Couple that with how full and firm his ass felt and how glorious his legs were, I knew I could get a lot of cash for him, if I was willing to risk it.

But there was no need to rush things. If he did me right, I'd be happy to let him keep doing so as long as I wanted. And right then, I wanted forever.

I didn't even touch his balls till the second time I'd brought him to the brink. Then I slipped them out of the boxers' slit to caress and kiss and lick and nuzzle and get him close to firing without doing anything else. After that, I focused on his nips and his navel and the hair spread across his belly and ran my hands up and down his legs and over his amazingly hard ass, using the cloth of his pants to add to the sensations. Within half an hour, I had him close to insanity from need, his hands still behind him, his stance unchanged, his hips thrusting him into my mouth once I started swallowing his shaft. It takes me a little while, but once I loosen up I deep throat with the best of 'em.

"C'mon, goddammit," he gasped when I pulled back, again. "Stop teasin'. Shit."

"You like my blow job?" I asked, on so innocently.

"Fuck, you do it better'n any girl ever has."

"You get sucked off by girls, too?"

"I don't give a fuck who does the suckin', so long as it's good, and you...you're deadly."

I chuckled and cupped my hands around his ass to finger between his cheeks, through the pants. He gasped and shoved his dick at me. I kissed its head.

"I'm gonna show you what deadly really means," I muttered. Then I went to town on him. Sucked him all the way in and worked him with my tongue and rolled his balls in one hand while I groped an ass cheek in the other and shifted his pants down so I could toy with his hole and make him whine and grunt and push at my mouth and kept going and kept going and kept going until he cried out and fired straight into the back of my throat. Over and over. His gasps were like those of a man who's found heaven as a river of semen flowing out of him. I choked, it was so such. Swallowed. Kept sucking and fondling and groping and he tried to pull away but I wouldn't let go till I knew he'd been drained. He was close to crying from my non-stop abuse.

Finally, I stood up and pulled him close and he leaned against me. Shit, he was a heavy fucker, so I curled around and laid him back on the bed, his breath deep and harsh, his chest pumping, his dick still hard and painful to look at. That's when I felt something wet in my briefs. I opened my pants and chuckled.

"Bitch, look what you did," I said.

He made himself rise up to rest on his elbows and holy shit, was he lovely, right then. His shirt parted to reveal his glorious pecs and nips. His boxers halfway down his hips. His dick and balls elegantly sensual in the extreme as they lay across the thin cotton plaid. Half of his thighs visible, thanks to me lowering his pants, showing a light swirl of hair on them. He took a look at my briefs and saw I'd cum without realizing it, and a crooked grin crossed his face.

"Fuck," he gasped.

"Maybe next time."

He flopped back on the bed, still breathing hard. "Not me."

I nodded. "We'll see."

He just laughed.

I started going through Douglas every time I went down to pick up some new guys, and Horace and I got to be steady. We never did fuck; he was of the opinion you only fuck women, not men, and I got the feeling he had one girl he was doing it with, when I wasn't in town. So it was always me sucking him off.

Which I didn't mind.

It wasn't till I'd known him a year that I suggested he could help me when I brought merchandise back from Mexico. Just let me know when he'd be on duty and what lane. He'd do the inspection and pass me on...and I'd *pay him off*, later.

He thought I was talking drugs and that I'd been giving such fantastic blow jobs to get to him. But the fact that I kept giving them every time I went over, and even a couple times when I came back, empty-handed, finally relaxed him to the point where he agreed. I didn't tell him what my *merchandise* really was. This was why I started giving the guys a light booster shot, to keep them quiet in the hide-a-ways. I also started slipping money into his pants after our sessions.

He never turned it down.

But then one day he was supposed to be on duty...only when I got to his window, his sloe-eyed workout partner had taken over. The guy's name was Meriquez and it was too late for me to change direction, so I figured I was cooked. I had three guys in the cubby hole, this time, two of them half-naked; forget trying to explain that shit away. Of course, I wouldn't say a word about Horace; no need to get him caught up in this. So I just rolled on up.

To my surprise, even though he noticed the mattress in back, Meriquez didn't ask to have it moved. Instead, he passed me. I left, fast.

The next time I was headed down, I met with Horace and found out he'd been accused of *forcing* a Mexican kid to give him a blow job. He'd caught the guy trying to sneak across the border in the trunk of a Chevy. The investigation was ongoing, but since no one else had ever made that sort of complaint against Horace, before, and he'd been fucking a girl they all knew, they seemed about ready to dismiss the charges. I'd dealt with Meriquez just after the accusation had been made.

"Was it true?" I asked. We were lying on my king-size motel bed, him in uniform, shirt and t-shirt pulled up to show off his gorgeous chest and nips, his soft little belly rolling down to a crotch filled with sandy hair, his gorgeous dick flopped back and drained but still fat and sassy. Him still loving the overload of endorphins I'd just brought to him. I was also beginning to relax after firing. His pants had drifted down his knees, this time, and my fingers were running over his long, elegant treasure trail and the hair on his tree-trunk thighs.

He looked at me for a long time, then he sighed a reply. "I'm findin' that I'm missin' what you do. Want more of it, but you're not through here much. Thought it'd be the same as with you. Wasn't."

"How'd it happen?"

"He offered. An' he did it. An' I got off. But you, shit, you rock me senseless."

"What about your *girlfriend*?"

"She don't like doin' that. Just wants to fuck."

"You sound bored."

"She's okay. 'Sides, we're tryin' to have a kid. That ain't gonna happen with a blow job."

I rolled on top of him, rubbing my dick against his. "Next time I come through, maybe I'll liven things up a little, for you."

He squirmed under me, wary. "I ain't fuckin' you and you sure as hell ain't fuckin' me."

Wanna bet? hit my brain, but all I said was, "I know."

"Then what you plannin'?"

"You'll see. I'll be back across in two days, and gettin' in late. I'll stay overnight, this time."

He looked at me, uncertain. "I'm back on duty, then. Off at midnight."

"Perfect." Then I kissed my way down his belly to his crotch and nuzzled his pubes, and reversed the softening, and proved he wasn't as drained as he thought.

So here I was, on my way back, only with a lot more cargo than I'd planned on. I was set to arrive just about dusk, and the Sheriff was meeting me outside Douglas instead of our usual transfer point at Wickenburg, so it was going to be up to Vermin to help bring Horace into the fold, as it were.

Meaning, I was going to fuck Horace, that night. Full and complete and show him what he's been missing. Hopefully as he fucked Vermin. Or got sucked off by him. I got the feeling my new little buddy wouldn't mind.

Things went like usual, when I crossed back. The sun was just setting when I gave all the guys a light booster. There were too many for the cubby hole, so I scrounged up a bunch of cardboard boxes and bought a few sets of sheets. I stacked the empty boxes over the guys and covered that with the loose sheets. It looked like shit but Horace wouldn't care. I sent him a message, *DQ*, and got back a quick response, *3*. That was his lane.

I pulled in, my passport out, and he looked as hot and horny as ever. He actually licked his lips when he saw me. I ran my tongue around mine to remind him of what's in store. He let out a huge sigh and we went through the ritual.

Where were you?
How long?
Why?
Bringing anything back to declare?

And on and on. This time he took a bit longer and went into more detail, but then he waved me through.

Meriquez was the guy choosing cars to pull over and search. I waved at him, smiling. He frowned at me then turned away and stopped a Toyota SUV that was behind me. I headed on.

There was a spot up the 191 not far from the prison that the Sheriff had directed me to as a good transfer point. But two minutes after I'd crossed the border, I got a message from him.

Indian.

It meant there was a problem. Don't do anything.

I headed straight to my motel and checked in, like normal, then I parked the van two doors down from my room, under a sad pair of trees. I pulled out everything of mine and put it in the room, all nice and casual. Then I took a lovely swim in the pool's warm water, followed by a nice long hot shower, and used the facility's laundry to wash my clothes, wrapped only in a towel.

I'd have felt very risqué if anyone else had been around.

Along about eight a massive honey wagon wandered up and stopped crossways behind the van. It was the type with four small dressing rooms and two smaller toilets; one for the boys and one for girls, I guess. Its engine kept running so the AC would work. The doors all faced the motel's.

A moment later, a fifty-three foot semi-rig rolled up and sort of blocked the view from one direction. A wing of the motel sort of blocked the other direction. It all looked very calm, casual and incidental in the way it was done. I was bringing my dried clothes back from the laundry when it happened so just sauntered up without a care in the world, damn near naked. I'd left the van unlocked and the windows down, and the drugs were only just now set to wear off.

The Sheriff came out of the honey wagon's front room; six burly men in holey jeans and athletic tees came out of the others, looking like an Olympics wrestling team, in all races, colors and creeds, I guess.

I set the bundle of clothes in my room, tightened my towel, and opened the back of the van. They pulled off the boxes and sheets and cardboard to reveal the cargo. Sure enough, Juan and Reuben were almost conscious. No smiles from anyone, no words except for me pointing to Vermin and saying, "Not him."

The Sheriff saw him and growled, "Oh, they fuckin' didn't."

I nodded.

"Son-of-a-bitch, I thought you was just bein' paranoid. You gonna handle this?"

I nodded. "But that terminates Mexico."

He nodded and motioned to his men. Each one took a guy, and while Juan and Reuben struggled a little, they didn't have the focus needed to break free so were handled with little trouble. Their bindings were cut off and clothes torn away, completely. Soon all of them were naked, their rags in a trash bag.

Then the one holding Theo motioned the Sheriff over.

I followed him, saying, "That one's from Mexico, but I think he's Muslim."

The Sheriff eyed Theo. He was moaning and starting to squirm as the man inspected every square inch of him, including his surprisingly elegant feet. It made me proud to see how amazingly perfect he looked, naked.

"He been tested?" the Sheriff finally asked, holding Theo's dick in his hand.

I nodded. "He grew to about eight inches."

He nodded, did one last look over Theo's lovely ass, then he flipped his hand and Theo was taken into the second dressing room. Oscar, Juan and Tomás were carried into the first dressing room as Emilio and Reuben were each hauled into numbers three and four. I heard every door lock. Now they'd be bathed and shackled naked to a bed, then videotaped and offered up for sale.

Except for Theo.

"He's goin' to the guy I told you 'bout," the Sheriff said, escorting me back to the van. "His ass is gonna cover the cost of all this shit, twice over, by himself."

I smiled. "So long as he's not hurt; he's too pretty."

"That an absolute?"

"Yes."

"No need worryin' 'bout that. This client's high-end. He ain't goin' off-roadin' in no Ferrari."

I laughed.

The Sheriff continued, "If you'd just brought him, we'd been happy. Dumb as shit, what you did, an' goddamn lucky you got away with it, but a nice profit."

"I had an ace."

"Not no more. He's turned."

That jolted me. He knew about Horace? And he was warning me? I flashed to the legal trouble my own private Customs Cop was in and realized he'd been off-center, the other day. Almost like it was going to be his last time with me. Now it made sense.

Stupid little Hunter had let his dick do the thinking instead of his brain.

I nearly growled with sudden anger. "Turned, huh?"

He nodded. "They think they're gonna find drugs. Got a raid set for tonight. Right here. Prob'ly under surveillance, now."

"But I must be under surveillance, now. Isn't all this suspicious?"

"Yep. But...there's a movie shootin' out in the desert. Honey wagon's headin' out there. Told 'em I'd do a search. If they stop the semi, nothin' in it but car parts. Just a guy got lost, stopped by, and you give him directions. GPS sucks out here. Dressed like you are, with your history, they can put two an' two together an' make if forty seven, if they want. As of now, they think your dealer's comin' in through Lordsburg, after midnight."

"Horace shows up, at midnight. So he's in on bustin' me."

"He's buyin' his way out of trouble."

Suddenly, I was sad. "Doesn't work," I said. "They'll fuck him over, anyway."

The Sheriff shrugged. "Leave the van," he continued. "Got a Chevy 'round front. Take that." He gave me a set of keys. "See Phil in Anaheim. He'll set you up fresh docs. Coordinator's got a setup in LA you're perfect for. We'll handle your boy..."

"No," I said, cold and angry. "Don't."

The Sheriff eyed me. "What you up to?"

I pulled up that photo I'd shot of Horace standing at parade rest, hands behind him, his dick at full attention, and showed it to him.

The Sheriff hesitated. For the first time, I sensed a bit of flush to his face. And wariness. "He's border patrol."

"Who's in big trouble. Who might run."

"Still pretty iffy. Trouble ain't that bad."

"Makin' a Mexican boy suck you off isn't that bad?"

That jolted the Sheriff. "I heard it's a girl did it."

"He thinks women don't know how to give a decent blowjob."

The Sheriff focused on the image. "Ass?"

"Virgin, he says."

"Mouth?"

"Virgin, he says."

"Can you verify?"

"I will."

"When?"

"Give me a week. How much?"

He looked long and hard at the photo. It was a hot one, I knew. But the Sheriff's eyes were cold, calculating and unmoved. Me? I was getting hard just thinking about taking Horace down.

"Gotta do some checkin'," he said, "but I'd say half a mill." Then he shot me a glare. "No strings."

I nodded. "Him? They can do whatever they want."

Vermin was starting to come around so the Sheriff helped me move him into the room and flop him on the bed. Then he left without another word.

I was cutting off Vermin's bindings when I heard both trucks trundle away.

I stripped Vermin, and even though I'd already seen his dick in action and pretty much knew what he looked like, I still checked out every square inch of him. Man, I really appreciated the way he looked. A lot. Smooth skin with only those couple of tatts. An ass that was too damned inviting that flowed into his legs, just right. I lingered in some areas, and he didn't seem to mind.

I emptied the pockets of his jeans. Nothing but a truly battered wallet, a driver's license showing he was twenty, some coins and set of keys. I left him wrapped in the sheets, and took his things to the hotel's laundry. When I got back, he was sitting up and looking around, still a bit dopey and lost.

"What?" he murmured at seeing me. "What?"

"Why don't you take a shower?" I said as I dressed. "It'll help clear the cobwebs. I'll get us something to eat, then we'll be headin' out."

He still had a stupid look on his face, so I motioned to the bathroom. "Over there. Shower. Here's some good soap."

I tossed a bar of Dove at him and he caught it, without a thought. He looked at it then slowly rose and wandered into the bathroom, completely naked. I loved how that tattoo emphasized the way his ass moved.

I ordered in pizza and bought some beer from a gas station next to the place. He looked at both for a good five minutes before taking a slice and nibbling it. Then biting into it. Then devouring it along with three more slices and two cans of beer.

Finally, he leaned back on the chair, still focused on the pizza, wearing nothing but a pair of my Hanes boxer briefs, his skin still gleaming from the shower, and asked, "What you gonna do with me?"

"That's up to you," I said.

"Is it?"

"Yes. I'm headin' west. I can drop you, wherever you like."

He looked at me, startled. "Just like that?"

I nodded.

"Where are we?"

"Douglas, Arizona."

"Where's that?"

I almost snarled, thinking he was trying to fuck with me, but then he added, "No, wait...that's a border town, ain't it?"

I nodded. "I'll be goin' through Tucson. You got a bank you want to be left at?"

He nodded, wary, then frowned. "It's in Texas. El Paso. But it's a Chase. They...they got branches all over, don't they?" He grabbed his wallet and pulled out his debit card. "I can use this there, right?"

"You can use that in any ATM."

"Yeah, but they charge you like five bucks."

I chuckled. "Do you have your ID?"

"Yeah. Texas DL. Took my Army ID away, so..." Then he looked at me, amazed. "Wait, didn't you check?"

I smiled and said, "You weren't who I was worried about."

He sort of flumped back in the chair. "You were worried about them. They were pulling some kind of shit. And they set me up for it."

I didn't say a thing. Just let him piece it together.

He took another slice of pizza and nibbled at it, saying, "Pepperoni and black olives. How'd you know I like it this way?"

"It's how I like pizza."

He nodded and sipped some beer. His awareness was catching up to him. Watching him fight with the understanding of it touched me in ways I didn't think possible, anymore.

I hurt for him.

Finally, he shook his head, over and over, saying, "I got myself into somethin' really stupid, didn't I? Real bad." He was close to tears. "You got me out of it."

Okay, I couldn't have this, so I jumped in with, "How old're you?"

"Huh? Uh...I'm twenty-one, end of March."

I gave a wild grimace and pointed at the beer. "Oops, then that is illegal."

He chuckled, despite himself. "Lots of stuff is, but it still happens, right?"

I smiled, nodding. "You're not stupid. Just inexperienced. Trusting. Eventually you'll catch on that trust is great, but always verify what they say."

"Jeez, you sound like my dad, but you're not nearly as old as him."

"I'll bet I've been around a lot more than he has."

He nodded then cast me a sideways glance. "If you're really gonna let me go, you can drop me at the bus station. I can catch one back to E-P. If...if you really mean it."

I did something I do not like to do — jump feet first into the deep end by saying, "Why not come with me to LA?"

He chuckled. "I don't have enough to get started, there and..."

"You've got another five-thousand due you."

Now he laughed. "Those guys're gonna pay me? Bullshit."

"They already have. Let's find a Chase, in Tucson. I'll prove it to you."

He eyed me for a long moment then murmured, "Do I wanna know what happened with 'em?"

I did something I'd never done, before. I said, "If you ask me, I'll tell you, but you won't like it."

He looked me straight in the eyes, unwavering. Not scared. Not wary. Not hurt or angry. Just accepting. He finally shook his head. "I'll never ask, again."

That answer filled me with such joy, I reached across the table and kissed him. Tasted the beer and pepperoni and cheese and red sauce and it was so fucking lovely I didn't want it to stop. He caressed my face and drew me closer. Held me there until we had to come up just to breathe.

I sort of chuckled as I asked, "Were you really kicked out of the army for bein' gay? Even with DADT?"

He half-laughed. "I got caught with my captain in the gym. He said I forced him to let me suck him off." His voice went whiny. "*I got a wife and kids and I'm not like that.*"

I laughed.

"Officers closed ranks. I made 'em give me a general discharge in exchange for not yellin' about it."

I huffed. "Fuckin' closet cases."

"Oh, he wasn't."

"Huh?"

"He was so fuckin' hot, I was jackin' off to him. Then I found out he was bangin' this pretty little PFC and told him if he didn't let me have him, I'd tell his wife. Too bad his dick wasn't as pretty as he was."

"Vermin! My kind of guy!" I laughed.

"I hope so," he said, then he kissed me, again.

He stood up, still kissing me, and held me close. Tighter than I've ever been held, before. Our bodies trying to become one. His erection tenting the boxer-briefs between my legs and up against the base of my balls. Feeling it through my jeans me was like eroticism defined.

My hands caressed down his back and over his ass. His glorious ass. Not round or flat or awkward in any way, just perfect on him. His hands flowed around the small of my back to let his fingers dig into me and pull me even closer, not touching my ass but almost...almost...almost...

To say I was hard and ready to go would be like saying a tornado's a light Spring storm. My heart was pounding in ways I didn't know possible. Every nerve in my body was howling with delight. My lips refused to let themselves be parted from his. In the back of my mind I realized it had been a year since I'd actually made love with another man. I'd done my testing. Fucked a few guys for fun, so long as it didn't interfere with the profit. Considered keeping a few for myself...like Theo. But this?

This?

This.

Just holding Vermin was like being reborn.

Suddenly I hated his name. It was so wrong for him. He was an angel, not something vile or debased. But Frank didn't fit him, either, so I finally had to pull back from his kisses and ask, "What's your full name?"

"Franklin Howard Verminsky," he whispered as he ran his lips up over my nose and across my cheek. "Pretty fuckin' weird, ain't it?"

"What can I call you? Howie. Lin?"

He looked at me, cock-eyed. "What's wrong with Vermin?"

"It's like...I feel like I'm callin' you a rat."

A lovely lopsided grin filled his face. "I had a rat as a pet. He was fuckin' awesome. If rats got souls, his was part of mine." He kissed me, his hands slipping down to cup my ass. "When my folks'd send me to bed with no dinner, he'd sneak food to me. Like he knew I was hungry."

"Your parents did that to you?"

He shrugged. "I wasn't a good kid."

He shoved me back to land on the bed then fell on top of me and ground against me, holding my head in place for more kisses.

I pulled the boxer briefs off his ass and grabbed his cheeks, nearly screaming with need.

He rose to sit on my stomach. Felt up my pecs. Rubbed his ass against my readier-than-ready dick. That lopsided grin grew wicked as he said, "You're hungry. All the guys you had, and you're still hungry."

"Haven't had 'em like this," I managed to say.

He gave a deep, guttural laugh and shifted back so he could shift his briefs down. Slowly. Teasingly. His fingers tickling all around my groin and making me squirm with pleasure...until he groped me.

I damn near came, right then. I know I gasped. He laughed and undid my jeans and yanked my briefs completely out of the way to reveal me.

To say I was erect would be an understatement. I know I'm good-sized. Not what you find in a porn studio but I'd satisfied more than a few men in my life. Still he gave my dick a good long look, then looked at me, then tickled my balls, then dove in and swallowed all of me in his mouth.

I did scream, then. Shit, I'm good at giving a blow jobs, but he could teach me a thing or two. Oh. My. God.

I released him from his undies and stroked him, at the same time, then he pulled back, let my now fiercely hard dick flop onto my belly, shifted up and took me in hand and positioned me straight up and sat his ass down on me and slipped me in, no condom, no grease, and he laughed as his hole swallowed me up.

Then he grabbed my hands and held them just over my head and began sucking on my tits, one after the other, as he rode me straight to heaven.

Hard.

Biting my left nip.

Clenching around me.

Rubbing up and down on me.

Bouncing and twisting and clenching.

Harder.

Sucking on my right nip.

His balls riding up my pubes.

His dick bouncing around on my belly.

Oh, the tightness of his body as I kissed his pecs. The beauty of his nips as I bit at them. The fullness of his dick bouncing in front of me and balls rubbing me, it was like they'd doubled in volume since this morning. He rode me and rode me and rode me, every second of him fucking himself on me sending screaming lightning throughout my body in waves of ecstasy until this wave of perfection roared over me and I couldn't help but scream, again, as I exploded inside of him. Over and over and over and over as he gripped me tighter and tighter and...

And then he fired his own cum straight into my face. Twice. Three times. Trailing down my chin and neck. Slapping across my chest and shirt. Being smeared onto my nips by his wicked fingers as his greedy tongue licked it off at the hair on my belly. I nearly blacked out, it was so intense.

I finally had an idea of what Horace had been experiencing, and I couldn't believe he'd give that up to keep out of jail. Idiot.

Then Vermin melted down on top of me, holding me with a warm heartless tenderness. His cheek to my chest. His hands still gently holding mine. Both of us gasping for air.

I think we lay like that for half an hour before I could pull together any form of mental awareness. And even then all I could think to say was, "Father. Fucking. Son. Of a. Bitch."

He chuckled and shifted to give my right nip a soft bite and said, "And that's without foreplay."

"Come with me," whispered from me before I could even think about it.

"Just did," he murmured.

"You know what I mean."

He rose to rest on his elbows and look at me, wary.

"I'm settin' up in LA," I said. "You could join me. Live together?"

"After one fuck?" He took in a deep breath, but I could see his eyes were anything but disapproving. "What'll we be doin'? What you did in Mexico?"

Okay, kidnapping might be a problem, for him. "If you don't wanna work with me, that's fine, I'll keep you, but..."

"But I wanna fuck you. Long and hard." He leaned down to whisper in my ears, "Decided that when I figured out what you were doin'. When you were messin' with Theo, I got a *hard*-on."

I looked at him. "I kind of wondered."

He nodded. "So you make lots of money at it, huh?"

"Theo, alone, is bringing in half a million, gross."

He jolted up, his mouth agape. "Fuck me!"

"Um...I just did."

He laughed and dropped to lie on me, face to face. "How much of that do you get?"

"Thirty-five percent."

"Whoa."

"So maybe you're interested in developing a partnership?"

He laughed and rolled off me to lie face-up. "Y'know, you didn't need to knock me out. In the van. If you'd asked me to help you, then, I would've."

"Why?"

"Sounded like fun."

I rose to rest on my elbows and look at him. "Maybe Vermin is a good name for you."

He chuckled, low and deep, grabbed my dick with one hand and pulled my face closer with the other and said, "Bitch, you got no idea." Then he kissed me and slipped his fingers into my ass and led me straight to heaven.

And hell.

HUNTER

BOOK TWO
"...This is my prey"

ONE

"His name's Tony," Vermin said as we parked. We were in one of those LA neighborhoods off mid-Venice where you don't want to be, after dark, sitting in front of an old bungalow that looked totally abandoned. Fortunately, we were in this gray beat-up '98 Taurus that wouldn't light anybody's car-jacking fire. I wasn't crazy about how secretive he was being, but Vermin's ideas had been more good than bad, since we joined forces, so I was willing to go along.

To a point.

We'd been together eight months, now, living the good life in LA. It's one of those towns where, if you've got money it's got what you need. I only had a fair idea of what the neighborhoods and areas were like, but Vermin — he'd been born in the city. Well, Manhattan Beach, but he lived and breathed every square inch of SoCal.

It had been a long ride, getting here from Douglas. We had to sneak out of my hotel and take a car left for me by the Sheriff I was aligned with, then drive all night to avoid probable arrest by Border Patrol. I'm the only one they were looking for because they thought I'd been transporting drugs into the US.

As if.

No imagination to those idiots.

Y'know, I'd never liked the desert; too brown and dead for my taste. But then, I'd never driven it at night on empty, desolate, two-lane blacktops under a bright full moon. The land almost white. Mountains dark in the distance. The bare vegetation black. A sky exploding with stars. It was like we were on another planet, and I'd felt freer than I ever had before in my life. I finally let my brain run free.

Which may not be a good thing for me to do. I was already planning my revenge for the betrayal that had set me up. Goal was to get way more than a single pound of flesh, for that.

Like the whole 205 pounds of him.

And I do mean set *me* up. Vermin would've been seen as a victim, not part of my operation. I'd only smuggled him back across the border to keep even worse trouble from exploding around me and those I worked with. Like I've said before, nobody really cares if you're making Latinos disappear into the night; but when an Anglo guy goes missing, cops can be pressured into paying attention. So best not risk it.

We'd hit LA at 5am and stayed at a hotel off East Third, the first few nights. I'd contacted my Coordinator the only way I knew how — text to a short-form number — and we'd met face-to-face for the first time...

And I really did *not* like him.

Granted, I'd never been fond of this guy's voice, but then I saw he was small and fey in ways that give all gay men a bad image. Oh, so pastel. So carefully coiffed. Meticulously dressed. Watery eyes. If the Sheriff hadn't been the one to connect us, I'd never have gone near him. And then to see how he gazed at Vermin, the first time he saw him? Like he was a hungry kitty and had just seen his dinner?

Hunter don't share with mealy-mouthed jackals.

What added to my dislike was, I couldn't tell what he was up to. The Sheriff? I'd got him down from day one; he had people who wanted something and he supplied it, like any good businessman. It was a couple of years before I'd even found out he worked with this character, someone to put another layer of safety between what we were doing and the clients, themselves. But supposedly I was now stepping up a level in the Network, the organization I'd been supplying the last seven years.

Bullshit on that.

It took me no time at all to figure out this little freak was only dealing with *new money* clients. Fools who thought a Ferrari was the same as a Porsche was the same as a Bentley; all that mattered was status of ownership. Idiots who had no idea that money was just a tool, and most of the things you could buy weren't worth it. I hate that *nouveau riche* shit. It meant we had to up the quality of the merchandise to suit their peculiarities, which were nothing more than middle-class crap caught up in pretentiousness beyond imagining with no true appreciation for our efforts. Focus on Anglo guys, now. *Maybe* some higher-end Hispanic ones, so long as they looked like Ricky Martin or a young Antonio Banderas. That is dangerous. But...he was all I had, at the moment.

It was a real chore, because in person his whiny queeny voice grated on my nerves. He's like someone who just knows he's better than you and is really fighting not to let it be too-too obvious. Oh, and would he carry on about expenses, which also bugged the shit out of me. There's such a thing as the cost of doing business; if you can't handle it, go sell grapefruit on a roadside.

No increase in my fee, but least one thing helped keep *my* expenses low. He insisted we live in a fourth floor loft on East Pico, in a building he owned. I think he wanted that as a way of keeping track of whatever we did. I almost said no, but Vermin flipped over the towering windows, and the glorious view of downtown, and the thick walls of whitewashed brick, and the central air and heat — "Trust me," he'd said, "you'll love it in the summer," — and the solid wood floor that offered so much open space you could roller-blade or skateboard in it. What made it okay for me was how the alley behind it gave access to a garage entrance, where we could keep our cars. That Taurus as well as a '66 Mustang convertible and an old Econoline 250 van I'd bought *for business purposes.*

And I do mean old.

I'd got it off this ancient stoner who'd bought it new in 1980. He was going blind from glaucoma, thanks to too much acid in his past...or maybe he'd smoked too much pot; I dunno. It was a long white beast with plain hubcaps on questionable tires. He'd tricked it out with a mattress inside and wood paneling all over, including behind the driver's seat. The bed was locked down across from the swing-out doors, on top of this nasty avocado green shag carpet, with a couple of bean-bag chairs around it. The damn thing even had a blacklight fixed to the dome and a silk tie-dyed curtain slung behind the passenger seat. The back right corner had a small cabinet for his *medicine* atop a mini-fridge. It still smelled a little from all the pot and ciggies he'd smoked.

Well, I dumped the bean-bags, and that blacklight was now a couple of soft LEDs to give us illumination when we needed it. But the cabinet, fridge and mattress remained, and the carpet became this flat brown indoor-outdoor thing that was so damn much easier to clean. We'd also added...oh, various *accoutrements of restraint*, shall we say, around the mattress, and the cabinet now held handcuffs, ball-gags and packing tape.

It pretty much served our purpose.

Of course, that's the main reason I wanted off-street parking — not just to keep the Mustang from getting stolen, but also because I didn't want some nosy cop asking questions about the van's new decor.

Unless he was cute...in which case I might be happy to show the little bastard the true meaning of life.

We only took the van out when we were going to use it. The Taurus was for scouting. Which was what we were doing, now.

"In fuckin' gang-banger central," I snapped.

Vermin chuckled. "Hermanos Mayan."

Okay, that sent a jump down to my gut. "Are you fuckin' crazy?" I snarled. "They carry machetes."

"Who doesn't, these days?"

"Us, Vermin! This is *not* the place for a couple of whiter 'n white guys, this time of night."

"That's why I brought these."

He handed me a black hoodie and yanked his own on. I growled and sighed...and slipped into mine. And I started wondering what he was up to. He'd gone out prowling several times in the last couple of weeks, like he was restless or bored or out to cause trouble just for the sake of trouble. It bugged me because I didn't want him to go overboard and bring issues back to the loft. But nothing seemed to be happening on that front so I was letting it ride.

For now.

Reality was, the last eight months had been pretty damn good. We'd settled into a nice rhythm. I'd decorated the joint with faux-walls and plants and minimalist furniture in a Japanese motif, with bamboo pads on the floor and furniture in blacks and deep blues. I used tall plants to build a foyer around the elevator's door and made sure we had plenty of food, beer, wine and whiskey available for company...something Vermin loved but seemed surprised I went along with it.

"Dude," he'd said, "I'd never have picked you for the type who likes to nest."

"What's wrong with having a comfortable place to live?" I'd snapped, a bit insulted. I'd had a nice place in Arizona but had to give it up and let the Network clear it out...and I still was kind of pissed about that.

Vermin had laughed and yanked me onto the couch and held me close to say, "Nothin'! But next thing you know, you're gonna want a dog or cats or a parrot, and I don't do animals."

"Me, neither," I'd said, before kissing him. "Unless they're like you. I'm an Air Force brat and we moved around too much for 'em to handle it."

"They couldn't go with you?"

"We tried that with a poodle my mom adopted. When we wound up in Spain, it went into quarantine...and thought it had been abandoned, so died of a broken heart. No more pets, after that."

"Wow," he'd said, caressing my face. "I just don't like 'em. It's like havin' a kid."

Then he'd kissed me, long and deep, like a river of heaven, and we'd held each other and fondled each other and fucked and sucked and slept on that couch, the whole night, and showered together the next morning...and I wanted it to stay like this, forever.

Yeah, I know, I know, and I'd already warned myself, several times, *Keep it physical, Hunter; don't get too close to him. That'll fuck you up.*

It was proving to be harder than I thought.

To my shock, he joined a writing group. Screenplays. He swore to me he'd always been interested in making movies, but not Hollywood style things.

"Experimental narratives," he'd told me, before another gathering of his fellow scribes. "Usin' images and edits to tell the story, along with music and narrative and juxtapositions of lights and darks."

"Were you doin' this in the Army?" I asked.

"Naw, just standin' guard. These're for me. Put up some quickie stuff on YouTube, Facebook, Instagram..."

He showed me a few of them, and they were quick dirty videos of lean, lovely guys on the street in the middle of the night, no females, not even transvestites hawking their wares. Some smoking various types of tobacco. Some looking lost. Some sharp and cruel, mixed with butch buff bears doing their *working out thing* on the beach by Venice or Santa Monica or Manhattan Beach and surfers wandering about Malibu and Zuma. All ranging in age from college to really hot daddies. Intercut were images of self-cutting and booze and pills and needles and guns firing and steam and smoke and shadowy alleys and rain-wetted streets.

What's wild is, they actually did have non-verbal stories in their three or four minute lengths. Like one showing a bright college kid on a wide open campus, who descended into drugs, prostitution and finally death at the hands of two figures in black, who raped him as they choked him then stabbed him in flashes of glinting steel as his blood trailed down the gutter.

I'd just said, "Vermin, you're another Scorsese."

He'd snorted a laugh. "In my dreams."

But it did make me wonder what had happened to him in his twenty-one years on this earth, only he never would talk family or life prior to joining the Army. He'd shut down or leave if I tried to get him to open up. And he never asked me about my life. In a way, that was good; kept up a reserve, between us...still, I'd like to have known more.

His group was made up dumpy people, for the most part, with a couple of good-looking actor-types mixed in who just knew they were the sexiest guys in the room. And in truth, I'd have used this one adorable little otter to fulfill a contract we'd been handed...if I'd just seen him on the street and there hadn't been this connection to us. I was almost sorry.

Y'know, that's how I judged men — by whether or not they could make me a buck. And I was pretty good at figuring it up, because I didn't get locked into this one look or race or body type. What mattered to me was how he came together and the feel he projected. I'd shrugged off white guys who were really good-looking but weren't quite right, in some way. Out of proportion. Built to where their muscles seemed like they'd been blown up like a balloon. Thick neck or thin chin. Skinny calves. No form to their torso. Shaved everywhere.

I wasn't picky; I was selective. On top of this, we were given specific parameters of what the new clients wanted, and I had to stick within those. I mean seriously, if a guy's looking for a Porsche and you bring him a Beemer, you ain't lasting long in this business.

That's not to say there couldn't be extremely specific types requested, like one order for an Asian who looked like a too-soon-deceased actor-model named Godfrey Gao. Wow, talk about a beautiful man, by any standard. He'd died of a heart attack while still in his thirties. So tragic. Took us a week, but we managed to find someone very close in every way to him, in Korea-town.

Got good feedback on that transaction, and a bump-up in my five-figure payout. I suppose to anyone else, that would seem like a lot of cash, but I was used to making more for something that high-end.

Anyway, the group kept Vermin happy and busy writing, reading, planning, and rewriting. And dragging me to bed every time he could. I think the script he was working on got his inner animal going. It was some erotic horror thing about a nine-hundred year old vampire and a young mixed-race jazz musician in New Orleans, and he made me his outlet.

"The vampire's female," he'd told me after one meeting, "'cause that'll sell to Hollywood, but in my mind, she's a he. Just an extra letter on the pronoun."

"Does she suck his blood through his dick?" I'd chuckled.

Vermin had grabbed me and shoved me onto the bed to bounce on top of me, then ground his already hard dick into mine and laughed, saying, "That'd be perfect. Feed on where life begins."

Then he'd given me a blow job for the ages, almost making me pass out from its beauty, before yanking off my clothes and fucking me to within an inch of my sanity. What was even better was, he didn't go out prowling for a week, after.

So obviously, I didn't mind being that outlet.

We'd been all over each other since I saved his ass in Mexico, and

I'd enjoyed every inch of that ass. Shit, I damn near worshiped it. I'd never been so happy with anyone, ever. He would get so deep into the joy of me pounding away at him, it's like he was on another planet.

Conversely, when I was being fucked by him, while he would squirm and writhe and gasp and giggle under me, when he was on top I'd wrap my arms and legs around him and try to pull him in tighter to me as he fucked away, and use every trick I knew to make it last as long as I could...which would drive him crazy with need.

He was also into games, like me wearing a wedding ring and pretending to be sleeping when he pounced on me. Then he would tie my hands to the bars of the headboard as he *forced me* to let him suck me off and then throw my legs in the air and, holy shit, the feel of his dick as he slipped in and humped me. His pubes as he pushed into me. The sensation of his lips on my nips as his teeth nibbled and sucked on them and his body shifted atop me in ways that flashed images of lions and tigers and bears, oh my, rutting in the wild through my brain till I exploded everywhere and tightened my ass around him like a suction cup and pulled his own ejaculation from him.

It was death and destruction and rebirth, every time. Exactly like I wanted life to be.

I really loved it when Vermin was home, not out prowling. When I could hear him pattering around, talking to himself as he worked out his story. It was like a dozen people all coming out of his mouth, sometimes.

It reminded me a bit of when I'd lived in Spain. Our floors had been tile and the apartment older but open and cool, even in the summer. Ceiling fans instead of central air. Siestas...and tall glasses of mint tea on ice, oh so very American. Me working out how to make piles of money as my brothers and sister chased each other about, shouting happily or angrily, didn't matter which.

Until mom would howl she was getting one of her headaches so we should all go outside. I used that as my implicit okay to ride my bike to the base and hit the BX, hoping to see someone cute to gaze upon. Which I usually did.

But that had also reminded me that living there was the last time I'd been truly happy. Of course, I didn't know it, at the time; I was so full of angst and confusion. But I'd felt safe. Comfortable. Wanted. Alive. Hopeful. With a world of dreams in my notebook. More than once I've considered returning. There was a lot of beauty outside Madrid and Barcelona, and I wanted that in my life, again.

Then I'd look at Vermin and smile and return to LA's truth. I'd focus on expanding my investment portfolio. Doing what I could to make up for the okay income while keeping the dream that someday Spain would be my choice of final destination.

And wondering if Vermin would join me.

Unfortunately, I was growing less and less sure about that. The last few weeks, he'd had these moments, every few days, where he'd get all quiet and vanish and be gone half the night. In truth, deep down I was hoping he'd find someone else, because I felt myself becoming addicted to him and I despise addiction, no matter how glorious it is. That's why I never touched drugs, myself, or even had more than a beer or glass of wine with dinner. Maybe a cocktail. So while I was dreading the possibility it might be over between us, I also figured it would be for the best. I had no hold on him and had determined long ago that jealousy or possessiveness were for children, so I refused to allow them space in my heart.

However, we were joined at the hip in this business, and I did not want him branching off on his own. But I felt more and more like that's what he was doing, and tonight's hunt was his first move. He'd pushed for it, hard, almost like he wanted me to back away from it. It set off warning bells in my brain.

I should have listened to them.

TWO

I was already in anything but the right frame of mind to go scouting, that night. On top of Vermin's insistence, the request from the Coordinator had hit me wrong, and I was still trying to figure out why.

I mean, aside from his usual condescending whine.

"Bring us this," he'd sneered as he handed me photos of a nice-looking guy — sleepy-sexy eyes, pouty-snarly lips, a trim body and legs, smooth skin, a lovely curve of an ass, and a dick to die for. He had dark floppy hair partially slicked back in this old-fashioned style and a tattoo of a shrunken head on his right bicep.

"Cute," I said as I showed the photos to Vermin. He let out his little growl to let me know he agreed. "Is he local?"

"His name's Joey Stefano," the guy said. "He's been dead for some time."

"Shame," I said. The name didn't sound familiar, but I didn't want this guy to think I was a dumb shit so figured I'd look him up, later. "He's different from the other guys you've wanted. All smooth and small. Not very built up."

"He was taller than you. And more beautiful than this in person. Unfortunately, he was also a junkie. These were taken before he began to lose his beauty to drugs. The men must look as much like him as they possibly can."

"Men?"

He nodded. "Twelve like him. All virgins."

Twelve? That was a big step up, and awfully damn sudden.

I glanced at Vermin. He had his little smirk going that said he was up to something, so I looked closer at the pictures. While Joey was cute he wasn't what I'd call the hottest thing that ever existed, not by a long shot. He looked a bit slutty, even, and his face could easily turn surly. Good for a night or two and no more; not up to my usual standards.

"He's cut," I said, pointing to a dick that really *was* nice-looking.

"I know."

"Can't guarantee that, every time."

"So long as the foreskin doesn't show when he's erect. If you can't get that, he's not what I want."

What the fuck...?

Okay...something was going on, here. This twerp had never been so specific about that little detail or casual about the reality of the enterprise. Previously, it had always been *Get me one who looks like this superhero actor,* or, *I want one with the appearance of that musician.* Which could take a week of scouting before finding one like him. Then so long as we could basically match what he wanted, could show he'd get hard, and prove he'd shoot his wad under duress, he was happy. The guys hadn't even needed to be virgins, which made Vermin especially happy. But now? What if we grabbed a guy and found out he wouldn't or couldn't meet this new requirement? What were we supposed to do? Let him go? After testing him out? Even loading him up with peyote wouldn't work, not every time.

He seemed to sense my growing wariness, because he added, "I'd be more careful as to whom I select, from now on. I will not pay for anyone who does not meet these full and complete specifications."

"Okay, the base fee as it currently stands is not..."

"Is insufficient. I recognize that. The rate will be increased."

"Something like this? I want two-fifty, each."

The twerp had almost laughed. "Um, no, we were thinking fifty instead of forty."

"Forget it. Not enough, though I will come down to two-hundred."

"Preposterous." He got all huffy and snitty. "I'm authorized to go seventy-five, not a penny more."

"Still a No. You're talkin' a huge time expense and lots of product to be tossed aside, so..."

"One-hundred. If you find one exactly like him, we will *consider* doubling it."

Well...not great, but better. "All as smooth as this?"

He sneered. "Just not as hairy as you."

Shit, like I'm an ape or something? Yeah, I got hair on my chest, belly...arms and legs...and a little on the small of my back...and on my ass. But it's not massive. Shit.

He turned to Vermin. "Take your shirt off."

Vermin stiffened, and I was not at all crazy about it.

"Please," he continued. "For comparison."

Vermin sighed and pulled off his tee-shirt. Then he stood in that sloping casual pose he's got that shows off his pecs and abs in ways that are so wickedly erotic, I wanted to rip his shorts off and fuck him, right there.

The guy smiled, eyeing him in that hungry way. "I like how you're a true blond..." His voice trailed off as he lowered his eyes down Vermin's treasure trail to his crotch. Jesus, all he needed to do was start biting his pinky.

Vermin just nodded.

Then I wondered why he was mentioning that. Was hair color another determinant?

"You are as hairy as we will accept," the guy said.

Well, that was something that could be handled with a pair of clippers, so I said, "Okay."

"I mean it," the guy said. "I'm putting up a great deal of money, so if you can't meet my standards..."

Great deal of money my fucking ass. I'd brought him twelve guys in the last eight months and hadn't even clicked half a mill, yet. Not a lot, in LA, even if we aren't paying rent.

"We will," I said, making my voice stay calm.

"All white?" Vermin sneered. I could have kissed him for being such an ass. And kicked him. But since the client actually liked him, better he ask the hard questions than me.

To my surprise, the guy just got this faraway look in his eyes and said, "Honestly, what race he is means nothing. I've seen African-Americans with a cafe-au-lait complexion who would do nicely. Same for Hispanics and Asians. So long as they match Joey in body and general looks."

"And dick," I said.

"What about experience?" Vermin asked.

The guy's eyes grew cold. "As I said, virgins only."

I was about to tell him he was asking for too damn much, even for that price, but Vermin gave me one of his sneaky little half-winks. He'd asked that because he already had somebody in mind and just wanted to make sure it was okay to consider him as a starting point.

Which was probably why we were in this area, a few hours later.

Shit, I was even less in the mood, now. I'd wanted time to sort my thoughts out. Understand why this job was bugging me, so damn much. See if I could figure out what Vermin was up to, but he was already leading me into the abandoned house's yard.

"This is somebody's place," I growled.

He had his jokey voice going when he whispered back, "The bank's."

"Bullshit."

"Nope. They're in Germany and the loan's covered by the Feds. They foreclosed and tossed the people rentin' it out. Then they gave up on it. They don't give a shit about LA."

"What d'you expect? Fucking Republicans runnin' things."

I got a grunt of agreement as we entered the house...and sure enough, talk about neglect; obviously everything of value had been ripped out by scavengers, considering how shredded the walls and floor were. I heard rats and cats and bats and all kinds of skittery noises, and nearly fell face forward twice thanks to crap scattered everywhere. I've never been so relieved as when Vermin led me into the overgrown back yard and to an opening in the left corner of the fence. He put a finger to his lips and slipped through. I followed.

We crept up to a decent-enough stucco bungalow. Not much grass for the yard. Folding chairs set up near an old cable-roller used as a table; I never could figure out what those things were called. A couple of plants hung from hooks screwed into the eaves and were barely alive. The narrow windows had bars with vines growing up and over them, and a ten-year-old Corolla sat in a driveway that was barely big enough for it.

Vermin stopped and smiled then pointed to an ear.

I listened...but only heard a shower running so shrugged.

He grinned and nodded then whispered, "Right on time."

"How many times you been here?" I barely whispered back.

He held up three fingers.

Shit, Vermin was a peeping tom! "What the fuck?"

"Just layin' groundwork for a possible."

Groundwork? Bullshit. Why didn't I know this about the little snake? Now I was sure he'd gone scouting on his own, and probably for the Coordinator. Like with an early clue on what this job was. Well, if he thought he was going to shove me aside in my own business, he was fucking crazier than I gave him credit for. Just because you're a good fuck doesn't mean you can fuck me over.

We slipped up to a window, my heart pounding. Never in my life would I have thought me capable of sneaking a peek in somebody's private home, late into the night, but here we were, aiming to do just that.

He held me back and looked in, first, carefully moving vines aside to do so. I heard the shower cut off, and he all but jiggled with excitement. He motioned me over and stepped back.

I held my breath and looked inside.

It was a small bedroom jammed with a queen-sized bed, dresser, chest of drawers, night stands and a couple of straight-backed chairs. A closet door was open and clothes hung from it, loose and haphazard. A pretty Hispanic woman sat on the bed, cross-legged, her hair long and black, her skin tawny, reading a folder of papers. She wore nothing but panties.

I scowled at Vermin. Women were NOT on the request form, idiot; someone else handles them. He frantically indicated I should look back, so I did — and a moment later one naked Latino male exited the bathroom, still drying his hair.

And I took in a very happy breath.

He was built almost exactly like what our client wanted, had light wisps of hair on his trim torso and exquisite hips while a nice amount swirled down his legs, and he had that lovely macho swagger. But the best part was, swinging from a thick bush that danced up into a perfect treasure trail was a long, gorgeous dick and set of balls to match. He was uncut, but experience told me he had the kind of foreskin that'd stop showing halfway into his erection.

"That's Tony?" I mouthed to Vermin.

He nodded.

Then the guy took the towel off his head and I froze. He had a Telenovella face — all square cheekbones and bright eyes and perfect lips with a chin to make any man envious. Now that his arms were down, I could see his pecs were a bit fuller than Joey's, and he had a pair of truly adorable nips. And definitely was no older than twenty-five, if that.

Vermin punched me in the arm to say, *Told you so.*

"Your turn," Tony said in Spanish, but without a Mexican inflection. Maybe South American?

I frowned at Vermin, mouthing, "Where's he from?"

He whispered, "Uh...Colombia."

The woman got up. "Any hot water left?" She spoke in plain English, not like it was her second language.

Tony nodded. "You still work?" No question English was his second language.

"Gotta be ready for tomorrow's meeting," she said. "Gonna be a real winner, this time."

Tony grabbed one of her breasts, playfully, and said, *"I'll help you to be less tense."*

She swatted his hand away, laughing. "Tomorrow."

"You say this last night," he said in a seductive voice as he spooned her.

"I told you, not till after the meeting," she giggled, pulling away. "Tomorrow night, okay?"

He sighed...and I nearly sighed with him, because he'd started to get an erection, and what an exquisite one it would be.

She vanished into the bathroom and he flopped back on the bed...and his dick flopped back with him. He started to play with himself.

I kept still, wondering if he could hear my heart pounding, it was so loud. Then he dipped down next to the bed and I finally got a good look at a nearly perfect ass. He reappeared with a pair of basketball shorts and yanked them on. The top of them didn't quite hide the top of his tan line, but the way they draped over him made my heart do backflips.

Vermin nudged me and we backed away from the house.

Man, I had a boner like you wouldn't believe as we slipped back to the other yard and returned to the car. It wasn't until then that I could formulate enough of a thought to say, "He's perfect."

"Told ya."

"Too perfect." And my voice was very wary.

Vermin jolted. "Bullshit..."

"And you know him. That's dumb..."

"No, no, no, he's Army reserves."

"So he's legal."

"He's married to that pushy bitch and she's born here. He's got a green card."

I unlocked the car and got behind the wheel, saying, "You've been workin' the research. Why?"

"He fucked over one of my Latino buddies, about a year ago. Got him written up for takin' too many supplies, or somethin'."

"It's still too close to us."

"Not if you blame immigration. You even look Mexican, these days, they kick you out of the country."

"But he has a green card."

"You think they fuckin' care?" he asked as he got in the car. Then he held up a roll of packing tape. "He drives home the same way, every day. Eats at the same time. Showers at the same time. Goes to bed at the same time."

"What does he do?"

"Dunno. Some kind of temp work, right now."

"Right now?" I grew warier. "Vermin...are you his own private stalker?"

"What? You gonna lecture me?"

"No, you're gonna tell me what the fuck's goin' on. You've been plannin' this for a while, and all of a sudden we get an order for a guy just like him and..."

The front door to Tony's house opened and he hopped out, flipping through a key ring as he headed for the Corolla.

We both jolted around to look at him and I have to say, even in the dark, the way those loose shorts barely clung to his hips and swirled beautifully around his legs and crotch and ass? Shit, maybe I'd have stalked him, myself.

Vermin caught his breath and smirked at me. I knew instantly what he was going to do, but before I could stop him, he'd bolted from the car and leapt over the chain link fence around the front yard.

Shit, what could I do? I glanced up and down the street, started the car and left it in park...and raced after him.

Vermin jumped Tony before the guy even heard him and I was there two seconds later.

Tony twisted away from Vermin, his eyes wide with shock as he said, "Wait, wait," but then I had him in a choke hold and Vermin had wrapped tape around one wrist. He moved so fast, it caught part of my hand as he whipped it around Tony's other wrist. The guy started kicking and trying to yell but I jammed my other arm across his mouth, then yanked him to the ground. He fought me but my legs were around his waist as I rolled onto my back, then Vermin managed to tape his ankles together. I lowered my arm just enough so Vermin could slap tape over his mouth. He yanked me to my feet by grabbing Tony's ankles and lifting him up by his legs.

Shit, the guy fought us like crazy, twisting and turning and jolting as we scurried back to the car. We slapped through the front gate then, since I was partially taped to Tony, I fell into the back seat and wrapped my legs around him to hold him down as Vermin got behind the wheel and we took off.

In all, it took maybe thirty seconds.

"Anybody see us?" I gasped.

"Some people came out," said Vermin, "but I don't think they got a good look."

"Don't stop," I said. "We're fine back here."

Oh, were we ever. Because Tony was crushed between the seats with me, his tight lovely body struggling and tensing and wriggling and shifting against my dick and balls. Any hesitation I'd had flew out the window. I was loving every second of this. His butt wasn't the most solid I'd ever felt, but it was full enough and smooth enough to make it even sexier than a hard-body's.

My left arm was still taped to him, but my right hand was free so I used it to find one of his tits and pinch it. Startled the hell out of him. I'm sure by this point he'd noticed my dick was raging and pressing against his ass cheeks. What it wanted was obvious, even with me wearing briefs, so he really fought me...because it was obvious he was gonna get gang-banged.

Unless he kept massaging my dick like he was, brushing his hips and those basketball shorts up and down because, even through my jeans it got me too damn close to shooting, and that would not be cool.

"Fight all you want, bitch," I whispered in his ear, in Spanish. *"I like it when you struggle. Gets me all hot."*

He began shaking his head...well, as much as he could...and moaning as best he could, *"No, no, you can't, I don't want to, you can't,"* over and over.

I just kept playing with his lovely little tit.

We zipped up Venice to the 10 and headed for town. This time of night, traffic was relatively easy so Vermin took the liberty of glancing back at Tony and me to see what he'd done, and he giggled.

"Shit, I gotta get pictures of how you look."

"Could've done this right if you hadn't jumped the gun," I snickered back.

Vermin just giggled some more then pulled out his cell phone and shot video of us, along with a couple of snapshots. As we neared the 110 overpass, he reached down and groped Tony, almost like he was rearranging the merchandise. That set the guy to struggling, again, so I pinched his tit hard enough to all but tear it off and he screamed.

"You're ours, bitch," I snarled. *"So give it up."* Then I ran my hand up his leg and under the shorts to fondle his balls, and he kept twisting and squirming and trying to kick and push me away.

Hell, by that point I was hotter 'n shit ready to have more fun than I'd had with Horace.

Good ol' Horace.

The fucker.

Remembering him put me in even more of a mood to have fun with Tony.

THREE

Lemme tell you — if you're going to commit a crime, always be in league with a Sheriff. They got sources out the ass.

Mine happened to be notified of a *pending arrest* in Douglas, Arizona and had worked out it was aimed at me only because of the timing. He didn't know I was blowjob boy for Little Sir Horace till after the fact. He just learned a Customs Officer had turned and was helping the DEA set me up because they thought I was running drugs.

As mentioned before, *As if.*

There's just too damn much competition over drugs and too damn many people wanting to fuck you up for them. But sneaking in good-looking young Latino males to be used by the Network? I was in a far more exclusive realm.

Which got fucked up by fucking Horace. He got himself into some trouble and tried to use me to get out of it. In doing so, he'd come damn close to costing us half a million bucks, and did force my move to LA, so I was not in the mood to be forgiving...and was on my way to exact my revenge.

I spent the night in Tucson because I wanted to drive into Douglas about two pm. I'd already called the same motel I'd stayed in to let them know I'd like the same room as before. The way the clerk hesitated told me the cops had probably caused all kinds of shit, the week prior, but I knew they hadn't found a damn thing of use.

When I learned of what was about to go down, I'd been smart enough to disable the cargo van I'd been using and had left a call for it to be towed to a junk yard. I'm sure it was searched and the cubby hole I'd used to smuggle in my male cargo was found. I was also sure they'd assumed it was meant to carry tons of coke or heroin or trash bags full of pot or just lots and lots of pills, not drugged-up men. I bet they'd kicked themselves for not grabbing me the moment I crossed back in from Mexico. But like most cops, they'd gotten greedy and thought they'd get the Big Cheese (yes, I was told they really did use that term) instead of just a little rat.

So I checked in, set the room's AC to full blast, then sent Horace a text — *Sorry for missing last week. Crossing into Mexico, tomorrow. Stop by before work for my full apology.*

Fifteen minutes later, he agreed.

Fifteen minutes!? When it'd never taken him more than five seconds to reply, before? That son-of-a-bitch. He'd probably let everyone know they could have a second go at me. Well, I'd be ready for him, the asshole.

If he did come in asking questions, I had the perfect excuse to hold them off, for now — *the van had broken down in Agua Prieta and I'd barely got it back across the border.* That's why I was heading over to Mexico in the morning. *Had an appointment, in Moctezuma.* They would want to wait till I was returning from that. See if my new car had hidie-holes, as well.

He went on duty at four so would drop by at three, decked out to perfection in his uniform. He loved getting sucked off in that thing, so would not be wearing a wire; wouldn't want the Feds to know how much he loved getting his knob polished. So I had time for a few phone calls on my new phone before yanking on a pair of boardies. Those gave me the look of a college brat on Spring Break, especially as I jumped in the pool.

The water was nice but on the warm side; would've been better if the pool had been covered.

After a few laps, his SUV pulled in, right on time. I deliberately did another lap as he knocked on my door, then gave a happy yelp in the shallow end, to draw his attention.

"Hey!" he called as he strode across the parking lot. I looked and waved and wiped the water from my eyes and shit, he looked so goddamned perfect. But something else that had popped up in my head was how he had never called me by my name.

"Hi!" I called and jumped out of the pool, dripping wet. This always makes me look good. I toweled off and met him at the gate. "You're early."

"No...right on time."

"Shit, I should've brought my watch. C'mon, I got some beer on ice."

I led him towards my room, making sure my ass swayed enough to make him more than notice. I hadn't seen any cars nearby that might have be there for a stakeout, but that meant nothing. If the mule ain't got the stuff, yet, no sense in spooking him.

"Gonna pass on the beer," he said, his footsteps tight behind me. "On duty in an hour."

"C'mon, it's light beer."

"Piss water."

"Okay, I got cans of Coke, too. Prissy."

I laughed when I said it, and he took the joke well. Of course, he then sounded me out about what happened, last time, and I laid out my story. He seemed to believe every bit of it.

"So what's in Moctezuma?" he asked, feigning disinterest.

"My grandmother's from there," I said. "Got cousins and stuff. You know how it goes."

"You're Mexican?"

"Who isn't, in this part of the country?"

"I ain't."

"You take a DNA test?"

"Don't need to."

I laughed. Typical Anglo arrogance. I remembered reading about a bunch of white folk in Louisiana, years and years ago, who had found out the state classified them as black because their great-great-great grandmother had been a slave, or something. Oh, the howling and rending of garments in reaction to learning they weren't lily-white. It was childish. Race is a human concept, not a biological one.

Once inside, I popped a Coke, dropped in a Roofie and handed it over, then wiggled out of my boardies.

"What you doin'?" he asked after he took a long sip.

"They're wet. And...to be honest..." I took a condom off the nightstand and slipped up to him to rub it against his left nipple. "I was wonderin' if you'd like to fuck me, this time?"

He blinked. "Fuck you?"

"Yeah. Full on fuckin'." I let my right hand cup his crotch through his uniform to find he was way more than ready. "On my back. Doggy style. Whatever. Show you what else I can do. Trust me, I got muscles you never ever felt before."

He gulped down more of the coke and said, "I...I like what we've been doin'."

I cupped his ass with both hands. "Kind of one-sided, ain't it?"

He backed away. "You been gettin' off."

"Okay, okay, okay," I said, pouting a little. "I like that, too. Just thought you'd like a bit more, this time. But fiiiiiiine."

I sat on the bed and leaned back, erect, looking at him and licking my lips as lasciviously as I could. Despite himself, he ran his eyes over me with a lot more interest than just in how naked I was. He put the Coke down and stretched. Holy fucking shit, was he gorgeous doing that. I halfway thought I should double the price I'd been quoted, for him.

I motioned him closer, saying, "Parade rest."

He stood before me. Legs slightly apart. Hands behind him. Breathing deep. Dick pressing to be released from its prison.

I undid his belt. Lowered the zipper. Caressed his dick out from behind the tight boxers. He was so rich and full, he'd have cum the second my tongue touched him, I was sure. Must have been saving all his lovin' for me.

"Jesus, God, you have got such a pretty dick," I sighed as I caressed it with long, easy strokes. It rewarded me by growing longer and fuller.

"Thanks, it's my pride and joy."

"Lots of demand?"

"Yeah, I never had to worry...about..." Then he staggered a little. "Whoa, that was...that was weird..."

He wasn't looking at me so I snuck my hand under the pillow to pull out a roll of packing tape, asking in a very concerned voice, "What was that, sweet cheeks?"

Before he could answer, I jumped up and whipped a strip of the tape over his mouth and wrapped it around his head. Then I shoved him face-down onto the bed, grabbed his arms and wrapped tape around his wrists, as well. He struggled but I held his face in the pillow so he couldn't be heard...and the feel of him twisting and pushing under me had been intoxicating. His ass was firm, thanks to him being a gym bunny. Getting to sneak some feels of it almost made my day. My dick slipped between his legs so I had to fight to keep from firing a load onto his uniform. Finally, he slowed and stopped moving. I rolled him over to make sure he was still breathing; he was.

Good for me; bad for him.

I cut the tape off his wrists then undressed him, nice and slow. Tie drifting around his lovely neck. Unbuttoning his shirt, gentle and methodical, revealing he wore a v-neck t-shirt. It had looked lovely on him. I rolled him onto his belly then pulled the uniform's shirt away from his shoulders and down his arms to lay it aside. After rolling him back over, I undid his pants, lowering them in stages to reveal legs that had a lovely shape but were really white and barely hairy. Until his knees. Then his skin was golden and his hair swirled over calves...that were on the thin side. I left him in his tight boxers and tee, white boot socks on his feet.

Oh, fuck, I wanted to fuck him.

But there wasn't much time; I needed to be gone by four. So I bound his ankles with the tape, then his knees, then his wrists behind him, then used a rag to cover his mouth before I wrapping tape around that, as well. I lay him prone on the bed, copping a lot more than a couple of feels and placing my lips in several once-forbidden areas.

Oh, and his ass had passed my virginity check.

So far, so good.

His uniform was large on me, so I pulled on jeans and a hoodie to wear under it. His boots were a bit tight, as was his hat, but soon I was done. Then I strolled outside, got in his SUV and drove it around to a Macdonald's. There, I stripped out of the uniform and left both it and Horace's cell phone in the back. I'd brought a pair of sandals so yanked those on, handed the keys off to a guy who knew a guy who knew a guy I knew. Then a buddy of the guy, who was driving an old Sentra, dropped me in back of the motel. I went straight to my room.

Horace was still out, cold.

I fondled him, some more, making him grow, and caressed him and, man...there was nothing I wanted more than to stick my dick up his ass or into his mouth. But I'd promised the Network a virgin and I knew they'd know if he wasn't one, so I stuck to my agreement, even though it was harder than hell, in every way you can think of.

Now came the dangerous part — getting him out of that motel.

I called another guy who knew a guy I knew, who had an old UHaul cube truck, and he backed it up next to my room. I sprayed shaving cream on the CCTV camera, then he helped me load Horace and my things into the tail, before the shaving cream evaporated. We drove off, me riding shotgun, looking as bad-ass as I could in my hoody.

It was dusk and pretty spooky when we arrived at a junk yard on the east side of town. I paid cash for an old F150 with a camper, then we transferred Horace into the back of that. I gave the UHaul guy the keys to the Impala and drove straight to Sierra Vista. I got there just as I heard Horace waking up.

Of course, he started freaking out and making noise, so I found a side road, parked and crawled in the back to sit next to him, cross-legged.

He glared at me with hate and more than a little fear.

"I know what you're up to," I said. "Not the details but enough. Probably has somethin' to do with that bullshit story about you gettin' in trouble for some other guy's blow-job."

He grunted and pleaded in some garbled language, his cowboy-eyes as wide as they could go.

I just shook my head...and tore open his t-shirt to reveal a pair of pecs that were very round and only lightly hairy, two large pink nips well-positioned in them.

"You should've let things go like they were, Horace. We could've had so much more fun."

He howled as I pinched his nips, hard, and tried to kick me, but we were in too tight quarters for that to work. Instead, I gave his ass a good smack.

"I'd have got you, eventually. Your type, it's just knowin' the right way in. The right time. And you were close."

I caressed his pecs and belly. He started sweating, though not from heat, and his abs had begun to quiver.

"But now that's off the table. Too bad."

I forced him on his belly and tore open the tight boxers. He had a light fluff of hair on his cheeks, so I plunged into it and stuck my tongue against his hole.

He howled in shock.

I pulled back, caressing his hole with my thumbs.

"Damn, I wish I could pop your cherry."

I rolled him onto his back and tore the front of his boxers open, then I'd taken my time working him up into a nice erection. Long and fat and full, as usual. Spent an hour playing with it and pinching his nips and exploring every inch of his body as he tried to curse me and fight me. I also got video and took hundreds of photos of him in all stages of being serviced.

It was well after sunset before I let him cum. By then, he'd have happily sucked me off or let me fuck him in exchange for relief. To add to the insult of the whole situation, I jacked off into his face, causing him to scream and bounce in anger. He tried to head-butt me, but got nowhere. Finally, I drove on up to the 10 in the coolness of the desert night, and headed west through Tucson and Phoenix to Wickenburg.

The final transfer point.

I arrived well before dawn to find a Chevy minivan camper. The Sheriff got out, along with a couple of his muscle men, so I stopped by it and popped open the tail. He looked in to see Horace all but cowering against the back. I could tell he was more than pleased. The muscle-men had grabbed Horace by the legs and pulled him out then carried him into the camper, not the least bit troubled by his struggles.

I stood by the Sheriff to watch as they gently lay him face down on a nicely-made bed. That magnificent ass finally got to be shown to full effect.

I sighed. "The Network's gonna be very happy."

"They do like what they see," the Sheriff had said.

I noticed his earbud was flashing.

"They got a request," he continued, "if you're up for it. And considerin' the money he's bringin'...well, they'd like to watch you test the merchandise." My expression must have been way more wary than I thought, because he'd added, "The camper's connected to Satellite TV."

I'd been irritated. "Photos and video ain't enough?"

"Request just come through. Of course, they like you, too."

"That's comforting."

"Don't worry. *We* know you can get more like this."

"Dunno if I should. I'm gonna be hot, for a while."

"Not in LA."

"Yeah, that guy..." I let my distaste show in my voice.

The Sheriff had nodded, smiling. "He has access to a higher end clientele. Don't ask me how."

"So I test each one on live feed, now? YouTube? FaceTime?"

He'd shrugged a *yes*.

"For the price I'm gettin'?"

"Take it easy...for now."

I huffed then snarled, "Lemme comb my hair, first." I dug into my bag for a brush. "Y'know, it may take me a while." I showed him my phone. "I shot that shit, just a few hours ago."

"He looks healthy enough to go, again."

"It's kind of open country for us to sit here while I jack him off. And already groin' hot. I'll be too tired to drive back to LA, so..."

"No drivin'. Truck gets destroyed. The Impala's now in Mexico. We'll transport you to Phoenix airport and..."

I shook my head. "Bus terminal. I don't want anything to connect me to here, past yesterday."

He looked at me. "So you'll do it."

"Love to. But let's do it on the way."

"Ain't all that far."

"Oh, ye of little faith."

"You're the one bitched about takin' time."

"Crank up the AC. This'll be my partin' gift to him."

So they'd set fire to the F150 and off we drove. And I gave Horace the hardest, cruelest, most powerful blow job I'd ever given anyone. One for the ages. Lips and tongue and fingers on his dick and balls and up his ass massaging his prostate and mauling him without mercy. My hands touched every square inch of his body, and I loved doing it. Loved how he fought me. And I really loved how we only had to do one loop around downtown before he came. Then I pulled back and held his dick upright and let it spurt straight up and out like he was Old Faithful, over and over and over as I kept stroking him and milking his balls. He groaned and moaned and whined and cursed and proved himself worthy of every penny he'd be bringing in for us.

Then they dumped me a block from the Bus terminal.

I bought a ticket for LA but got off in Rancho Cucamonga, checked my bank account at a branch, found I was now a one-percenter, bought myself that old Econoline van and drove back to meet up with Vermin.

Who now seemed to think he was running things, the little fuck.

We'd see about that.

FOUR

We got off the freeway and in minutes were at the loft. Another really great thing about where we were located was how everything was pretty much shut down by 6pm. Streets all but deserted. Some homeless, here and there, but they didn't bother you if you didn't bother them.

Vermin had to get out to unlock the rolling-door so the controls could open it. But moments later, we were inside, the car was shut off, the rolling door was locked, again, and he was at the passenger door grabbing Tony's ankles. I scooted over on my butt.

Tony tried to kick Vermin away but couldn't get the right angle or leverage. Instead, my guy got a good hold on him at mid-calf and helped me up by pulling him out of the car. It was not easy.

The garage was connected to the upper floors by a nice big freight elevator that opened straight into our loft, but we also had been told to arrange a space on the third floor as a way-station for the guys we brought in. It had been closed off from half the floor by padded walls on three sides, done in deep purple cloth. A full-size bedroom suite straight out of Ethan Allen was set up in its center, and lights and cameras were positioned on runners along the ceiling. More cameras with tripods were also placed around. The deal was, we tested the merchandise here.

On camera.

There wasn't all that much to do. We'd bind the guy to the bed, I'd set the cameras going from a control box that was next to the elevator door, and either Vermin or I would get him to cum. We could also show him off by stringing him up to a chain from the ceiling, but that never seemed to get as good a response, so bed it was, every time, lately. Then we'd leave him there, head up to floor four, and let the Coordinator and his representatives slip in to take him away.

It was all very cheesy and dangerous, to me.

But the Coordinator insisted, so I made it part of the deal that neither Vermin's nor my face could be seen on any video copies. Otherwise, the contract would be terminated. That sounds like a weak threat, I know, but reality is I had some heavy-duty backup to it. The Network did not take any breach of contract lightly. At best, the violator would be banned. At worst?

Well...as I once said, the desert has swallowed a lot of blood.

So we carried Tony to the bed. I flopped us onto it and held him in place as Vermin cuffed one of his ankles to a thirty inch long pole that was chained to the floor. Then he cut the tape and forced his other ankle into a cuff at the other end of it. Through the whole thing, the guy was kicking and shaking and twisting and cursing us with every bad Spanish word he could think of...and I was loving it. Just like a cat loves playing with the mouse it caught. His squirming and pushing against me was almost like foreplay. Then Vermin wrapped more tape around Tony's arms to keep him in place, and cut me loose.

Once I was free, I stepped back to watch him glare at us and hurl muffled threats and fight the tape. Man, even with his arms crossed in front of his chest and hiding his pecs, he was a joy to behold. His shoulders were broad and smooth, and his treasure trail flowed from his belly button in ways that defy simple description. His shorts were halfway down his lovely hips, showing off that amazingly sexy tan line, and one of its legs had ridden up far enough to reveal his balls. On top of it, the outline of his dick was obvious in the folds of the shorts. His hair flopped in his face and his eyes kept shifting from fury to pleading to fear to *You have got to be kidding me!*

Oh, he was gonna be fun.

"So now what?" Vermin asked.

"He's your boy," I said as I backed to the cameras' control box.

"You think they'll like him?"

"Don't see why not."

"He's Latino."

"So was the guy we grabbed in Long Beach."

That's when Vermin got a weird look on his face and pulled me aside to whisper, "But they wanted him. What happens if they don't want Tony?"

He was asking me that *now*?! After all the guys we'd already done?

Granted, we hadn't been faced with one being unable to get it up or cum, yet, and yeah...this time the requirements were more strict...so what if this guy was the one who didn't meet them? What then?

Truth is, I'd never had to wonder that, before. I'd been able to work around any possibility of failure with a bit of dope and the knowledge I'd grabbed a guy who didn't matter or would be paid no real attention to. But Tony? He had a house. A wife. A life that wasn't in the shadows. Wasn't underground or connected to anything criminal. If he didn't work out, would we have to kill him?

Could we?

Vermin must have seen the thoughts in my eyes, because he said, "We can't do that."

Don't be so sure, is what I thought. What I said was, "We won't need to. Think positive."

"I mean it, Hunter. I can't hurt anything pretty."

No, you're just willing to procure them for some guy to do with as he wants...and God only knew what that was. I wasn't stupid enough to think those guys who'd vanished, thanks to the Sheriff, weren't actually buried in the desert. Hadn't actually been killed by a client who got carried away. I'd been able to handle an electrified probe up the ass, but I could see some straight guy freaking out and getting snuffed over it.

I could be honest about the possibilities because they weren't really actualities, to me. They were thoughts, not facts. That's how you have to do business, sometimes — by compartmentalizing the truth of what you're up to.

I thought Vermin understood that.

I lost a little respect for him, right then.

"I got a contingency plan," I said, even and calm. "The ass he's got — my contact in Arizona'll take him off our hands. Pass him around some. Probably dump him back in Bogota."

"Caracas."

"Whatever...wait, I thought you said he's from Columbia."

"Yeah, yeah, yeah, right. Bogota."

"Okay..." That felt weird, but we were in the middle of it all so I just said, "You ready? The cameras are."

He looked at Tony and licked his lips, his breath soft and deep. He was torn between fear and desire...which could be a very erotic combination. "Yeah," he finally said.

"Need my help?"

"No." He shook his head and pulled off his shirt. "No. Not for this."

I set all eight cameras to running as Vermin strode over to Tony and walked around him, rubbing himself through his jeans and ignoring the guy's pleading and twisting. Still fighting the tape and the pole, Tony managed to sit up, but Vermin shoved him back on the bed then slipped his knees between his legs, worked his hands under his ass, gripped him around the hips and pulled him onto his crotch.

Tony tried to fight him, tried to scream that he wasn't this way, but Vermin just laughed and groped him through the shorts then slipped a hand up his leg to fondle him...then tore the shorts open, revealing him to the world.

Tony cried out in horror as Vermin groped him, some more, and dipped down to start sucking on his flaccid dick.

I checked the cameras' viewfinders. The reason we'd been set up with eight was so we could focus a close and medium shot on any of the four play areas we'd been given.

"Mouth, tits, dick and legs," the Coordinator had said. "Don't be consistent. That's the death of creativity."

Creativity, my ass. This kind of shit requires nothing but showing what's being done where. That's it.

So all eight were trained on the bed, getting great angles of Tony being orally assaulted by some unknown guy as he grimaced and shook his head and almost seemed ready to cry. Vermin gripped his lovely ass through the remnants of the shorts as his lovely legs pulled at the cuffs. He howled and cursed and fought Vermin's every touch, for all the good it did.

By this point, I'd decided that if I had to, I could slip a finger up Tony's ass and massage his prostate till he became erect. One of my tricks to make sure I never had to face that final decision. But to do that, I already had to be playing with him, in some way, so I grabbed a pair of handcuffs and clipped them around Tony's wrists. They were linked to a chain in the ceiling that looped through a hook on the headboard. Then I cut the tape off with surgical scissors and used the chain to yank his hands back up over his head. Now we had a full view of his sweet nips. When I pulled off the rest of the tape, it left marks, but it also yanked at his nips, making them a bit perky and adding to his sexiness.

Now that he was completely secure, I could focus on his trim tight body. Help Vermin work the guy up, if need be. I caressed the light hair in his pits. Ran my fingers up his sides and felt his muscles trying to pull him free of his restraints. What's even better is, the camera above my head afforded a perfect view down his torso, showing round pecs that had only hints of hair on them. Just enough to emphasize his lovely nips. Seriously, they were examples of how a man should look. The hair was soft and almost not there as it trailed down to this heaving navel and then blossomed to encompass his crotch...where Vermin was hard at work letting Tony's lovely dick play hide-and-seek in his mouth.

Fortunately, it looked like he would not need any of my tricks to get the guy off.

There's something exquisite about this view of a man as he's getting a blow job. It's like his nips're begging to be played with, so I did. First with my fingers, then I bent over to kiss and suck on the lovely little things, one after the other, shifting around on the bed to do it so I wouldn't come between the camera and Vermin at work. I also made sure I always had a nice view of my guy's lips and tongue doing their jobs as his fingers fondled an exquisite set of balls.

Now the deal was, once he cums, we're done. Absolutely no penetration by our dicks.

Dammit.

"We are mainly interested in making certain he is capable of ejaculating under duress," said the Coordinator.

"What happens if he won't?" I asked, irritated I was being told how to do a job I'd been doing for years, and in a very condescending fashion.

"Surely you have certain tricks up your sleeve to help force the issue."

Yes, as I said, I did, but you always have to put out the disclaimer. "I know some things I can try, but no guarantees of success. Some guys won't even get a hard-on."

He'd given me a long whine of a sigh and said, "You're being well-paid. Don't offer us one who won't."

Well paid for fifty years ago, maybe. Saying this guy was fronting for a high-end clientele was like saying a Chevy's the same as a Jaguar.

Anyway, to my relief, there was no way Tony would be a disappointment. I guess it helped that his wife'd been holding out on him for a few days. Get a guy who's horny and, no matter what, they're yours. Of course, a large part of it came from Vermin really knowing how to use his oral experience to enhance the electrifying sensations one can get from a well-placed pair of lips and nicely swirling tongue.

I sat back on the bed and idly toyed with Tony's nips, Happy to watch Vermin work...because he was art defined. He didn't just plunge down Tony's dick, acting like a suction device that'd been fixed to a cow's tit; he slid and glided, almost tender in his caresses and need. Every third time, he'd slip all the way to its base, nuzzling his nose in the guy's thick pubes, but two sets of sucking motions stayed focused on the upper third of Tony's dick, where the majority of nerve endings were.

Sometimes he'd give the head of Tony's dick a puckery kiss as the fingers of one hand tickled around just under the head while his other fingers would gently roll his balls. Other times he'd swirl his tongue around the head's base as he stroked the shaft and caressed the hair on Tony's thighs, up from knee to pubes and down after a quick fondling of his sack.

Man...just seeing him go was enough to fire me up even more. I loved being the recipient of Vermin's blow-jobs, so I knew the sensations Tony was going through, even though I'm cut; apparently uncut guys get it ten times more intense, and he'd done the research to prove it.

"When I was still in El Paso," he'd told me once, "I took this straight Austrian student to my room and let him sleep over. Not a great-lookin' guy but a nice pair of bandy legs and tight body, so about two AM I snuck a blow-job on him. He woke up. Asked me to stop...but he's already really hard and never pushed me away. When he came, it fired halfway across the room. That's what got him to let me talk him into fuckin' him. He didn't like that so much, till I got him to cum, again. You play with the foreskin right, they can't even begin to control themselves. Little fuck bought me a massive lunch the next day, 'fore he left on a Greyhound."

So he was having at it with Tony, and fight as the guy might Vermin was bringing him closer and closer to out of control mode. His grunts and moans were now laced with shock at the explosions of need shooting through him. Vermin kept shooting quick glances up at Tony's face to see how he was reacting, to make sure he didn't get the guy so far gone he couldn't be kept from cumming. That was another torture tool of Vermin's — edging.

"Get 'em to the point and stop. It makes 'em crazy."

Man, was he right about that. So I stayed where I was and played with Tony's nips and caressed his abs and ran my hands up and down his arms and played in his pits and eyed his hips, where the shorts had been torn almost completely off. Only a few threads of material were left to connect fabric to elastic, and I loved the look of the blue strands clinging to each other across his pubes and tan line.

Shit, he was so beautiful.

He stopped fighting us and just let himself go, his eyes jammed shut. Makes sense that a guy'll do that once they realize they've got no choice in the matter. Even me touching him in places that were brutally intimate didn't make him flinch, anymore. His nips were erect. His breath deep and fast. Laying my hands on his hips, I could feel his ass beginning to clench as he tried to force himself deeper into Vermin's mouth.

That's when Vermin stopped. It took Tony a moment to realize he wasn't going to be sucked off, just yet. He moaned, nearly weeping. In answer, Vermin nuzzled his pubes and sucked his balls into his mouth to flip them about with his tongue. Tony just groaned from the intensity of it and squeezed his ass so tight, if anyone'd been inside him he'd probably have ripped their dick off.

Now came the fun stuff.

Vermin got off the bed, grabbed the bar Tony's legs were attached to and flipped him onto his belly before he could even think. His gorgeous ass twitched and shifted under the blue material, and he screamed at thinking he knew what was coming next, pun intended. In answer, Vermin groped both of Tony's cheeks, gripped the material with his fingers, then tore the shorts apart to reveal his amazing butt.

Tony struggled and cursed and shook his head and pulled at the handcuffs, but all that did was add to the beauty of the moment. Then Vermin dove in and began licking Tony's hole. The guy began to shriek with anger.

Well, as much as he could, seeing as how he was still tape-gagged.

Vermin chuckled and looked up at me, saying, "He is so tight."

Then this feral glare roared into his eyes. "We haven't notified 'em about him, yet..."

I jolted and looked at him, not at all sure about this sudden change in direction. "You wanna have fun with him?"

He nodded, his body taut like an animal in the wild who's about to spring for his evening meal. His hands were massaging Tony's ass and his thumbs were rubbing against the guy's hole.

I knelt by the side of the bed, my eyes locked on Vermin's. "What're you up to?"

"I've been dreamin' about him..." he whispered.

I was beginning to see, now. "You've been to that house more'n three times."

He nodded. "Since last month. Saw him. Followed him home. Watched him go in. I want him. Been wantin' him. Need him."

"Then what? What do we do with him?"

"We could hand him over to ICE? They'd ship him out of the country and won't care and..."

"No." I shook my head, smiling. "Too iffy. I've got some peyote, upstairs. We can get him junked up, dump him back home. He'll think it's just a dream. All safe and sound."

Vermin's eyes brightened. "That work?"

"Yeah, I've done it."

Well...a few years ago, when one asshole in Mexico tried to give me a guy who was half-Latino. It turned out his mom was a judge in Texas. I left him behind a gas station in Fort Stockton and he wound up in rehab. Never a peep of anything else.

"That's your backup, huh?"

I nodded at him. No need to tell him I hadn't learned who the guy was till after I'd tested him, paid for him and got him back to the States. The dumb kid had tried to rip off a second-rate pusher for a couple keys of coke, and this was how the idiot handled it. When I told the bastard we wanted back the money I'd paid, he'd told me to fuck off. What made it worse? We could've made a couple hundred thousand on that kid...dammit.

The Sheriff was not pleased and found out the sneaky prick had a brother and a cousin. They were good-looking enough to make up for some of the payment. I'd have suggested taking the idiot, himself, but he was past forty and had lost the battle of the bulge, so wouldn't have brought in more than a buck-ninety-eight. Meaning brother and cousin it was, and while they only brought in a hundred-K, total, it was better than a total loss.

I heard the son-of-a-bitch shot himself, after he learned what had happened. I wasn't sorry; you don't fuck with people in this business.

"If you're gonna do it, so am I," I said, running my hand down Tony's back to cup his ass.

He squirmed and tried to twist away.

Breathless, Vermin rose to his knees, undid his shorts and pulled himself out. He was raging hard. Damn he had a lovely dick. I was bigger, but not by much, and mine curved to the right more than I liked. Having Vermin pop this guy's cherry was probably better for him. I could have just as much fun once he was done.

He slid his dick into the valley between Tony's cheeks and slipped it back and forth.

Tony was damn near in hysterics before Vermin moved back down to slip his tongue into the guy's hole, again. After a moment, he rose and positioned his dick to start sliding in and I was about to remind him to use a condom, for this one, and...

"Stop!"

We both jolted around to see the Coordinator striding towards us, his right hand up and a couple of overdone muscle queens behind him, wearing what looked like one-piece leotards with wife-beater straps and neon shorts, like something out of an 80s exercise video.

These were his backup? Seriously? I actually laughed.

"What the fuck?" said Vermin. "He's not yours!"

"Yes, he is," the guy said in his irritating tone.

"We're not due for the first delivery till tomorrow," I snapped.

"That's immaterial. We're taking delivery of him."

The muscle queens shoved Vermin aside and the Coordinator slipped his hand in-between Tony's legs. The guy screamed and shifted around, and the man nodded and smiled at me. "Good, he's still a virgin." He pulled his hand back and looked at Vermin, saying, "You may finish making him ejaculate."

"No way, motherfucker," he snarled. "He's mine!"

"Not if you want to be paid," said the little fuck. "And if you bring us more like him, who will struggle and fight as well as he, payment will increase to the two-fifty you requested."

"Two-fifty?" I murmured.

"Give you some incentive."

"Base, right?"

"Yes, so long as they remain virgins to male intercourse, oral *and* anal, and have been brought to ejaculation under your, shall we say, *less-than-tender* ministrations. Nothing more."

Vermin was about to tear into the Coordinator, which could have been really messy since the muscle queens really wanted to have a go at him, so I moved to between him and the guy and said, "You're increasin' our fee without me even negotiating? Why?"

He huffed. "We don't want you to get carried away, like you almost did."

"Will you update the contract and get me a copy?"

The Coordinator rolled his eyes. "Of course."

Vermin wasn't going along with it, but I learned a long time ago not to argue with this bastard's monetary logic. So I used an old wrestling trick to trip Vermin, sending him to the floor, then I looked at Tony.

"Okay," I said. "I'll bring him to fruition."

The client sent that creepy hungry look at Vermin, again, saying, "Your associate seems to have the gift."

His inflection caught even Vermin by surprise. In answer, I sat on the bed and ran my hand down Tony's lovely back, saying, "You've seen me work. That's all that counts, right?"

I was only half-bragging. I really did not want Vermin to have to put on a show for this bastard. I did not trust him.

"Vermin," I said, turning to him, "why don't you run a camera and zoom it in on me? Make a video for the ages." I smiled at the Coordinator. "He's better at the visuals than I am. And I'll waive the rule about not showin' my face. This time."

"If that's what it takes," the bastard whined. Then stepped back and waited.

And the muscle queens waited.

They were going to watch, live? Damn...

I took in a deep breath. I was going to have to make this as much of a show as possible.

I rolled Tony over. His dick was soft, again, and his foreskin obvious. His eyes were begging me to leave him alone. He made such a beautiful picture, his muscles now pumped and taut and showing how little fat there was on him. No wonder Vermin was so obsessed. To be honest, if there hadn't been so much money involved, I might have told the little bastard to fuck off.

Instead, I dug my tongue into Tony's navel and worked my way down his glorious treasure trail to his dick and took his balls in my mouth and rolled them about as I drew my fingers up his shaft, over and over and over...sometimes playing with his foreskin...sometimes tickling his pubes...sometimes caressing his skin over his hips and along his thighs and around the shredded shorts.

He squirmed and moaned and whimpered, and his skin quivered under my touch, especially right at the edge of his pubes. If I let my fingers just brush over the short curly hairs, he nearly always jolted from the sensation to the point where his dick would bounce a little, in response.

It took a few minutes, but he was finally back to being rich and full and elegant and standing erect, and his gut was heaving and his ass was clinching and my lips kissing him added nothing but feelings of lightning to his body, so I began diving down on him like Vermin had, dip-suck-lick-dip-suck-lick-dip-suck-lick-dip-suck-lick, rolling his balls and pulling at them and fondling them and holding them for five solid minutes until he jolted and I pulled back and his balls contracted and his hips flexed and he grunted in pure horror and he shot a lovely stream straight up in the air and over my shoulder, followed a second later by another and another and the beginnings of another before he collapsed on the bed, whimpering and twitching and gasping as his still amazingly beautiful dick flopped about on his heaving abs. More cum flowed from him and spread over his tan line and the shorts' elastic and torn material.

I almost creamed my pants just looking at him.

"That's what we want, every time now," said the Coordinator in a voice that was too fucking even and cool.

I looked at him and stood up and backed away from the bed. His muscle queens undid the hand and ankle cuffs. Tony still tried to get away, but they had no problem scooping under his arms and picking him up around his knees, and carrying him to the elevator. The blue shorts weren't even trying to cover him, anymore, just drooped and whispered back and forth.

I was actually sorry to see him go. And for the first time I decided one of my goals was to be a client of the Network. I wanted to own men like Tony, not merely supply them.

The Coordinator looked at me, his eyes black as coal, and he said, "Same time tomorrow?"

"That...that soon?" I managed to ask.

"No need to prolong this more than need be," he said. Then he followed them into the elevator and down they went.

Wow...that left me with a hollow spot in my heart.

FIVE

When I finally looked at Vermin, I saw hate in his face. Then he said, "They took him away from me."

I half-chuckled. "He was never ours, Vermin."

He looked back at me and said, "What the fuck've we done?"

"What?!"

"What the fuck've we done!?"

"Uh, become one of the one-percenters," I said.

"What're they gonna do with him?"

Excuse me? "Vermin, you chose him! You were about to rape him! That's not exactly makin' love!"

"I know, but..."

"But?"

"But that was before I understood..."

"Understood what?"

"Why you call yourself a hunter. I hunted him. I caught him. He was my feast, not theirs. Fuckin' jackals."

"What the fuck, were you gonna eat him?"

"I was eatin' him. I was turnin' him!"

"By stickin' your tongue in his ass? Are you fuckin' crazy?"

"He was gonna be like us, Hunter. With us!"

"Or maybe in place of me..."

"No, with you! You and me and him, together. We'd be as one 'cause he is the one and..."

"Fuckin' shit, you sound like a character from one of your fuckin' scripts, and just as unrealistic."

"No, no, no, it's not like that. I connected with him. I wanted him beside me. My companion."

"What the fuck am I!?"

"I don't know what you are! I don't know who we are! I just know I want...I just wanted him..."

I howled and spun around, unable to figure out what the hell was going on.

By this point, it was one in the morning, and Vermin was pacing, back and forth like a caged lion, all but howling. "How'd they know we'd bring him, same day? Tonight, even!?" Vermin slammed his fist against the stone wall. "We didn't even know."

"The cameras," I said. "Or when we drove into the garage. Something alerted 'em and they got ready. They had time."

"Bullshit," he shot back. "We had him for half an hour 'fore they walked in. Not even that long. And they took him away from me.

Motherfuckers took him away from me."

"Jesus Christ, get a grip! When has that not been part of the deal?" I made my voice as soothing as I could. "C'mon, Vermin, let's go upstairs. Away from this shit. You can do whatever you want with me. C'mon..."

"I want Tony! And they took him from me!"

I tried to joke. "You...you're just pissed 'cause you didn't get to pop inside of his pretty little ass."

"It's not like that! It's weird. Fuckin' weird. But I felt — I felt protective of him."

"What?!"

"Shit, he was so beautiful, I wanted to keep him. Forever."

"Like a fuckin' pet?! That is fuckin' crazy! You can't do that! How *could* you do that? Put him on a leash? Lock him in a cell? Shit, not only is that ridiculous, we'd get a reputation as guys who can't be trusted to deliver. And in this business, it's a sure way to get fucked over."

"I know. But if I'd gone back down him, instead of you, I'd have fought 'em for him."

"Are you fuckin' telling me you're in love with him?"

He stopped and looked at the elevator. "Where you think they took him?"

Oh, no, no, he can't go that way. "Uh, how...how the fuck should I know?"

"We gotta go find him. We gotta get him back."

"What the hell is wrong with you?"

"We can't do this. We can't let them have him."

"You think we can just give the money back and take him home and it's no harm, no foul? Really? We signed a contract! We kidnapped a man, Vermin. And sexually assaulted him. And handed him over to some asshole for money. A LOT of money. Three million dollars' worth of money, once the deal's fulfilled. And you wanna give that up and go to jail?"

"But I need him! I felt a connection and..."

I looked closer at him. He had this shaky, unfocused thing going in his eyes, like he was jonesing for a fix. I figured there was only one way to handle this.

I slapped him.

Hard.

Twice, again.

Then I shoved him into the elevator. We went down to ground level, where I dragged him to the van and threw him in its tail. I got us out of the garage and drove us straight to Silver Lake, fast as I could. He stayed crouched in the back, lost in his anger and softly muttering, still locked on the thought of Tony.

The bars along Sunset were shutting down. It being a weeknight, there wasn't much of a crowd out, so the over-pumped guys going in and out of them in search of the right fit for their intended experience were giving up their own hunts.

Then I saw one that was interesting. Broad shoulders, solid legs, a bubble butt packed into distressed jeans, Doc Martens and a wife beater. Cool uniform...for the Eighties, maybe. It was dark and he was turning down a side street but I could just make out his head was half-shaved and he had elaborate tattoos on his shoulders.

He'd do.

I turned to follow him down the street then drew the curtain behind the passenger seat aside and snarled in the back of the van, "Vermin!"

I saw him jump, confused.

"You remember Theo? The guy we grabbed in Mexico? Remember how we did it?"

It took him a moment, but he finally nodded and looked around. "You...you want me to drive?"

"No, I want you to come here. Check out that guy in the wife beater, up ahead."

He scrambled up to behind the passenger seat and saw him.

He wasn't the most muscular man ever, and had some love handles bulging over those too-tight jeans. I wouldn't have given him a glance as a possible piece of meat, except his ass did move in ways that anyone would be proud of. Then he passed under a light to show he had an eagle's wings tattooed across his upper back.

I heard Vermin whimper. "Yeah."

"Get out. I'll stop a little ways down. When he passes, get him in the van. Take some tape. I'll have more ready."

I heard Vermin chuckle then giggle, like a cat seeing a mouse that's about to be din-din.

I stopped the van.

Vermin snuck out through the back door.

I quietly drove on by the guy. In profile he actually looked pretty good. Straight nose. Nice pecs. Michelangelo lips. Bit more belly than I like but not like it's rolling over his belt. Mid-thirties, probably.

Oh, and a goatee!? Really?

Okay...whatever...

I stopped at the corner of the next street, opened the side door and waited. Watched the guy approach, striding along like he was pleased as shit with the world. Legs strutting, even, showing off their form. Yeah, definite love handles, but not bad ones.

And there was Vermin, prowling up behind him.

When the guy started to pass the van, Vermin jumped him, wrapping tape around his mouth. The guy yelped but Vermin had the momentum and they tumbled through the side door. I yanked it closed and pounced on the guy to hold him down as Vermin bound him with tape. He fought and twisted and squirmed and he was strong but we had control and he felt very nice. Not as nice as Tony, but more than livable. We flopped him on the mattress and I got behind the wheel and drove us up to circle the lake.

No need to see what Vermin was doing. It's easy to tell the difference between a wife beater tearing and a pair of jeans, and I heard both. Between the gagged grunts and cries of a man in fear and the pain of one who's being fucked against his will, and I heard both. I drove around and around the lake, for an hour, listening to Vermin grunt and growl like an animal. I even heard the disbelieving groans that mean the man was being made to cum, and Vermin's little whimpers as he joined him in ejaculating. It brought a sort of peace to my heart.

I kept driving and driving until there was complete silence in the back, then I pulled over.

Vermin was lying atop the man like a feral beast protecting its meat. The guy was on his side, shirt torn to bits, revealing he had a nice enough chest covered with hair, and both nips were pierced. His jeans were way beyond distressed now, and he'd been wearing an overpriced designer jockstrap that was barely in place, anymore. God damn he was sexy, like that. He was moaning so softly you had to listen for it. But I could tell from the gentle flow of Vermin's breath he was satiated. He looked up at me, almost seeming to be drunk.

"Feelin' better?" I asked.

He let a slow smile cross his lips. Jesus Christ, he looked dangerous. And so fucking erotic.

I smiled back. "Can you drive?"

That guttural chuckle whispered from him.

I got out of the driver's seat. My own dick was ready for some relief. "I'll let you know when I'm done."

He rose and didn't bother tucking himself away as he took the wheel. I gave his dick a caress and he all but purred then ran his hand up my leg to my ass and I went in for a kiss. He tasted of the man's cum, and that really fired me up.

For the next half-hour I had my turn with the guy. Caressed his nice enough butt. Legs. Back. Abs. Played with his pierced nips. Sucked on his dick. And finally slipped into his ass and pumped him almost as hard as I'd heard Vermin doing.

The guy whimpered and tried to get away but he was ours, right then. Nothing he could do to stop it.

After I came inside him, I took the wheel and let Vermin have him, again. It was dawn before we were finished.

We dumped him behind a bar on Santa Monica and headed home, both feeling very Zen.

Showered together.

Fell in bed, naked, together.

Nestled in each other's arms and kissed, both of us tasting of clove toothpaste, sending electricity zinging through me.

"So that what you think?" Vermin finally asked, his voice carrying an odd, sleepy sort of echo. "One to make them happy, and one for us? Any kind we want?"

I nodded, caressing his left tit. Anything to keep him from freaking out on me, again.

He purred and drifted to sleep, and I finally relaxed, completely. Now I knew how to handle Vermin, let him be as evil as he wanted to be.

And if you're gonna be evil, why not do it all the way?

SIX

It was eleven days later, and Vermin saw him first, of course. Heading away from the surf, dripping wet, long-board under one arm, a pair of boardies rocking halfway down trim hips that barely held them above his pubes as he swaggered across the beach. Dark, wet curls caressed by a soft breeze. Shoulders tan and formed just right. And what was even better? Nice wet hair swirled around his trim well-formed legs and a lovely treasure trail danced up across his abs to fan out just a little over a pair of neat pecs. Man, calling him hot would be like saying California's coastline is okay. No, he was exactly what we needed to complete the contract.

Which would be none-too-soon, since the legal freaks were beginning to take notice of our...oh, let's just say, *less-than-legal* actions.

Problem was, we were not alone on the beach. Nor was he. We'd thought since it was on the chilly side, for SoCal, there wouldn't be many people out...except some truly die-hard surfer boys to choose from, but it was the exact opposite, which made the hunt pointless.

But this guy, he was still fun to think about.

Contemplate the possibilities.

Of course, Vermin had his camera out before he nudged me, so he caught some beauty shots along with a bit of decent video thanks to the road having fresh asphalt. I slowed down to get a better look of my own and I have to admit, my heart started racing.

"Turn around and do a slow pass back," Vermin said. "Betcha he's headed for that blue SUV."

I nodded. I'd noticed it as we approached. Apparently, someone didn't want to pay for parking since all the free space along the road was taken. So they'd left the SUV with its driver's side next to the curb on the wrong side of the road. Which could get you a ticket even faster if CHiPs was in a mood to be their usual asshole selves.

Not sure why I thought this, but if that was his car, it now seemed likely he'd do one of those surfer-boy change of clothes — wrap around a towel, off with the boardies, on with the jeans...maybe undies, first, but not necessarily.

I hoped he *would* pull on some briefs. I love tighty-whities and even enjoy boxers, so long as they're snug. But hey — if he did go commando, it'd be okay, too, because he was just that gorgeous. As for Vermin, he didn't give a shit either way.

I hit a wide spot in the road and turned the van. As we coasted back, sure enough the surfer stopped at the SUV and opened the back passenger door then propped his board against it. Shit, he looked even better in profile, with a Roman nose and Greek lips, truly porno tits and an ass meant to lust after. Not big and bubbly, like some guys have, but just the right size and shape for him and his colt-like legs.

I looked out over the water and noticed a couple more nice-enough-looking dudes striding up to their rides, while several others were still catching waves. More people were lounging on the sand as others played in the surf or walked around.

Shit, shit, shit. There was no way taking him would not be noticed.

But man, the more I saw of him, the more I thought he was exactly what we needed. I could barely breathe from just the sight of him.

Vermin was already playing with himself, of course. In the passenger seat of the van. In the middle of the day. Where anybody could look in. He's got all the propriety of a rat in a dumpster. He even started whimpering like a cat about to jump a canary.

"What the fuck, bitch?" I smirked at him. "You 'bout to cum?"

"No fuckin' way, asshole," he sneered back. "Just primin' the pump."

I reached over and grabbed his dick, felt how thick and hard it was. I'd had fun with his cock on many an occasion, and he'd had fun with mine, too, so it felt right to have my hand on it like I owned it.

"Two pulls," I snickered, "maybe three, and we'll have to clean the windshield."

He slapped my hand away, letting his dick bounce back and forth like one of those stupid plastic birds that keeps dipping its beak into a glass of water. "Don't fuck with the animal," he growled.

"You sound hungry."

"Look at him! Look at him. Who wouldn't be? Who wouldn't need him? Want to feed on him?"

Feed on him. That shit, again? It's how junkies talk, and he'd drifted too close to that too damn many times since Tony. That *been too long since my last fix* kind of shit that always gets you into trouble, especially since I knew we couldn't take this guy, not with all the people around.

What really bugged me was, it had only been twenty-four hours since we had a Korean guy, who was an adorable bear cub, in Mid-Wilshire to make use of after we turned a Muslim guy we'd grabbed in Fairfax over to the Coordinator. Now Vermin was, yakking like he's in some kind of withdrawal. That could be dangerous...not just to me but to the Network.

"Calm down, Vermin," I snapped. "We're not takin' him."

"What? Why fuckin' not?"

"Look at the crowd, idiot. Somebody'll get our license plate and..."

"So what? It's fake."

"The van isn't! And it's more than an hour back to the loft, even in the best traffic."

"No, no, they won't notice anything till we're gone..."

His soft, breathy tone made me look at him...and man, you want to talk about a great image — Vermin leaning back in the seat, jeans tight against his legs, wife-beater stretched across his tits, dick flopping back up to his belly button, hard and ready to unload. I felt my own heart jump into fourth gear.

Shit, I came damn close to parking the van, dragging him onto the mattress and playing our game just between ourselves. Calm him down before we got back to business.

He must've read my mind because he tucked himself away and snarled, "No. No fuckin' way. Not now."

"Bored with me?" I asked, sounding sweet and innocent, but halfway thinking the answer was, *yes*.

"No, but I need a fight, and you won't do that with me. You can't. Fakin' it just don't work."

"We're close to havin' a real fight now, bitch."

"Oh, shut up. Okay...you're right. Let's check the colleges."

Which we'd already done, once. Hell, we'd been cruising half the day looking for a suitable subject. You'd think in the whole fucking city of Los Angeles you'd find dozens of guys who'd be the right fit for the Coordinator's specifications. Not skinny little Mexicans or overbuilt thugs or HIV-junkies or black drag queen whores. And don't think I'm spouting racist crap here. Vermin and I've brought everybody into his fold. Latino. Pakistani. Black as well another Korean. He didn't care so long as they had the same feel as Joey fucking Stefano.

I'd looked him up and seen some of his work, and I still didn't get it. He was a snarly little punk who I wouldn't have trusted to walk my dog. There were lots of dead porn stars with better bodies and dicks. Brett Mycles, Kyle McKenna, Tom Farrell, Cameron Fox...but it wasn't my obsession I was wasting money on, and the customer is always right.

Dammit.

Vermin sulked all the way back to Santa Monica. Considering we saw nothing of value at this one University we drove through, he was getting to be in a nasty mood.

But then we hit a junior college and caught a look at this one black kid strutting down an empty street. Tall, sleek body with café-au-lait skin and all the right form to it, almond eyes and sculpted lips centering a lean, open face. Hair cropped close to show off a nicely shaped head. He wore a white, sleeveless athletic tee with an open plaid shirt half off his shoulders. His walk, alone, would have caught our attention, even without the baggy jeans around his hips and purple boxer briefs peeking out, because the shirt's tail was happily dancing in the breeze. His butt also had a lovely roll to it, so I couldn't help but go for him.

Vermin liked him, too, but had to wonder if the Coordinator would be happy with another black guy.

"He told us from the start," I said, "he didn't care what they are so long as they fit the parameters."

"C'mon, Hunter, white guys like him like white guys like him."

"It's not for him! It's for a client."

Vermin snorted then leaned back and sighed as he shifted in the seat, still not happy about losing out on our first catch.

But then I noticed his hand was tickling his crotch.

"Well," I chirped, "you know what they say about black guys..."

"Shit, you racist fuck."

"If I was racist, I wouldn't even consider him. So let's try him out; see what happens. If he's a no, he's our fun for the night."

"You said I could choose 'em."

"So you don't like him."

"I didn't say that," he huffed. "But I'll betcha he's got skinny legs."

"Look through your camera, you stupid fuck." Him and his fixation on legs with meat on 'em.

He watched the kid in his camera's monitor and straightened up and let out a slow growl and nodded. "Okay, I see it, now."

I shook my head. For some weird reason, Vermin could not figure out just how good-looking a guy was until he'd taken some photos or video of him. It's like reality was too real and he needed that one little step of removal to make it all right to accept what his eyes had already told him. I'd found hours of video of Tony on a USB drive, and while it spooked me, it also helped me understand why Vermin had been so obsessed with him. His usual uniform was tight jeans and a tee-shirt, and he was almost as gorgeous as Horace had been.

This kid, it looked like he was headed for the college, so I drove past and dropped Vermin off a block ahead him, then I drove around the block. If I timed it right, I'd swing past just as he reached my guy. What happened next was rarely problematic, though I still double-checked to make sure a roll of tape was by the mattress, in easy reach. And a sock, since we'd found they work best at muffling their cries.

The kid had walked faster than I expected because when I got back around, Vermin had stopped him and was talking to him. No problem there; he had this great stupid act he'd use — "I'm tryin' t' find this here ad-dress. Know where it is?" Spoken in some Kentucky-Tennessee trash tone of voice that always put people off their guard. And sure enough, the kid was deep in thought trying to figure out what the hell Vermin had scribbled on a sheet of paper when I pulled up next to them. Vermin had stopped him right by a fire hydrant where the curb was open.

"Is that a Y or a G?" the kid asked in a gentle voice.

"It's an F, motherfucker," snapped Vermin as I popped the side doors open. Then he grabbed the kid around the waist and tackled him into the back of the van so fast, it was like they'd never even been in the street.

The kid started to yell and fight but I wrapped an arm around his neck in a tight hold and twisted one of his arms behind him in a way that hurt if you even thought about moving. Vermin let go and yanked the door closed then grabbed the tape. The kid still kicked and squirmed and howled as I fell back on the mattress and held him there so Vermin could ram the sock into his mouth and tape it shut, which he managed to do even though the kid was twisting and squirming and close to getting away from me. Little fucker was stronger than he looked.

Man, I gotta say, I love having a guy's ass pushing and shifting and clenching against my crotch at a time like this. It always got my dick close to exploding, it was so fucking hot, and every nerve in my body was aching from the joy of holding his wiggling body close to mine.

Of course, that's half the reason I'd loved wrestling in high school. You could tumble around with guys all you wanted and even get a raging boner and nobody'd pay any attention. And man, some of the action I'd get after meets and practice...it still fuels nights when I'm on my own.

But this kid — he was fuckin' strong. It helped that I had my legs locked around his waist, keeping him in a position that made it hard for him to reach around and grab at me, because even then it took Vermin close to another minute to gain control and tape his ankles across each other. He had to whip the tape around four or five times to make it tight enough, thanks to the kid's floppy jeans. But that only ended some of the fight.

I rolled over onto him, crushing my dick against his ass, and just about passed out from the beauty of how solid it was. How it kept rubbing against me. How my balls cried out from happiness as Vermin dug under me to get both the kid's wrists and bind them behind him. Every second was a fight.

When he was done I fell back, breathless and damned close to passing out from the near ejaculation I'd just experienced. Shit, I could barely move, my dick was still so damned sensitive. It was intense.

Vermin saw its outline in my jeans and laughed. "You handle him," he said, then he jumped behind the wheel and we drove away. We had to be gone quick in case someone'd seen us and called the cops.

That's when it hit me — we'd pulled this off in the middle of the day by a college. We'd done exactly what I did NOT want to do by the beach. Shit. The only saving grace was how deserted the street had been; we were lucky with that.

The kid struggled and fought and slammed against the walls and tried to scream, and he looked so fucking beautiful as he did it I didn't want to stop him, but I had to. He might still call attention to the van and we couldn't have that. So I slammed him face down on the mattress and lay on top of him, crushing my hard-as-a-rock dick against his ass and said, "If you don't cut it out, I'll break your fuckin' neck."

He was breathing hard and fast, but he quit struggling and started trying to free his hands or legs from the tape. Vermin had wound him too tight and neat for that. Meaning, he was ours, now. Completely, totally and for as long as we wanted.

He was ours.

What a thing to say. I have to admit, the thought almost made me laugh. Slavery's been dead more than a hundred and fifty years but now I owned this black kid's pretty, perky ass. I chuckled. And then I wondered if his ancestors had been grabbed in the same way. And used in the same way. It'd be interesting to find out more about that, sometime. See if the real-good-lookers caught by the slavers were sent to male brothels for the closet cases who ran the country, even back then. Or if they were so racist, they couldn't even see a kid like this as human enough to consider sticking their dick up his ass or in his mouth. Would they have considered it just like fucking a goat or horse or steer?

Me, I didn't care. If a guy's good-looking, he could be black, brown, yellow, pink or purple polka-dotted — I'd go for him. Vermin's the same way. We'd already proven it with Tony, who's Mexican...okay, Columbian, and a Korean with a lovely swimmer's body as well as a few white guys. Shit, we don't fetishize anything in the way of skin color. As for the guys Vermin then chose to have fun with, they turned out to fall in the bear cub or otter range. Almost the anti-Tonys.

Well, the Coordinator had been more than pleased with our choices, so far. Even the ones that weren't cut, since we'd been able to meet those requirements about that, too.

Now here we were, about to offer him a kid with skin the color of creamy coffee. And if he did say *Nope, not what I'm looking for*? I was more than willing for him to be our fun guy.

*****

We were on the 10 before the kid finally calmed down enough for me to get off him. He rolled onto his back to look at me with anger instead of fear, and damn...I knew right then the Coordinator would not refuse him. Not only did he have these amazingly beautiful dark eyes, there was this elegant flow of his tight body from broad shoulders down to trim hips just wide enough to legs that managed to prove themselves exquisite even under baggy trousers. His shirt was halfway down his arms and the athletic tee had been slightly ripped, so part of one pec could be seen. It was covered with gentle hair in a smooth, flowing way; I doubted we'd have to do any shaving.

I grabbed his belt and flipped him back onto his stomach to feel up his ass and make certain I wasn't wrong about it. I noticed he'd actually twisted his hands around to where he could pick at the tape around his wrists, and was doing a good enough job at it to where he might have gotten free...if given a couple hours alone to work at it.

"Damn," I muttered. "I better keep an eye on you."

Then I dug into his back pockets, finding nothing...except that his ass really did not disappoint. Next, I tried the cargo pockets and found a student ID and driver's license along with a couple of twenties in the right one. Turned out his name was Jerome Orion Carter, and he was twenty. Five-eleven. One-sixty-eight. Within the parameters as set forth, thus far. A pen and small notebook were in the left pocket. Looked like Jerome was en route to a speech class and had some notes of what he was going to say.

Guess he'd be dropping that class.

Something else I noticed was, as I was digging around in his pockets and grabbing his ass, he hadn't flinched much or tried to twist away. He'd just breathed hard, his eyes closed. I mean, his legs and butt had tensed a little when my hands were on his cheeks, but usually guys try to toss me off when

I do that. It made me wonder.

"You gay, Jerome?" I asked.

He took in a deep breath then shook his head.

"Molested by a priest or coach or something?"

He cast a glare around at me, actually pissed off as he shook his head. He almost seemed insulted I'd even asked the question.

Okay.

"Get roughed up much by the cops?"

He just glared at me then looked away, rolling his eyes in answer. So...Jerome had been pushed around by the boys in blue. Probably because he'd been walking down the street while black.

I grabbed his belt and flipped him onto his back. He grunted in pain when he landed on his hands. His dark eyes looked at me, confused and afraid and accusing. I dug into his front pockets, finding only a few coins and a house key...or apartment, I really couldn't tell. I tossed them all into a Ziplock bag, closed it then tossed it to the back of the van. Now it was time to inspect the merchandise.

Y'know, it's weird...but I'd said that with each of our other guys. Even the other black guy we'd sourced...well, black man; he was closing in on thirty. Never any thought about it. But now that I'm dealing with Jerome, it seemed...I dunno, wrong to think.

Of course, it didn't stop me. I wanted to see what we had to work with.

I finally noticed his ears were pierced and had ruby studs in them. Plus his right ear had a silver star and crescent moon above the blood-red gem. No wait — blood red made them garnets. That was interesting; Jerome didn't go for diamonds or rubies, but what was really just a crystal.

He had a couple of silver chains around his neck, as well...simple things that had a sort of elegance to them, and they shifted about as his chest heaved. His shoulders were nice and strong, not pumped up, and were accentuated by the torn tee. I decided to leave the undershirt on because of how hot it looked on him and how it didn't hide the fact that he had a bit of hair on his chest. It also hinted that he had a pair of tits that would fit my mouth perfectly. But that could come later.

I grabbed his legs around his knees and shifted him to where he was completely on the bed, then I straddled his thighs and leaned back on my butt to gaze upon him. Damn, he was pretty, his flat little tummy moving up and down in fear, his neck long but not gangly or thin, his hips slim and looking just right being wrapped up by the purple boxer briefs. The jeans were probably a size too large and held in place by a thick, well-worn belt.

I started to undo the belt and he jolted, his eyes wide with shock. He grunted something along the lines of *What're you doing?* and tried to buck me off him, but I'd held bigger guys than him down for the count so all he did was wriggle around under me and make me even hornier. I pulled the belt off and tossed it into a corner of the van then unbuttoned his jeans.

Man, he started struggling, then, and came close to making me lose my leverage. But that was half the fun. I leaned down, laid my full weight on him and pinched his tits through the tee, hard enough to make him grunt in pain. I'm sure he could feel my dick was thick and ready to get started as I ground my crotch against his. Then I whispered in his right ear, "Cut it out, bitch. All I want to do is suck you off. That's it. You work with me, you get a blow job, a hundred bucks and cab fare home. Okay?"

He grunted and shook his head as he moaned, "Uh-uh, uh-uh."

So I sighed and added, "It's that or I fuck you." He looked at me, horrified. "If you won't let me be happy with your dick in my mouth, I'll have to be happy with my dick up your ass. Choice is yours."

Then I made eye contact with him and let nothing show in my face. If you try to convince them you really, really mean what you say when you make promises like this, it never works. Being blank sells better than sincerity.

He looked at me for a long moment, trying to read me, then he closed his eyes.

That meant, *Okay*.

I slowly unzipped his fly. He tensed and gulped, but let me pull the flaps open to reveal his crotch. The purple boxer briefs revealed he had something of value inside, for damn sure. Even soft he was bigger than average. And his balls looked like they hadn't been milked in years, they were so fat and round. Oh, he was going to be lovely, I just knew it.

I ran my hands up his belly, riding the tee up with them to expose a nice chest. Not as pumped or defined as mine but just right for him. The hair curled down the center of it and, sure enough, his tits were lovely ellipses of chocolate brown. I bent down to suck on one and he whimpered. I tickled the other one then switched to suck on it and went back and forth like that for a few minutes. And every time my tongue started on the opposite tit, he groaned from the sensation. I knew he was reacting to my mouth because his tits got perkier and perkier, and I could feel a bit of growth in his crotch.

I finally trailed my lips down the light swirl of hair to his navel then on down to his pubes. I tickled them with my tongue, for a few moments then leaned up and ran my hands down his sides to the elastic in his undies. Now I could see for sure, he was beginning to grow. Not by much, but he already had a nice head on him.

I leaned back down and took the elastic in my teeth and pulled it down to reveal about half of his dick. Man, the bush surrounding it was exquisite. Thick without being wild. No hint of trimming. Smelling a bit of bath soap, not the perfumed kind but the clean stuff. I nuzzled my nose in the hair, brushing it around the base of his dick as my hands traveled up the inside of his thighs. I'd rather he not still be in his jeans when I did that; I loved it when the guy's leg hairs tickled my fingers as I toyed with them. But then I groped his balls, feeling them for size and flexibility...and even through the cloth of his boxers, I could tell they were dropping down from his scrotum and soon would be just right to milk.

I pulled the elastic down from his dick and positioned it behind his balls, so he was completely exposed. And I smiled. His shaft was still soft but had an elegant form to it — longish, not perfectly round, a well-defined urethra traveling under it with a couple of veins already starting to thicken.

And he was cut, to my surprise. The black man we'd taken wasn't. But then I thought of the star and crescent stud in his ear. He was probably Muslim, like Theo had been, in Mexico.

I ran my right fingers up the length of his dick as my left hand toyed with his balls. He grunted and tried to shift away from me but could not move. And his dick responded with a light little bounce. He was getting ready to let me have my way.

Not just yet, buddy. I should wait till we were back to the loft, where everything was ready and waiting.

Except his dick as so fucking beautiful. Long and curved and fat and perfectly formed. What could I do but lean down and take him in my mouth?

He gasped in and I almost did the same, because he actually tasted sweet. And he fit my mouth perfectly. I swirled my tongue around the shaft and up to the head and stayed there, sucking and playing and twisting as my left hand kept rolling his balls. My own dick and balls were damned near screaming from it all so I pulled back to give myself a breather...and release myself.

I pulled out my own dick, and I have to say it's not one to be ashamed of. But this kid's...not only his size but his head — it was a classic shape and positioned in a way that seemed to be leading the charge. And it was getting more and more flush. He was going to let me take him off. Perfect.

I maneuvered his dick into line with mine and gripped them both, letting my balls brush against his as I swiveled my hips to rub everything together. His eyes were still closed and he was still shaking his head and grunting, "Uh-uh, uh-uh," over and over, but he was also growing bigger and bigger.

And lovelier and lovelier.

I noticed he had a slight tan line, like he wore low-riding shorts in the sun one afternoon. I'd never thought of a black guy tanning, before, but his skin was so creamy I guess it made sense.

I kept grinding my hips as I leaned down and sucked on his tits, again, one after the other. I found his left one was more sensitive than the right so stayed on that.

He whimpered and groaned and his dick grew even larger. He was bigger than me, now, both in length and width. And his ass was clenching almost in rhythm with my grinding. I was getting closer and closer to that moment when I wouldn't be able to control myself...but I didn't care. I loved the feel of him under me. Didn't ever want to let go. Didn't want to even think about stopping.

By this point, his dick was at full size and I wanted to see it more than anything, right then, so I made myself take a deep breath and sit back and holy shit. Ten inches, if anything. Probably five...five and a half in circumference following this slow curve from stem to his lovely head. His urethra was in perfect proportion to the rest and the veins that had started out so neatly were thick and dancing around him. It took me maybe half a second to decide to bend down and take him in my mouth, again.

Then I got going hard on him. The hell with waiting. I wanted him now, now, now. So I got to sucking and swirling and rubbing and kissing and toying and stroking and reaching up to pinch his left tit and rolling his balls and working him and working him and working him and working him until he started to grunt in unison with everything I was doing and he shoved himself deeper into my mouth and all but cried out as he jolted and shot a massive load of the sweetest cum I'd ever tasted into me and I pulled back and kept stroking and he fired another load up over his chest and onto his face, once, twice, again, covering himself in his cum and I couldn't keep myself from rubbing my own dick against his throbbing one and firing my own load to mingle with his. I even managed to aim some onto his face, which he howled about, before I collapsed onto him, mixing our semen together and smearing it all over my shirt and his belly. My dick kept caressing his and my balls kept rubbing against his and my legs kept holding him in place and I nearly passed out from the beauty of it.

Then wondered how'll we get him off, again?

"You done?"

Vermin's voice jolted me out of my stupor and I bolted back off Jerome, still breathing heavy. He didn't move, his eyes still jammed shut...but God, the picture he made. His hands tied behind him, forcing his chest to raise a little and emphasizing his perfect tits. His stomach heaving, glimmers from the light dancing up and down the wet, sticky cum. His pubes soaked with it. His dick lying to one side, curving, semen still dripping from the slit. His balls wet with my cum. His boxer briefs also stained from it. His jeans halfway down his hips. All of it sent something stirring within me, again, and I knew, even after this massive ejaculation on my part, I could have taken him up the ass, right then.

Vermin seemed to read my thoughts and snarled, "No need for Viagra, right?"

I just shook my head. Then I looked around and saw we were in the garage. As I was busy blowing Jerome, Vermin had pulled the truck up to the door, unlocked it, driven in and closed it as I was in the midst of a...well, truth be told, it was like a religious fervor.

"You really like him," Vermin said.

I nodded, still unable to formulate words.

"Now you know how I feel about...well, felt about...about the first guy."

I nodded, again.

"Let's get him upstairs so I can work on him. Let the powers that be see what they're gettin'." He got in the back of the van and squatted next to Jerome...and hesitated. "Unless you wanna make him the fun one?"

I just looked at him then forced myself to rise and shake my head. "Let's finish it."

I tucked myself away as Vermin pulled Jerome to the side door, then I took his legs and we carried him to the elevator and went up to the third floor. We laid him on the bed and I backed away to take a good look at him.

Yes, I finally understood Vermin's nearly violent obsession with Tony. Jerome was lying on his back, arms bound behind him, body and crotch revealed in a way that I found brutally erotic. I wanted his dick, again. I wanted to hold his ass. I needed more than just a hand job to remove the desperate want boiling inside of me.

This also explained why Vermin had needed to have a guy to fuck after struggling with one like Tony and the others. There's an animal that hides behind your heart but won't reveal itself until you're losing control of your lusts. Then it growls and tickles your tits from the inside and draws its claws across your balls and lets you know it needs to be fed. And watching lovely

Jerome twist and pull at his bindings, I could all but hear it shriek within me. This time we'd need to find a guy for me to fuck, and fast. I almost wished we'd taken someone else with Jerome. Anyone else. All I cared about then was it was male and has an asshole to violate.

Oh, wait...I hadn't checked to see if he was a virgin, yet.

With a shocking sense of joy, I bounced onto the bed to kneel beside him and tore the boxer briefs open. Fuck, that looked so erotic — Jerome's dick and balls bouncing around as the bits of material danced away, leaving the elastic around the kid's waist along with shreds of the purple material, just enough to caress his skin and pubes and the beginning of the hair on his legs. Then I rolled him onto his belly...and he was still picking at the tape. I ripped the back of the briefs open and smacked his ass and God, he was so smooth. So nicely formed. Such a natural flow to him. I grabbed his cheeks and dove down to shove my pinkie up into his hole...and he was tight.

He shrieked and bucked and forced me off. I laughed. I knew he met the final requirement but I desperately wanted to be the one who took his cherry so dove back down to slide my tongue into him and was losing myself like Vermin had, with Tony.

The kid tried to scream but not a lot of sound came out. He twisted himself away from me and kicked me back from him but I just shifted and grabbed his tee and tore it open and yanked him back under me and flopped to on top of him and bit his left nip and flicked it with my tongue and used my legs to hold him in place as one of my hands yanked at my own jeans to pull them down and reveal me and...

I was shoved off the bed.

I landed on the floor, hard, and looked around.

The muscle queens now flanked the bed and the Coordinator was looking at me.

"I thought *you* had better control," he giggled.

"Sorry," I said. "I...I did get a bit carried away."

"Understandable. He is a beauty."

"No shit," Vermin sneered. I finally realized there were two other muscle queens in the room, standing between him and me. "I got some good shots of you praying to his god, so those'll make the client happy."

I rose and adjusted my clothing. "Not to mention that he's gettin' himself a virgin."

The Coordinator smiled, "We'll take him, now."

"You...you haven't seen us get him off, yet," I said.

"I see the ejaculatory fluids on him, still wet and gleaming. Those are proof enough."

"They could be mine."

"No, his are rich-looking; yours tend to be clearer, a bit watery."

Well, excuse the fuck out of me. Bitch.

He nodded to his boys. One grabbed Jerome around the chest as the other took him around the knees, and they brought him back to the Coordinator. The kid still struggled and twisted around, but they had him under control as the man gripped Jerome's balls and ran a hand along his dick and nodded.

"Yes...excellent choice," he muttered.

Then his boys shoved Vermin onto the bed and carried Jerome away.

"That completes the contract," he said. "You're free from obligation to me."

"What do you mean?" I snapped.

"Los Angeles is too difficult to work with, now. The police are suspicious about what's been happening. I lay that on you both. Had you stuck with the agreement and taken only one man a day instead of two, and at least not left the second ones lying around to complain, we wouldn't be faced with this dilemma." He glanced at Vermin them back to me and added, "It's up to you to rectify it."

With that, he turned and followed his boys out the door.

I went cold. I'd seen the news talking about the disappearances and finding men who were turning up raped. Junking them up with peyote or hash hadn't fooled anyone. The cops were on the hunt. So the van was now marked, as were Vermin and I. And the Network knew it.

Shit.

I'd fucked up, letting it happen, but I knew what needed to be done.

Vermin was lying on the bed, snarling. "You got all fun, this time. I didn't even get to touch him and..."

I put a finger to my lips and looked at the cameras. They were still running. He grew wary.

I went to the mini-fridge and pulled out a couple of beers and my kit of syringes then led him back to the elevator and we went downstairs. He raised the rollie door then I drove the van out. He lowered the door and locked it then jumped in the back, with the beers. I drove us away.

He held the beers up. "You want one?"

"Don't drink the beer," I said. "They're laced with peyote."

"Shit." He put them both in a cup holder between the seats. He'd opened one.

As I drove us through the middle of downtown in rush hour traffic, I asked, "What time is it?"

Vermin sat cross-legged on the bed, scowling. "Shit, I dunno? Four? Five?"

"No," I said. "It's time to go hunting, for each of us."

"Each of us?"

I nodded. "You pick first."

"Now?"

"Yes."

"Where?"

"Griffith Park'll have some nice joggers. But choose careful. We're goin' underground, so you'll want something we can keep till this is over."

"What you mean?"

"Cops're onto us. I know a place we can hide, near Phoenix. Take our boys with us. Keep 'em. Make 'em ours."

He crawled up to behind the passenger seat.

"You sure about this?"

"It's that or I fuck you and you fuck me. And you want somethin' that'll struggle, right?"

He let the hint of a smile flit over his lips. "I want a virgin."

I chuckled. "Then we better hit Simi Valley. Find somethin' with a wedding ring. Outside a gym, maybe."

"He'll be missed."

I nodded. "Then what about West Covina? Azusa? Riverside? They got some cowboys. That spread out enough? Different towns? Who's gonna know? Look at how long it took the cops to figure out the *Freeway Killers*, and that was with dead bodies turnin' up. They won't care."

"Can I pick 'em both out?"

Jesus, just like a kid. "Yeah, I trust your taste."

He chuckled. "You've tasted me enough."

"You're my favorite."

"This time of day it's gonna take hours to get anywhere, no matter where."

"Your choice."

"Manhattan Beach. Veteran's Parkway. Always somebody there, if you time it right, 'cause everybody's focused on the ocean..."

So I headed the van onto the 101 and aimed for the 105.

It took an hour to get there, and then there were four false starts before we found the right guy — a nice slab of beef running down North Ardmore just as dusk was descending. He was on the strip of park along Valley Drive and had a good head of sweat on him. Full legs. Bubble butt. Pecs that begged to be manhandled. Broad well-formed shoulders and a nice "V" to his back. What made it best was, Vermin saw a thick gold band around his finger when we drove past.

Around Eighth Street we hit an area of no traffic, no people, no nothing...so we waited till he ran up.

Then we jumped him.

Got him in the van.

He fought us and I loved wrestling with him till we gagged him and Vermin locked him up.

In moments, he was shackled face-down on the bed, looking hotter than hot, and I was behind the wheel, driving us away. Before the guy even knew what was happening, Vermin had yanked his shorts down past his butt to reveal he wore a real jock, and his ass was on the hairy side but still nice.

"How long we keepin' him" Vermin grunted. "How long?"

"Long as you want," I said.

Vermin giggled then rammed his dick up into him and started fucking away without even trying to get the guy hard or feel him up. The guy screamed and fought, but that did nothing to stop the assault.

I turned the van around and headed down Valley, calmly driving along as I listened to them struggle. The man continued to scream and fight, while Vermin just giggled. It was glorious.

We were headed up into Palos Verdes Estates when I heard Vermin cum in big, shuddering gasps. It had taken him a whole five minutes. No question, he was interested in having a few more goes at the guy.

That's why I stopped at a small park just as the sun was setting.

Vermin looked at me, almost drunk. "Keep driving. I ain't done."

"No time."

"What d'you mean? You said I could keep him."

"I...I saw one I want."

"Oh, right, right." A wicked grin crossed his face. "Can I have yours, when you're done?"

"You want them both?"

"I wanna make 'em suck each other off. I'll get 'em up and they can finish each other off."

I made myself laugh. "You're a sick fuck."

He grunted his agreement.

I slipped out of the van and looked around. It was quiet moment, so I opened the side door and Vermin looked at me.

"What you doin'?"

I slipped a shot of Ketamine into his ass. He jolted and looked at me, confused, saying, "Hunter..." before he passed out. It was a strong dose. He nearly rolled out the door so I grabbed him and lay him halfway into the van. He looked so lovely, his jeans open and his dick lying back on his belly, his shirt halfway up his body.

I focused on the man. He was in shock, so I ungagged him and poured some beer into him. He gasped and gulped and drank some then coughed and tried to spit and talk but I had a hand over his mouth. Kept it there till the drug had taken effect, then I unshackled him, taped his hands and feet together, dragged him to a bench and lay him across it, face down, leaving his shorts around his knees. Next, I lay Vermin atop him as if he'd fallen asleep on the guy.

Then I drove the van halfway up on the curb, looked around, saw no one wandering about and scurried into the vegetation to make my way down to a church. There I called an Uber and had him take me to LAX, where I rented a car and drove back to the loft.

I contacted the Coordinator. His muscle queens cleaned out the studio and took the rental and Taurus away as I loaded a few clothes and other things in the Mustang. By ten pm, I was heading for the easiest city in the world to hide in — Las Vegas.

I was just across the Nevada state line when it hit the news.

Gay Rapist Captured. Suspect in multiple assaults and disappearances now in custody. I didn't like how they put it. A rapist is a rapist, be it against men or women. It came across as just another excuse to vilify the gay community as perverts and dangerous to your little boys, but it didn't really matter. The narrative was already set in the media and they were copying each other's horror stories. More than a dozen men were known to have been kidnapped and sexually assaulted. As many more were missing and suspected to be dead, *including the suspect's roommate*. The whole situation was explosive, even for LA.

So there I was, driving through the desert at night, just like I'd done when leaving Arizona. Headed for a city that has no honest reason to exist. The Coordinator had already indicated he'd have more work for me, soon, so it seemed I was still on the Network's good side. Just needed a base of operations.

I was bothered by the suddenness of everything falling apart. And wary of the coordinator's casual attitude about it. There had been no hint of trouble prior to this evening. It made me even warier of him.

But I had too much invested in this situation to walk away, now.

Shit, I was going to miss Vermin. Miss having fun with him. But in truth, he was spinning out of control and was dragging me and the Network with him, which was not acceptable. I had a business to run, and business is business.

And the first rule of business is, the company comes first.

No pun intended.

Dammit.

HUNTER

BOOK THREE
"Each one I capture..."

ONE

You hate me.

As you probably should.

My story thus far has been one of offenses against the law, society and humanity in general. What I have done violates every conceivable notion of decency, morality and respect for others in today's world, and you'd be right to think so.

You'd also be wrong.

Because what actually offends you is how I don't cloak myself in the hypocrisy that passes for civilization, these days. I don't claim to be one thing when I am, in truth, the opposite. I told you who I am from the outset, to put it bluntly.

I'm a hunter.

You should believe me when I say this.

Something I learned a long, long time ago was civilization did not really begin forming until a guy like John discovered he could make a dude named Joe do the whole job while John-boy kept the fruits of that labor. That led to slavery and employees and a two-tiered strata in society — those who take and those who are taken. Nothing new about it or even unusual. Ants have slaves and chimpanzees go to war for territory. Female lions do the hunting so their cubs can eat as the males get to be lazy assholes good only for fucking. Then jackals come along and steal it from them all. Not nice, but reality.

I was on my way to being one of the taken when I latched onto the Sheriff with my plan and began remaking myself into one who takes. A true entrepreneur who saw through the veneer of morality in today's world, recognized an opportunity and figured out he'd make a buck off it. Capitalism at its best. Granted, it's by selling men to other men, but consider this: the first ones I went for were men destined to be killed and buried in the desert. I kept them alive. I see that as a good thing. Makes me close to philanthropic. A true humanitarian who gave the doomed a chance at a new life.

So long as they met my criteria.

Unfortunately, not all of them did...but them's the breaks.

Now keep in mind, men and women have been taken and forced to build munitions and clear paths for roads and work the fields and provide sexual favors since forever, and nothing's really going to change that. The only difference now is how the chains tend to be more symbolic than actual. Debt. Desire. Destitution. Renumeration that comes only by adhering to a particular belief that no one else matters as much as you do, so let others handle themselves. Human beings are beasts who live by a hierarchy that allows little deviation from top to bottom, and anyone who tells you we're not is either a liar or a fool.

I'd like to think I'm neither.

I'm just someone who realized sometimes the beast needs to be fed in ways that cannot be openly acknowledged. I don't ask my clients what they plan to do with those I bring them; I just provide the merchandise.

Many would call me evil and amoral and unacceptable for this attitude, and they'd be right...by their claim to morality and decency and all the hypocritical accoutrements that adjoin it.

They would also be full of shit.

They don't truly care about a WASPy little someone like me taking non-WASPy someones to be used and abused and disposed of in ways no one knows about. It's a given to them that some of us are worth more than others; it's just considered *unseemly* that I have the nerve to put a price tag on that reality.

I don't associate with those two-faced fools; I deal with those who are honest about their hunger. Clients who want things they cannot gain by conventional means but don't want to be associated with getting them by...oh, let's just say *un-conventional means*. To a hunter, their wish is our desire, and we fulfill any request...within our stated parameters.

Now that I'm higher up in the Network, I know there aren't many of us. Not true professionals. I know of two who work with pieces of art. Another has brought about land acquisitions, no matter what the hurdles. One is believed to have toppled three governments for her clients. And just to balance the scale, there is another woman who acquires well-known females for hers.

Turns out, I'm the only one whose specialty is young men. Twenty to thirty-five years old. Good-looking and well-built being a given. An associate I've never met procures older males, for whom there may not be as much demand but is far more costly, thanks to the delicacy of the hunt. I know of no one in our Network who provides anyone underage. Not because of moral objections. No, it's just like I said...if an adult vanishes it's halfway assumed they just walked away to another life and eventually will return to their home and family.

So long as there is no body to be found.

But when children disappear people notice, and that is dangerous. The news will use their disappearance to work up ratings and fear and panic, not only in the US and Canada but also Europe.

So I focus my hunts on areas of the world where you can disappear anybody. Places like that have always existed. Hell, in just the last hundred or so years we've had two world wars in Europe (with the Pacific Rim tossed in during the second one); Russia in the 20s and 30s; America in the 30s, 60s and 70s; Central and South America since forever, and same for the Middle East; Eastern Europe from the 40s to the 90s; and India and Pakistan since no matter when.

There's always someone willing to make it worth your while, to do what others will not. The one percent of the one percent of the one percent who like to get their kicks and have the cash to do it, and the legal and political power to hide it while keeping even a specialist like me busy. For example, in the three years since leaving LA, I have fulfilled ninety-three contracts for sixty-seven clients. Made my banker very happy, and when you make a banker that happy, they never ask where the money came from.

Same for my portfolio. I was finally at the point where I could afford anything I wanted without asking the price, and liked being in that position.

All because I've graduated to big game. I don't have to go hunting for simple deer or elk or bears, anymore. Now it was more exotic fare, worthy of higher fees and greater expertise. I'd shown myself worthy of joining this club by handling a delicate issue in Los Angeles, a few years back. I proved it, again, when one chosen lad grew so panicky, once we handed him over, he couldn't even get it up for the client.

He was a young actor who'd been on a couple of Venezuelan Telenovelas, but he'd run afoul of one of the cartels...or maybe the rebels; it never was really explained why he was chosen. Which always makes me leery. However, the Sheriff had pulled this deal together with some new Coordinator, whom I had yet to meet, and he'd talked me into going along with it.

The guy's photo was very promising; on the short side but built like a college wrestler, with hair everywhere there should be, big brown eyes, round jaw under a fine face, and a damn good ass. All I had to do was hop on down, bring him back, run my usual test and hand him over with his semen in condiment cup. That was the new requirement — physical proof of ejaculation. Seems the hunter who handled older men had faked his evidence, a couple of times, and this was to remedy the situation.

By this point, part of the deal was I flew private jets and got handled by upscale customs folk, who were usually more amenable to a little cash in hand than the border guards had been.

I still planned to be a billionaire by the age of forty and lemme tell ya, that is exactly why. No border bullshit, anymore. Being alone in a cabin that was beyond plush, with cold champagne, sodas, beer, wine, hand-prepped food to nuke and a couch that shifted into an amazingly comfortable bed — oh, was this the life.

On trips like this, I'd have no attendant, due to the nature of the trip; just the two pilots in the cockpit, neither of whom was usually very interesting. But since it was an overnight flight, no need for anything more. In fact, the actor-wrestler was brought to me, blindfolded and handcuffed, put on my plane, shackled to a seat and away we went.

Well...this guy lived up to his photo, but the moment I saw him, I knew he'd be difficult. He struck me as one of those macho twerps who hates even the thought of being touched by another man. Once we were in the air, I got down to business and, well...it took me almost the entire trip to get him up and off, and then he only half-filled the cup. Saving grace was, he had a dick that was amazingly big and flat out. gorgeous, once it got hard. With a bit of care, he could be a lovely play-toy.

Once he got over his hatred of male intimacy.

Because this was mainly just a transport job, I only made fifty off him, plus expenses. I wouldn't make a big deal about that except this bastard client wound up bitching and moaning and claiming the guy wouldn't get it up. I learned from the Sheriff that it seemed the second the guy was delivered, he'd been strung up, whipped and fucked really hard. What was worse. He was then tossed back at my new Coordinator, and the client was demanding a replacement.

At no additional cost.

I didn't want to do it. I'd given clear instructions on that guy's use. Gentle caresses through his pubes and up his shaft brought out a lovely reaction. And no touching of the ass till he'd cum. I mean, it's not like he was the first lad we'd had who was difficult. That's why we had disclaimers to specify how the more high-strung ones should be treated. It was the client's own damn fault for not reading or following them. No, he'd decided he wanted hard dick now and fucky-fucky-fucky too fucking fast. To my mind, it was like he'd bought a car then driven like a maniac and wrecked it, and now was demanding the dealership replace it with a new one because it wasn't working like he wanted. The hell with that.

But the Sheriff told me this new Coordinator was making noises at him like *This is not why we signed up with you* and *We expected better service* and shit. He also reminded me this new jerk had contacts all over Spanish-speaking South America, thus widening the hunting field for raw product. Which didn't impress me all that much; I have my own contacts because I speak Spanish. What did get to me was how this threatened to be a hit to my reputation, so I reluctantly let him arrange for a replacement. In fucking Maracaibo, of all places. But I still headed down to fetch him.

Like I was fucking FedEx.

And I had to pay for the jet, myself. Shit.

You cannot enjoy luxury when in a mood like that.

So I sulked the first hour of the flight. Tried to watch some DVDs. Surfed the web. Glared out the window at the Gulf, far below. It wasn't till I indulged in a killer cheesecake with strawberries and champagne that I lifted myself out of my foul mood. Then I managed to sleep a solid six hours to wake refreshed. For breakfast, I nuked waffles and sausage and made coffee. By the time we arrived, just after nine, I was back to being bright-eyed and bushy-tailed, and willing to live with the assholiness of it all.

We landed at a private airfield, near the Atlantic. I had no idea if we were north, south or anywhere near the city; it looked very rural. We pulled to a halt, then the pilot opened the door and both he and his buddy exited without a word. I was about to follow them out, as usual, when four truly vicious-looking characters approached, carrying a trim young man who was bound with duct tape and wearing a hood. I was forced back as he was carried in and dumped on that couch. Then they got off the plane, without a word. I started down the steps to talk to them, but the most vicious of the four stood at the foot and shook his head, a pistol in hand.

"Stay on the plane until you are home," he snarled, in what sounded like Columbian Spanish, not Venezuelan. Not a huge difference between the

two but enough to notice.

I smiled and climbed down a couple more steps, saying, *"I just want to stretch my legs and..."*

He pointed the pistol at my head. *"Stay on the plane!"*

Okay...I backed up and stayed.

Talk about feeling unwanted.

Two new pilots strolled up, one of them a taut blond hunk in his mid-thirties, who spoke with a Slavic accent and whose uniform barely held his muscles inside it. He looked vaguely familiar...but I finally decided he just reminded me of a porn star I'd once had a crush on. The other was younger, darker and not as tight, but he was still in damn good shape. Neither of them even glanced at the bound guy on the bed. They started their inspections and preparations, so as everything was being taken care of, I inspected the replacement.

He was athletic, with a neatly pumped chest, flat belly and trim hips. His long legs had good form, as did his arms, and his crotch was rich and full. A lovely specimen.

And the complete opposite of the actor-wrestler he was replacing. His slacks very expensive, as was his striped Polo shirt. Even the flip-flops on his lean long feet were designer. Binding him with duct tape instead of shackles was like a sacrilege.

I took his hood off...and damn near gasped like a girl seeing her favorite boy from her favorite boy band. Oh, my God, he could have given Ricky Martin a run for his money when it came to Latin male beauty. Around twenty. Creamy skin. Big eyes dark as umber. Brunette hair, thick, wavy and on the long side. Small nose but right for his face. He was gagged with a bandana and some cloth shoved into his mouth, so I couldn't see what his lips were like, but my bet was they would be perfect, too. I doubted our client would squawk.

Good choice, I told myself...except I was also thinking, *This kid's not a narco. He's too classy for that. Too neat.*

The actor-wrestler had been the near opposite — nervous eyes darting around from wariness, tremors in his hands, nostrils raw from snorting the bad stuff.

But this guy...while he was shivering with fear and his big brown eyes were searching to see if he had any chance of escape, it wasn't the same as the actor. And while I was supposed to test him en route back to the States, his fear told me it would take a while to calm him down into an erection, so it was not going to be fun.

I maneuvered him to an upright seat and buckled him in, saying, *"Don't worry, little one, I'm not going to hurt you."*

He managed to focus his eyes on me and saw me smiling at him.

"I do not know what you did," I continued, *"but where I am taking you is a lot better than what they were going to do."*

He frowned, confused, trying really hard to understand or believe what I was saying. Which threw me, a little. Granted, Venezuelan Spanish has a different inflection in many words from Castilian, but it was close enough to work for most of South America. So I winked and pinched a tit, and he glared at me, shocked. I got the feeling he'd been pinched like that, before.

By this point, the jet was refueled and the pilots ready to go, but before the vicious guys could close the door, a Suburban roared up, the driver laying on its horn, and skidded to a halt by the steps. Two more vicious men got out, grabbed a limp bundle wrapped in a sheet from the back, carried it over to the plane's door and tossed it in, on the floor.

"What the fuck is this?!" I yelled, pissed.

"Your tip, faggot," snapped the vicious guy, laughing. Then he slammed the door closed.

The Slavic pilot came out to finish locking it.

"Son-of-a-bitch," I snapped. "I'm supposed to watch both these guys by myself, the whole fuckin' flight?"

Slavic smiled at me, ice cold, then said, "If trouble you have, call," and calmly opened the nastiest looking buck knife ever, just by using his thumb. Then he winked, said, "Buckle up," and got in the cockpit.

Well, that let out any fun with the first guy. An audience is not conducive to my form of playtime. I halfway wished it was Slavic replacing the wrestler. Testing him would have been a joy and a half.

I snarled and unwrapped the sheet to find an unconscious kid, and by kid I mean a boy who looked like he was fifteen or sixteen. He was in nothing but a pair of still damp boardies that smelled of the ocean, and he was bound in that goddamned duct tape. Holy shit, did that piss me off. My contract was clear — no one under the age of twenty, so unless they could prove he was at least that old, no deal. I hauled him into another seat and buckled him in, then sat my own ass down.

Moments later we were in the air.

What kind of shit was this? I'm sent for one guy and they throw two at me, like a fucking courier? Both treated like sides of beef? What, was I supposed to test them both? Even though one was clearly out of bounds? And even at no charge? I mean, what the fuck was going on?

As soon as we were at cruising altitude and the Wifi fired up, I sent the Sheriff and new Coordinator a quick message to bitch about the extra cargo, then I got up to inspect the kid.

He had the clean limbs and smooth chest of a surfer-boy, with sun-bleached blond hair. Small nose and a few freckles over his cheeks and shoulders. Trim body. Sweet little nips. Tan all over except for a line that hovered just above the belt of the boardies. And he was breathing very, very softly.

Oh...this did not feel at all right.

I sent a photo of him to the Sheriff then focused on my dark-haired cargo. He'd calmed down enough to remove the gag.

"We are at twenty-thousand feet," I told him, *"so it will be a waste of breath to call for help. Let us talk, instead."*

When he spit out a cloth soaked in his saliva and I held a bottle of water to his lips. He guzzled it all down, spilling very little. He was breathing heavy but less from fear than the simple exertion of trying to stop shivering.

"*What's your name?*" I asked. "*How are you called?*"

He frowned and thought then said in a soft voice, "*You. Spanish? Brazil.*"

Wait, wait, wait, wait...I pointed at him. "*Are you Brazilian?*"

He nodded. "*São Paulo.*"

I bolted to my feet and paced the length of that jet, back and forth. "Those motherfuckin' bastard sons-of-bitches! What the fuck're they tryin' to pull with this bullshit?!"

Slavic opened the cockpit door and cast a look into the cabin. "Is problem?"

Shit, careful, Hunter. Don't know who this guy is. "No, cut my finger. Stupid."

"Toilet has first aid."

"Thanks."

Brazil sort of chuckled in a kind of scared way and said, "You. English. Speak English. American?"

I looked at him. Fought my anger. Put a finger to my lips to indicate we should keep it quiet. "Yeah. Speak English?"

"Little." He almost seemed hopeful...and fuck, was he beautiful with that expression on his face.

"What happened?" I whispered. "Why are you here?"

He took a moment to translate it in his head then shrugged and murmured, "Bar. Drink. Friend. Sleep. Here. Where here?"

"Sleep? Like him?" I pointed to the unconscious guy.

He frowned, looked around his seat to see him and nodded.

Okay... "Here...well, here was Venezuela."

"Venezuela!?"

I grimaced and put a finger to his lips then knelt beside him. "Did you hurt someone there? In Venezuela?"

"Hurt?" He shook his head. "Never to Venezuela. Never. No good there. Ever. No work."

"No work?" I sat cross-legged and eyed him. "What kind of work?"

He didn't understand me.

"*Trabajar. ¿Cuál es su trabajo?*"

"Ah, *trabalha.*" He gave me a half-smile. "*Modél.*"

"Model. Clothes? *¿Vestimentos?*"

He nodded.

"Photos on the internet?"

He nodded. "Facebook. Instagram. YouTube."

"What is your name?"

"Name? Ah, Luiz Monteleone. Please, *banheiro.* Toilet."

I knew there was a plastic knife with a serrated edge in a drawer so used it to cut the duct tape on Luiz. I figured Slavic had his buck knife, if I needed backup...but I had a feeling I wouldn't.

Luiz struggled to his feet, still shaking, so I helped him to the lavatory and he crushed himself inside. Then I sat in a seat, silly knife at the ready, and went online.

Sure enough, Google brought up images of Luiz doing his modeling thing — clothes, runway, beachwear, and even some paparazzi shots of him at clubs with a girl or a nice-looking buddy. Or on the beach playing volleyball. Or diving around. And did the camera love him? Man...

Okay, this didn't make sense. Taking a guy who's known by the general public? The actor-wrestler had already pretty much fallen out of favor with them, so he wasn't that big a deal. But this? Taking a guy like this would take some serious finessing, and it had the feeling of anything but that. Besides, the only reason I could think of for him to run afoul of anybody in Venezuela was by fucking up a drug deal or owing a shitload for a drug habit, but I didn't see anything like that in him. His skin was clear. His eyes, too. No tracks on his arms. Didn't even seem to have any tattoos. He looked like a good clean healthy guy.

And then to have this other kid thrown in at the last minute? Without any kind of warning or information?

Kitteh was not at all happy about the current situation.

I went to a Facebook page then Twitter and Instagram and found nothing but more nice-guy images and stories. It wasn't making sense...

Until I hit Grindr.

He had a profile.

It came up just as he came out of the lavatory. I showed it to him, on my phone...and got a *So what* shrug, in answer.

I pointed to myself. "Gay." Then I pointed to him. "Gay?"

Again, a *So what* shrug.

Suddenly, our client's ass-holiness was coming into focus.

"Luiz, did someone try to buy you? On Grindr?"

He frowned, not really understanding.

"*¿Prostituta?*" I asked.

He jolted, more than a little insulted. "*¿Me?! ¿Una meretriz?! ¡No! No...*" Then he stopped and dropped into a seat. "*Grindr...*"

He dropped his head into his hands and went on a rage of words that, even though I didn't know Portuguese, I was pretty sure were along the same lines as my tirade, earlier.

I made coffee and set two meals to nuking, then he and I had a nice quiet sort-of conversation as they cooked, and as we ate.

First, I managed to tell him we were en route to America, and I could not get the jet turned around; we'd have to deal with this new situation once we landed. He took that fairly well; only a thirty second tirade of low-down Portuguese. Then he stumbled out that he'd been contacted by someone on Grindr who wanted to bring him to the States for a weekend, but it had sounded too much like the man expected more than just company so he'd turned it down. He wasn't a whore, and he had a sort-of boyfriend, who was not invited. In fact, they had been out at the bar, on Saturday night. When I told him it was now Monday, he lost it, entirely, and it took me several minutes to calm him down. Slavic even tossed a few glances back at us to make sure I wasn't dead yet.

Luiz wanted to send a message to his family and boyfriend to let them know he was okay, but I did a quick check of the Brazilian media and found there was nothing about him vanishing so convinced him to wait till we landed.

Again, something was feeling totally, totally wrong.

Now don't go thinking I'm one of those super-smart guys who can figure all kinds of shit out after catching just a couple of clues. I wasn't. What I was is sharp enough to listen and not seem like I'm listening, and use the information I pulled together over time to help me. After all, I'd been doing jobs like this for eight, almost nine, years, now; so you catch onto some of the bullshit, even if you aren't paying attention...and trust me, I paid attention.

Of course, it was pretty obvious that our client was the one who'd contacted him and was using me...using us to bring him into the States without bothering to fill us in on what he was using us for.

Not acceptable. And once the Network found out he'd pulled this kind of shit, he'd be lucky if he was just banned.

Of course, that raised lots of questions. Like, did he pull this stunt with my actor-wrestler as an excuse to make us bring Luiz to him? Was that the plan, all along? Had he set this up with this new Coordinator? Because Luiz and that guy looked nothing alike, so why would one be chosen as a substitute for the other? If so, that really pissed me off because to start with it made me look like an idiot who could be used. What was worse, it also made the suggestion that I'd delivered the wrong merchandise, which REALLY pissed me off.

I'll put up with a lot of shit, but not if it's going to stain my reputation as a businessman.

Then there was the blond in the boardies. How did he play into this? Looked like I was about to find out, because he was starting to wake, and no matter how you looked at it he made the situation worse than bad. If he was American, the media would have all kinds of fun screaming stories about him being kidnapped, and the FBI would get involved. Didn't matter where he was in the world; pretty blond boys are the most important thing there is...I mean, next to pretty blond girls, of course. If he was European, their press would go even more bonkers with half-true exclusives and lies and horror stories, and Interpol would definitely start looking into it. Canadians would simply get down to business and find out what the fuck was going on, and you did not want to mess with the Mounties; they are polite little sadists, as I learned, not so long ago (and that story is for another time).

So not one of those scenarios was acceptable, especially since I had no idea why he'd been tossed into the mix. And right then I didn't give a shit if this new asshole I was dealing with *had* taken an order for him, despite the age restriction; at the very least I should've been informed so I could tell them to fuck off.

But my gut was telling me there was something else going on, thanks to the way he was tossed in so dramatically at the last minute. Almost like an afterthought...a way too deliberate *afterthought*. That got me to wondering if he might be the real reason for the whole trip. That it was done so casually was meant to distract me from thinking much about him. Maybe the deal with Luiz was concocted as an excuse to get me to bring Blondie back to the States in a way that was under the radar.

So...do I sound paranoid enough, yet?

One way or the other, that fucking Coordinator was seeming more and more like a skank, and while I do enjoy skanky, at times, doing it without my input was not cool.

Blondie opened his eyes and looked around, groggy. He tried to move and realized his hands were tied and he was gagged and he started to freak, all in the space of a few seconds, so I crouched beside him and held him down by the shoulders.

"Calm down!" I snapped. "Calm down! Do you speak English?"

His big blue eyes focused on me and he nodded, barely under control.

"We're in an airplane," I continued. "I'm gonna take your gag off and we're gonna talk, okay? Just be cool. You'll be okay. Okay? Understand?"

He glanced between me and Luiz and made himself give a jerky nod.

I used the knife to carefully slice the duct tape behind his left ear then slowly pulled it away from his face and hair. He hadn't had anything stuffed into his mouth.

"Get him some water, will ya?" I asked Luiz.

He looked at me, confused.

"Water. *Agua*."

He finally jerked a nod and grabbed a bottle from the mini-fridge. I put it to the kid's nicely-formed mouth and he gulped some down, his eyes locked on me.

Then he jerked his mouth away, letting some spill on himself, and said, "You got the wrong guy. My folks don't have any money. Please, just lemme go..."

American. Oh, holy fucking shit!

"I don't care about that. What's your name?"

"I mean it! My dad's a doctor but we don't have a lot..."

"What is your name?!"

He looked at me, lost. "You...you don't know who I am? Who do you *think* I am? Why'd you kidnap me?"

"I didn't. I'm tryin' to figure out why you're here. So what's your name?"

It took him a moment to finally say, "Ryan. Ingersoll."

"Where're you from?"

"Chi...Chicago. My folks don't have a lot of money."

"I'm not after that!"

"Then what's this all about?"

"I don't know, yet."

He looked around. Saw Luiz sitting on the bed, watching him, confused. "Where are we?"

"Told you, in a plane. En route back to the States. Why were you in Venezuela?"

"Venezuela? I wasn't."

Uh...okay... "Where were you?"

"Um...Aruba. With my mom...dad...brother. They okay?"

He was starting to panic, so I said, "I'm sure they are, but let me check. This is Luiz. He's in the same situation as you." I gave Luiz the knife. "Will you cut him free?"

I made a sawing motion at the tape; he took it and nodded.

Okay, you may think that was a stupid thing to do, but it was deliberate. I wanted them to trust me, and the fastest way to gain that trust is to give them a weapon they can use against me. Besides, we're in a jet flying over the Caribbean Sea; what the hell good's it going to do them to go after me?

I checked the Aruban news and there was a blurb about a search for a boy who'd gone missing during an early-morning snorkeling trip. The family was down for a vacation after one of them had beaten cancer, but no names were mentioned. At least it did say his parents and brother were frantic.

I showed him the story. That seemed to relax him, a little.

"Today's Monday," I said. "Was that this morning?"

He nodded.

Well, that explained why the story was minimal and he was so last-minute and wet; they'd grabbed him in Aruba and had barely had time to get him to the jet.

He was rubbing his wrists and starting to shiver so I grabbed the sheet. It was still damp.

"Luiz, can you see if there's a blanket?"

He was pulling the duct tape off Ryan's ankles so looked at me, confused. "No understand."

"Blanket," I said. *"Cobija."* Then I motioned putting it around Ryan's shoulders.

Luiz nodded and started checking the drawers. He found one under the couch and gently draped it over Ryan.

I sat cross legged on the floor next to Ryan and asked, "What were you doin' in Aruba? The story said somethin' about cancer."

He nodded. "My...my mom. Beat breast cancer. Came down to celebrate. My...my grandparents...dad's folks...they paid for the trip. That's why we don't have a lot of money. It all went to mom's treatment."

"Your *father's* parents paid for the trip..."

"Yeah. Air fare. Hotel. Mom's folks..." His face screwed up with an intense dislike that spoke volumes. "You...you got anything to eat? I...I skipped breakfast for the dive and they were gonna feed us on the boat, after, and...and..."

"Yeah, right, sorry..."

I looked around but Luiz had already pulled out a meal and was showing it to Ryan. Looked like some kind of chicken dish. He smiled and nodded, so Luiz put it into the microwave. Then he showed cans of Coke and Sprite, and Ryan brightened.

"Sprite's cool," he said.

Luiz gave him one. He popped it and guzzled down half, then sighed, almost happy. "Thanks."

"So you don't like your mother's parents?" I asked.

"Fuckin' assholes," he grumbled. "Richer'n shit and they — oh, wait, if you think you'll get a fuckin' dime from them for me, you're fuckin' crazy. They wouldn't even help pay for mom's chemo, their own daughter and — "

"I told you, this isn't a kidnapping for money. Who's your grandfather? Your mother's father?"

He eyed me, wary, then finally said, "John Mueller."

BAM! Oh, man...this could now make sense, but only if...

"Mueller Industries? Based in Chicago?"

Ryan was still wary, but he nodded.

Well...HIM I had heard of. Worth tens of billions, every penny verifiable thanks to investments and corporations owned and lots of press on the business news front. Mansion in Lake Forest. Penthouse on Lake Shore Drive. Offices on the great and glorious Magnificent Mile. One of my heroes, in fact, since he'd started with fuck all and now was in the one-tenth-of-one-tenth-of-one-percent. My goal to be a billionaire was to make it ten years earlier than he'd done it.

Needless to say, I was a bit behind schedule.

I locked in on Ryan. "You have two uncles, right?"

Ryan shrugged. "Probably, but I haven't seen 'em since I was six."

"How old are you, now?"

"Fifteen."

Okay. At least now I had something to go on — one of America's richest families was involved in this budding fiasco, and it looked like my long-time buddy, the Sheriff, and this new Coordinator were pulling some shit. Question was, what were they up to, and why?

"Can you two talk to each other, for a while?" I asked them. "I need to see if I can get in contact with my people in the States. Ryan, if you know any Spanish you can get an okay idea of what's being said in Portuguese."

"No, I've been takin' French. Was gonna go to Paris, after graduation, but that got totally fucked."

Luiz, however, bounced up to kneel beside Ryan, saying, *"Vous parlez français?"*

The kid looked at him, almost bright. *"Un peu. Je l'étude depuis quatre ans."*

"Ma mère est français! Elle est née à Orléans!"

"C'est vrai? Ma mère a étudié à la Sorbonne."

"Ma mère, aussi!"

"Merde."

Luiz offered him a hand. *"¡Luiz!"*

"Ryan," he replied, taking Luiz's hand. *"Et je suis tres heureux de faire votre connaissance."*

"¡Et moi!"

And off they went. I just hoped they were talking boy stuff instead of planning to gut me and steal the plane. Slavic would not appreciate that.

But it got me thinking. Spanish is enough like French to sort of make out similar words. Like, I knew *etude* was the same as *estudio*, which meant *to study*, and that the Sorbonne's a university in Paris...and I'd once made the dumbass mistake of thinking *aussi* meant *oh, yes* and got corrected, after a lot of laughter, to let me know it was really *también*, in Spanish.

So I asked Ryan, "Did your mother go to the Sorbonne? And his, too?"

"Yeah, weird, ain't it?"

"Did they know each other?"

He blinked, catching on to what I was wondering, and asked Luiz something that I'm pretty sure was *Did your mom know mine?*

Luiz shrugged, a frown entering his exquisite face, and he said, *"Sais pas. Peut-être."*

Those words I knew — *Dunno, maybe.*

"Ryan, ask him what his full name is."

He did, and Luiz looked at me, wary, before responding, *"Luiz Francisco de Carvalho Monteleone."*

He'd taken his mother's name? *"¿Carvalho? ¿Sus padre?"*

He gave me a weird look. *"¿Católico? No, Ele é..."* Then he jumped and understood. *"Oh! Meu pai!* Father. Yes."

"What's goin' on?" Ryan asked. "What's the deal?"

"Hold on," I said. "I think I got somethin'."

I did a cross-reference of Carvalho-Mueller and came up with a four month old article about plans for a roster of projects in South America developed by *Investimentos Cuidadosos* and Mueller Industries.

And one Nestor Carvalho Sexto was the main man in São Paulo.

Motherfucking son-of-a-bitch, was I being used to help in TWO kidnappings?

Oh, kitteh did not like that idea, at all.

"I think you guys were targeted," I said. "Your families are in business together."

"What!?" burst out of Ryan.

Luiz was confused so Ryan quickly translated, in French. He leaned back, stunned, and murmured, *"Merde."*

That word, I knew.

"What the fuck's goin' on?!" Ryan cried.

"I dunno. But I know someone who can find out."

They got back to talking in French, now comparing notes and trying to see if they had any ideas of their own. The microwave dinged so they sat at a fold-up table and shared the dinner after Luiz poured them both some wine.

Yeah, right, Ryan was underage for that, but this was neither the time nor the place to police it.

First thing I did was send a message to the Sheriff, telling him, *Cargo checked and cleared.*

He sent back a snarky, *Good for you.*

Motherfucker had no idea...and now I knew he'd gotten my earlier texts.

Then I sent a message to that pastel Coordinator. I wasn't even supposed to have his cell phone number, but I'd caught a glimpse of it when my IT-guy was digging into a file I...oh, let's just say I wasn't supposed to have any idea existed, and I'd input it into my phone. My inner critter never lets rules stand in the way of protecting himself, especially when he feels like he's being shortchanged...which it showed I was, by the way, which was why the Sheriff had suggested shifting to this new guy...and I digress. The son-of-a-bitch had always been squeaky about money, but then again...he'd had my back, in LA.

Sure enough, just I was starting to sift through an article on Mueller's daughter and two sons, which laid out how said daughter had fought breast cancer, with a photo attached of Ryan with his WASPy parents and younger brother, I got a response.

Are you fucking kidding me?!?!

I snuck a snap of my boys finishing their lunch and sent it to him, and I would swear I actually heard him scream clear from California. He sent back links to two news stories. The first was fifteen minutes old — *American Kidnapped in Aruba*; the second was in Portuguese but offered an English translation to show the same thing, for Luiz, from this morning. Total ransom demanded was equal to twenty million dollars.

Holy fucking shit, this was not something you could bury in the desert.

That's when Slavic came out of the cockpit, aiming for the toilet. He sent a wary glance at Ryan and Luiz, chatting and eating at the table.

I popped up with, "How's it goin', in there?"

He cast me a wary look. "Is okay."

"Cool. Y'know what time we're gonna land?"

"Is five more hours."

I let myself look as dumb as I could and said, "I dunno what that means. Five o'clock? Six o'clock?" Then I let him see me toying with a roll of packing tape.

He nodded and almost smiled. "We land fifteen-thirty."

"Fifteen...oh, oh, right. Got it. Thanks." Three-thirty.

He went on into the lavatory and damn, did his ass move nice in those slacks.

Focus, Hunter, focus.

I let the pastel Coordinator know the time of arrival and that both boys were fine and safe, with me.

I got a message back — *Sounds like Kino.*

That made me freeze.

Kino's in Arizona, just across the border from Mexico, where there's a small packed-earth landing strip that this fancy little jet I was paying for would not enjoy. So first, it meant the Sheriff had fixed it with Border Patrol to not be paying attention when we came in.

Second, we would not be taking off.

Man, was I glad I'd sprung for the extra insurance in the rental.

So...it looked like the Sheriff was going to put a dead-end to the set-up with me by doing the old school thing. Why? I hadn't a clue. We'd been doing really well. In fact, it was me who got him into a far more lucrative business than just providing inmates to rich assholes to be fucked.

But then again...the boys had seen my face, so I guess I had to be vanished in a way that no one would ever find. That desert has swallowed up more blood than anyone could ever even begin to imagine. In short, so what if I was damn good at what I do? So could somebody else be.

This game was apparently much bigger than I thought.

Of course, that meant the pilots would probably meet the same fate. Slavic's blade wouldn't work against a 9mm or .45, unless he was Ninja Knife and could deflect the bullets.

Shit...such a waste of good male flesh.

I looked at Luiz and Ryan, still chattering in French like a couple of school boys. Pawns in some bigger game of money and power and business they knew nothing about. Hell, I had an idea as to what was up, now, and even I wasn't totally sure about where, how, who and when. But that's the way of the world, isn't it? The innocents get used and die so those using them can live on.

It's life's bottom line.

TWO

I figured the only way to stop this budding catastrophe was through a combination of alliance, blackmail and bribery.

Slavic passed back through to the cockpit so I snuck a shot of his amazing ass and legs as he squatted to grab a Coke from the fridge. Got a good shot of his profile, too. He slipped into his seat and the other pilot made the trek to the lavatory. While he wasn't nearly as interesting, I still copped a shot when he did the same thing as Slavic and sent both to the pastel Coordinator, telling him who they were.

He responded with, *We'd make a nice pile off the blond.*

So be it, was my response, because not all lives really matter. You can say all the right words you want, but when push comes to shove it's me who counts, not you. Just being honest enough to admit it.

I spent another hour digging through articles about the new projects between Carvalho and Mueller, projects set up in Brazil, Paraguay, Uruguay and Argentina, before finding a very interesting pair of tidbits.

One of Mueller's real estate groups owned lots and lots of property in and around Phoenix...including a high-rise condo on North Central Avenue that was *oh-so-very high-end.*

I had a strong suspicion I'd been to the penthouse, there.

Mainly because another article mentioned Mueller's younger son, Edward, was executive producer on three of my action movie star's films, the last being three years ago. Which was that monster flop.

Well, in the States; it made its money back, in China.

Zing, did that catch my focus, or what? I quickly located a photo of Eddie-boy, a big grinning, semi-buff, full-of-himself man nearing forty in a well-tailored suit, with a dark widow's peak touched by silver, cold blue eyes, long nose and weak chin. And what was best? I got more than a few pings off my gaydar. Next to him was his photogenic Stepford Wife and three Stepford Children, almost like they were out of central casting.

In comparison, while Ryan's folks were just as WASPy as Eddie's, it was in neither a plastic nor scary way. They were merely an attractive white upper middle class family who looked fortunate in life while Eddie's belonged in a wax museum.

So...could Eddie be involved in this mess? Could *he* be the target for extortion by some assholes? Using his nephew and the son of a business partner? No, that kind of crap would have been aimed at big daddy, because it didn't look like Eddie was in control of anything at Mueller Industries. Yeah, too weak. Nor was there mention anywhere of money troubles, not even after the movie fiasco, so him doing it to get cash seemed unlikely.

But if he was connected with the Sheriff in any way...and if I could prove that high-rise on North Central *was* where I spent my weekend getting fucked, thanks to the Sheriff...well, that might be useful.

Of course, I doubted Eddie knew anything about Kino because it was at least three-four hours from Phoenix, and it only tied in as being a nice quiet place to end somebody. Still, I now had a pretty good idea of the *who* so the *why* didn't matter as much as the counterattack. I didn't know what the pastel Coordinator had in the way of abilities in the death prevention department, so I played it safe and sent off another text.

To my old friend, Hernandez.

Let him know I was in need of his expertise. I figured if anybody could help me keep my boys out of this, he could.

And yes, I now saw them as *my* boys.

The son-of-a-bitch actually called me! Saying, *"Hunter, good to hear from you. Has Julio been in contact?"*

"Uh, no. What's up?"

"You may congratulate me. I am going to be a grandfather."

"They're having a baby?! Oh, my God, that is excellent!"

"And it is your doing. Julio is proving to be a good son. Good lawyer. He is so good, I am now a legitimate businessman, and just as boring."

"Oh, that is good for you, but it might be a problem for me."

"Yes, I did not think you texted me to just talk. Has that fat old bastard finally turned on you? You would not be the first he has done this to."

"I know and have heard of this, so with him I am ready. The problem is, we have a new man involved."

"Ah...so I am glad we stopped doing business, years ago."

"Yes, it is good. I am not comfortable with him. I like to think I can talk my way out of any trouble because of insurance I have arranged, but now I am not so sure."

"What is the problem with this new bastard?"

I laid it out for him, as much as I knew...and for the first time since I'd known him, he sounded angry.

"I knew the fat son-of-a-bitch was stupid, but this is insane. He risks all for a few dollars. Idiot. You must not worry, Hunter; I have many reasons to help you."

"Thank you!"

"Do you know where you land?"

"Yes, there is a landing strip in Kino..."

"Kino!? It is to Kino he takes you!? Mother of God. When do you arrive?"

"The pilot says three-thirty, but we are making good time."

"And the boys who are with you? How are they?"

"They are fine. Eating. Drinking."

"Do they know what has happened?"

"Not everything."

"Did you...well...?"

"No! I am more concerned with getting out of this alive."

"Good. What about the pilots."

"I think they are part of it, but I will want to...to keep them."

"Do so. It is best to keep things simple, in a situation like this. I will see you in Kino, mijo. Do not be afraid."

"With friends like you, how could I be?"

He laughed. *"You are full of shit."*

Then he disconnected the call.

And I felt ready for lunch.

As I ate, I let the boys know we had protection coming, so the rest of the trip was almost festive. I had a decent paella and a couple of cokes, no beer; I wanted all my wits about me upon landing. I also found out more about the kids.

First of all, Luiz was Jewish. His great-grandparents had been worried about the rise of fascism in Europe and seen hints of it coming to Portugal, so had established a branch of the family in São Paolo and assimilated their name. His mother was actually a distant cousin to them, via Spain, and had met his father during a family get-together in Orleans.

"My mother asked if this blood link is why I am gay," he laughed, in French; Ryan was translating. *"But I have two brothers and four sisters and none of them are interested like this, so she has grandbabies and no longer cares."*

"Wow, that's cool," Ryan said, also saying he wasn't gay.

I let him keep his illusion that sex can be delineated in so simple a manner.

Man, I really enjoyed just sitting there and talking with these kids. And yeah, I know, I know, I was only twenty-nine so calling Luiz a kid was silly, but I'd done so much more than they had and been through so many more situations, sometimes I felt three-times my age. I guess that's what privilege does for you, no matter what country you're in. If you don't have to fight for a living...fight just to make it, day-to-day, but instead have family that support you and money enough not to have to worry...you can keep your innocence intact for much longer. Maybe even your whole life.

I'd had that till I was seventeen. Dad didn't make a lot of cash, but being military helped cut the costs a bit. Hitting the BX. Housing supplements. Mom working in home care...well, not in Spain; three years there and she learned nothing of the language, so couldn't find a job. But the country was cheap enough to make even a Captain's wages seem like a General's.

It wasn't till we were back in the States that everything fell apart. We settled near her family, all good conservative Lutherans whose one true party was Republican and all else was spawn of the devil. Church on Sunday and family dinner in the grandparents' massive yard afterwards, with lots of sniping about *liberals* and *socialists* and *those people* (now that they weren't allowed to use the N-word) and the like.

Needless to say, we did not get along well.

It was a dumpy second cousin who figured out I was gay and let the whole family in on it. How she figured it out, I never did learn. She just spread the word and it fit too neatly into their disdainful view of my less-than-popular attitudes to be disregarded. Took one long Sunday afternoon for me to go from *that fool liberal Mexican-lover, Hunter*, to *that fag, Hunter*. With lovely mom and dad joining in.

I put up with it till I was eighteen and had some savings, then I split and haven't seen them since. And I realized it was eleven years past, almost to the day.

I watched Luiz and Ryan chatter like happy puppies playing at being big dogs. And felt an odd mix of pride and joy and pleasure...and anger at how easy life had been for them. How neatly they would become one with the world. Neither of them a renegade, like me. Neither of them fighting to have a comfortable life, like me.

Except...that comfortable life had set them up to be victimized. And scroungy, growly, angry me was the only thing keeping them from what could easily have been a disaster. I've heard of too many occasions where kidnap victims wound up dead...and there was no guarantee this would not be the same, if things didn't come together, right...but kitteh was ready for trouble. Ready to spin into wildcat mode, if need be. And I actually felt proud of myself for being willing to do so with no promise of payment from them.

Well, Hunter, weren't we just full of ourself?

*****

We reached Kino not long after three, flying in low and easy. I could hear the pilots chattering to each other in some kind of East European tongue, meaning Slavic and his buddy were from the same place, and I could tell from their tone they were not the least bit happy about setting down here.

I'd already laid out a quick plan for when we landed, which was basically, "Lock yourselves in the lavatory and do not come out willingly." And I made sure Luiz had the knife. Ryan held onto a couple of forks, and I got the feeling he could turn into a real terror, if he wanted to.

I almost felt like a proud papa.

I looked out the window and, of course, there was nothing but desert scrub and distant hills in every direction, all brown and deadly. To think people actually crossed this on foot, once upon a time. Shit.

We touched down and bounced, kicking up too much dust to be able to see out the windows, and rumbled to a fairly quick halt. More dust swirled around us like yellow fog. The plane also felt off-balance. After a bit of cursing in his native tongue, Slavic came out to unlock the door. It was pulled down...

And there was the Sheriff, looking as much like a junkyard dog as ever. A stiff hot breeze whipped more dust around him. He had five men at his back. Four were big, butch bastards of varying lumpiness, the same damn scowl evident on all of them despite all wearing sunglasses. The fifth was a trim man standing next to a Mercedes sedan, in designer desert wear and mirrored aviation sunglasses...under an Australian outback hat?!

I had to fight to keep from laughing.

"Out," was all Slavic said. I heard his associate behind him, getting out of the cockpit.

"After you," I smiled back at him, then cast my boys a wink and added. "I hope you brought sunscreen. If not, there's some in the lavatory."

Ryan translated into French and they bolted into it, taking Slavic by surprise. Same for the co-pilot, whom I shall now call Bear. He's the one I grabbed, then I slammed him against Slavic and kicked them down the steps before happily following.

"Hi, guys, how you doin'?" I said, cheerful and carefree.

Both pilots rose from the dirt, just furious and using many, many bad Slavic words on me, I'm sure.

I noticed two silver SUVs parked close by...then froze.

There was no one else around.

None of Hernandez's men. None from the pastel Coordinator. Nothing but these scowling monkeys.

Oh, shit. Where was my backup?

"What the fuck's this all about, Hunter?" the Sheriff snarled, red in the face. He was sweating from the heat, despite how dry it was.

To no surprise, Aussie-hat-guy wasn't even perspiring.

"What the fuck's the big idea gettin' me mixed up in a kidnapping?" I shot back, forcing that smile to stay on my face.

"Figured that out, did ya?" the Sheriff sneered.

I nodded. "I also figured out you guys ain't smart enough to come up with this shit, yourselves. Somebody else did it for you. All you did was make a real mess of it."

"You got too much mouth on you."

The Sheriff started for the steps and I pushed him back.

"Don't do it," I said, almost pleading. "You'll wish to God you hadn't."

He hesitated. He knew me too damn well to dismiss any warning I gave him. But Aussie-hat-guy? He didn't know jack from shit. He motioned to the plane, saying to the men, "Bring the boys out."

"Don't do it, guys," I said. "He ain't as smart as he tells you he is, so you'll just wind up six feet under."

Hat-guy gave me a look-over then said, smiling, "You have no idea what you're involved with."

"The kidnapping of two kids belongin' to Mueller-Carvalho's main people? For a ransom that's ludicrous on the face of it? Gimme a break. You're after somethin' more than just the money. My bet is, you got me to help in a negotiating ploy, and a really fuckin' stupid one, to boot."

I'd have said Aussie-hat-guy blinked at my amazing summation, but his sunglasses hid his eyes. Instead, the Sheriff grabbed me and slammed me against the side of the jet. The metal was already getting hot from the sun.

"You been gettin' too fuckin' full of yourself, you little fuck," he snapped. "Any of these guys can do your shit."

"Even test the merchandise?" I asked in as queeny a tone as I could muster, batting my eyes at him. I called over to the Scowling Monkeys, "Didn't know you guys were family! Let's have a kiki."

"You sick fuck," he growled. "That Ingersoll boy is just fifteen."

I all but spit. "You think I'd diddle a kid? I thought you knew me better than that! Or have you got him set up for the same pleasure you got me into, asshole?"

The motherfucker hit me. I slammed to the dirt and looked up, ready to spin into howling beast mode...

But then I saw it.

A drone floating in from the north. Soft. Light and airy. Almost gentle as it cut through the breeze. Followed by another. And another. And another. Each of them dancing around the jet, camera lenses focused on us.

Aussie-hat-guy noticed them, first, and spun on the Sheriff, snarling, "You said Border Patrol was taken care of."

The Sheriff looked around to gape at the drones, murmuring, "Those ain't BP." He turned on me, growling...then jolted and spun back around.

I followed his gaze and saw dust rising in the near distance, signaling a bunch of cars were coming, fast and furious, and more drones circled in to hover around us like flies over shit.

The Sheriff was speechless.

The Scowling Monkeys pulled guns and, with both pilots and Aussie-hat-guy, started scrambling into the jet.

So I sat up, whistled to get their attention and pointed to the jet's front tires to show one of them was caught in a rut.

"Sorry, guys," I chirped, "you ain't goin' nowhere in this puppy. That gear'll collapse before you're halfway to liftoff."

The monkeys scowled, but the pilots knew I was right.

Moments later, a caravan of black SUVs surrounded us, then men in dark suits and darker sunglasses got out with pistols at the ready. They almost looked like Feds, but every damn one of them was big, buff, butch and Latino. The drones kept circling, now seeming more like buzzards waiting to feast.

Last but not least, Hernandez exited one of the SUVs.

I rose to my feet as he took everything in, at a glance, then he strode over to me. He eyed a cut to my cheek, nodding.

"Have you been talking too much?" he asked, smiling.

I shrugged. *"Had to keep the assholes busy till you got here. What took you so long?"*

"You told us three-thirty."

"We made good time.

He glanced back through the group. *"Where are the boys?"*

"In the lavatory. They will not come out until I say so, and one has a knife."

"So they know to be wary of you." Said with a wink.

I nodded. *"They know I am on their side."*

"This means you may have to lie low for a while. Perhaps a couple of years."

I shrugged. *"I have some savings and investments...and if the substitute merchandise brings in enough..."*

He nodded. *"Which two?"*

"The pilot's uniforms."

He eyed them, nodding. *"I can see why. Go into the plane. Do not come out until I text you."*

I did. Knocked on the lavatory door and asked, "You guys okay?"

"Yeah," Ryan said. "What's goin' on? Kinda hot in here."

I barely managed to keep from saying, *I'll bet, with you two beauties rubbing against each other.* Instead I said, "Couple more minutes, then it's over."

It was five minutes later that I heard the SUVs drive away. I looked out a window to see the drones following them, like a murder of crows. A moment later, Hernandez texted me the all clear. I looked out the door and saw all but one of the SUVs were gone. No garbage around. No tire tracks in the dust. Not even blood in the dirt.

For all his claims of going legit, Hernandez could still be one very vicious, very efficient motherfucker.

I called, "Okay, guys, it's safe."

Ryan and Luiz all but tumbled out of the tiny room, both drenched in sweat, and staggered over to the door to see the same as me — no one around...except for that one and only SUV.

In basic black, of course.

I guided them outside, made sure each had a bottle of water. I also pulled out some sodas, no beer and wine, and sprayed the kids with more water to cool them down then herded them into the SUV. It was a push-button starter with the keys in a cup holder, so I fired it up and cranked the AC to max. After that, I transferred my things into it. I was about to wipe down the jet when I noticed a fat box of matches resting on one of the wings.

I sighed; thank God I got the extra insurance.

I went back to the jet, struck a couple of matches and stuck them so they would burn down to light the full box, set them on the couch and scrambled back to the SUV to lead-foot it away.

In the rearview mirror, I saw smoke begin to billow through the jet's door.

The navigation system had been set to a location on North Central in Phoenix. *Gee, could that be what I think it is? Hmm. Seemed awfully precise a destination.*

There was also a pre-paid cell phone attached to the dash. I let Ryan call his folks and Luiz call his, and the joy being expressed all around damn near gave me a sugar rush. Of course, they wanted to talk to me, but I refused to take the phone *since I was driving*, and I would not tell them where we were. Wouldn't even say where we were going; just let them know they'd be safe in a couple hours. That had to be sufficient, for now.

It was, but they were very reluctant about it.

After an hour, we hit the 10 then headed straight for Phoenix. Of course, these kids weren't dumb; they could read road signs. They kept speaking to each other in French, but by this point they trusted me. They'd heard everyone's voices as we spoke, outside the jet, but couldn't make out what was being said, so I was able to deflect their questions by saying, "I knew someone who owed me a favor."

Best to keep it as detail free as possible.

We arrived during rush hour, of course, so it was slow-going for a while. But then I got off on 7th Street, cut over to North Central and headed away from downtown. It was a nice, wide boulevard lined with palm trees and upscale shops and overpriced condos and open spaces. After a couple more miles of evening traffic, we approached this tall structure of pale concrete, golden windows and solid balconies that gave off the attitude it wanted you to pay just for being allowed to look at it.

I drove past, once, to scope it out, and the fact that there were no police cars or fed cars around the building told me none of the Muellers were there.

I did a series of right turns to get back around to North Central and stopped before turning onto it. The main driveway entrance was half a block away.

I turned to Ryan. "Your grandfather's company owns that building. You two go inside. Tell security who you are. They'll contact the police and get you home."

"What about you?" he asked.

I looked him over. Even after the hell he'd been through he was still young and pretty. And Luiz, while he was a bit more rumpled, looked as heartbreakingly beautiful as ever. The image of them being used and abused made my heart contract...but all I did was give his chest a fist-bump and say, "I don't exist."

I drove up to the entrance and Ryan got out. Luiz followed him, looking around in shock. I hit the gas and roared away as a doorman approached. In the rearview mirror, I saw them watching me go, then Ryan spoke to the doorman.

Oh, man, I hated leaving such profitable cargo behind, but I was glad I'd done it. Which didn't make sense, to me...well, except in Ryan's case, since he was way too young. But Luiz, his beauty and even being circumcised...shit, I could have unloaded him with no trouble. Made a good seven figures off him. But money's no good if you're in prison or dead, and deep down I knew it was an all or nothing situation, thanks to how clumsily the whole transfer had been handled. How stupidly. So I could live with it.

And it wouldn't be a total loss. I pretty much suspected this SUV had a space added in to hold couple of pilots to trade for enough to at least break even.

Which brought a song to my heart.

*****

I headed straight up the 60 for Wickenberg, where I was to connect with the pastel Coordinator. I found my turn off, drove down a two-lane blacktop then up a lovely dirt road...and there was a nice big Winnebago sitting off to one side, its canopy extended and a card table with two chairs placed under it. Its engine was humming so the AC would be on, but it had started to cool down for the evening so the outdoors wasn't completely unpleasant.

A grill was set up next to it, the lovely aroma of fajitas caught in its smoke. I stopped near the canopy and got out. By the time I was at the table, a glass of iced tea had been poured for me by a serious muscle queen who could have killed me with a flick of his or her or their finger, whichever pronoun fit.

The Coordinator came out dressed in his usual pastels. He took a seat, I sat diagonal to him and the muscle queen began prepping the fajita fixings. I drank down the full glass of tea before I even looked at him.

"Feeling better?" he asked in that whiny, grating voice.

I nodded.

"The boys are well?" he continued.

"It's not on the news, yet?"

"I'm asking you."

"Right. Right. Right. I did not even think of touchin' either one. I was too unhappy about how it was bein' handled."

He sneered. "Liar."

"Okay, okay, I thought about it. Especially Luiz. He is too fuckin' gorgeous."

I gave him my phone to show him the photos.

He looked at them, saying, "That's why we like you, Hunter; you think on your feet instead of with your dick." Then he handed it to the muscle queen, who did some tickety-tackety thing on it before going to the grill to pull perfectly-cooked strips of flank steak onto a plate...

Then toss the phone into the hot coals.

The Coordinator handed me another phone. "The images are gone from the Cloud. Use this one, from now on. Never call or text me, again. *I*..." and he drew the word out for a good three seconds, "...will contact *you*."

I nodded, then noticed a couple of muscle princesses were hauling the pilots out of a space behind the back seat of the SUV. They were unconscious and soaked with sweat, but that only enhanced how good both of them looked. Blond and smooth...brown and burly...they'd have made the perfect wrestling tag-team. Both were carried into the Winnebago, like sacks of potatoes.

We feasted, first, and I wanted to hire that muscle queen to be my personal chef. Hot DAMN, those fajitas were like nectar from heaven. I ate WAY more than I should have, and didn't care. Kitteh loves being fat and sassy after a job well-done.

The sun was just setting when the Coordinator rose, saying, "Shall we inspect the merchandise?" Then he headed for the door.

Oh, so much for lazing. I poured another tall glass of tea and followed him in.

Both pilots were laid out on long benches that were facing each other across a narrow aisle. Hands and feet shackled, and ball-gagged. They hadn't needed to be. Whatever Hernandez had done to quiet them was still working.

As if reading my mind, the Coordinator said, "It's the same anesthetic you use, but a different dosage."

Confirming in my head that he and Hernandez had been in contact, and might even be working together. Time to be extra careful, my boy.

"Do you know anything about them?" he continued.

I shrugged. "Eastern European; maybe Russian. The blond is good with a knife."

"Yes, we found one on him. *He* has started a bidding war. Of course, he must be cleaned up..." His voice trailed off but his meaning was obvious.

"Happy to do it," I said. "I could use a bath, right about now. What about Bear?"

"I haven't heard back, yet. Should know by tomorrow."

I saw lots of Old Spice accoutrements on the shelves so asked, "Does this thing have a shower?"

He chuckled and led me into the back, where a magnificent jacuzzi setup covered the whole tail. Pipes ran up the corners to make a shower, and one-way windows looked out to give it even more of an open feel. There were steps up to the counter that surrounded the deep clean basin, and I could see plenty of room in it for two or three or even a dozen men.

Damn, I wanted one of these.

"It's good to know you didn't test either of those boys," he said, casually. "One is the son of a very dear friend. I think the trauma of having been kidnapped, alone, will be hard enough for him to handle. To have added your actions to that...well..."

Stupid Hunter still had to ask, "*Friend* or *client*?"

He looked at me, his icy eyes growing icier, if that was possible. "She was never a client." He was silent for a moment, then added, "But an asshole brother of hers was. Got himself into a bit of a hole with the Network, and he foolishly believed we would ignore it. But then he always did think more of himself than he should. We have determined that is why this happened — a way to pay off his debt without going to daddy. Further proof the rich know nothing about obligation."

Holy shit, that froze me. He had just given me info I did not need to know, and had proven another supposition of mine was correct. That new Coordinator and my old buddy, the Sheriff, had joined forces with Eddie to kidnap two high-profile sons, then stupidly...or arrogantly, whichever...had thought they could dupe greedy little me into transporting them from Venezuela to the US. The only thing that kept this from becoming the end of Hunter and his pilots was how I'd been able to access outside help. The fact that Hernandez had directed me to drop both kids at the doorstep of the very condo Eddie and the Sheriff had been using to let his buddies fuck men in, well, that just solidified the thoughts in my head.

So in answer to the Coordinator's comment, I simply started water flowing into the tub, nice and hot.

Oh...and it was scented with rose oil. How lovely.

The Coordinator looked back at the guys and asked, "Which one first?"

I heard Slavic moan and smiled. "Does it matter? Only thing I need to know is — any holds barred on them?"

He eyed me for a moment then said, "None, for the blond. For the brunette, I may need proof of virginity. We have a group interested solely in bears, as you call him, and virgins are always in high demand."

"Proof ye shall have," I said, with a wink.

He nodded then said, "Be sure and drain the tub after each, when you're done. And leave them on the couches, well-shackled."

Aw, for fuck's sake...little bitch was still telling me how to do this? To keep from snapping at him, I tested the water. Just hot enough. I heard the guys starting to come around so asked, "Aren't you worried about 'em makin' noise as your people drive this thing down the road?"

He chuckled. "I'm not taking them through Phoenix. The SUV is being disposed of. You'll have a car outside, to use."

"You got somethin' in a nice hybrid?"

He almost rolled his eyes, at that comment. "Now...as to where do you set up shop, next..."

Next? I wasn't crazy about the sound of that. "I was just gonna head back to Vegas."

"You might want to rethink that." Meaning, *Oh, no, you don't.*

I huffed. "It's a nice anonymous city. Lots of people in and out. Even good for shoppin'..."

"No! Nothing from North America. It's grown too dangerous."

"Okay...I could always do..."

"Miami area."

"I don't like Miami."

"But it has excellent access to South America. We'd like you to be there." Meaning, *Fuck what you want or like.*

Shit. "Okay...you got an apartment there?"

"You have enough money to get your own."

Whoa...meaning, *Get back in contact with your hacker, Hunter, and increase your security to Mach Ten, because these motherfuckers were keeping way too tight an eye on you.*

"Besides," the Coordinator continued, "I have a project in the works and it's best if you're situated there. I'll be in contact." He started for the door then stopped and said, "Watch the news, tonight. It should prove very illuminating."

I sat beside Slavic and caressed his pecs. "I might be busy."

"You won't regret making time. May even help you decide you like Miami." Then he left.

And if that wasn't the softest, subtlest threat I'd ever heard...

THREE

I was so glad I wouldn't have to be gentle with Slavic. I needed someone to take my frustration out on, and he looked like he could handle it.

I checked the restraints on his feet. Nice and tight, and linked to a solid iron bar screwed into the floor. The key was in the ankle cuffs lock. I think that was the Coordinator's subtle suggestion I work with him first. Get my jollies out of the way so no risk to the other's virginity.

I had to chuckle. One time, one fucking time I come close to losing control and I'm forever marked by it? Dude's got the memory of an elephant.

I looked at Bear, who was taking in deep breaths as he came out of his slumber. He was cuffed the same. I took the key from Slavic's lock and tried it on his shackles, and they opened. So I linked his feet to his hands, effectively hog-tying him, then I let my own hands go exploring.

Man, I loved the sensation of my fingers trailing over him, outlining his pecs and following his tummy down to his belt. He had a layer of flesh covering his muscles that made him feel real and human. I even liked how he had slight love-handles in just the right proportion to his body. I let my right hand envelop his crotch as my left toyed with a nip through his shirt. My big, butch, brawny bruin was bursting at the seams of his clothes and desperately needed to be liberated from them as soon as possible. And I was just the man to do it...oh, yeah...

He regained full consciousness, realized what I was doing, and tried to bolt away from me. I lay on top of him. I giggled and kept running my hands up and down his sides and legs and shoulders and chest as he twisted and squirmed and kicked and fought to get me off. But I'd been able to hold wrestlers down with no trouble, so his moves did nothing but increase my need.

Shit, too bad he had to stay a virgin.

It was a good thing I'd left the gags on. Bear howled and cursed as I pinched and pulled and flicked and fingered both of his nips. He was not the least bit confused as to what was about to happen, as was evident in his dark, wide, lovely eyes. I looked over, saw Slavic awake and watching us in horror, and laughed. That only made me more excited.

"Don't worry; I'll save plenty for you."

Then I gripped Bear's shirt and tore it open.

Buttons flew everywhere. I could now see his lovely full round pecs swirled with hair and had nips that were made to be sucked on. Well, I never was one to resist temptation. He jolted and really started to fight me, but I had too good of a hold on him. Oh, did he howl, then.

Slavic joined in the howling and I rejoiced in the sound of them. I had control, and they were trying to tell me I really couldn't...and I shouldn't...but honestly, it wouldn't do them one damn bit of good. Ownership is 99% of the law.

I sat back on Bear's hips and tore his shirt the rest of the way off, revealing a soft little belly also swirling with hair and a cute little innie of a belly button. His right shoulder and bicep had an elaborate tattoo of geometric features covering it, adding to his beauty. He rocked me like he was one of those mechanical bulls, adding more and more to my sense of entitlement. I unbuckled his belt and unbuttoned his trousers and lowered his zipper to find he was a boxers kind of guy. Not my favorite underwear, but I didn't care. They were bunched in a nice plaid bundle around his dick and balls, all of which quivered behind the light cotton material.

I took a glance at Slavic, who was now focused on trying to get his feet or hands free. His struggles gave him an amazingly gorgeous look. I reached over and pinched one of his nips, saying, "No rush, honey; your little buddy's just the appetizer. You'll be the main course."

Then I stood up and heaved Bear across a shoulder to carry him back to the hot tub. One of the great things about wrestling is you learn to handle guys close to twice your size, no matter how much they struggle, and while he wasn't *that* big, he wasn't a lightweight. But this gave me a chance to smack his ass a couple times, which made him buck even harder at me.

The tub was full and had shut off, automatically, so I dumped him in. Water sloshed over the sides but drained into a couple of funnels without letting a drop hit the floor. The sudden immersion shocked him so much, it gave me a chance to yank off his shoes and one of his socks before he started kicking at me. I left the other sock on and raised his legs up, which put his head underwater. Then I yanked his trousers down to his knees. I let him back up for air, and water streamed over him as he fought to cough and breathe through his nose.

It took me ten seconds to strip off my shirt, jeans and shoes. I left my briefs on because he wasn't the one I was going to fuck, dammit, and I didn't want my dick to get carried away.

Not again.

I flipped Bear onto his belly, in the tub, and he snorted out a lot of the water that had gone up his nose. That took all his concentration, so I whipped off his belt and tore his trousers into strips, starting at the inner seam of the legs. Next, I shredded his boxers, revealing his ass and lower back had a fine layer of hair, and he had a rather sweet swimming trunks kind of tan line. I still preferred the Speedo look, but since his legs also flowed from his cheeks in a smooth, very lovely, very soft and creamy way, this type just seemed right for gentle caressing. Now he was naked...well, except for one sock.

It pleased me, aesthetically, so I left it on.

I flipped him back to face up, got in the tub and straddled him as the water whooshed around us. His chest heaved. Water dashed through the hair, matting it to his lovely tan skin in a way that was startlingly erotic. His nips were round and perky. His shoulders and neck were elegant as he puffed and strained against the handcuffs.

I felt like I'd scored the winning Lotto number.

I kissed his throat and whispered, "All I wanna do is suck you off. Be smart and let me. If you don't, I get to fuck you, and I can go for hours...and hours..."

I knew he spoke English; as a pilot, it's required.

He shook his head and muttered *No, no,* as I sucked on his left nip and then his right and back and forth, repeating what I said. He fought to control his breath then finally became still. I looked at him. He was just gazing at a corner of the hot tub.

He'd surrendered to the inevitable.

I kissed my way down his belly to his pubes. Pulled at them with my teeth. Kissed along the side of his dick. Brushed water away with my lips and nose. He was uncut and soft but I could feel him beginning to fill in, so I lifted him slightly out of the boiling wetness and engulfed him with my lips, swirling my tongue around him and inside his foreskin. I decided to let him experience the full force of my abilities.

I pulled back and saw his balls were hanging low. I gobbled both of them into my mouth and rolled them around with my tongue, making him almost squeal from the sensation. It's a lot more intense than just fondling them with your fingers; it's like joining them with a universe meant solely for pleasure and joy and nirvana, and it connects with every part of your being, from nose to nips to thighs to ass to your heart and soul. Once started you can't stop it and want it to go forever.

So he got harder.

A LOT harder.

In fact, I began to wonder if I'd misread him, that maybe he was family and I hadn't seen it, because he clenched his ass to push his dick against me as I kept sucking his balls and used my right hand to stroke him, soft and easy and steady. The full length of him. Toying with his foreskin. I made him squirm from the overwhelmingly erotic sensations.

I finally pulled back to look at him and he had become glorious. Yeah, he could've lost twenty pounds and been perfect. Yeah, his dick wasn't the biggest in the land. But no question he'd be worth any price we charged for him. The way his torso flowed into his legs. The lovely tan line. His balls bouncing between massive thighs designed by Michelangelo. His pedigree was obvious to any and all.

I dove back in and sucked on him like I was in starvation mode and he was my nourishment. I was a starving kitten drawing sustenance from momma cat. I was a lion feasting on his dinner. I was a machine drawing milk out of a cow's udder. It was so fucking perfect, I was close to losing myself in just the steady pumping and slurping and fondling of it all.

He moaned in horrified enjoyment and clenched and squirmed and pushed harder and harder at me and just about lost it when I slipped a pinky between his ass cheeks to toy with his anus and slip it into him...and find he was just tight enough to pass for virgin as he grunted and bucked.

In fact, that last little tickle from my finger sent him careening over the edge and made him shoot his wad into my mouth.

Without even asking! The bitch.

I grabbed one of the plastic condiment cups on the counter and spit into it, then let him fill it with his semen as he fired, again. I kept rolling his balls and licking his dick to get more and more and more until he was whining from being so tender. Finally, the cup was full so I sat back, clipped its lid on and looked at him.

He was looking back, shocked and bewildered in that so-called straight guy way, so I patted his cheek and said, "Good boy," then grabbed a bar of soap that smelled of spices to lather him up from head to foot. I made sure to go as slow and invasive as I could.

He started to get hard, again, to his shock and awe.

And to mine. Maybe he was bi, and I've never been a hundred percent on my gaydar, with them. Too many variables.

So I took special care to clean inside his foreskin, not that it was needed; he'd kept himself clean. But that adds a layer of pure unadulterated pleasure to the experience. And...it got him hard, again. So I sucked him off, again, this time just for me.

That really fucks with their brains.

The water was barely warm by the time I was done and he was rinsed off. I set the tub to draining and guided him to his feet and dried him with slow brushes of an elegant towel, then carried him back to his couch. He let me attach the shackles to an iron bar then rolled over as if to hide from me, revealing the lovely line of his body to his ass and down his legs. I had to caress him, once more, he was so beautiful.

Then I started the tub filling, again, and returned to Slavic.

"Next..."

He pushed back deeper onto the couch, in horror. He could see the outline of my erection in my wet briefs. His eyes whipped from me to Bear and back. Neck straining. Chest pumping. Arms flexing to pull at the cuffs. Legs pressing together and pulling at the shackles attached to the iron bar, making his crotch nice and full. He was sweating, despite the AC, and the moisture made his shirt cling to him in ways that screamed perfection.

I started by removing his shoes and socks. He sat up and tried to head-bump me, a couple of times, but he couldn't get the leverage to really hurt me so I ignored him. Because all it did was add to my need to fuck him...and fuck him good.

Mmph.

I rose to face him and he tried to head-bump me, again, but I just shoved him back and used his momentum to tear his shirt open. More buttons flew all over. He gasped and tried to twist away but it did him no good. He wore an undershirt that was soaked with sweat and showed off his pecs in elegant fashion. I pinched his nips through it, making him howl and buck, then I ripped the rest of his outer shirt away. After removing his belt, I tore his pants off, too. Finally, I stood up to look at what was going to be my main course.

His struggling and bucking and twisting only added to how lovely his body looked, still encased in that t-shirt and a pair of red *Meat* boxer briefs that covered a very promising crotch.

But what was the absolute best? A monochrome tattoo on his left thigh...of a rearing horse.

I recognized it, and finally knew why he'd looked familiar.

Slavic was Pavel Jakettov, a porn star with what had to be the dumbest made-up name, ever, but who was so fucking beautiful it didn't matter. Tall. Blond. Perfectly built with a covering of soft golden down over his chest, arms and legs. A longish face. A ten-inch dick that never looked like it was uncut, even though I knew it was. Oh, man...I'd jacked off to his image and videos for years before I'd found my calling.

I looked closer at his face. He'd beefed up a lot and it looked like he used muscle enhancers, because he was at least forty pounds heavier and his face was a lot fuller. But now I could see his eyes were the same — big and blue and a hint of hurt behind the anger and fear in them. He'd quit the porn biz more than ten years ago and gotten married. Supposedly. Claimed he'd only fucked with guys for the money to buy a farm.

Well...flying a private jet is hardly farming.

Of course, that explained the bidding war for him. My bet was, others had recognized Pavel in the photo I'd sent to the Coordinator, or he had and made it known who was being offered. That was why there were no limits with him. He was anything but a virgin, yet who wouldn't want to have their own porn star to play with? And Pavel was one of the hottest pieces of meat ever put on this planet.

I think he realized I recognized him, because his eyes grew angrier and his nostrils flared. He stopped bucking against me and let me take a long look at his rebuilt body. The fucker thought him being pretty was going to work me into being on his side, did he? This could prove to be a lot of fun.

I flipped him onto his belly, unhooked the shackles from the bar, grabbed him around the waist and lifted him up to carry him back to the hot tub. It was almost full, again. I set him into it, feet first, then let him topple over to lean against one side. He shifted around to look at me, giving me a good look at his ripe red crotch as the water washed around it. Even soft, he was big...but I already knew what to expect from him.

What's wild is, I really wanted to talk with him, once we were done. Have a post-fuck conversation. Learn the truth behind why he quit the biz and became what is, in effect, a narco-pilot.

Who had assisted in two kidnappings! There was no other description for what he'd just done. I now wondered if this was another way of reinventing himself, and if his current bosses would miss him.

Or if he was more cannon-fodder in the service of the rich?

I slipped into the tub and straddled his thighs. Oh, my God, how lovely they felt between my legs. Then I rolled his t-shirt up his body to reveal his nips. Small and round and tan against a big slab of muscle that actually now felt a bit over-developed, in comparison to how he'd been. Now shaved and smooth instead of soft golden down. I fingered them both. Toyed with them. Pulled lightly at them, making him gasp from sensations he may well have hidden in the background of his mind, sensations brought to him by other beautiful men as they fucked and sucked and kissed and fondled him.

I traced my fingers down the center of his abs, so very well-defined. Heaving less from fear and more from uncertainty as to what I was going to do. Or certainty, since he'd been through a lot of this, before.

Including the bondage...my favorite videos.

I reached the elastic of the boxer briefs. Toyed with them. Pulled them down...down...down to reveal his uncut dick was exactly as I remembered and his balls were begging to be caressed.

I honestly think the warm water swirling around us added to the erotic need within me. Added to the lightning exploding through me as I felt his wet skin. How smooth it was, and golden and tight and elegant. Nothing sharp or angular to him.

My jaw was worn out from the hard suckings I'd given Bear, so I'd intended to just jack Slavic...no, Pavel off. But now it seemed like sacrilege not to go all the way, so I pulled my briefs off. And sat so my dick and balls brushed against his. And fondled both of us, together. Stroked and pulled. Watched him grow and expand and lengthen and stiffen.

Man, touching him was like a religious experience; there's no other way to put it. I adjusted my movements as he got harder and harder. My hands encompassed his ass and massaged it and held him in place as I rubbed my own hard-as-shit dick against him harder. Stronger. Then, when he was as hard as he'd ever been, I rose and held his dick up in the air and shifted so I could sit back down on it.

"I've always wanted to be fucked by you," I murmured.

And I all but swooned at the feeling of him sliding into me, filling the inside of me. It was beyond exquisite. Once I was fully impaled on him, I started working him with more intensity than I'd worked anyone before. I barely had to move my hips to make him shiver from the sensation of me squeezing tight against him. My fingers twisting his nips added a hundred times more electricity to what he was feeling; I could tell from how he squirmed under me. Not once did I touch any other part of his body.

I felt him tensing and clenching and pushing at me in steps and stages until he was participating in my rape of him, and still I kept on and on and on and he grunted and gasped and groaned and whined and yelped.

Finally, I felt he was ready to fire so I slipped off him and got the condiment cup under his dick just as he exploded with a near wail. Shot so hard into it half splashed out. He shot more and more and I kept working him until he started to grow soft. Only when I saw the condiment cup was overflowing with his semen did I release him and affix the lid.

His hips slipped back into the water, bubbles from it rushing around his lovely dick and balls as he leaned against the side and looked out a window. He was perfection, at that moment. The epitome of what it means to be male. Glorious in his beauty and willingness to allow me to view it.

Wait...*allow* me?

He was lying in the swirling water in a way that emphasized his beauty, and he was *allowing me* to witness this?

Fuck that.

I grabbed his Meat undies, flipped him over, and yanked them down past his exquisite ass. I dug my fingers into his cheeks. Ran my thumbs between them. Felt every fiber of my being screaming at me to get on with it, so I sank my tongue into his anus. Pushed it in. Licked and tickled and rolled it around, making him squirm, something I'd seen done to him dozens of times.

He groaned in that way I'd heard so many times, suggesting he was loving every second of my worship.

I suddenly exploded with anger at being just another guy rimming a porn god...being so unimaginative and basic and common to think that this was heaven. I growled and jolted up and grabbed my own dick and pushed it into him without adding grease or anything.

He yelped in pain as I slapped up against his cheeks with my hips and began to fuck him like an animal. Felt him fight to get away from me. Felt his core finally start to accept me and surround me and love me as he grunted and struggled a little more...but then let me fuck him, since he now knew, without question, he couldn't get free.

Holy shit, having him wrapped around me was like heaven. Life as it was meant to be. I'd dive in as deep as I could go and hold here, then slowly pull back and every part of my body would cry with happiness. Pure joy. Exquisite pleasure. Sometimes fast. Sometimes slow. Sometimes pulling all the way out before plunging back in, again. Shifting in ways that made my dick rub his prostate like I never had before. Mauling his glorious ass cheeks as if they were the most virginal in the world.

I made damn sure I fucked him like that for a good half an hour. Loved molding myself to him. Spooning him. Bumping slightly against him as I did short, sharp jigs in and out of him. Rolling inside him and fondling him until I could feel his own dick was hard as a rock, again. And going and going and going until he fired, again, before I pulled out and shot my own all over his back and ass. Over and over to the point I was close to fainting from the joy of it all. The overwhelming sense of heaven.

It was about then I started hoping the Coordinator had set up cameras, in the Winnebago, and was recording everything I was doing, because I really wanted to watch me raping Pavel. Fucking him and sucking him against his will. Bear, I didn't care about. Yeah, he was lovely, but Pavel...he'd been in the porn world and I got the feeling he was really, deep down enjoying this. That he'd wanted this. Hoped for this. And used me to get it.

Which infuriated me.

That made absolutely no sense, whatsoever. Seriously, he was only involved in the kidnapping. While that was bad, it didn't explain the level of anger I suddenly felt against him. I now know that deep in the back of my mind, I was thinking he had really been helping transport Luiz and Ryan to the Network. Maybe as part of the ransom demand. *Pay up or they get sold to someone so they could be fucked and fucked up.* My beautiful boys, destroyed as casually as you smack a fly. When he knew what it meant. He fucking knew.

Now reality is, I should have known that Pavel wasn't part of such hideousness. He and Bear were really just more cogs in the machine, just doing a job like billions of people, all over the world. When you help manufacture pharmaceutical drugs, you don't worry about who will overdose from them. If you drive a cab, you don't worry about whether or not your passenger is en route to kill someone. If you're working in a brewery, you don't worry about the beer you make causing some alcoholic to drive drunk and take out a family of six. You just do your job and leave the rest of it up to others. And that's really all I could honestly say Pavel and Bear were doing.

But sometimes my anger just explodes, and no excuses were allowed for whoever caused it. So I whipped my hand against his ass. Over and over and over, furious. Kept at it until he was crying out and whimpering.

And I found I was hard again.

So I fucked him, again.

And I wasn't happy till I saw he was weeping.

Only then was I able to regain control of myself. I cut his briefs and t-shirt off him, very neatly because I planned to keep them, then bathed him in the same spiced soap with the same slow intimacy that had brought Bear back to a semi-erection.

Didn't work, on Pavel; I'd both drained and hurt him.

And I actually felt bad about it. Weird.

I dried him and carried him back to the other couch and attached him like I had Bear. He lay on his back, glaring at me with pure hate. His body was no longer as beautiful as I'd thought. He actually looked better dressed or half-hidden by the hot tub's water. He should have kept his old figure; that was him as perfection. Now that I was satiated, he looked a bit overblown.

I sighed, showered and dressed, realizing the whole adage about never meeting your heroes was too goddamn based in reality. Before I left, I gave Bear one last caress, which he did not appreciate, then sat beside Pavel and pinched his left tit, hard.

"The only reason you're still alive is because of me," I told him. "You should never have helped them carry those boys up here."

And I slapped him.

Then I exited to find an amazingly glorious night sky filled with ten billion stars and no moon for them to argue with...and a ten year-old Blazer waiting for me. The canopy and tables and everything had already been put away, and the muscle queen was sitting by the driver's door, all set to leave.

I bid him/her/them a fond farewell and headed up the 93 for Vegas. Fortunately, being an Air Force brat had trained me how to shut down and pack what little I needed in record time, and since I was being transferred to Miami, best to get it done ASAP.

I didn't think about the news until I was passing through Kingman. It took ten minutes to find a radio station with the huge story about the kidnapping of the son and grandson of two of the world's wealthiest men. Which had come to a happy ending by payment of the ransom.

Which I knew was bullshit, but never can stop the spin.

The story continued with word of a raid on a camp in Venezuela that might have been connected to Ryan's kidnapping, and the arrest of Luiz's boyfriend, in Rio, who was suspected of having slipped him a roofie so he could be taken.

Then came a separate story of a fiery three-car collision on the 17 by New River. Six men were known dead. Seemed a Mercedes owned by some guy named Blake Coal had crossed the median at a high rate of speed and slammed headlong into an SUV carrying what were thought to be migrant workers. It had then flipped onto an SUV. The only reason it engendered a story on the broadcast is that SUV was registered to my old friend, the Sheriff, and his death was too important to shrug off. Police were still trying to figure out what had happened because there were no witnesses, no skid marks, and the bodies had been burned down to near nothing. The wreck had been heard by people working at a nearby gas station, who'd come out to find the fire already hot.

I didn't want to know how Hernandez had pulled this off. My suspicion was, the pastel Coordinator was part of it.

I knew the Network couldn't really touch Eddie; he was surrounded with legal whores who'd fight back as down and dirty as rabid canines. But they had let him know that they were onto his bullshit, so he'd better play nice from now on...and pay up. Even legal mad dogs can't stop a bullet.

As for the actor-wrestler who'd been tossed back at me, I worked on him for a week in a private compound outside Vegas, I think — bathing him, massaging him, caressing him, feeding him, fondling him, teasing the length of him over and over until I had released his inner gay man...or bi, whichever. All men have one. Then the Coordinator took him off my hands and provided him to an even better client. One who truly appreciated his beauty.

I quietly asked him to contact me, at the end of a year, to tell me how he was doing. After lavishing so much care and attention on him, I really did want to know...and it turned out he was living a life of absolute luxury and grace in a penthouse in Bahrain. He has an ankle monitor but can walk freely anywhere in Manama. And three or four nights a week he's...oh, let's just say *used* by both a very attractive sheikh and his lovely wife.

At the same time, like meat in a sandwich.

Which he found, to his surprise, he actually enjoys.

"Makes me bi, doesn't it?" he'd asked, in Spanish.

I agreed.

Unfortunately, he first had to be circumcised and agree to convert to the Islamic faith, before they'd accept him...which he'd begun studying...and found, again, to his surprise, it offered him a new sort of inner peace. No more drugs. No more drinking. He actually thanked me for leading him to this place.

Well...that was a first.

Apparently, the couple who support him, now, were trying to have a baby but the sheikh was shooting blanks. I looked up a photo of the man, and to my shock...he and my actor-wrestler looked enough alike to be brothers. I guess that was the main sales point.

Now she's pregnant, and everybody's happy because it seems they feel...well, since the sheik was fucking my actor-wrestler as the guy was fucking his wife, then it was like he was fucking his wife himself, right? That way the baby is his.

Which makes absolutely no sense.

But hey...people can talk themselves into anything.

FOUR

So now I'm stuck in Miami, and I really do not like that fucking town. The heat and humidity and political crap are way beyond what I normally tolerate. The people are assholes on and off the road. The beaches aren't anywhere near the level of LA's. Not a mountain to be seen. Miami's airport is ridiculous to deal with, not like LAX or Las Vegas. But it's quicker access to our main hunting ground in South America and, since I'm now closing in on the first step of my main goal, I figured I could handle it for a while longer. Especially since my condo looks out over Biscayne Bay and downtown Miami, and I've hooked up with both a nice Jewish guy and a sweet Muslim for fun.

Oh, no rapey-rapey stuff there; just *Hi, how you doin', come on over for a few drinks and a fuck* kind of thing. Helps that I'm easing nicely into daddy territory and have been told, more than once by my chosen ones, that I look like a major movie star who's part of the Marvel Universe...which I do not mind, at all. I even dressed up as him in his character for a Halloween Party and had people begging me for selfies, thinking I really was him.

It was cute.

Of course, hunting *could* be good here, if I needed something quick for an order. Miami's always on the verge of chaos, especially after a good storm passes through. Lots of young men here could go missing and no one would care...Cuban, Caribbean, black, Latino, even some low-rent Anglo boys, if need be; I've always thought they could bring as good a price as I got for them in LA. I mean, so long as I was just as careful in my pickings...

It's just...now I was in a jet on approach to an airfield near Recife with fresh merchandise and bonus cargo, and thinking about Luiz and Ryan made something about this whole setup feel even more wrong, all of a sudden. The rush job aspect of a specific request by a client for a high-end guy in Rio. The lesser plane. The change in pilot. Turning the cargo over in a town still in Brazil. And the way I was going to disappear Thiago so we could get away with kidnapping him — deliberately crashing the plane in the Atlantic, with no one on board...that now reeked of stupidity. Hell, I didn't know if this stupid turbo-prop even had a black box to show it had gone down.

I was finally paying attention to the alarms going off in the back of my head, and I was beginning to wonder if I'd lost my edge. Because this had not felt right from the first moment.

So why had I gone through with it? It's not like I needed the cash, anymore; I was doing extremely well with my other investments. I had my Miami boys to fulfill my whims, both of whom were *so* into whims. Besides, I really wanted to leave that fucking town and couldn't, not so long as I was working with this pastel Coordinator. So why *was* I doing this job? Was it just from force of habit?

Maybe that was it — I just plain wasn't enjoying myself, anymore. It was all by rote. The previous jobs had been fun and I'd taken pleasure in checking the merchandise. Looked forward to it. I loved owning a man's dick. Loved making them grow and pulling forth their nectar. Even on the few occasions where nothing would happen and I'd have to reject the man I'd taken, I could gain joy in fucking him and then finding ways to dump him back into the world without him really knowing or understanding what he'd been through.

I looked at Rey, who was beginning to wake. So nice and buff. So much like what I go for, personally. I would love to fuck him. Keep him, even. He looked a bit like that jogger Vermin had taken in LA, a few years ago. Wait...five years? Six? I'd had to forego that guy, too, since I couldn't leave behind any DNA on him, just Vermin's. But if Rey was mine to keep, I'd never have to worry about that.

I shifted my gaze to William. Another gorgeous man with creamy skin. Reminded me a little of Jerome, this black guy we'd sourced for the Coordinator. He was lovely and fun to suck off. Another young man I couldn't fuck because I had to supply a virgin. Of course, William was larger. Much more buff. But his face had the same general look. A pleasant awareness. In fact, he looked like what Jerome would have grown into.

I wondered where he was. What had ever happened to him? He was handed over the same day Vermin took that jogger...

Oh, man, this didn't make sense. Why was I reminiscing about guys I hadn't given a thought to in years?

I moved to sit next to Thiago and caressed his face. He was pretty, but not for me. I loved the Latino look, but I was growing tired of grabbing young men for other people. I was assuming the client base was male, but some could be female, I suppose. Forcing my boys to fuck God knows what kind of pussy. Or even...oh Jesus, even fat ugly old men. Not all turned out like that actor-wrestler. That was not fun to think about.

Maybe it was time for me to retire. Become one of the buyers instead of suppliers. Find out more regarding the market for guys like this. Did they actually have a lust for uncut men? Or did the dick not matter? No, it had to, to some. That sheikh had my actor-wrester circumcised before he'd let the guy fuck his wife. I looked at Rey and William and wondered if I could do that with them. Keep them in a holding center till I'd arranged for a place to keep them. Let them get cut and heal. Shit, their dicks would be lovely.

And then what, Hunter? Lock them in your condo on South Beach? I don't think so. Too many nosy old ladies. That compound outside Vegas? One look at a night sky with any clouds in it and they'd see there's a city nearby and make a run. Not good. I'd have to find someplace else to build my own peaceful little world.

But all that inferred a permanence I'd never sought. A consistency of companionship I'd never wanted. Was I old enough, at thirty-two, to be having thoughts of settling down and making myself a life in one place? I couldn't think of a single man I'd been with who I'd want to live my life out with.

Except for Vermin.

Eight months together and I'd enjoyed all but the last one. Grown comfortable. Watched him write his screenplays with his group like you watch your puppy on a play date. Except he was more than a puppy, wasn't he? He was fresh and alive and exactly what I liked in a guy, and I'd loved being with him. I'd loved him fucking me and me fucking him and it never being an issue who did what, when or how. We'd clicked.

And I'd let fear cut me off from him.

No, not fear. Greed.

And stupidity.

I'd built up enough money to walk away, with him, even then. I could have, if I'd stopped to think about it. But I still had my eyes on the prize...

Shit.

I'd learned he was in a prison for the criminally insane. His maniacal stories about a man named Hunter telling him what to do and helping him do it had made the cops and DA leery. Him claiming the loft's third floor was wired for transmitting videos when all they'd found was a mattress stained with cum, like that's where he'd taken some of his victims...it only added to their wariness. Forensics had also found traces of blood, but the van was covered in so many fingerprints, they couldn't match them all. It was just too freaky for them to process. As for the fourth floor, with my clothes still on hangars, my laptop on a kitchen counter, my LA wallet next to it, but with me nowhere to be found? His screenwriting people had all acknowledged I lived there, but I'd always just been referred to as his roomie, nothing more, and the name on my California driver's license was not Hunter. So I wound up being counted among the missing.

Him swearing the missing men had been carried off someplace by some queenie freak called the Coordinator sealed the deal. Three psychiatrists, two psychological specialists and a clinical researcher in psychotic behaviors had said his psychoses were too deeply rooted to be cured, so his public defender and the prosecution had given up on finding any bodies and agreed to have him committed.

For life.

Short of murder, the safest way in the world to keep a witness to your actions silent is to have them put in a mental institution.

I wondered what it would take to spring him.

Of course, that meant I thought he might forgive me for betraying him. Knowing Vermin, he wouldn't.

Oh well.

I looked out the jet's window. We were still a few thousand feet off the ground, floating in over the ocean. The water was a blue that is just plain unearthly. Whitecaps. Dolphins splashing about. It brought a sigh to me.

I looked at Thiago, again. He hadn't moved...not since I drugged him. Which was odd.

In fact, he was barely breathing. Which was even more disconcerting.

I took a closer look. Checked his pulse. Very light. His skin was very pale. He was completely out of it...so much so, I grew very uncomfortable. Joey Stefano had died from an overdose of this drug, as had many other people who had it administered to them.

I pulled out the vial of Ketamine and looked at it. Everything seemed right...until I noticed a small bit of torn paper sticking out from behind the label. I dug at the label with my nail...and it peeled away with no trouble...to show it covered the remains of another label.

Oh, holy shit, no, no, no, NO...what the fuck was in this vial!? I didn't know if it was even really Ketamine!

I checked his eyes. Rolled back. I slapped him. He did not wake. Again. He just kept lying there, looking as beautiful as any man had a right to.

Oh, fuck, this was not good.

"Jose," I called, "is there a hospital close by?"

"What do you mean?"

"A HOSPITAL! An Emergency Room? Close to the field?"

"There's a clinic in the north of João Pessoa."

"How far?"

"From where we land? Thirty-forty minutes."

"No, no, no, no, no, no, no, can you land by the hospital?"

"No! There is no space and the wires in the streets..."

"We gotta get to a hospital, now! Thiago's havin' a reaction to the anesthetic."

"He...he's what!? Very bad?"

"I think he's close to his heart stoppin'."

"Shit. Shit. Uh." I could hear him breathing and muttering, then he said, "Aero club. Paraiba. That is good. A hospital is close by it."

"Call ahead. Have a medic meet us."

He nodded and did so, in Portuguese, then gunned the plane and banked left to fly across an urban area just south of us. Tall buildings dotted the area and more and more of the ground was covered with tile-topped houses.

As we closed in and flew lower and lower, I shoved the vial into my pants pocket, tore the bindings off Rey and William and slapped them awake, saying, in Spanish, *"We are about to land."*

As they shook themselves back to awareness, I undid the tape binding Thiago.

Rey looked around, confused, and said, in Spanish, *"Did I go to sleep? I did not sleep?"*

"I drugged you," I replied.

Rey looked at me, his expression dumber than dumb. *"You what? You fucking what!?"* He staggered to his feet, checking his clothing. He could feel it wasn't exactly right. He all but roared and loomed over me, screaming, *"What did you do to me, faggot? Did you rape me? I will fucking kill you!"*

I didn't have time for this, so I kicked him in the gut and he fell on his ass.

"Sit down and listen!" I snapped.

Which did make William snap to full awareness.

"You have done something to make your boss angry, so he gave you to me. But there has been a change in plans."

"I do not understand," William said. *"Vinicius is not angry with me. I always do what he wants."*

"Well, I think he wants to get rid of you both."

Rey sat up, holding his stomach. *"What are you talking about? You say he gave us to you? That is stupid."*

"I find men to sell." I nodded to Thiago. *"You were both assigned to assist me in kidnapping him, but when we landed I planned also to sell you."*

"You think us male whores?" Rey snapped.

"No, I think you are idiots! I think this is a murder. Thiago...I injected him with the Ketamine Vinicius provided, but I now see the label on the vial has been changed. I think this was a murder and you both were to be blamed for it, with me."

"But why would Vinicius take a contract on Thiago Belo?"

William just looked at Thiago then leaned back, his mind whirring. *"Anjelica."*

Rey frowned. *"What does your wife have to do with this?"*

"Vinicius wants her."

That made something click — Vinicius grabbing his maids in lewd ways. *"He loves to fuck women,"* I said. *"You guys work as a team. If one goes missing, the other will try to find out why."*

They both nodded.

"Vinicius...around my wife," said William. *"I have seen how he looks at her. He thinks she is too beautiful for me. If he touched her while I was alive, I would kill him."*

"Or he would kill you then I would kill him," said Rey.

"We are cousins," William told me, pointing to Rey. *"My father and his mother."*

"Do you know who the pilot is?" I asked. *"He was given to me, as well. I was expecting a different man and a better plane than this."*

"I do not know. The plan was given to us by Vinicius. Now I see why."

Rey looked out the window. *"We are landing in the city?"*

"In a few minutes," I said. *"Near a hospital. Medics and police will meet us."*

"We will be arrested!" Rey cried.

True, that, but I quickly said, *"No, if you open the door, very fast, I will take Thiago out of the plane. Then you close the door and fly away. Will this work?"*

"I will ask," he said then went up to the cockpit to speak with Jose in Portuguese.

"You did not trust Vinicius," William said. *"Why?"*

"This boy should be awake by now...and it bothers me when things happen that I do not expect."

Rey called, in Spanish, *"His name is Jonas and he is from Porto*

Alegre. His brother asked him to fly this job. His brother is Carlos de Almadiriz Saldana."

William jolted. *"Carlos!? Shit."*

"Interesting," I said, wary. *"What is Carlos all about?"*

"I...I cannot tell you," said William. *"But Jonas would not be here without Carlos knowing what was going to happen. Not even Vinicius will cross him."*

"You think he sold out his own brother?"

William gave me a crooked smile. *"Some men will do anything for money."*

Okay, I got your meaning, bitch. I'll let you have this snap.

I looked out the windows to see rooftops whizzing past. *"We are landing."*

"I see the medics at the other end," said Jonas. "And the police. Do it fast. Keep them busy."

"I will."

The wheels touched down and the plane bounced and rumbled as it danced over the ground. Rey had the door half open before we'd stopped. Jonas kept the engine running. William helped me take Thiago in a fireman's hold...then the second there was no further motion, Rey dropped the door and William helped me guide Thiago out. I stumbled away from them and the plane circled around and headed back down the runway. The cops yelled in Portuguese and chased after it, pulling out their weapons, but I paid them little attention. I flopped Thiago onto a gurney and said, "It's an overdose of this."

I gave the vial to a lovely medic with the biggest brown eyes I'd ever seen on a man and the sweetest mouth. He said, "You American?"

I nodded. "I don't speak Portuguese."

He nodded and pointed to his patient. "Name?"

"Thiago Belo."

BAM! That made him jolt and he screamed for the cops to come back. I actually watched them skid to a halt, do a reverse just like some cops in a comedy, and in seconds I was surrounded by them and being peppered with questions, in Portuguese. I paid full attention to the medics, as they set up an intravenous line and injected something into Thiago. Then they wheeled him to a waiting EMS unit and raced away as I was left to tell the cops, in English, that I knew nothing, nothing.

For some reason, they did not believe me.

*****

Brazilian law is not quite the same as law in the States, but the cops are just as big of assholes. I was handcuffed, yanked around, slammed into a police car and whisked away to the closest police station to be shackled in a room with a table, chairs and four old CCTV cameras pointed at me.

They had to bring some fat sweaty guy in from the central station to speak to me in English, and his command of it wasn't all that great.

"You this boy have kidnap?" he snarled, thinking he was being intimidating.

I went the full sweetness and light of shocked horror mixed with a breathless chatter that thoroughly confused him. "No, no, no, he and I *both* were kidnapped and the men who did it were gonna make us give them money from our account, but he got scared and freaked out and they gave him a shot of somethin' and all of a sudden he's almost dead and I didn't understand a word of it but his skin got so pale and I began to think they'd killed him so the pilot spoke English a little and he called the paramedics and they dumped us out then headed off, and it all started in Rio and I just want to go home to Miami because I only came down here to meet with Thiago for a possible show on Telemundo and maybe sign up with my agency and we were gonna talk on the plane trip to Brasilia so I was gonna meet him at the airport but then I got grabbed and he was grabbed and we were flyin' here for some stupid reason and I got no idea what's goin' on! Is he okay? He was almost dead and I was so scared."

They called in an English teacher from the university.

I repeated everything to her and she translated. The guy interrogating me didn't believe a word of it, from his body language, but he had nothing else to go on.

I did find out Thiago was in critical care but was doing better. It was Ketamine in the vial, but a much stronger solution than I'd ever used. The only reason he hadn't died on the flight was due to him being young, strong and healthy, but it had damaged his heart and that had been close to failing. Apparently we were lucky he hadn't eaten; he could have vomited and choked to death before we even realized.

Okay...THAT damn near freaked ME out. I did not want to be held responsible for delivering merchandise that was damaged in transit; I had a reputation to maintain.

The cops were trying really hard to get into my phone, but I'd had it set up with a three-tier system that hid one profile completely while offering one that was more acceptable to those who felt it was their right to tell others what was and was not acceptable. *To be magnanimous*, I happily showed them the safe profile...which also happened to reference not only who I was but how wealthy I was.

And yes...I was rich. Nowhere near a billion, as already noted, but damned comfortable.

It was almost five before the national investigator, who introduced himself as Wilson Caramiz, arrived...and his attitude was rather deferential. In fact, everyone started treating me like gold...albeit still kept in a vault.

"Mr. Hunter," he said in well-modulated English, "I apologize for the circumstances, but we have many questions regarding the events as presented and would like to have them answered before we determine a course of action."

"Anything I can do," I said. "But y'know, I haven't eaten since an early breakfast at the hotel, and I've got a splittin' headache, so I don't know

171

how much good I can be..."

"Oh, of course." He turned to the sweaty cop and asked for something before shifting his focus back to me. "We will have a meal here for you, in a moment. I see you have a bottle of...is that sparkling water?" I nodded. "Would you care for something else to drink?"

Okay, time to really play. "Oh, man, I'd kill for a beer, right now."

The hint of a smile flickered over his face. It's a lot easier to get a man with booze in him to talk, as if I didn't know that. He sent another cop off. Two minutes later, I had not only a bottle of *Brahma Maltzbier* but a couple of Advil.

I didn't even know they were available in Brazil.

We talked around the issue, for a while, and I'm sure he did this to give the beer time to have its tongue-loosening effect, then my meal arrived...some sort of chicken stew he called Galinhada on a bed of rice, and damn was it good.

So once I was fed and acting like a happy kitty, he got back down to it. By this point, he had a fat folder in front of him, into which he glanced every now and then.

"To start with," he said, his politician's voice in full swing, "none of Mr. Belo's people knew about you meeting with him on the flight."

"No, they didn't," I said, smiling.

"Wouldn't that be rather odd?"

"Not if I asked him to keep it quiet till we were on our way."

"Why would you do that?"

I leaned in, conspiratorially. "Univision is after him, too, and I didn't want 'em to find out."

"What is the name of your company?"

"Cazador. Know what it means?"

He smiled. "It is caçador, in Portuguese. *Hunter*. So very interesting."

"Really? I thought it was kind of obvious..."

"And this is your talent agency?"

"Will be. I'm just checkin' into it. See if it'll be a good add-on."

He nodded. "What else does your company do?"

"Investments. Financial stuff. What's this got to do with me and Thiago bein' kidnapped?"

"That depends. You see, your photograph has now been in the press and on the news programs."

Oh, shit, what photograph? I didn't have any photos...except on my driver's license and passport. Oh man, I hoped they weren't using those; I looked like a low-rent hood, but I didn't recall any paparazzi snapping one when I was being hauled into the police station.

"I received a phone call." Wilson continued, "just before I arrived here. We had a very confusing conversation."

Shit. Time to stop being *Mary Poppins* and turn into Mr. Hard Ass.

I nodded. "Luiz Francisco de Carvalho Monteleone."

Wilson leaned back, his eyes locked on me. "So now you will tell me the truth?" No politician's voice there, baby.

"I can't."

"Why not?"

"I want to speak with an attorney."

He chuckled. "You think this is the United States and you have access to such automatic privileges?"

I did not move as I said, "I will speak with an attorney."

"You will talk with me, and you will talk with me, now, or you will go to jail for kidnapping."

"I will not discuss anything with a bureaucrat."

That got his back up. He rose and snapped something in Portuguese at an officer behind him.

Two men came in to grab me and unshackle me and drag me away, so I said, "You should ask Mr. Carvalho about Cazador. Ask Mr. Mueller, too."

They yanked me out the door and down a filthy hall to remove the shackles and slam me into a tiny cell. It stank and was wet from condensation, and the heat index was well above tolerable. Only good thing about it was, it gave me time to think. So I sat my ass down on a really disgusting bench that I think was supposed to be a bed, and I let myself go all Zen.

Empty the mind and the brain will follow.

What I finally saw was, this was the third time I'd been set up to fail, on a job, and it fucking pissed me off. Same goddamn bullshit, too! Almost. Like I'm a fucking idiot. That or those arranging things have zero fucking creativity. Like the Sheriff, who had actually been partly behind the kidnappings of Luiz and Ryan. But what about the first time, with Vermin? He'd really seemed pissed about that. But now? Now it was more like some sort of intense irritation and plans going wrong. But there was no way he could be involved in this fiasco, boo; he was long dead.

Wait...I think he was. Didn't they say his body was burned beyond recognition?

Okay, here comes Mr. Paranoia, knocking on my mental door.

No, calm down, Hunter; he'd have to be dead. They'd have verified his body through DNA or teeth or something.

So...what if it was someone trying to get rid of me? Someone in the Network, and he'd just been part of it? And the only reason I wasn't long dead is because I'd been able to work around the situations. I could see me being underestimated. I was just twenty-six when Vermin's kidnapping happened. Twenty-nine when handling Luiz and Ryan. Old people like to think anyone under the age of thirty is dumb as a brick, so they go with something silly and shallow, like...oh...*first time he got lucky. Second time, we were dumb to use an underage kid and he got paranoid.*

Which brings us to now. *Don't give him a chance to get out of it. Kill the victim in another country and let him hang.*

Motherfucking son-of-a-bitch...that made too much fucking sense to be dismissed as paranoia.

So I was in the middle of a situation that had nine kinds of hell attached to it. How the fuck can I get myself out of this? Because I *was* in a foreign country. With a language I really did not speak. It was only blind luck I'd realized Thiago was sinking. Or that maybe it was just that he was stronger than they'd figured and that had given me time to save him. I don't know.

Hell, I don't even know if he *is* saved. He could still die. That shit can mess with your heart, when given in too high of doses or over too long a time. It's killed a lot of people, and he still might get fucked over by it.

Shit.

And I'd already been thinking I didn't like doing this crap, anymore. But now? Now I was done. Totally done.

I was also positively ready to bring the house down.

Motherfuckers wanna play? I'll show 'em who wrote the fucking rules.

If I ever get out of this cell, alive.

FIVE

What seemed like years later, four guards crashed into the cell, shackled me and dragged me out. I was taken up an elevator to an air conditioned office. It was big, spacious and luxuriously furnished, with not only a massive desk but couches and chairs and plants and tables and everything you could want for comfort. Windows showed it was night, and I got the feeling it was very late...maybe nearly midnight.

Wilson greeted me with manners a-plenty, as did a portly officious man who never introduced himself and was easily twice my age. He was wearing a suit that was way too elegant for him. Next to him was a birdlike woman whose eyes were dark and cruel. Her suit was so sharp, you could cut tomatoes with it...and, again, no introduction.

She was the only one in that room who made me nervous.

Set up next to the desk were three large monitors. One showed a calm, bright, good-looking daddy in casual wear seated in what was probably his massive home's living room; one had Luiz by a window overlooking a modern boulevard of glistening high-rises, just as lovely as ever but now with a light goatee and longer hair; the last had Ryan in one of those living rooms that's so American in style and comfort I got homesick. He didn't seem to have changed a bit.

The moment I walked in, both Luiz and Ryan grinned and said, "That's him!" Luiz's accent was thick but understandable.

The daddy did not move, just asked, "Are you sure of this, Luiz? Ryan?"

"Yes, papa," said Luiz. "I speak with him, much. He is very good with us."

Wow, Luiz had been taking English lessons.

Wilson asked, "Did he not tell you who he was?"

"No," said Ryan. "I asked him and he said he didn't exist. This is my mom..."

A lovely healthy-looking woman snuck into the frame, beaming. "I just wanted to thank you, personally, for protecting my son. We were so frantic and...and..."

She was near tears, so I just said. "Don't worry about it. He's a good kid. Same for you, Luiz."

"My mother, in Orleans, she is...so she not is here, but she tells to me to thanks to you."

"You've been learnin' English."

"Yes, a little. Ryan is help with me."

"I'm glad you two're friends."

Both of them beamed. I didn't dare; in the side of my eye I could see

Carvalho Senior watching me like a cat watches a bird it's about to feast upon.

Then he said, "All right, boys, it is late and we have legal matters to discuss, so I must ask you to excuse us."

"Sim, Papa," said Luiz, then to me added, "A bientôt."

"Yeah," said Ryan. "Later. Thanks, again."

"Yes," said Mrs. Ingersoll. "Many thanks to you."

Their screens went dark.

And the weirdest emotion washed over me. I almost felt like a proud father and without thinking said, "I'm so glad they're doin' all right."

"Why?" cut into me. Carvalho was asking.

I looked at him...and if we had been in the same room, together, I knew without question he'd have cut my throat. That killed my mood and brought forth danger kitty.

"Because it's nice to see a couple of rich kids turn out decent instead of like complete assholes. Got a problem with that?"

"I have many problems with it." His glare did not shift one bit.

"We found the aircraft." Wilson said. "The one used to transport the boys into the US." He opened his folder. "Near a place in Arizona called Kino. Almost totally destroyed. Except for a few items. Like a metallic toilet bowl that had the following words scratched into it. *Ryan Ingersoll* and *Luiz de Carvalho Monteleone.*"

"As well as your fingerprints," said Carvalho. "And now a positive identification."

I glanced at him and the others. All of them had their eyes locked on me, but I knew who was running this and wondered why. From what little I knew about him, Carvalho was not in law enforcement, and this was overstepping the bounds, even by Brazilian standards. I kept my focus on him.

"Why were you on that plane when my son was brought aboard?"

"Where's Mueller in this?" I asked.

"Answer my question."

"No...you answer mine. His grandson was kidnapped, too..."

"That is of no importance."

"It was, to Eddie."

"Who is this Eddie?"

"Oh, cut it out; you know damn well who. Lost a shitload of cash on a really bad movie. Had to get some of it back, ASAP."

Of course, this was bullshit, but one should never let reality interfere with a good counterattack...and that made everyone in the room and on-screen stiffen.

The sharper-than-sharp suit leaned forward to ask, "You suggest Edward Mueller was somehow involved in his nephew's kidnapping?"

I just smiled at her. I'd said enough to get their minds going.

Carvalho all but hissed, "Why would someone like you be involved with Edward Mueller?"

"I'm not. I owned a specialty courier service and went to Venezuela to collect a package, because I'm fluent in Spanish. Your son's kidnappers put their own pilots in my chartered jet and forced me to bring him and Ryan back into the US to be held till the ransom was paid. That gave me no choice but to go along with it, since both of the boys were now aboard. However, I have contacts throughout South America. Well, the Spanish-speaking parts. The moment I knew who the boys were, I contacted my contacts and we...oh, we changed the direction things were goin'. The boys' safety was my first priority...that, and I didn't want my contacts to get involved, so I dropped 'em to a safe place and vanished."

"You expect us to believe that?" Carvalho growled.

Sharp suit added in, "But his story does match what the boys have told us."

Wilson leaned closer to me. "How does this new kidnapping work into the scheme?"

"It wasn't a kidnapping," I snapped. "It was an attempted murder. For revenge. High profile. Grab me when I can't prove anything, then take a well-known person and have him die while with me. I'm not quiet about bein' gay. Throw in it was a plan to rape him that went horribly wrong? Paint all fags with the molester brush? You can connect the dots."

"This is nonsense!" Carvalho sneered.

"Ask Eddie," I said. "He's not above gettin' even, since I messed up a really nice deal he had goin' in Phoenix. C'mon, haven't you wondered why I dropped the boys at that particular buildin'?"

One of the screens flared on and a brutal man with a strong resemblance to Edward Mueller, only in his seventies, appeared, and if I'd thought the Sheriff was a junkyard dog, this bastard was the whole damn pack.

"What the fuck kind of game're you playin', you little shit!? Tryin' to drag my son into this?!"

I grinned. "Hello, Mr. Mueller. Good to see you. I've long been a fan, and so glad to finally meet. You're one of my idols, so much so, I've even invested in Mueller Industries." I turned to Carvalho. "I put money into *Investimentos Cuidadosos,* too."

Carvalho sighed. "Yes, Cazador," he whispered.

"The one and only. I liked how your son handled himself, and I figured it ran in the family, so..."

Wilson glanced between us, confused. "Are the three of you in business, together?"

"Impossible!" Mueller snarled. "I don't know this fuck."

I looked straight at him and said, "Two four...four nine three...eight nine nine point six eight."

"Bunch of goddamn numbers. Don't mean shit."

But Carvalho was silent. Obviously, he practiced due diligence, because he knew what I was saying.

A moment later, a sheet of white paper appeared before Mueller...and he went just as white.

"The value of my investment," I sighed. "Granted, it's only five percent of the projects' total worth, but it'd be a shame if I had to let an automatic sell order I have go through instead of postpone it. Like I've been doin' for the last three years. Might kill the project."

"Explain to me," said Carvalho, "why you involved yourself in our company then kidnapped two young relatives of mine."

I was so exasperated, I snapped, "I didn't kidnap any..." Then it hit me. "Wait...*two* young relatives?"

"Thiago Belo is my nephew, by my sister."

Oh, shit...now I knew without question, I *was* the target, and Thiago had been grabbed to deliberately link me back to the initial kidnapping, making it seem like I was responsible for that one, too. Kill not only him but any good-will Carvalho might have had for me. Eddie was out for revenge over me screwing up the earlier kidnapping.

Oh, shit...he'd have killed Thiago to get back at me? A guy who was completely innocent? That motherfucking son-of-a-bitch...

Again, I'm not a brilliant guy; I'm just properly paranoid. I think of the first thing I'd do in order to crush someone and project that onto them. I'd say it's saved me more than once. I didn't need to know the details, yet; the outline of probability was enough, and no way in hell was I going to let them know what I thought it was about. Fact is, I still had no honest idea of what the full goddamned story was. So I merely asked, "How is Thiago doing?"

I kept my voice calm and even, and my outward emotions were under control, but Carvalho was too sharp not to notice the slight change in my manner...and better grammar. He was already scrolling through his mental list of contacts, wondering who might have helped in the targeting me and, by extension, him. He almost let a smile come to his lips as he said, "He is healing. He is strong."

"But I don't get it," snapped Mueller. "How the hell'd you get mixed up in this kidnappin' after being part of the one against me?"

I looked at Wilson and the suits. They were being far too silent and calm for my liking, which could mean they were on Carvalho's side...probably were, since Mueller had injected himself into this mess. That's when I decided to stop playing poker and go for Russian Roulette.

"Eddie," I said.

Mueller went white hot. "I fuckin' told you not to — "

"He and I go way back," I snapped. "You want to know how I knew to drop Luiz and your grandson off where I did? I knew it was owned by your company. I've been to that building before. Spent a looooooooong weekend in the penthouse. I was nineteen."

"What the fuck're you talkin' about?"

"It was all handled through a certain Sheriff, who loved doin' favors for your son. Granted, I didn't see Eddie, himself; I was blindfolded. But I sure felt him. Every inch of him. For a full weekend. Which the Sheriff knew about. Which got him killed."

If you're gonna pull a good lie, gotta sprinkle in some truth.

Now Wilson's eyes were locked on me. The suits were focused on each other. Carvalho was saying nothing, but I noticed his phone was by his hand and his fingers were not still. Well...I'd pulled the trigger three times and no bullets in the brain, yet.

"Who's this man who was killed?" Wilson asked.

I told him all about the Sheriff's *accident*, leaving out Hernandez and the pastel Coordinator. Instead, I made up a lovely story about the two pilots helping me get the boys away from the kidnappers, *probably at the cost of their own lives*, finally suggesting, "I think the Sheriff losin' the boys was sufficient to get him and his helpers all done in, as a safety measure."

"This is slander," Mueller growled, his face gone from red to white and his voice barely even. "This is libel!"

I smiled at him. "Sue me. Discovery'll be a bitch."

"You can back this up with proof?" Wilson asked.

I sighed. "Well, I don't know all the ins and outs of what does and doesn't constitute evidence, but I do have enough information stashed away, nice and safe, to at least initiate a very big investigation. I mean, we're talkin' about the murder of a Sheriff. In Arizona. Law enforcement don't like that shit, and it don't matter how dirty he was; you don't go killin' cops. It's just not nice."

That's when Wilson stood up and said, "Senhor Carvalho, Senhor Mueller, may I ask that we terminate this meeting? I have many things which must be considered, now."

Carvalho glanced up from his phone and gave his blessing with a wave of his hand. "Thank you for allowing me to be part of this conference, Senhor Caramiz. Mr. Hunter, I wish to join my son and the grandson of my business partner in thanking you. I am certain my nephew will also appreciate what you have done for him. Until we meet, again. Good day."

And he was gone.

Mueller's screen just went to black. I would not want to be his son, at that moment. Because the truth is, he wasn't the only one trying to fuck me over, and I was going to find some way of getting to the bottom of it.

And then I'd make goddamned sure hell would come calling.

HUNTER

BOOK FOUR
"...He's all yours...for pay"

ONE

It finally became clear that every time I got hit with a near-catastrophic kidnapping, be it Vermin or Luiz and Ryan or Thiago, it was when I was doing well in my career. When I felt I was proving myself as a key member of the Network. It was almost like someone was trying to undermine me. But I decided to consider another possibility.

What if each one was really a test to see how I'd handle the situation?

I gained support in this supposition by how the sharp suit, who asked me to call her Senhorita Julião even though she was well over fifty, took over my case and got Wilson to let me go, all without giving any true sort of explanation. The way she put it was, *I'd also been kidnapped, yet I'd still managed to talk the men into releasing Thiago and myself so they wouldn't have to deal with a famous young man dying from an overdose, thanks to their actions*. Her smooth words were all in Portuguese but nicely translated for me by her assistant. That, plus the fact that the Brazilian media was in love with me because I actually had saved Thiago's life...well, that sealed the deal.

No need to mention I gave him the shot that almost killed him.

The story Wilson handed the media was ludicrously basic. Unknown criminals had kidnapped me and Thiago to hold for ransom and drugged us both, but they had given Thiago too much. When I came to I realized this and convinced them to let us go, using the pilot's command of English to negotiate. The plane had been stolen and was located in Porto Seguro, in a small private air field, out of fuel. Two witnesses said it had glided in, silent as death, and three men had jumped out, stolen a car and driven south. The police were now *searching for that vehicle*.

Yeah, real hard, I'm sure.

On a side note, there was a report of three men gunning down a criminal boss, just a couple hours later in one of Rio's favelas. He was known only as Vinicius, and his killers made their escape...in what was thought to be a stolen vehicle. Since it was in Portuguese, I had to use my Spanish to approximate what it said...but if it was Rey, William and Jonas, first off, they made damn good time to do the murder, and second...those aren't their real names, just to let everybody know.

Third, I'll bet the drive down to Rio was lovely.

When the reporters asked to talk with me, Wilson told them I was very shaken by the events and had already returned to the States, but I was *willing to do anything needed to assist in the arrest of these criminals*. And the little shit just had to add, *"He also feels somewhat responsible for what happened, since it was his journey here that caused young Mr. Belo to let down his guard enough to be taken. But neither Thiago nor his uncle, Mr. Carvalho, hold this against him."* Connecting this to the Carvalho family was enough to distract them, since a couple recalled Luiz's kidnapping and all but decided the two were connected. I quickly became last minute's news.

Senhorita Julião was *kind enough* to translate it all for me, as we watched the live broadcast. We both knew what Wilson was really saying. *I know you had something to do with this, but if you stay away we'll let it go. Unless Mr. Carvalho says otherwise. Then? I will tear you a new one.*

I deliberately huffed and growled in mock insult, which I don't think fooled her for one second. In fact, I'd almost swear her suit got even sharper as she calmly watched me act.

They had my passport records so I hadn't even tried to lie about when or how I'd arrived, what hotel I'd stayed at or whom I'd met with, but they said nothing about the length of my stay or how none of my luggage could be found, or even that I'd bought a one-way ticket. Instead, they simply had Senhorita Julião escort me to the main airport to make certain I left.

Whereupon I was taken to a private terminal, where a supremely cushy little jet was waiting to fly me away.

Okay...that gave me pause. I'd rather have flown commercial because I halfway suspected this had not been arranged by either Wilson or Carvalho. I hoped my vague threats of information ready to be released and potential investment chaos would be sufficient to protect me...at least till I had a chance to figure out what was what.

The moment I was on the jet, ground attendants slapped the door closed. It actually bumped me in the ass. Then a very soothing voice locked it, behind me, murmuring, "Please be seated and buckle in," with a gentle accent.

I smiled at him and nodded...

And froze.

It was Tony.

A bit bigger, much more buff and the personification of golden masculine beauty, with a nice layer of scruff around his chin. I actually licked my lips, felling disgusting and dirty, next to him. His dark elegant eyes locked onto mine, hate shining from them and daring me not to do what he said.

I turned to take a seat...and froze, again.

One of the neatly-overstuffed leather-bound seats held the pastel Coordinator, looking over his shoulder at me.

Okay...so we were not headed for Miami.

By this point, we were already halfway to the head of the runway, so I sat facing the Coordinator. Tony took a seat across the aisle from us, his eyes never leaving me.

Oh well, I've been looked at, before. I just widened my smile.

In moments we'd lifted into the sky and were on our way.

Not one word was spoken by any of us as Tony set up a table between the Coordinator and myself and served a plate of fruit and cheese with glasses of champagne. I made no secret of inspecting him. Appreciating how he had filled in so nicely. Good arms had become strong and lovely. A trim, well-formed body had taken on lines that promised perfection under his just-tight-enough shirt and tie. His hips fit belt-less trousers just right, showing off an ass that I'd already thought was elegant. And his thighs added to the sleek profile of his body. I almost caressed him to see if he was real.

Once done, he sat where I could see him, in a forward seat, casting me another glance of pure hate, then he crossed his ankles so his rich full crotch was brutally evident. From that point, he paid me no further attention; just read a book of Lorca's poems, in Spanish.

I wondered if I should tell him I studied those in school, when dad was stationed at Morón Air Force Base. Could that be a way into his pants, again? I mean, if he wasn't still pissed off at me for kidnapping him, raping him and selling him into slavery.

All water under the bridge, right?

The Coordinator's whiny voice brought me back to earth.

"The cheese is Spanish, too," he said with more than the hint of a sneer. Little fuck was letting me know he knew my background...and my interest in Tony. "We have Arzúa-Ulloa, Manchego curado, and Mahón curado." Jesus, Christ, did he mangle those words in his piss-poor approximation of the language. "The grapes are from Chile."

Pronounced, *chilly*? Oh, for God's sake, how hard is it to say Chill-EH?

"This is true champagne,' he continued, "vintage 1947. And the crackers are from Pittsburgh. Please indulge to your heart's content."

I shrugged and did so, not sure why I needed to be told any of that crap. I hadn't cared what cheese or wine was called since we'd lived in Spain; either I liked it or I didn't.

Except it did remind me of my first real crush. When I was twelve. Fernando Airaudo. His father owned the market around the corner from our apartment, in Arahal, and he would tell me all about the cheeses and wines they offered. He was tall with creamy golden skin, thick black lashes around deep brown eyes, body by Adonis, and always wore a light dress shirt, tight faded jeans and boots, showing off his magnificent form in ways that should have been illegal. He was at university in Madrid for much of the year, but whenever he came home he helped in the shop, and I made every excuse I could to drop by and speak to him. He was the reason I learned Spanish, so I'd seem cool in his eyes, and he was kind enough to work with me on it.

Help me.

Correct me with the sweetest of smiles.

Nothing ever happened between us. I was just the American chico whose dad preferred beer to his family, though I do think he knew what I was all about. He either wasn't interested or didn't let it bother him. Either way, it didn't matter. I had no idea what was going on inside of me, at the time; I just knew I'd have done anything he asked me to...even if I didn't know how.

He's also the reason I'm so focused on circumcised dicks. I happened to catch him taking a piss behind the market, one day, without him noticing. He had one that was long and fat with a helmet head that only added to its clean lovely outline. Of course, I now know he'd just pulled back his foreskin to pee, but at the time it looked like he didn't have one, just like me, and that picture of him was seared into my mind as the ideal.

Silly, I know, and hardly an absolute requirement in a man, for me, but still...every guy I'd been with had to measure up to him, in the back of my mind. Few had. Vermin was close, and I halfway think Luiz would have if I'd done my testing with him. Tony's dick had been right, except for the foreskin, but back then he hadn't had the same beauty of body.

Not like he had now.

I kept casting glances at him as I nibbled. Oh, but he had built himself up nicely. No more boyishness, just the vision of a man. His face was even better-looking with a few more years of experience in it. He kept sitting there for me to gaze upon, lazing like a lovely tomcat pretending not to care but begging to be petted. Damn, I got myself worked up into a nice horny state and came so close to going to talk with him about that book. See if I could feel up a few more parts of his body.

"He's yours, if you want him," said the Coordinator.

I did...and granted, I was being obvious about it. But I also noticed the slight tightening of Tony's mouth when the bastard said that. It bothered me, and for the first time in my life I replied, "Only if he agrees."

"Don't you want him as yours?"

"Yes," I snapped, "but only if he agrees."

"I'm sorry to hear that."

"Are you?"

"It strongly suggests you're still too middle-class to join with us."

Okay...nice cannonball into murky business waters. "Is that what this is all about?"

"You handle yourself well. You've had more luck than you should, but half of that is due to you not losing your head in the middle of a situation. We thought you'd be a fine addition to our crew, as a Coordinator."

I chuckled. "Glorified logistics manager. Cut above just handling the phones. I'm worth more than that."

"Arrogance is unbecoming."

"Truth is not arrogance."

"A humble man would see there are other rungs in the ladder, once this is done."

"An honest man looks at the offer and sees how it takes him out of the fun. I mean, it does, don't it?"

"Are you asking if I sampled the wares, as you have?"

"Tested."

He smiled. "It's not permitted from this point."

"Then why would I want that?"

"Well, you are allowed to keep one, per cycle. One that's been used, of course." He cast a slight glance back at Tony.

Son-of-a-bitch, was this whiny-assed little motherfucker telling me he got to make use of a guy as lovely as him? I cannot believe how angry that made me.

"That's not enough," I snapped.

"Greed is also unbecoming."

"You don't know what my counter-offer is."

"You want to own the store."

I snorted half a laugh. "I already do. Partly."

Now he chuckled. "Through Cazador? Do you honestly think you're in the correct league to consider doing a full buyout?"

I leaned back and focused on the Coordinator. "Y'know, I never would have expected you people to have such a limited view of others. It's rather disappointing."

"It's based in reality and experience."

I chuckled. I had a feeling he was digging at me to see what he could find out, and I didn't want to play that game, not till I knew the rules...if there were any.

After a moment's silence, he continued, "I do find it interesting that you haven't asked where we're going."

"It's not the States."

"Are you so certain?"

Um, yes, I was, because if we'd been headed for the US we'd be over land, and we were out over water. But I just smiled.

He eyed me. "You think you're smart. Tough. Protected. *Your* view of the world is what's limited."

I chuckled. "Tony, come here."

He took in a deep breath, looked at me, placed a marker in his book and rose to come over, looking even more like a cat stretching and rising to figure out where it next wanted to take a nice long lovely nap. He stood beside us and I wrapped a hand around his leg. Felt the strength of it. Let my thumb nudge the base of his balls. Felt him grow tense. He was wearing briefs, just as I liked. I dug my fingers into his thigh. He didn't flinch, not one bit.

"Reveal yourself," I said, looking straight into his eyes.

The Coordinator watched me, tight and unsure. I guess I wasn't going by his playbook.

Tony took in a deep breath and unbuttoned his trousers. He pulled down the zipper and opened them to show he wore plain white CKs, and they were fucking gorgeous on him, especially as contrasted against his golden skin. He lowered the front of them to show his pubes and then his dick, in stages...and then the head, and I blinked.

"You had a foreskin," I said.

He nodded. "It was removed after I was...after I was taken away from you and your...your *helper*."

I cast a confused glance at the Coordinator. "But he fit the requirements; it wasn't evident when he was erect."

The man shrugged.

I caressed the length of Tony's penis. He let me. I tickled my fingers through his pubes, causing him to start growing. Suddenly, I was back in Arahal, watching Fernando finish peeing. Then shaking his dick. Then tucking back into his briefs. And I was feeling this odd sense of...I hate to put it this way, but of reverence. As if I was witnessing the beginning of my love for men's genitals. Having it reborn. Which was stupid. That had started with Fernando. After watching him, that time, I'd had the hardest erection ever and had to slip into a dark shadow to get relief before going near him so I wouldn't say or done something to embarrass myself. Something that might have turned him away from me.

If he'd stopped wanting to be around me, anymore, I'd have died. I damn near did collapse into depression when dad was transferred back to the States. I'd wept when I said goodbye to him, and he'd just patted my shoulder, smiling...and that's when I'd started hating my father; he took me away from Fernando. And now I was feeling the exact same thing.

Shit.

My heart hesitated and its beat increased. Something about this was wrong. Brutally wrong. Doing this to Tony was a...it was a desecration. I could barely breathe. I had to slip him back into his briefs and pull up the zipper and button his trousers to keep from losing myself in a weird form of lightheadedness. I didn't care what the pastel motherfucker thought of my actions. All that mattered was he not get to see any more of my Tony.

Mine.

Except...

"Do you want to come with me?" I asked, looking up at him, just managing to keep my voice even and calm.

He did not look at me as he said, "If you want me to."

"I want to know if you want to."

"I have no choice in this." He still would not look at me.

I released him. Let my fingers touch his hand. "I'm givin' you a choice. One night with me. Then you may stay or return to your wife."

He still did not look at me. In fact, he closed his eyes and his hand trembled as he said, "I will go with you."

I kept my eyes on him but could sense the Coordinator was growing irritated.

"Good," I said. *"You may return to Lorca. We can talk about him, later; he's a fine poet."*

He didn't hesitate, just sat back in his seat and opened the book, but his whole demeanor had changed, just a little. He was a bit more alert. Less tight. And vaguely confused.

Perfect.

I turned back to the Coordinator. He was not confused.

"You cannot set him free. It's against — "

"We're still in negotiations," I said, smiling.

"There are certain rules and requirements for — "

"I will not have an errand boy tell me what I can and cannot do with my own property, unless it's specified in the contract. Which has not yet been put forward, let alone signed."

My English is always more precise when I'm dealing with an asshole.

I finally saw some real emotion behind the bastard's eyes, and it was not joy. His voice dropped the whine to become sharp and cold as he spat, "You have no authority to set conditions."

"Don't be silly," I sighed. "I'm Cazador. Your accountants have only scratched the surface of what I have and don't have. What I can and cannot do. Who I am and am not. I advise against making any threats until you've contacted the Network."

"A puppy thinks itself a wolf!"

"Snap. Snarl. Growl. Grr. Ask!"

"The Network has nothing to do with someone of your low stature, nor anything to fear."

"Don't be so sure."

"We already know."

"Anyone who feels the need to make that claim, doesn't."

"We have more resources than you can even imagine."

"You keep minimizing my intellectual ability. Why?"

"As I said, you've proven lucky, but luck does not last forever."

"You also said I think on my feet."

"When you have options. I see nothing available for you to use against me or us, right now, so..."

"Oooohh...so maybe you should ask your *bo-ossss*." I sing-songed it.

"I am the one making the decisions, here, and..."

"What the fuck? Just ask her."

He hesitated, barely. "Why *her*?"

I only smiled...because in truth, it'd just sounded good.

That's when his earbud blinked, startling him. He tapped it and said, "Sorry, but this is not the time..."

Then his face went white.

"Are you sure?"

He huffed and made himself pull out his cell phone and put it on facetime. He pointed it at me.

The screen showed a desk before a window overlooking one of the most beautiful gardens ever developed, and seated at it was a thin shadow of a person who could be male or female or someone in-between, since light from the window was blaring them into near darkness. But I didn't need to see their face; the voice could be either male or female, but it was also wary and irritated, just as I wanted.

"What about Cazador?" they asked. No accent whatsoever.

"You know what it means?" I shot back.

"It's Spanish for tracker."

"I prefer *Hunter*."

They did not budge. "Let's have it."

"*¿Comprendes Español?*"

I got nothing in response.

"I am Cazador."

"That has already been established." Still nothing.

"Silent partner with *Investimentos Cuidadosos.*"

"Silent, no longer."

"They're not the only ones I've partnered with."

"We know."

"Do you?"

"There are five others in your portfolio. Mueller is the only one even remotely connected to the Network."

"I think arranging for kidnapping the son and nephew of another company associated with Mueller would be a *very close* connection. Especially since you tried to kill said nephew."

"That is nonsense."

"And slanderous," said the Coordinator, "and impossible to prove."

"Okay, okay, okay, okay," I said, with deep sigh. "Let's get off that nonsense. Try doubling the number of my partners, to the tune of six-hundred-fifty-million, verifiable reserves."

As I said, I wasn't quite to my main goal, yet, but on my way.

They stiffened and snapped, "Make this call private."

The Coordinator jolted and said, "But I..."

"Make this call private!" And the voice was adamant.

The Coordinator handed me the earbuds and took the phone off speaker. I slipped them into my ears...and not happily, considering they'd been in his, but one does what one must.

While arranging myself, I noticed Tony's eyes on me, wary. I winked at him. He quickly looked away.

Of course, the Coordinator noticed, but that was what I wanted. Tony was mine, now, and he had no say in what I did with him. So deal with it.

The person on the phone yanked me back to them. "How did you build that sort of investment? You're merely a supplier, not involved in the end market. Your best year brought you a mere three-point-three million."

"Investments. Not on the scale of Warren Buffet but I did pretty good in the market run-up under Obama and even DJT. Cashed some out before the downturn and have the rest in other venues, including yours."

"We are not publicly held..."

"Not this particular aspect of your organization." That made them sit back. "But there are other branches which claim to be more...oh, let's just say, legitimate and *vaguely affiliated,* and are publicly traded on Euronext. Under *Importations et commerce du Pieuvre.* I hope I said that right. Anyway, I'm also proxy for a number of investors in other companies and work a couple of hedge funds. Keeps me out of trouble in-between jobs. But that's where the big numbers come from — paper profits. Oh, and I have a standing sell order for certain ones that I have to cancel, at the end of each week. Otherwise two-hundred-million of your group's stock gets dumped on the market with rumors that it's junk. I'll lose probably ten percent in value. You could lose as much as fifty."

"You're talking about minimal monetary amounts in an organization worth hundreds of billions and..."

"It's not the money; it's the message. Doesn't take much to spark auto-sales. Once those get going, try and stop 'em. Only way that happens is shutting down all trading. Other groups won't like that."

They lifted their phone and the light almost illuminated their face. All I could see was a wrinkled neck and sharp chin before it was put away and their focus was shifted back to me, but this time it was a bit less certain. Obviously, my claims had just been verified by their people.

"What do you want?"

I'd intended to say, *Partnership*, but for some reason went with, "Freedom," whispered from me. "I don't want to be part of the process, anymore; I just want to be a client."

That took everyone by surprise, even Tony.

"But we require a ten million dollar bond to be in place, for new clients, and restrict their access..."

"No restrictions. And I'll set up the bond."

"Surely you're not arranging for this in Miami?"

"God, no. I'll let you know where after a good night's sleep."

"We have a minimum purchase of two cycles per twelve months, at a base of one-point-five million."

And that's when Greedy Guts came stupidly roaring up. "Aw, man," I snapped, "you motherfuckers were rippin' me off, left and right. I take all the risk and you reap all the reward? How fuckin' typical."

"You were well-paid."

"Like hell! One-point-five as a base?! I wasn't even making three percent on three-quarters of the guys I brought you! A fuckin' agent in Hollywood gets ten for talkin' on a phone!"

"You agreed to the rate," snapped the Coordinator. "And beginning with this one," he nodded back at Tony, "you were paid a great deal more."

"You didn't get one-five for him. No fuckin' way. He was lovely even before he buffed up, and customizing him by cuttin' off his foreskin? With him a virgin? That means he was brought in for a specific client. High-end even to your high-end. If you got less than six million, per cycle, I'll lose all respect for your business acumen."

"You have no idea of his worth and..."

"STOP IT!" Tony bolted to his feet, nearly in hysterics. "I'm not a fuckin' dog! You can't talk about me like I'm a fuckin' dog!"

Then he screamed and grabbed his head and dropped to his knees, in pain.

I bolted to my feet but the Coordinator stopped me.

"Tony," he said, "take your medicine."

He stayed on the floor, groaning, and it was all I could do to keep from kneeling beside him and taking him in my arms and holding him and soothing him as best I could.

"Tony, your medicine," whispered from the bastard.

Still grunting in pain, he forced himself to his feet. Used the armrest to help himself up.

I could barely keep my voice level as I asked, "What've you done to him?"

"It's just an implant. You'll be given the code."

An implant. Told to me in the calmest, coldest voice I'd ever heard, as if he was talking about an extension to a computer or an option on a car. Fury exploded within me, but I didn't dare do anything until Tony was all right, again.

Oh, Jesus, God, how I hated seeing him like that. Hurt and broken, almost cowering. He was too beautiful to be treated this way. It wasn't right and I finally lost all control and glared at the Coordinator to growl, "You motherfucking son-of-a-bitch, how dare you mess with my property?"

"He's not yours, yet."

"By oral agreement! So I will decide what happens with him. Override your command, right now!"

The Coordinator just smiled at me, now very much amused.

"Tony, don't do it," I said.

He sent me a pitiful look, still gasping, and pulled a bottle from a small satchel.

I bolted over and grabbed the bottle from him and slung it down the aisle. Pills flew everywhere.

He cried out in absolute horror. "No! They help me! Make me okay! Stop the pain! Make it all...all okay!"

I took him in my arms. "I'll make it okay."

"No...no...you don't know what they did to me. Everything they did to me. You don't understand....you can't...they take the pain away and...and..." And he started moaning...no, keening as he held his head.

Oh, my God, the pain I felt at hearing him. Seeing him. The full-scale destruction within me. It tore through my whole body. Shredded me in ways I have never felt, before.

Never.

I had no idea it was possible to fall into a well of sorrow so deep...so never-ending...

Jesus, Hunter, you dumb father-fucking son-of-a-bitch, you have totally fucked up.

I drew him close to me. Held him. Caressed the back of his neck. Felt the implant's nub at the base of his skull.

Felt ill from knowing I had helped put it there.

I guided him down to the seat then found a pill lodged in the corner of the cushion and gave it to him, with some water. He swallowed it, almost greedy and shaking. I stayed by him till he grew calm. Put his book in his hands and he held it tight...but just looked out the window.

No tears in his eyes.

All but cowering like a dog that's been abused.

I returned to my seat, unable to process the boiling emotions inside me. Hate. Anger. Shame. Pain. Sorrow. All of them new and frightening and making me ice cold from self-loathing. I made myself finish the last of the champagne in my glass, just to give me something to focus on besides the chaos within, then looked the Coordinator dead in the eyes and said, "If you ever mess with anything of mine, again, I will rip your fuckin' heart out...if you have one."

"You growl at me like a dog over a bone. Pathetic."

I held the fluted champagne glass tight and snapped the bowl off the stem and pointed the now sharp edge at his throat. "Don't think I won't do it."

It didn't seem to faze him. "All of this emotion over a pretty boy you chose to give to us, for money."

Aimed straight for my heart...only a memory flashed through me — Vermin and his vanishing act prior to this motherfucker's last request. Me thinking Vermin was out to replace me...

Holy fucking shit.

"I didn't choose him," I said. "You did."

He almost chuckled. "I suppose it was I who kidnapped and molested him."

"You were workin' with Vermin. I knew somethin' was wrong, but I was too unsure about you and too close to him to see you were doin' this, together. What'd he do? Scout most of 'em out? Maybe even set it up with 'em? *Be around this area about this time for a game we want to play, and we'll pay you.* Did they have any idea what they were gettin' into?"

"Don't be ridiculous," the Coordinator said. "Did we arrange with Tony for him to be taken from his own home in the middle of the night? The logistics, alone, are impossible."

He could say whatever he wanted, but I could see it, now. Vermin *had* been working with the bastard. My bet was, he'd chosen Tony and they'd come up with Joey Stefano to use as the sample because of their basic resemblance. And the others? I'd found it odd we were able to track down so many guys over the space of twelve days to fit the same description...but my eyes were on the money it was bringing in. Now I also remembered, it had always been going to spaces Vermin suggested.

Taking guys Vermin saw first.

But then Vermin began slipping into instability. Grew untrustworthy. Left a trail of assaulted men behind him, all slathered with his DNA, since I'd consistently used a condom. The cops were narrowing their search to him, so they'd silently shifted back to me. Seen me as better for business. Greedy. Predictable. Malleable. All but told me to get rid of him. And like a stupid fucking dog trained to obey, I'd sent him to hell in order to protect the Network.

I looked out the window at the dark water, far below, punctuated by moments of cloud cover. A wave of weariness swept over me. Deep and harsh. I wanted nothing but sleep, night now.

Sleep? How could I want to sleep? Not now...not...unless...

Shit...the last of the champagne...probably drugged.

"Where we goin'?" I asked, fighting to keep focus.

"I thought you didn't care," said the person on the phone.

I'd forgotten about them. "Fuck off," I said, then I ended the call, yanked out the ear buds and looked at the Coordinator. "Where we goin'?"

More emotion, this time almost pleased. "Lisbon."

"And then?"

He was pure evil, now. All masks were down. "Bucharest. Then Moscow."

I sighed. "I'm on the menu."

"We don't believe your claim about having safety measures in place to protect yourself. We've scoured our system and our stock listings, in Paris, and found nothing to suggest it's anything more than a bluff. We've also searched your condominium and computer. Nothing to find."

"What day is it?"

"We should arrive tomorrow, about 7pm, their time."

"What day is it, now?"

"Thursday."

Thursday? I was caught up with the Brazilian cops for two fucking days? No wonder I'd lost track of time.

"How far behind them is Paris? Hour? Two Hours?"

"Are you still trying to bluff? The game is over."

I was hard to formulate the words. "Just answer me. Shit."

"Two hours."

I nodded. "What's gonna happen with Tony?"

"The order is for you both." His voice sounded hollow. Thousands of miles away.

"Good," I whispered. "You ain't worthy of him."

"You're taking this rather calmly."

"We're in a jet...twenty thousand feet...over middle...of the ocean. What'm I supposed to do, jump? Naw, let's see what happens in Moscow." I looked at the grapes. Had a couple more, anything to keep moving. Asked, "Do I at least get to know why you're doin' it? Thought I was...doin' a good job."

"You brought in a fine selection," he said. "Unlike others, none had to be refused, up front. But then you began increasing your rate. When it reached a certain point, it was untenable."

"*You* increased it, in LA."

"As incentive, to keep pleasing a certain clientele. But you pushed for more, so we decided to work in a new supplier. Unfortunately, you know too much about the business and were being too secretive in so many way, so you couldn't just be sidelined. Only you kept avoiding our traps."

"Traps? The kidnappings. Was Vermin's one of 'em?"

"Vermin?"

"Verminsky. Guy I let take the rap...in Manhattan Beach."

"That was too clumsy for us, but did give us the idea."

"Suuuuurrrre," I murmured. I had more grapes. The simple act of maneuvering out the seeds before eating them helped me keep focus. "You got control here, bitch. Why can't I know...real fuckin' story, already?"

He eyed me then let a smile cross his face, and that spooked me more than anything ever had.

"All right," he said. "Yes, we had him taken, and you were supposed to be caught bringing him back across the border. But you didn't fall for it and overwhelmed the Mayor with your new plan. That's why he directed you to some local boys, thinking you'd never get away with transporting them. He overestimated your ability to think on the fly. And your contacts. When you turned those boys over to the Sheriff and kept Verminsky, we had to do a great deal of work to silence what happened."

"Kill 'em?"

"Are you out of your mind? The Mayor is Emilio's father-in-law; that's why he was helping him. Reuben's parents are well-to-do. We worked it out so they remained silent, then used your playbook and drugged three others so they'd think everything that happened to them was a nightmare. We did keep one, to cover our costs."

I nodded, to keep from crashing into sleep. "Theo."

"A nice Muslim boy. Disdained by many in the town. His parents sold their pharmacy to the Mayor and left, thinking he'd been killed. He's been a good investment."

"The other guys...I brought...from Mexico...do them like Tony?"

"All of our merchandise is chipped..."

"Not what I mean." I was close to losing the battle of the sleep waves.

"Oh, circumcise them? One or two, by special request. And you're correct, Tony was a special order, and did bring in a great deal more than one-point-five million. In fact, he was kept four cycles by the initial client."

"What's this...cycles thing?"

"Ah, right, you don't know the full business plan. Each young man is first *conditioned*, then the client is given control of him for ninety days, at the end of which time he is returned and put into our catalogue. Theo has just been kept for five cycles, at five-point-five per. He's still rather popular, but he's reaching the end of his usefulness. However, there have been indications his current client will keep him. You never know. If they're willing to pay the premium, then we are open to agreement. Tony's have balked at the cost, so far. Had you become a client, we'd have provided you with the full costing schedule."

"And they go willingly?"

"As I said, they are conditioned beforehand. The chip provides a very strong incentive."

"Any kill themselves?"

"That's not allowed."

I finally gave in and yawned. "Am I gettin' chipped?"

"No. You are to be brought untouched, for immediate use. They like the idea of you being unwilling."

"Well, it's been a rough day, and I'm tired, so I'll take a nap."

"Be my guest."

I yawned, again, and noticed Tony was lying very still, asleep, his book about to fall from his hands. Looking like an angel.

An angel destroyed by little-ol'-devil me.

A final wave of sleepiness washed over me. I sighed, leaned my seat back, made certain my belt was well-secured and relaxed. Nothing I could do about it, now.

"Good night...then...motherfucker..." I managed to murmur before I slipped away.

Guest we'd see what happens when I wake.

TWO

The plane was on the ground, when I came to, and my hands and feet had been shackled. I yawned a groan as I said, "Guys, c'mon, I need to pee and my mouth's a swamp. I wanna brush my teeth."

The Coordinator came up, not smiling. Which made me glad.

"The Paris stock exchange has been closed for an hour," he said. "So far, nothing's happened."

I chuckled. "Oopsie. Guess you called my bluff. I'm hungry. Where's the grub?"

"You'll be fed, shortly."

I super-pouted as I said, "But I'm hungry noooooowwww."

He nodded and a sack was whipped over my head.

"Oh, for Christ's sake," I snapped, "what the fuck am I gonna do? Run away? Call a cop? I don't even know where the fuck we are, so unless it's Spain or England, I don't even speak the lingo. Shit. This is stupid and amateurish."

But the bastards left it on as they lifted me up and carried me out the door. I was then hefted into the back of what I think was a minivan and laid on a mattress...sort of like what I'd done with my guys coming up from Mexico, so many times. I felt someone beside me and asked, "Tony?"

"Yeah."

Shit. *"Listen,"* I said in Spanish, *"follow my lead and I will try to get us out of this. I will protect you."*

"It doesn't work," he said in a voice that was flat and uncaring. *"Nothing works. I even tried to kill myself and they stopped that, too."*

"But...but why would you want to do that?"

"What a stupid question."

Yeah, I guess it was.

"If I get us out of this, will you come with me?"

"Do I have a choice?"

"You will."

"I will believe you when it happens."

"Fair enough."

"If either of you says one more word in Spanish, I will hurt Tony." Said in the Coordinator's voice.

"Yeah," I snarled, "you're just bitch enough to do that."

"I would rather not. I very much enjoyed having him as my companion, the last three months. He is a lovely young man. But I will not hesitate. That's the bottom line."

"Errand boy speak; Hunter takes note."

"Be as insolent as you wish. It matters not, to me."

I both heard and felt the door close and two pats on the wall, then the van zipped off...and a siren sounded. From the uneven whine, it reminded me of ambulances I'd heard in some movies based in Europe.

Wow, they'd called out the high-priced crowd.

We rambled through some massive city, with cars and trucks honking and people yelling in a language that made no sense. I'd like to believe it was Moscow, but I couldn't make out any of the words I heard, and I didn't trust that motherfucker as far as I could spit.

When I'd transported my cargo, I'd made certain they were unconscious to what was happening. That was mainly to keep them from causing any noise issues, but mixed in was the idea that it was a bit easier on them, emotionally. Less time to be scared.

Now I understood what bullshit that was. Truth is, I'd used their sudden fear upon waking as a sort of aphrodisiac, to help prove to them they no longer had control over themselves. Their fates were in my hands, and while they probably had a good idea they were going to be used, sexually, they had to be wondering if they were also going to be killed. Like Tony probably had. When the muscle queens had carted him off, he'd been awake. He'd known what he was being taken for. Same for that black kid. What was his name? Jerome, that's it. And the others in LA.

And that cut into me. Because now that I was the prey instead of the hunter, I knew what they'd gone through, and I couldn't be so damn flippant about it.

Shit.

Finally, the siren stopped and we turned and went down a ramp. Curled around and down at least two more levels...and finally squealed to a halt. The doors opened, someone grabbed my feet, and I got pulled out to be slung over somebody's shoulders and carried off, fireman style.

"Y'know, I hope it's more than Micky D's when you feed me," I yelled. "I'm ready for a ten-course meal!"

In response, I got a harsh slap on the ass.

And fingers that dug into my crack just a little more than necessary...and stayed there.

I made myself laugh and say, "Careful, big boy, I'm about ready to take a dump, so you might get your fingers dirty."

The hand moved away.

So...the motherfucker knew English.

I was carried into what seemed like a hallway, according to the sudden change in echoes, and maneuvered into a room then dumped on a narrow couch. Off came the sack.

And it was Bear who'd carried me, looking a bit less beefy than before and with a Mohawk and a tattoo cuff of flames on his right arm. He wore a loose fleece outfit, like he was at the gym, and had a light beard on his pleasant chin.

"Dude, we meet, again," I said. "Where's Pavel?"

As if in answer, Pavel walked in with Tony, shackled and hooded, like I was. He was dressed the same as Bear and looked just as hot as ever, touches of white nearly blending into his hair to give him a real *Daddy* aura. He saw me and snarled, "Shit, I tell you that one was mine."

Bear shrugged and exited.

Pavel sat Tony on the couch and removed the sack. He barely even blinked at the sudden onslaught of light.

"Bathroom," said Pavel, pointing to an opening in the wall, in fake hotel clerk fashion. "Clothes." He pointed to a plain shopping bag with handles, by that opening.

I looked around the rest of the room. It was painted a dark blank gray and had a small dressing table and mirror attached to the wall by the door, nothing else. The bathroom opening showed it was fully-appointed, with a walk-in shower.

"Not exactly the Hilton, is it?" I sighed.

Then Bear entered holding foil-wrapped plates of what must have been the most wonderfully aromatic food ever put on the face of the earth.

"Dinner," Pavel added, needlessly. "We are back in two hours. Make ready."

Then he tossed a key on the bed, between us, and he and Bear left. I heard the door not only lock but the sound of a bar scrape across it. Guess they wanted us to stay here.

"Jesus," I growled, "just like a Hollywood movie."

I took the key and managed to unlock the shackles on Tony's wrists. He rubbed them, unlocked his leg restraints and stood up, to stretch, saying, "Here we go, again." Then he unlocked mine.

"Your second time in the room?" I asked.

He shrugged. "This or one like it."

"Were you kept unconscious the whole way, then, too?"

"What do you care?" He nodded to the bathroom. "You or me, first?"

"Aren't you hungry?"

"I need to pee."

"Have at it." I bolted for the nearest plate and unfolded the foil to find an amazing beef goulash on a bed of scalloped potatoes seated in a large paper bowl...and no utensils to eat with. Fingers only. With it was a paper cup of sparkling water.

Okay, knowing where my fingers have been and not having washed them since the dawn of time, I hesitated in digging in. The last thing I wanted was an issue with my internal organs. But I needed something in my belly, now, now, now, so I used the foil to scoop some up and licked it off. It helped, a little.

Tony was pissing away, so I looked through the opening at the sink, saw a small dispenser of soap.

"You mind if I wash my hands?" He nodded to the sink so I slipped in and scrubbed my fingers like crazy.

"It's hand to mouth," I said. "No utensils."

He just nodded.

I looked at the back of his head. You couldn't see the chip thanks to his hair being so black and thick. But I knew it was there. That I'd put it there.

And I think for the first time I noticed how elegant a man's skull and neck can be.

To my shock, it hurt me.

I actually stopped washing and let the water rinse the soap away as I kept gazing upon him...and for some reason, two words I had never spoken before welled up, deep inside me, and I had to whisper, "I'm sorry."

"Are you?" No commitment in his voice.

"Did you hear any of what we talked about on the plane? Before we were drugged?"

He finished peeing and tucked away before looking at me. His voice took on a derisive sneer. "Yes, you were *tricked* into kidnapping me. How sad for you."

"I...uh, yeah, that's what it looks like."

"May I wash my hands, now, sir?"

I realized I still had my hands under the running water. I stepped aside and grabbed a couple of paper towels to dry them. I also needed to pee, but hunger took preference so I stormed back to the bowls and began chowing down. It tasted as good as it smelled.

After stuffing a fourth bite into my mouth, I said, "Tony, there has to be a reason you were selected. My partner scoped you out, several times. What did you do, before all this?"

"Does it matter?"

"Please, I'm tryin' to understand..."

"Why?" he sneered as he dried his hands. "Oh, you want to become my friend. We talk and find common ground? I tell you about my first experience being raped, and then I like you and you like me and all becomes good, again? So sweet and pure."

Now there was hate in his voice. He came over to the dressing table.

"I don't know why you chose me. I only know what happened. How you...how you kidnapped me and groped me and pinched me and forced me to do things I'd never done, before. The fear I was going to be tortured to death. To be killed with a man inside me. That's all I know. *Sir*."

Tortured to death. As he's being raped. Shit.

"I...I've never hurt anyone like that."

"Of course not. Why would I even think it?"

He unwrapped the other bowl to reveal the same meal. He grabbed a piece of the meat and set a slice of potato on it.

"Please," I said, "just tell me what you did before you were taken."

He was about to bite into it but stopped and looked at it, almost in awe. His voice was soft and soul-destroying. "Listen to how you say this. So general and bland. *Before I was taken.* Not that *you* took me. Not that *you* kidnapped me and are the reason I am here. No..."

Then he put the whole thing in his mouth.

"Tony, I'm tryin' to figure a way out of this, and if I know why you were chosen...why we were asked to take you..."

He glared at me and bit into another piece of meat. He wasn't giving me an inch, and it's because I was being a wuss about the whole situation and the lead-up to it.

So fine. Pull your big-boy pants on, Hunter.

I made myself ask, "Why I was given a requisition for you."

That made him frown. "Requisition?"

"Yes. An order. Like in a diner or online shoppin'. I was told to bring in a guy who looks a certain way, and you fit the bill. And it sounds like you were not only chosen; you were the reason for that specific description."

"So I *am* nothing but a dog to you."

"Well, we did, effectively, crop your ears, so..." I tried to make it a joke. Big mistake.

He looked at me in absolute horror, muttering, *"Jesus Christ, Almighty, what kind of devil are you?"* In Spanish.

"If you want to speak to me in this language," I quickly said, *"that is fine. I am fluent. In fact, it may be a good idea. If we are in Russia, there will be few who know it, and we can talk more freely."*

He looked away and absently helped himself to another bite of the goulash before finally murmuring, *"I drove for movies."*

"Drove for movies?"

"Yes. People. Things. Whatever was needed. My driver's license was good for livery. Trucks if not too big."

"And...and on movies you would drive actors?"

He nodded. *"And crew. And equipment. Documents. Food."*

And he took another bite of the goulash.

I dug in on my own bowl, thinking. Wondering.

"Well-known actors?" I asked.

"Sometimes."

Oh, no, no, no. It couldn't be...

"The man who took you the first time..."

He glared at me. *"Are you not man enough to use the right words for this?"*

Shit, I'm trying to help you, dammit, and yes...I'm the reason you're in this and I understand you're pissed off about it, but c'mon, cut me some slack, here.

I took another bite of the goulash and potato and said, *"The man who raped you the first time..."*

"You and your friend raped me, the first time."

"We only sucked you off," I snapped.

"You are of the devil," he murmured, his voice thick with loathing.

"I am referring to the man who took you in the ass, idiot!"

His hand shook as he put some potato in his mouth and whispered, *"Men."*

That jolted me. Killed my irritation. *"More than one?"*

"That is what the word means. Two of them. The first time I had

ever...ever been used like that." He didn't move for at least a minute, and I didn't dare say a word. *"I...I had already been trained to let them have me. To fight back, but not too much...just enough to make them happy. I did well. So well."* It took him another long moment to continue. Watching him struggle with the memories tore me to shreds. *"They kept me for nearly a year. Fucked me every weekend, many times. Together. Always together."*

"Did you...did you recognize either of them?"

He shook his head. *"I wore a mask. A blindfold, every time. I never saw their faces. Never saw any part of them. Only felt them. Felt their hands. Their dicks. The rest of the time I was kept in some ranch house in the middle of the desert. Middle of nothing. I already had this..."* He motioned vaguely to the chip in his head. *"And I had been...healed..."* He motioned to his groin. *"I could wander the grounds within an acceptable area. But I could find no way out. No Wi-Fi or phone. I had only computer games. A hundred channels of cable. A library with thousands of books, many of them in Spanish. A big pool. All very luxurious...but a prison."*

"Completely alone? All the time?"

"No. There were two people in knitted masks..."

"Balaclavas?"

He looked at me, confused. *"Is that the ski mask, with holes for the eyes and mouth?"*

I nodded.

"Yes, like that. There were always two of them. They would feed me any meal I wanted. Give me any drink that was not alcohol. Clean my clothes. See that I bathed and dressed and exercised. But no other form of human contact with anyone. Except when my owners came to rape me. Put their mouths and hands wherever they wanted.

"It was always the same. Wear this outfit and blindfold. My caretakers would check to make sure it was on correctly. Stand me where I was supposed to be. Then they would leave, and moments later I would be grabbed and bound and...and my clothes torn away and...and I had to let them do what they wanted. If I did not, they...they hurt me."

Again, he motioned to the chip in his head. I felt sympathy pains in my groin.

"When they...when they were finished...the caretakers would help me clean myself. Mend myself, if needed."

"Mend yourself?"

His hands trembled as he processed that memory. *"Sometimes I would be chained. Strung up. Clips used. Electricity. Whipped and made bloody. Not too much of that. They also had to stay within boundaries, it seems. I heard one was angry about them. He enjoyed causing me pain. After those times, I would be given something to sleep. And when I woke, the torn clothes would be gone...and healing begun...and I knew the next weekend would not be so bad."*

"Did they say anything else, as they were abusing you?"

He glared at me. *"They said many things. I will not repeat them."*

"Anything like, 'You're done'?"

He hesitated. *"No. I do not remember anything like that. That phrase...that is an actor. Movie star."*

I nodded.

"I drove him, on my first movie," Tony said. *"I picked him up from his home, every day for a month."*

Uh, what the fuck?! *"Which movie?"*

"World's End."

Ouch, that was his monster flop. Six years ago? Seven?

"He never said anything to me," Tony continued. *"Just would get in the car...him and his assistant, some older woman...and they would talk or he would use his phone the whole time. Every time."* He half-chuckled. *"I was surprised at how old he is."*

"How old were you, then?"

"Twenty-one. I was afraid to say anything to him."

"He never came on to you?"

He looked at me, almost laughing. *"He has had two wives and some daughters. Why would he want to be with me? With any man?"*

I finished the last of my meal as I said, *"I cannot tell you how many men have wives and children and still like fucking men."*

He looked at me for a moment. *"Did you take them like you did me?"*

"No, not usually."

"But...but you have done this to others, who were married."

The sharp coldness of his voice cut into me. I hadn't meant to be that open and honest. But too late, now. I took in a deep breath, looked him in the eye and saw there was no room for spin in this one, so I said, *"Yes. A couple."*

He stepped back from me. *"Jesus Christ, Almighty, you are of the devil."*

"If you want to believe in that shit."

"What other way is there to look at it?!" he all but cried. *"To kidnap a man from his family!? To hand him over to others to be abused in this way!? That is evil!"*

"What do you think slavery was?" I snapped. *"A picnic?"*

He backed over to a corner of the room, unwilling to look at me. He was almost keening, again.

I couldn't believe how hurt I was by...well, to be honest, by having hurt him, even more. It damn near tore me up. For the first time in my life, I was truly ashamed of myself. Ashamed of what I'd done to him, and I wanted to hide.

And rip him to shreds for doing that to me.

"Tony..." I started to say, but he put his hands to his ears. He was close to weeping. My irritation exploded and I growled, "Answer me one more question!"

He refused to lower his hands.

"Tony, listen to me!"

He hesitated then began to shake and slowly, slowly his hands drifted down to his sides.

"*Think,*" I said, in Spanish. "*Are you certain the actor said nothing to you, at all?*"

He took in a deep breath and finally said, "*Nothing, after the first day. Just hello and thanks.*"

"*What did he say the first day?*"

"*Nothing. Only asked where I was from.*"

I nodded. "*Columbia. Probably thought you were escaping the cartels and...*"

He looked at me, confused. "*I am from Argentina.*"

I blinked. "*Not Columbia?*"

"*No. Why would you think that? Can you not tell from my Spanish?*"

"*I...I speak Castilian and it is good anywhere, really.*"

He snorted in derision.

I accepted it and continued with, "*So you're from Argentina.*"

He nodded. "*My family has a ranch, in the Pampa. Close to Santa Rosa. Cattle and sheep. My father brought us to Los Angeles to handle business for my grandfather. We lived there many years, before grandfather died. Then he returned and I stayed.*"

What the actual fuck?

"*You have a green card?*"

"*No, I am an American citizen since I became eighteen. Papá wanted me to return with him, said the country was going crazy, but I liked it there. I wanted to work in movies.*" He turned to the corner. Lay his head into it. "*I was stupid. I could now be riding horses instead of...instead of...of...I should have listened to him. I should have listened to my Papá.*"

He fought back into control. Finally, slowly, he turned and wandered back to his meal.

Watching him go through it shredded me. Fucking shredded me. It's like he was my child. My soulmate. And he was in pain. Pain I had caused and could do nothing to alleviate. I'd knifed him and thought putting a Band-Aid on the wound was making everything okay, again. But it wasn't. It couldn't. There was no way.

I had no idea what to say. First time in my life, for that. As I've said, I'd never once thought about what it meant to the guys I took to be used...

No, be a man, Hunter. The guys you bought or kidnapped and sold into sexual slavery. A couple of whom you grabbed away from their wives and, maybe, kids. No sugarcoating allowed, anymore. It would be an insult to Tony.

The men I'd bought from Hernandez and the Mayor, those were...well, *supposedly* were nasty pieces of work. Criminals who'd have been shot and buried. Okay, except for the last set, with Vermin. And them...them, now I got the idea they'd been helping set me up, and they'd wound up being released, anyway. All except for Theo. He'd been kept and his parents driven off, for being Muslim.

Shit.

The men killed along with the Sheriff and New Coordinator, that was their own damn fault for intending to kill me. And Pavel and Bear, they'd been helping kidnap a couple of kids, so keeping them alive to get fucked didn't register as a bad thing, either. Especially since I now knew they'd become part of the Network.

I could toss all of them aside...but then I got to the guys in LA. They're the ones who dug into me. Twelve young men...

No.

No...twenty-six, if you go just by the Joey Stefano requisition. Thirty-eight, overall, including the ones we'd provided beforehand.

Fourteen of those were men Vermin and I just grabbed off the street and fucked, since we couldn't fuck the ones we handed over. Hunter! Stop trying to spin this into something nice. They weren't *grabbed*, they were kidnapped and brutalized and fucked and dumped on the side of the road like trash. Maybe terrified they were going to be killed. Like had happened in the 70s and 80s. No matter how I looked at it, those men hadn't been hired or set-up or done anything to deserve what happened to them. They'd just been in the wrong place at the right time for us.

And I'd laid it all off on Vermin.

Suddenly I did feel vile. I did feel evil.

I looked at Tony. He was forcing himself to eat and sip from the sparkling water. Beautiful, yes, but lost and dark and dying inside. No joy in him. He'd even tried to kill himself, once. And I did that to him. No one else. I did that.

Son-of-a-bitch, how I hated myself for it.

I had to get away from him for a moment, so I asked, *"You mind if I have the bathroom, for a little while? I need to take a dump, really bad."*

He shrugged and force-fed himself another bite of his meal.

Goddammit, I wish he'd yell at me or hit me or something to prove he still had life in him. Shit, the little fuck! Tearing into me without doing a goddamned thing and...and...

I bolted into the bathroom and realized the opening had a sliding door in it, so I yanked it closed. And stood there, looking around, now angry at myself for being angry.

I needed to break the self-loathing loop my mind was crashing into, so I looked the room over. A square of cement blocks half taken up by a large walk-in shower stall, to my left. It actually looked clean and comfortable. A metal toilet in front of me, no lid. That wasn't going to be comfortable, but I was at the point I didn't care. To my right, a shelf with an ugly metal sink. Two packets of toothpaste were on it, with teeny-tiny rubbing thing-ys instead of brushes. There were a couple of canisters of soap and shampoo fixed to the wall just below the shower head, but no towels. No facecloths. Nothing I could use as a weapon...well, except for the shackles, and those wouldn't do a damn bit of good in a close-in fight.

Dammit.

I huffed, peeled off my clothes as I ran hot water in the sink then used the pathetic toilet paper to run it over the metal so it wouldn't be too cold. I finally sat down and let myself have what is probably the finest shit ever in my life.

Except I couldn't fucking enjoy it!

Fucking Tony.

I was tearing myself up, inside, hoping I could figure things out before having to face him, again. Give him something to be happy about. To live for. Something.

But why?!

I'd never cared about guys like him, before. Even my fuck-buddies in Miami were there for release, not emotional contact. I'd learned better after Trax fucked me over, in Arizona — do not get involved.

Like I almost did with Vermin. Shit.

Fucking Trax. Christ, how I'd enjoyed being with him. Sucking on his lovely dick. Gulping in his balls like you gulp down oysters. Running my hands over every inch of his tight, perfect body. Exquisite legs. Pierced tits that begged to be bitten. Tracing his tatts with my fingers. Playing with the hair on his chest and abs. Holding his ass as he fucked me. The way he could swallow my cock and balls, all at once, drove me nearly insane, and his hands and lips doing to me what I'd done to him was like heaven. I'd never thought it would end. Till he used me as his get out of jail free card and vanished. I halfway hoped he'd been handed over to the Network and used to death. Just the thought gave my balls a tingle.

Fortunately, things had exploded with Vermin before we got that intense...but it was close.

Tony...he was way prettier than either of them. Fuck, the way he looked in that shirt and those pants, even after hours on a jet and being hauled about like a piece of meat...so fucking perfect. The beauty of his profile. His head. His face. His lips. I wanted to caress him. Feel every part of him. Hold his lovely dick in my hands, again. He'd improved since I had him, five years ago. He really was perfection, now. And I wanted nothing more than to strip him and shove myself into him and make him scream with joy as I fucked him. Like I had with Trax and Vermin, and show him what I could do, all the way...

And fuck him up, even more!

SHIT!

I *was* the devil!

I forced myself to focus on his connection to my fuck-buddy movie star; anything to take my mind off the bubbling sea of lust and self-loathing I was sinking into. Him picking the guy up for that piece of shit movie...it was minimal, but also too close to be a mere coincidence. And he drove the guy around for a month. To and from the set.

So imagine a month of seeing just how lovely Tony was, even then. How could anyone pay more attention to his phone than to the exquisite young man driving the car? Sweet. Innocent. Respectful. Letting you be. No fanboy shit, just doing his job and beautiful in it.

I finally locked down in my head that *World's End* had come out five years ago. August...no, around Labor Day...and we'd kidnapped Tony in October. If I figured it right, that meant the movie was shot a year earlier. Imagine a whole year of thinking about the beautiful boy behind the wheel. Maybe dreaming about him. Hiring other guys to be him...

Like during trips to Phoenix?

Lots of trips to Phoenix? You and Eddie, working together? Playing together? Using men provided by the Network? I'd had a slight taste of the shock treatment when I'd been used by him; could he have graduated into something stronger?

Maybe the movie flops and he thinks, *I need someone to take my mind off the pain and horror...off my fuck up...so what about that cute little driver on this film? Make things up to me, in a way?* So he puts in the order. And Vermin starts stalking him.

But it was all lining up too damn neatly.

After all, Tony was in a compound in the desert, not the penthouse. Locked away from the world. Surely not the first one there. Probably not the last. Kept until they grew bored with him. Then given back to the Network, like a library book. And checked out, again...and again...

Then offered to me and I blew it. He could've been mine if I hadn't been such a greedy, arrogant asshole.

So how old was he when we took him? He'd have been twenty-two. Meaning now he's twenty-seven. Lovely age. Old enough to know something of the world; young enough to still have hopes and dreams; too young to be feeling so dead.

Too young to be tossed aside.

Too beautiful to have been handled like a piece of meat.

Like a steer sent for slaughter.

SHIT, HUNTER, FOCUS!

I never believed in guilt. Shit happens to everybody, and I'd always figured it's not my fault if it happens to you. So I told myself, I must like Tony because he's pretty and he was the first guy to bring me a decent price. He set me on the road to being that billionaire I always wanted to be. Him and all the ones who followed. It was just luck of the draw that he was taken, that's all. Wrong place, wrong time. Could have been one of a million other guys, as we showed over the next eleven days.

Except Vermin had chosen him.

Known about him.

Lied to me about him, and in a way that made me think less of him.

Let's be honest, Hunter — you weren't above thinking everybody from Columbia was connected to the drug cartels, in some way. That made them worth less on your minimal scale of who is and is not due human consideration. It's stupid and racist, but it also provided some justification to the idea of taking him. Don't criminals deserve anything that happens to them?

But the guys we provided, before and after Tony, in LA. All to certain specifications. Were they criminals? Had they done something to warrant being taken? I had no idea.

Yes, I did. The last guy, Jerome. He was just a kid on the way to class, and I'd had to talk Vermin into going with him. Was that surfer on the beach the guy we were supposed to take and I'd fucked up the deal? Vermin hadn't been happy about that, could that be the reason why?

He had maneuvered me to the others.

Like the guy we took, after Tony. A curly-haired kid coming out of a Starbucks. Loose shirt on a neat body and fine legs in a pair of distressed jeans. Flip-flops on his feet. We'd been searching all over Studio City for the right guy...why there, I don't remember Vermin explaining...when he'd grabbed me and pointed to him.

"He'll work."

"Isn't that more of a swimmer's body? Or basketball? Not Joey."

Vermin had already taken photos of him so showed them to me. "See?" he said. "Looks good..."

"Looks like an actor so might be on the high-profile side."

"So what? Actors come and go." And he'd giggled at his pun.

I'd agreed, without another word. So we'd followed him as he turned down a residential street. Watched him stroll in that specific way actors have. Carefully casual. Jumped him in a shaded area.

He'd certainly felt good, during the struggle. I'd driven as Vermin played with him, in the back of the van. We'd carried him to the loft and shown that, while he didn't have much of an ass, he not only had a nice dick but it could be made hard as a rock and his cum would shoot a foot in the air.

The pastel Coordinator had almost smiled as they took him away.

So we had the new contract in order and my payments had been steady and Vermin was under control. At first. But then it went haywire, and since him, I'd been really careful not to connect too much with anyone. Keep my distance. That had done so well, since then, despite the Luiz/Ryan fiasco. Extremely well. Forty-one contracts for forty-six specific men, all fairly easy hunts. Very ABC.

Guess I'd been lulled into a false sense of security.

Until now...with Tony.

Bam, I almost screamed...and I was back to square one.

So...wipe out all the claims and promises and bullshit in the contracts and contacts and what do you have? What's actually happened, here? What do you *know* happened? Build up a scenario, Hunter.

Okay...first, a closeted movie star bought access to you through a law enforcement officer and fucked you for a full weekend in Phoenix. Second, it was in a business associate's penthouse. Third, he'd revealed who he was, but it was so unintentional, he might not even be aware he'd done it. Fourth, you haven't been in contact with him, since. Not even a hint of concern or interest. So it's not what I'd call a solid foundation to build any sort of conspiracy theory on.

On top of this, you were contracted to find eleven more guys, after Tony, with the same look and characteristics, so they would not have been for Mr. Movie Star. He had what he wanted. That might have been nothing but some accountant seeing the offer for Tony and thinking they could bring in more profit by offering something similar. It may have become an addendum to the order. A nice even twelve, one for every month of the year.

Except...Tony was used in the same way as you, Hunter. That is not minimal. Granted, his rape was by two men, but the same. Blindfold. Dressed. Grabbed and bound and rip-stripped and fucked six ways from Sunday, orally, anally, all over a weekend. With some electro-manipulation thrown in. Also, the actor had liked that I was cut. I could tell from a soft happy growl he gave when he saw my dick. I'd thought it might be because I wasn't exactly tiny, but that could also be the reason for it. So there was another link.

And Tony got customized to fit the client's preferences.

What's more, I seriously doubted Tony and I were the only ones who'd been used like that. Could it be Mr. Movie Star was working with Eddie to erase everyone he'd done this to? Every guy like me and Tony he'd used like this?

Like in some warped Hollywood thriller?

Nothing else even began to make sense.

But why?! Why the fuck would he care, now? He must be closing in on sixty. Isn't that the time to admit to the world you like dick, now that your kids are grown and career path is in the slow lane? Lots of actors were doing it in their thirties, lately, so why wait? Jump on the bandwagon and get praised for being *on-so-fucking-brave* to make such a revelation. Shit.

Still...it wouldn't let go. Those little links were all I had beyond this just being another one of life's shit-shows. And I only knew about the men I'd supplied; not if he'd gotten any from other sources. The other hunter I knew about, who dealt in women — maybe she'd done a few men as a favor or a sideline. Expanded her offerings. Nor did I really know what Eddie liked, other than he'd probably joined in with Mr. Movie Star in raping Tony. Maybe he'd been there and watched me getting fucked. Beating off in a corner or via closed-circuit TV. Been too chicken-shit to jump in till later.

Aw shit, was I just being paranoid? Or am I totally lost in full arrogance-mode, thinking I'd matter to somebody like him? Maybe all I was is another piece of meat. One that's reached its past-due date and had to be cooked or thrown out. Considering the cost of my continued participation, lately, I couldn't say I wouldn't do the same thing to help the bottom line.

But I couldn't let go of the thought. Couldn't let go of the idea this was a deliberate ploy by someone, somewhere aiming to remove a possible problem for some reason in a way that would satisfy all concerned.

After all, it's not paranoia if people really are out to get you.

Is it?

THREE

I finished my business and, despite the pathetic toilet paper, wiped. Then I stepped straight into the shower. I set the water to going, and just as it was getting hot I heard a knock at the door.

"Can you wait to bathe? I have need of the toilet, again."

"Aw, c'mon in. I'm way beyond shy, now."

"But I will need to..."

"I know, I know. I just did, so the seat's still warm. I'll keep my back to you."

I turned, letting the hot water pound on the side of my neck, and heard the door roll open. He said nothing, but I could hear the zipper go and the shuffle as he sat on the toilet. He was done, quickly, and the room must've had some major filtering going on, because I didn't smell a thing. What was especially nice was, when he flushed it didn't make the water change go cold.

I turned back to him. "Feelin' better?"

He was fixing his pants. "Sorry to bother you, sir."

"Join me," I said.

He looked at me, startled. "What?"

"They want us to shower, first, then dress in their new clothes, so come on in. Plenty of room and the water's fine."

He gave me a long look then sighed and unbuttoned his shirt. "I have no choice," he murmured.

I'd rather he have said, *Yes,* but I'll take what I can get.

I watched him remove each article of clothing and found myself barely breathing. His upper body was even lovelier than I'd thought. Well-defined muscles that were smooth without being sharp. Dustings of hair in all the right places. Arms lean and muscular, not overdone. His abs were visible but not looking like skin stretched over rocks...just flowing together, leading you to his groin, whether you intended for your eyes to go there, or not. No tatts. His round brown nips the only part of him not changed, but then...they were perfect from day one.

He dropped his trousers, next, and his hips were in just the right proportion for him. He'd built up his legs enough to add more form to them without bulk or hard lines, and even his calves fit just right. He had a square-cut Speedo tan-line showing creamy skin behind the golden shine of the rest of him. When he removed his briefs to reveal his...his genitals — shit, for some reason I could not refer to them as anything else, on him — I damn near stopped breathing. It was like I'd never seen him, before. Like I'd never touched him, before.

Yeah, let's *Madonna* it, *Like a Virgin.*

Shit, Hunter, maybe your development *is* arrested.

He opened the door and stepped in, and I let him move to under the shower-head. Water coursed over him and through the hair on his head and added to the form of his back as it tenderly trailed down to his rear...again, I could not call it an ass; that was too vulgar. I had to touch him, in some way, so I dolloped soap into my hand and rubbed it down his spine to his cheeks and caressed out to bathe him.

I took more soap and let my hands whisper around to wash under his arms and over his pecs, toying with his nips before drifting down over his abs to fondle his genitals.

He did not move, just let me do it.

"Did any of men who had you do this for you?" I asked.

He nodded. "One. With his wife. He washed my back; she washed my front; then they would have sex with each other, not with me. I was with them for two cycles."

I turned him to face me. Let the spray wash the suds off his back. Lowered myself to run soap over his legs and feet.

"They must've really liked you," I said.

He just shrugged. He was beginning to stiffen. Me? I was as hard as a rock.

Without thinking, I let my lips trail along him, growling, "Didn't they do this? Either one of them?"

"No. Only their hands. I was their foreplay."

"People are stupid."

I gently fondled him. Everything about him so lovely. Perfect size and shape. Water dancing through his pubes in ways so erotic, it had to be illegal. I leaned in and nuzzled them and licked him up one side and along the other and he grew harder and his breath deeper and...

He cried out in pain. Slammed his hands to the back of his head and fell against the wall before dropping to his knees, grunting and moaning.

I bolted to my feet, startled. "What? What?!"

I realized there was minimal steam on the glass, even though the water was hot, so looked at the vent and saw the tiny bulb next to it. A fucking camera, with the steam being sucked out so it wouldn't condense on the lens!

I yelled, "I...I...I won't do it! I won't touch him! I promise! I won't go after him, again!"

He kept kneeling and groaning and rocking from the pain.

I embraced him, saying, "I won't touch him, down there, again! I promise!"

He was still grunting from pain, almost whimpering.

"I swear! I won't. I won't. I won't." I was all but begging.

It seemed like the pain was going away. His whimpers were lessening, so I took him by the arms and guided him to his feet.

My voice was shaking as I said. "Here. Here."

I positioned him under the shower and let it massage the back of his head as I gently massaged the nape of his neck. The water cascaded over us. Mixed with the feel of his hair tickling my fingers. So tender. So kind. So decent and humane. So unlike me. It was exquisite in so many ways other than sensual.

"Better? Better?"

He leaned against me, like a child would a parent, gasping in breaths and letting them out just as sharply.

I began to weep.

"I won't touch you, again," I said, my voice breaking. "I won't let them hurt you, again. I won't. I won't. I'm so sorry, I'm so sorry," over and over and over as he slowly, oh-so-slowly recovered.

It took me longer to regain my composure. Knowing that the tremors in his hands were my fault. Knowing I had done this to him. I hated myself, so much.

The other men I'd taken didn't factor into my emotions, at that moment. All I cared about was Tony's pain. His suffering. He was here, with me, in front of me, and I could not ignore my cruelty. He was right. I'd treated him like a dog. Caught. Bred. Fixed. Sold. Only to be abused by his owners. It sickened me.

Finally, he looked at me, childlike, almost sleepy. I was barely able to focus on his eyes, I was so torn apart by hurt for him. All I could think to gasp was, "Better?"

He nodded and almost smiled. "All of this is new."

"I...I don't understand."

"This. Another man. Used with me. No blindfold. Never done this, before. Do you think...maybe...they will now kill us?"

A dagger of ice tore through me...and it wasn't for myself, it was for him. It was fear they'd do that to him. I'd wondered it, myself, I know, but having him say it...

I could barely say, "I'll be damned if I let that happen."

He chuckled, soft and vague. "You make big statements that mean nothing."

He shifted back and flexed his shoulders and neck then rubbed his eyes and let out a long sigh. "I think I am clean, now." He looked at me and stretched his back. "I am better. Thank you."

He opened the door and left the shower, and I stood there, numb.

Do you think they will now kill us?

Well...Truth whispered, *Yeah, makes sense. No one knows where you are. Hell, you don't even know where you are. How hard would it be?* The rest of me screamed, *No, you were an asset, an important part of the machine, and the investment into both you and Tony was massive and...*

And that bitch, Truth, slapped upside my face, again. We were talking about the sort of people who would wrap a candy bar in a hundred-thousand dollars worth of gold just so they could say they ate it. An item that is tasteless and has zero nutritional value being devoured solely as ludicrous proof they're really fucking rich, and that would make their shit as valuable as they thought they were. So the actual cost of that damned investment, even just in him, had already been made back a dozen times. Now he was close to the breaking point, so why not junk him? After a point, the cost of repairs probably outweighs the benefit.

Like a used car.

Shit...how immoral to even think such a thing...how vile...

*****

Somehow...I don't know how...I managed to remember I still needed to wash myself, so I focused on that. Arms. Chest. Belly. What I could reach of my back. Groin. Ass. Legs. Feet. Face. Hair. Each one chosen in order of need. When I finished, I wiped as much of the water off me as I could and left the bathroom.

Tony was standing by the dressing table, wearing a red and white striped Speedo, square cut to cover his tan-line. He was adjusting his hair with his fingers. My heart leapt at seeing him looking so lovely and normal.

He looked at me and pointed to a couple of vents in a corner by the bathroom door. "Those bring forth warm air to dry you. Not perfect, but works okay."

I went to them and the breeze felt good.

"How's your head?" I asked.

He shrugged an *Okay*.

"Did you have to take some meds?"

"I don't have any."

"Right. I threw 'em away."

He looked at me, sighing. "If they had wanted me to have some, I would."

Shit, no pussy-footing around with this guy.

"What do *you* think's gonna happen?" I asked, more from courtesy than anything.

"I think we are going to play one of their games. That's what these are for." He motioned to the Speedo. "And these."

He tossed the bag at me. It held a pair of CK briefs, distressed jeans, wife-beater, and flip-flop sandals.

I huffed. "Won't I look good in that Speedo?"

"Inside," he sighed.

An H was written on the waistbands of the CKs and jeans, and on the shirt's tag. He pulled the waist of the Speedo over to show an upside down T...and the way his treasure trail whispered up from behind it and over his lower belly made it hard for me to breathe, it was so perfect.

Oh, fuck, what the fuck had I done? I couldn't believe what I'd done. What kind of animal does this sort of shit to other creatures? Other human beings? And how many had I done it to?

Shit, Hunter. Focus! Fucking focus! You'll probably be dead in an hour, so beat yourself up, afterwards.

Okay, okay, okay...then...then games it is.

I pulled the briefs on then the jeans. Perfect fit. Once the shirt was on, I'd have looked at home in Ft. Lauderdale or Palm Springs.

"Have you had to play games?" I asked, in Spanish.

He leaned back against the dresser and looked at me.

"I have already told you," he said.

His eyes were dark and unwilling to be read. The line of his body was worthy of adoration. I could barely stand to look at him and could not imagine any artist refusing to paint or sculpt him, or photographer not to immortalize him. So why in God's name would anyone want to hurt him?

"Every weekend, the first year," he said, in Spanish, *"was a game. Always with a mask so I could not see them. Always with different clothes, each time...clothing I would not wear again. Shorts and polo shirt. Sandals. Jodhpurs and boots. With the shirt, not the jacket. Jeans and tee-shirt. Board shorts. Suits and ties. They would appear in my closet, the masked people would tell me what was to be worn, and when. And so it would be."*

"Is that why you kept working out?" I asked, trying to be jokey. *"Keep them coming back?"*

He rolled his eyes. *"If I do not maintain myself, they will make me."*

I grimaced at how stupid my question was, and motioned to the back of my head, indicating the chip that controlled him.

He nodded. *"Sometimes they even had me exercise immediately before...before...but this...this is my first time in a Speedo."*

"You look good in it."

He all but snarled, *"Is that supposed to please me?"*

I shook my head and slipped on the sandals. Maybe they would stop my foot-in-mouth disease.

"The man who followed them," he continued, *"when my first owners became bored with me...his ranch was in the prairie. I went to sleep in the desert and woke up surrounded by green fields. Not as big but just as nice. With two people to watch over me. His pleasure came from surprising me in bed. Like he had broken in. I would wear sleeping shorts or pants, sometimes a shirt, sometimes not, full pajamas, never nude. With a sleeping mask. He would bind me to the four corners and spend an hour fondling me. Making me service him. Servicing me."* He gave a crooked smirk. *"He thought he was very good at that, but he did not know how to use his teeth. I had to do all I could to ejaculate, because he would not finish it till I had. Then he would lift my ass up, kneel under me and...and let my body make me sink onto him. Enter me, that way. Then he would bounce on the bed until he came. Like an idiot child. He liked to slobber kisses on me as he did this. His breath stank of whiskey and sour beer. I hated every minute of it.*

"But the last few months, with him, he would bring someone else and...and they would play the game, instead. I think it was the same man, every time. Their breath always smelled of cloves. I think the one who owned me watched because still, sometimes, I would catch the scent of foul whiskey. Dead beer." It took him a moment to continue. *"The ones to follow...it was more games. All the same."*

He smirked at me, and if I thought I'd been blaming myself, before, he dug the knife in deep.

"Five years I have been doing this, now. I have been a good return on your investment, no?"

And that twisted it.

I made myself go to the dresser and run my hands through my hair, to give it some semblance of order. He did not move, just let his eyes follow me. I could not look at him.

I finally had enough control to say, *"You really hate me, do you not?"*

"The only reason I have not killed you is because of this thing in my head. If it were not there, you would have died the moment I saw you, again, and I would not have asked forgiveness. But I now know...of all the men you have done this to, I am the first you have had to face. To see what it means. I like that, because I am watching you come to understand that you are not a man; you are a beast. To you the world is the jungle. All of it, the jungle, and you are king of the jackals. Not a pretty sight, is it."

And that eviscerated me.

I looked at myself in the mirror and it was the same ol' Hunter, looking back. I may feel like shit, inside, but it was still my face and my body and my *fuck you* attitude...and I was pissed as hell. *I'm trying to help you, you little shit, and you spit on me? Fuck you, then. Deal with this shit, yourself; see how far you get, you fuck.*

Except then it hit me — Tony wasn't being hateful. Or angry. Or scared. He was just being honest. And goddammit...he was hopeful. He figured he was going to die, tonight, and he was hoping he would. He wanted to. Wanted to go sleep, forever. No more dreams. No more nightmares. Just peace. Solitude. Left alone.

He fucking wanted to die!

And I fucking did that to him.

BAM! That bitch, Truth, wasn't done with me, yet.

If he dies, you will have killed him, Hunter. No one else. Just you.

This latest load of clarity wiped away everything boiling in my brain except a deep, demanding, desperate need to protect him. Nothing else mattered but him.

Nothing.

"I am going to send you home, to your family," I murmured.

"More big promises," he sighed, turning away from me. *"When have you kept one?"*

"I do not make promises. Do you want to go home?"

He took a moment then soft words drifted from him. *"I would like to see my family, again. Yes."*

"And your wife?"

He almost laughed. *"You think she waited for me? Five years and no word?"* He shook his head. *"She is not that kind of woman."*

I remembered her brushing him off, that night, and had to agree. She'd probably divorced him for desertion and married some jackass with a portfolio who was just as *too-busy* as she was for anything but work.

"But your family's ranch. On the Pampa. Ride horses, again."

That almost broke through. I saw a tremor in his face as he whispered, *"How evil are you? Trying to build hope in me, now, at this time?"*

"I am going to send you home!" I snarled. And I fucking meant it.

He glared at me. *"How? HOW!? We do not even know where the fuck we are!"*

Then the bar was removed from the door, making both of us jump. It was time.

Well fuck that shit.

I dove over to the couch and lifted it partway to see the frame was made of metal bars. Welded, of course, so no way to break them off.

Dammit.

But the shackles were lying on the floor, next to the couch. I grabbed a set and looped them around the strongest bar.

"Sit and watch. Say nothing."

He just looked at me, confusion on his face. I bolted up to yank him onto the couch, then snapped the cuffs around his ankles before pulling his hands together and locking them up, as well. Then I broke the key off inside the ankle's lock.

"Say nothing!"

He stared at me, lost and wary and fighting to understand.

Well, I fucking understood. He looked on me as a beast? A jackal? A goddamn fucking jackal?! They're parasites. Sneaks. Hangers-on. They can't hunt for themselves but only steal the food out of other hunters' mouths. Compare me to a parasite? Fuck that shit, bitch; I'll show you otherwise. I've spent the last thirteen years surviving in this goddamn jungle. I'm no fucking jackal. *I'm* the fucking hunter, here! I'm a goddamn fucking lion!

And I was going in for the kill.

FOUR

I stood up just as the door swung open to reveal four men in tight black Spandex shirts and leggings, laced up shoes and balaclavas that had only eye openings. They all looked like a smash-up of Mexican wrestling and a muscle development magazine, they were so pumped up. I think I actually blinked at the sight of them as they stormed in.

"You first, little one," the biggest of them said to Tony in English that could be with a Russian accent.

"Forget it, bitch," I snapped.

That's when he noticed Tony was shackled to the couch. He growled and yanked at the chains as the others backed me into a corner. All he succeeded in doing was making the couch move and cause Tony to cry out in pain.

"Where is key?" number one snarled.

"Check the lock, you fuckin' idiot," I said.

He did and saw it was jammed in. He bolted to his feet, grabbed me and slammed me against a wall.

"What you fucking do?" burst from him, along with the aroma of what must have once been an onion sandwich. Oh, my God...

"You're takin' me, motherfucker." Then I smiled. "By the way, what time is it?"

Furious, he slung me onto the couch. I landed partway across Tony's lap so managed to wink at him as I rose to sit up.

Number one pulled out a phone and spoke into it in what sounded so much like Russian, I was now ninety-nine percent convinced.

Okay, then...if we actually had made it to Moscow, how did the time zones work? Paris is two hours behind, and London's an hour behind Paris...and New York's five hours behind London. But when was Tokyo? Shit. Uh...it's eight hours to New York, total. Was Tokyo another twelve hours? Eleven? Shit, I didn't remember.

I rose to my feet, straightened my clothes and stood at parade rest, just with my hands in the jeans' pockets. Out of the corner of my eye, I noticed two of the boys in black were watching me, and their postures were not defensive in feel. In fact, a glance at their crotches showed they were more like, *I wanna piece of that.*

Cool...I still had the look.

Number one spit and shoved his phone in a pocket.

"You make it worse for him, you know," he sneered. "Now *he* will hear *your* screams, and will wonder what is next."

I chuckled. "You're so cute when you're full of shit."

He snapped at the guards and they grabbed me. I don't know where the hell he was hiding it, in that outfit, but he pulled out a ball-gag and they forced it into my mouth.

I don't remember the exact words I used at the time, but I'm sure it was something along the lines of, "You motherfuckin' cocksuckin' assholes, why the fuck're you doin' this? Now I won't be able to suck your dicks and I know that's what you two-dollar whores like! Assholes."

Something to that effect.

Then they yanked my hands behind me and handcuffed me before hauling me from the room.

I was dragged down a short corridor by the two assholes who had seemed interested, each of them copping not only a feel of my ass and crotch but also pinching my tits, nice and hard. I guess they thought they were terrorizing me, but all it did was get me hard.

We stopped by a door that had Cyrillic lettering on it.

Woo-hoo, that made it a hundred percent. Russia, it is.

Or Belarus...or Ukraine...

Number One slammed a hand around my throat and damn near dented it. "You lucky I not let to hurt you," he growled. "I crush skull with one finger.

In answer, I bopped his nose with the ball-gag.

The door opened and he slung me inside.

And there were Pavel and Bear, again, now dressed in board shorts and athletic tee-shirts, and they had totally pumped themselves up. Pavel's hair was moussed to perfection while Bear had shaved his skull. Both also sported amazingly golden tans. Man, if I hadn't noticed it, before, now I knew — Pavel had trimmed back to being the hottest of hot daddies. And now that I could see Bear, it was obvious he had been slimming down. In fact, he was so toned, I actually looked forward to him manhandling me.

"Hello, boys," I tried to say around the gag, winking. It probably sounded like I was gargling.

Pavel came up to me, smiling. "So you we do first, and then your little friend. Is okay. We are flexible."

He groped me, and not gently, as Bear came up and lightly pinched my nips. I giggled, it felt so nice.

Until somebody grabbed my ass.

There was a third guy in the room.

He nuzzled the crook of my neck and spooned me as he whispered, "Hi-ya, bitch, guess who."

No need. It was fucking Horace. And he was pushing against me with his amazingly hot dick.

Okay...I think I knew this was where it was headed, so I got as queenie as I could and gargled, "Oh, honey, I never forget a dick." Then I laughed and added, "And by the time I'm done with you three, you won't have anything left for anybody else."

Pavel's grip on my crotch intensified as he snarled, "We will see."

I guess I'd actually made sense. Cool.

A buzzer sounded. Pavel grabbed one arm...and damn, that fucker was strong...then Bear grabbed the other, just as harsh, as Horace backed away. They lifted me off the floor and hauled me through a swinging door, in tandem.

After a short corridor, we entered what looked like an MMA arena, just four times the size and dressed in the appearance of an empty beach. Tons of sand covered the floor, brushing up against fake boulders and reeds. Bright lights burned down, as if it was noon. The sound of seagulls and waves washing in was just audible. Plastic palm trees swayed against walls that were ten feet high and painted green. Above them was cyclone fencing, and beyond the wires were the hints of people moving about.

"What the fuck?" I gargled. "We playin' *Weekend at Bernie's Sixty-Nine*?"

They slung me halfway across the sand. I stumbled and fell, then I rolled over to look at them as they approached, growling, veins in their muscles beginning to pop. I finally saw Horace just wore jeans. Good idea, considering his calves were nothing to crow about...not like Bear's or even Pavel's. But from the knees up he was hot shit, and he also had long lovely locks flopping about, kissed by the sun.

Pavel pointed at me. "You break in our house, last time!"

"We teach you lesson," sneered Bear in a heavily accented English.

"A nice long hard one," said Horace. "Maybe you'll live through it."

Were they fucking kidding? We really are putting on a play?!

Shit...a snuff play? Roman Gladiators updated? Instead of spears and swords they'll impale me on their dicks? Not sure whether I liked that idea or didn't. But hey...Horace was right; no way could I fight off three buff boys like this. I was getting it every which way you can.

I scrambled to my feet. Now I had an idea of what they had planned to do to Tony. My beautiful Tony? Oh, no, no, no, motherfuckers, you ain't scaring me; I'm too fucking pissed.

And...to be honest...my dick was also hard as fuck. It'd been a while since I'd played with more than one guy, and that had been me and my Muslim buddy ganging up on the Jewish one and taking him places he'd never been, before. He'd recently hinted at a repeat, so I knew he'd gotten everything he wanted from it.

Wow. So...I figured the best way to handle this was to make it fun! Meaning, play along, Hunter.

"I didn't do anything to you!" I tried to enunciate and make my voice as scared as possible...but I can't act. Didn't matter. It worked for the situation.

"Liar," snarled Pavel. "Check his pocket."

Man, his lines readings weren't bad, but I did remember him being a fairly good actor in his videos.

I seriously doubt anyone could tell what I was saying, but I still cried, "I don't have anything!"

Horace jumped me and used his police training to spin me and put me in a choke hold. Damn, he was strong, but I was still able to kick my feet up and use the downward momentum of them to yank him into a roll. A good wrestler move that startled the shit out of him.

Only it gave Bear a chance to grab me when I rolled up, and before I could maneuver, Pavel had jammed his paws into my back pockets...and torn the jeans open with one vicious yank. Now my ass was revealed, albeit still wrapped in the CKs.

By this point, Horace was back on his feet, pissed off, so he helped Bear twist me around and hold me as Pavel dug into my front pockets, rough and vicious. He tore my jeans there, too, as if they were made of paper. Ripped off a good chunk of them to reveal my left hip, completely.

I was trying to scream, "Is this what you fuckin' want to do? You want to fuckin' fuck me? Fuckin' faggots! I knew you were fuckin' faggots! All of you! Well c'mon! Have at it! I can take you all!" Hardly Shakespeare, I know, and all garbled and growly, not a roar. So much for my big moment.

Dammit.

Then Pavel ripped my shirt in half.

He sighed, "You'll be good," as he mauled my nips. Hard. Making me grunt from pain and pleasure. "Yes, very good."

And he tore the front of the jeans completely open and yanked the shreds down my legs to reveal the CKs...and show I had a raging hardon. Seriously, I was about ready to shoot, just from this little bit of foreplay.

What they'd never figured out about me is, I love being manhandled.

Bear groped me, from behind, pressing his not-so-erect dick against my ass and laughing. "He is ready."

"How we gonna do this?" asked Horace. "Who's first?"

Pavel kept pinching my nips, his eyes locked on mine as he said, "We all are going to fuck him. Maybe once. Maybe twice. What you think, mister? Maybe we keep you for week." He looked at the others. "Keep him? Use him? Fuck him lots and lots?"

"I dunno, guys. I think he likes that shit."

I froze. I knew that voice. That growly little sneer in it.

I managed to get a look past Pavel and see...

Vermin. Unchanged from the last time...except his hair was longer and a goatee framed his mouth. Oh, and his eyes gleamed with hate. But other than that...

He wore a pair of tight cutoffs and a cropped tee-shirt, with deck shoes, and he looked as 1990s slutty as you can imagine.

"I know his type," he said as he approached us. "Cock hungry whore who ain't happy with just one man's dick up their ass. Let's see how happy we can make him." Then he grabbed my balls and squeezed hard enough to make me cry out in pain.

"You are eager," said Pavel.

"Naw," said Vermin. "Boys just wanna have fun."

I didn't like the way he said that, so I made myself gurgle, "Don't get it. Thought you were locked in the loony bin."

He leaned in close, smiling in a way that was anything but

comforting, and whispered in my ear, "Paperwork says I still am. Funny what money can buy."

Horace grabbed my chin and forced me to look at him, saying, "I wanna fuck his mouth, but he's got that thing..."

"We fix that," said Bear. "Friend of mine is dentist. He give me opener. Be very good."

I managed to grunt, "Fuck, Horace, I'd like to suck your dick, again," around the gag. "I did it good, last time."

He smiled and whispered, "I don't trust you. Dunno why."

"He won't bite," said Vermin. "He worships cock."

Then he kissed me, hard. Over the gag. It was weird, but nice because he'd been chewing gum. I hoped others were, too...

Wait...gum? Clove gum? Fucking cloves? Tony mentioned it, when his second owner brought in a surrogate and...oh, fucking shit, had Vermin raped Tony for that guy?

Had Vermin actually got to fuck Tony, like he wanted?

He looked at me, his eyes narrowing, and he seemed to catch the idea I was thinking. He giggled and embraced me, ignoring Horace and Bear, and nibbled on my right ear as he whispered, "You should'a let me take Tony away from 'em. We'd have fucked him and drugged him up and dumped him, an' he'd be better off. We'd be done with him. Now we *are* done with him. But not you, bitch."

Done with him? *Done* with Tony? Oh, why did that sound like they *did* plan to end *him*, tonight, but not me? Like they were gonna keep me? That he was the intended victim of this fucking snuff play and no, no, no, no, no way was that acceptable and I'll fucking kill you before I let that happen and...

BAM! I jolted and kicked at Vermin, completely out of control, and he bounced back, laughing. I howled and fought and nearly freed myself from Horace and Bear.

Pavel slammed me in the stomach before I could formulate a word, knocking the breath out of me, then ran his hands down my belly to my crotch, squeezed my dick and balls enough to make me grunt with pain, then grabbed the jeans and yanked the last of them down to my ankles, where he used strips of them to tie my feet. He massaged up my calves and then my thighs to grope my dick and balls, again, this time more gently...which was a good thing, because I was still hurting...

And goddamn me, I was still raging hard!

"Get dentist tool," said Pavel.

Vermin took Bear's place to let him scurry off. Struggle as I might, I couldn't get the leverage to free myself from them as Pavel wrapped his arms around my legs and nuzzled my crotch.

"We play a game," he said. "We each suck your dick for three minutes while another fucks your mouth. If you cum, the one sucking on you is to fuck you, first, and the one you are sucking is to fuck you, second. And we keep you for another day. If you do not cum...I fuck you, first, then the others, and we start game, again. One man we keep for five days. He was fun."

"Fine with me," said Vermin. "It ain't like he's a virgin."

Bear brought back a dental expander, so Vermin, Pavel and Horace held me in place as he undid the bit-gag and pulled it out and I howled and cried, "If you think I'll put up with this bullshit — "

And the expander was shoved into my mouth, mid-sentence, cutting me off. Bastard cut into my cheek. Shit. Then he cranked it open, even wider.

That was not comfortable.

"This'll hold you till we got somethin' else ready to fill it with," Horace said.

Good thing he'd gagged me. I'd have laughed at how stupid that line was. Surely Vermin hadn't written this shit. What I'd read of his was actually pretty good.

"Me first," Horace continued.

Pavel nodded and grabbed the fly on the CKs and tore them open to let my dick spring out. "I begin here," he said just before he swallowed me almost whole...and holy shit did it feel nice. I remembered thinking his blow jobs looked most excellent in his videos, and by God, they were. Son-of-a-bitch.

FOCUS, HUNTER! GODAMMIT, FOCUS!

Bear and Vermin forced me to my knees, Pavel never missing a beat of suction, then Horace twisted my head around and unbuttoned his fly to release his dick, and it was as hard and lovely as ever when he shoved it into my mouth. I gagged because I had no control over how deep he went, and I wondered if he was going to choke me to death with it.

That would be jumping the gun, if I've figured out this stupid storyline right.

What kept me from losing it was knowing they would do this to Tony if I wasn't able to gain control of the situation. And now that I knew what they would do to him? That Vermin had been given access to Tony, just like he'd wanted? Had finished with him? Was going to hurt him in order to...to what? Hurt me? How could he know what I felt for the guy?

Oh, fuck...that fucking pastel Coordinator...

Oh, shit...and this was how he was getting even with me for betraying him. He was going to kill Tony. As I watched, I bet.

I fought to keep myself under control. Figured the best thing to do was keep them going for as long as I could. Drain them. Tire them out. Little fucks think I got no stamina or can't take it more than they did? Idiots. I'd already had every goddamn one of them and knew how to handle this. I could hold out till dawn, if need be.

But oh, shit, did Pavel know how to do suck dick! I was nothing compared to him. The way he slipped up and down me in near swirling motions, his tongue always caressing, fingers mauling my balls...shit, it was so damned hard to concentrate and I was really upset that I was finally raped by one of my long-term crushes.

God, I wanted him to fuck me first. Really fuck me. None of that silly riding his dick shit. I wanted him to pound me, deep.

I also wished I could have been really sucking on Horace's dick because that's the only way I could control it. I still managed to find a position where I could keep my tongue out of the way and even start to play with him. Stroking his shaft with it as he pushed in and out. Aiming to build him up them stop him. Get him to the edge then let go so he'd lose the momentum. By focusing on that, I kept him from cumming before the three minutes was up.

Nor did I let myself go; I still had *some* control.

Barely.

"He's fuckin' with you, Horace," Vermin said as he and Pavel switched places. "Keep at him."

Then he started in on me, and shit, he was even better than Pavel. He crashed into my concentration with tenderness and insistence and caresses and manipulation and suction that would drain a cow's udder in five second flat and I had to focus on holding back and Horace kept pounding at me and suddenly jolted and grabbed my head and shoved in deep and...

He filled my mouth, shot after shot after shot before he pulled out. I finally understood what they meant by buckets of cum. Shit. As much as I'd like to have swallowed, I had to let it drain from me into the sand so I wouldn't choke on it.

But that killed Vermin's control, for a moment. I felt him stop sucking and start me stroking, hard, as Bear swapped places with Horace and opened his boardies and pulled himself out to work himself into an erection. He wasn't flaccid, but neither was he ready to roar, either. Apparently, he still wasn't as into man on man sex as Horace was.

Good. That could take a nice chunk of time.

While he worked on himself, Vermin fondled me and juggled my balls. Sort of like an intermission. So I took the chance to look around as much as I could.

There wasn't a lot to see, thanks to the blare of the overhead lights...except the upper area was dark enough to show the red tips of cigarettes flaring to light as they were smoked. The scent of a dozen kinds of tobacco drifted past, from harsh to menthol to cigar-like.

Jesus, hadn't these people heard about the dangers of smoking?

Ah, but *we are Russian; we bow to nothing, not even lung cancer.*

Idiots.

FOCUS, HUNTER. Shit...focus! What else can you see?

The lights were harsh, heating the cage and keeping me from being able to make out anything more than the cigarettes...until I noticed a sign in green, in one corner. And above it, almost invisible thanks to the shining lights, were Cyrillic letters — двадцать два: Пятьдесят три — flashing in red.

Then it changed to 22:53.

Oh, shit, was that a clock?

Was that the time?

Bear shoved his dick into my mouth before I could even think. He wasn't completely hard, yet, just nice and full. If circumstances had been different, I'd have loved to make him rock solid. But man, if this was what he was going to fuck me with, he'd better go last so he can get it in...and hopefully, would not be able to get it up, at all.

Win by default, maybe?

Pavel and Horace were behind me, mauling my nips as they kissed my neck, and Vermin got back to working my dick in ways that were so fucking lovely, I didn't want him to stop. The way he'd tickle my balls with his fingers. The way his tongue swirled around my shaft. The way he added a bit more suction to around the head just before he pulled back, then dove in like he was a hungry little puppy. Holy fucking shit. How many years had it been since I last had him? Why had I agreed to dump him like that? I should've asked for him as my pet.

My head was swimming and my eyes burned and I was having a lot of trouble maintaining control, so I decided fuck it. There was no way Bear could fuck me, not with that soft sweet little thing he had in my mouth, and I know how to prolong a good fucking. I finally took a deep breath and let go of my control and let Vermin work me into near madness before I exploded in his mouth.

I actually groaned and growled and damn near let a wolf's cry drift from me, it was so lovely

Vermin stopped sucking and stroked me, hard. Drained me. Licked and kissed me as I shot my wad into the sand. He kept pulling out more and more, just like old times. If I hadn't had Bear's dick in my mouth, I really think I'd have passed out, it was so beautiful.

I realized Bear had withdrawn from me and was working himself, manually. Poor boy, he was still caught in sexual delineations from the last century. I managed to gurgle, "Take these things out and I'll help you."

He just glared at me.

I looked back up and could just make out the message light was now reading двадцать два: Пятьдесят восемь — which changed to 22:58...then 22:59.

Oh, shit, it *is* a clock. And I've got to keep this up for another hour? I dunno how much pleasure I can take. Or give.

Shut the fuck up, you whiny son-of-a-bitch; you're doing it for Tony.

"You get him first." It was Pavel's voice.

I looked around at him to see him smiling at Vermin.

Oh, I got it backwards. Vermin gets dibs on my ass. Good.

"Told you," Vermin said, "I don't want a go, yet. Got a special surprise."

"You?" Pavel asked Horace.

He shook his head, wiping off sweat. "I'll go after you."

Pavel nodded and they threw me over one of the fake boulders, face down. They tore away the strips of jeans and Bear gripped one ankle, Vermin the other, and Horace sat on my shoulders to hold me down, saying, "Not the usual position, is it, bitch?"

I felt Pavel slip between my legs and grope my ass through the

226

remains of the CKs and maul my cheeks and dig his fingers into my crack and then run his dick over it, over and over. Finally, he tore open the back of the briefs to reveal my ass, muttering, "You are pretty. I think we do keep you a week. Do this more times. Have more fun."

He shoved a couple of his fingers between my legs, rough and without grease, saying, "Good, a virgin."

Not in more than half my life, bitch.

Then he used some kind of wet cloth to wipe my ass, as if I was dirty! I'd cleaned and showered, you son-of-a-bitch, and you act like I'm just off the street? What the fuck?

I snapped and snarled like that...until he dug his tongue into my hole. Oh, I nearly cried out for joy. Man, there is NOTHING like a good rimming and he was doing it right. Shit, Pavel, why would you ever quit men to be with women? You are the best of the best of the best and keep it up, keep it up, keep it up, baby, I'm lovin' it...

But after a few moments, he pulled back, maneuvered the head of his dick down and began to push into me with nothing more than that little bit of spit as lube.

Okay...that hurt. A fucking lot. In fact, I howled, which is what I think they really wanted. He pushed in deeper and deeper and I'd never realized a man could feel so much larger than he really was when he was inside of you. I was relaxing as much as I could, but it was like he was going one millimeter at a time so I'd get the full effect. His skin driving past my sphincter and rubbing along my prostate was a combination of torture and heaven...I just couldn't settle on which, yet.

It seemed to take forever, but finally I felt his pubes brush against my ass, and hold there. Then he began rocking in and out and in and out and oh...the feel of him inside me. Rubbing my inner walls. Deep and lewd and wanton. Oh, I loved it. Hated it. Wanted it. Needed it. Would've torn his dick off, if I could.

It took a few minutes, but I got into the rhythm of him and began playing with his dick using the muscles in my ass. I can do that like you'd never believe. Relax as he pushes in, clench as he pulls out. Little bit of twisting and pulling and shifting of my own. I know fucking well how it can feel. I'd learned all about it from Trax and driven Vermin crazy doing it, more than once. Just a matter of keeping focus.

I also knew how to prolong things. Take time with the joy being dispensed. I didn't want Pavel to cum in me too quickly, so I did everything I could to milk his dick just enough so it would add to his pleasure and also would keep him going and going and going like that fucking battery bunny.

I could tell he was loving it. I felt his balls begin to slap against me along with his pubes. Then he'd hesitate before pulling back. He wanted it to last, too.

Fine...work with me, buddy...

Vermin must have caught on to what I was doing, because he grabbed one of my toes and twisted it, shocking me with the sudden plain. I jolted and tried to kick him away, but he had too good of a hold on my leg.

"You're not in control here, fatherfucker," he snarled, just loud enough for me to hear. Then I felt him scratch his nails into my back, cutting me. Drawing blood! Shit, when did he grow claws?

That's when Pavel got needy and started ramming me like a male lion fucks his mate. Push-push-push-harder-harder-harder.

I actually growled.

And got lost in the joy of it.

I know I was supposed to be pretending I hated being raped, but it's hard to do when you're enjoying it so fucking much. All other considerations fall aside, Jesus, the feel of him on me and in me. How he'd reach around and toy with my nips. Resting his body on my back. Rubbing his pecs against me. Rising back up to let his hands caress my back and ass and sides before leaning in to curl his fingers around my throat...and tighten...and play with letting me breathe. It all got me hotter.

I did everything I could to prolong it, half because of Tony and half because I just plain didn't *want* it to stop.

What was even better? I could see Horace was getting nice and full, again, thanks to my face rubbing his dick. I even started working him with my mouth, as best I could.

Poor Bear was missing out, being so damn straight. Idiot.

Then I felt Vermin's hand around my throat, his fingers digging into my skin. I could barely breathe. "You're still havin' too much fun, bitch," he whispered. "We'll see how long it lasts. Night's just gettin' started."

Shit.

Pavel was starting to grunt and gasp and slam into me harder and harder. I finally realized and loosened up...but it was too late. Suddenly he grabbed my shoulders and bit my neck and snarled and jolted up and pulled out of me and fired his load onto my back. I felt most of it slap onto my handcuffed hands and arms as he kept letting out little yelps of pleasure and his balls kept brushing over my cheeks. I remembered those little yelps when he'd cum in one of his videos, and he was giving out lots of them. Going slower...slower...but still grunting for joy. It took him a good two minutes before he could stop and sit back and relax, and I think he leaned against Bear, not Vermin. That's what it felt like.

Horace took Pavel's place and dove into me without a moment's hesitation, plunging deep on the first thrust, making me scream from the shock of it, and he started pumping in as hard as Pavel had, snarling the whole time, "You deserve this, you motherfuckin' bastard, you deserve this!" Over and over and harder and faster, so jerky and hard I could barely feel his balls slapping against me, not giving me the chance to slow him down before he jumped back and I felt his cum splash into my hair.

Goddammit, motherfucker, I'd just washed it!

He howled like a dog at the moon as he kept letting it out. Shit, guess I hadn't drained as much out of him as I'd thought.

Then he stood aside and Bear took his turn. Straddling my ass.

228

Pushing in deep. He didn't feel as big as them but that wasn't his fault. After the fucking Pavel and Horace had given me, a bazooka would have felt tiny. Shit.

He was easier to control. I got him going longer, slower, steadier into me. He tore the rest of the tee-shirt off as he fucked me. His rape was retribution. His pleasure was coming from going in as deep as he could as slow as he could to hurt me. He shredded the last of the briefs. Scratched at my back and sides and ass with his fingernails. Smeared the blood Vermin had drawn. Bit my shoulders as he leaned in to reach around and maul my nips. Shoved my face onto the boulder so I could barely breathe. Circled my neck with his fingers and squeezed. He made me squirm with discomfort as he kept going and going, and I had to remind myself this was a good thing. I needed to keep them busy till midnight.

At the same time, Vermin unzipped his cut-offs to show he was going commando, then shoved his dick in my mouth. The dental spacer was just wide enough for him. He slipped himself over my tongue, slow and easy, murmuring, "Remember this? I thought you loved it. But I was wrong. I'm not gonna cum. I'm savin' it for someone special. I'm...I'm gonna choke him with it, as you watch. Finish him, like he wants. Three times he's tried to kill himself, but we stopped him. Now he gets his wish. All thanks to you."

I fought to have a coherent response, but all that came to mind was...shit, three times, he tried? Three? No wonder he was so lost. No wonder he hated me so much. Vermin was right, I'd done that to him. I hated me, too.

When Bear finally came, his first shot was inside me and I felt it, it was so solid. Then he casually pulled out and aimed the rest onto my ass, shooting once more then dribbling and even smearing it with his dick. Finally, he slapped my cheeks, hard, saying, "Fucking whore."

Vermin pulled out and shoved me off the boulder. I landed on my back, and now I could see the other three were gloriously naked.

And still hard and ready to go, again.

Okay. Cool. I could handle another go-around. I'd do anything to keep them focused on me.

"What you think?" said Bear as he draped an arm over Pavel's shoulders.

"Yeah, keep him and keep fuckin' him," said Horace.

"Sounds great," said Vermin, zipping up his cut-offs as he joined them.

"But take this thing from his mouth," said Pavel. "He like what we did. He love for to suck dick."

Horace crouched to hold my head as Bear yanked the dental spacer out. He didn't need to immobilize me; I was glad to get rid of it. Shit, was my jaw sore. I could barely move it, but made myself do so, over and over, to make sure it hadn't been dislocated.

Horace and Bear rose.

Then Vermin pointed off to one side, saying, "Look over there."

Pavel looked around and said, "I see man in red Speedo. He suns on the beach."

Wait. What? What!? Wait, hold on! You ain't done with me, yet. I tried to speak but all I could do was croak and cough.

"Yeah," said Horace. "Yeah, he looks real pretty. His dick could be sucked by this bitch." He kicked sand at my face.

"You think he is lookout for this man?" asked Bear.

"He ain't doin' anything else," said Vermin, casting glances at me. "Just lyin' there."

"Waits to be plucked," said Pavel, and then the fucker started pissing on me! "Oooh, feel good. I think that man, we bring him over; make our new friend suck him as we fuck him. Make for fun weekend, yes?"

Oh, no...oh, no, no, no. "Don't," I managed to croak.

"Good idea," said Horace. "I love fuckin' straight guys." Then he started pissing on me, too, the bastard.

Goddammit, one thing I have NEVER liked is water sports. NEVER. I managed to spit out, "Motherfuckin' sons-of-bitches."

Bear laughed and joined in the pissing, aiming at my face. "Ah, yes...yes. We dress first? Or just go?"

"It's gettin' late," said Vermin. "Let's just go. We can sneak up on him. Get him 'fore the sun goes down. Use him alllllll night."

"So we go," said Pavel as he finished and shook off.

The other two were also done, so they slapped each other on the back and walked away, leaving me in the sand, dripping with piss. The lights began to come down.

Fury exploded in me. I rolled up to my knees and found myself screaming, "DON'T YOU DO IT! YOU TOUCH HIM, I'LL BRING THIS WHOLE FUCKIN' HOUSE DOWN AROUND YOU! CHECK NEW YORK, IF YOU THINK I CAN'T! CHECK NEW YORK!"

They laughed as they exited, and I heard Horace say, "Thinks he's Samson..."

Oh, fuck, fuck, fuck, fuck, fuck, fuck, I didn't know what to do; I didn't know what to say. It was too soon. The timing was off. I'd fucked up.

Shit, how could I have fucked up, so bad?

I kicked off the torn jeans and forced myself to my feet. There was a hint of light, as if it were a moonless night on the beach, but it was too dark for me to see where the swinging doors were. And it was dead silent; no coughing or breathing from above, so I had nothing to follow. I looked at the clock to see it now said двадцать три: тридцать восемь — then changed to 23:38.

Twenty-two more minutes. Twenty-two fucking more minutes. And no telling how long it would take word to arrive. And Vermin was going to kill Tony! He was going to fucking kill him. I roared with anger and disbelief. I'd failed. I'd fucking failed.

Well the motherfuckers had better fucking kill me, too, but...but Tony would be dead and I couldn't have that.

Couldn't accept it.

I'd make the bastards kill me, instead.

*****

After what seemed like ten years but was only five minutes, according to the clock, the lights went up, a little. Now it was like dusk.

The doors opened and those four little shits dragged Tony in. He had small cuts and scratches around his wrists and ankles; I guess they'd had to cut him free from the shackles. He was still in the red and white Speedo and looked so young and innocent and sweet, and it was tearing into me because I saw fear in his eyes and resignation and he was so fucking beautiful I exploded.

"LEAVE HIM ALONE! YOU DON'T FUCKIN' TOUCH HIM!"

Vermin locked an arm around Tony's neck and sneered at me. "So he is yours. Good to know."

Then he yanked the Speedo's front down to expose Tony's genitals and grabbed them, making Tony grunt and squirm. Held them as a tease to me. "This yours, too? You wanna have it all to yourself, don't ya?"

I roared and bolted up and ran at him. Didn't care that my hands were cuffed behind me; I was going to do damage to that motherfucker.

Horace laughed and tripped me and I crashed into the sand. Then he and Bear yanked me up and held me off my feet as Pavel slapped me. I was fucking naked and I couldn't free my hands and I had no way to put my wrestling to work and that motherfucker was manhandling Tony like he fucking owned him!

MY Tony!

MINE!

Pavel took Tony from Vermin and yanked the Speedo off his rear, saying, "No, this is what you want, I think. Lovely, yes? Smooth. Good shape."

He mauled Tony's cheeks as Vermin helped hold him in place. And Tony barely even squirmed.

I hissed and snarled, "I won't do it! Won't hurt him."

"Sure you will," said Horace, grabbing my dick.

Bear nodded. "Is not hard to make hard."

"Yeah," I growled, "that's why you fucked me with a limp dick! Couldn't get it up."

Bear slapped me. It stung, but helped keep me centered. If these fucking pieces of meat thought I'd go down without a fight, they were going to learn the truth about hunters.

Horace laughed. "Little valium to calm you down. Viagra to make you ready..."

"Maybe Special K to rock your world," Bear said, laughing.

"While we play with pretty boy," Vermin said. "And make you watch as we do all kinds of shit to him."

"I have pills here," said Bear, holding up one of each.

I laughed, harsh and cruel. "You're a fuckin' idiot! You ever try givin' pills to a dog or cat that won't take 'em? Don't work, motherfucker!"

"You do not know tricks I have," Bear smiled, then slapped me, again. He shoved a blue pill in my mouth before I could stop him, and tried to hold my mouth closed, but I managed to shake him off and spit it into the sand.

Dammit.

I was trying to hit his fucking face.

"I think we fuck him as you suck him." Pavel forced Tony around to fondle his genitals some more, caressing them, toying with them.

Vermin mauled Tony's nips, from behind, saying, "Or maybe we'll cut his dick off and fuck him with it." He looked at me and sneered. "You wanna see that?"

Oh, Jesus Christ, I so fucking hated Vermin, at the moment, I'd have ripped *his* beautiful dick off and shoved it up *his* ass.

Pavel grabbed Tony's chin and laughed and forced him into a kiss him and I howled, "I'll kill you, I'LL FUCKIN' KILL YOU!"

"You ain't killin' nobody, bitch," Vermin laughed.

"You better kill me first, you fatherfucker, 'cause if you don't..."

But I was out of words. I was into blind hate. Hell, blind panic, with no idea of what to do or say to stop this coming catastrophe...

And then I heard it.

This weird shuffle in the audience.

It was like someone rushing off. I realized I'd heard it, before, I just hadn't paid attention.

I stopped. Listened.

Someone *was* running.

I looked up.

Two cell phones fired up. The elegant women holding them gasped and hurried from the room. An older man quickly followed.

Oh, shit...was the clock reading the wrong time? I thought digital clocks were locked in on some universal timepiece in some unknown country, somewhere.

There was more shuffling. Then the regular lights came up and I caught a glimpse of maybe a hundred booths in the gallery holding well-dressed people of all races, religions, colors and creeds suddenly looking around, confused. Some hurried from the arena just before a screen encircled the cage to hide them.

Then it hit me...

Daylight fucking savings time!

The US switched over last week, but Europe wasn't doing it till this weekend. My timing was off by an hour! Oh, Hunter, you stupid fuck!

I began to laugh, hysterically.

Bear and Horace looked around, dazed and confused. Pavel still held Tony, just as lost, but I think Vermin caught on. He looked at me in near awe. "Oh, Hunter..."

A moment later, the Coordinator stormed into the arena, wearing an elegant tux, and cried, "What have you done?!"

I glared at him, probably looking as maniacal as the Joker in a Batman movie, and managed to choke out, "Oh...could it be that I wiped out...oh, I dunno...maybe twenty percent of your wealth...and the wealth of anyone even vaguely associated with the Network? Is that what you're askin' 'bout? Hmm?"

He stormed up and slapped me, three times. Drew blood. Nose and mouth. I could feel the warmth of it trail down my face and neck.

"Reverse it," he spit.

"Fuck you."

Oh, there was nothing cold or fey or even pastel about him, now. He was into beast mode. He stepped back and snapped his fingers...and Tony screamed in pain, startling Pavel into letting him drop to his knees, gripping his head. Even Vermin jolted back, in shock.

"Reverse it or he dies."

"You dumb fuck," I snarled. "You just guaranteed another ten percent's gonna vanish. No matter what happens! Now stop hurtin' him or every godDAMN PENNY IS GONE!"

The Coordinator hesitated then flicked his hand and Tony stopped screaming. He gasped in short sharp breaths and rolled into the sand, tiny grunts of pain still whispering from him.

I glared at the cold-blooded bastard and snarled, "I told you never to touch him. I warned you. Now you are gonna take that fuckin' thing out of his head if you want to protect even what little value you currently think you have."

"You're in no position to make demands..."

"You're a fuckin' idiot."

"We can initiate negotiations at a more..."

"Oh, you want to play international commerce, big business boy? Stocks. Bonds. Markets 'round the world. Fine, we can play. But I want to shower first and get dressed. Got plenty of time. Nothin' more's slated to happen with the markets till Monday. In Tokyo. Tony'll be with me, and if you hurt him in any way, form or fashion, it's all over. Every fuckin' penny will vanish. I promise you. Do you fuckin' understand me?"

The son-of-a-bitch just glared at me, tight and ready to rumble, a near smirk on his face. "You're claiming control of trillions in wealth, so there is no way you can — "

So I roared, "DO YOU FUCKING UNDERSTAND ME?!"

He finally hesitated and gave a slight nod, then said, "Uncuff him. Take them back to the room. Will you be ready to begin in an hour?"

"Two hours."

He huffed and stormed off.

Horace unlocked my handcuffs, saying, "What the fuck, Hunter?"

I adjusted my shoulders and rubbed my wrists and took some deep breaths before I said, "You fuckin' crossed me, bitch, and you're pissed 'cause I turned it back on you? What a childish little cunt you are."

He glared at me, but now there was a hint of subservience to it.

I glared at Vermin, snarling, "You really wanted to kill Tony?"

He took in a deep breath then gave a vague shrug.

His little *Whatever* shrug. I actually gasped at seeing it.

Oh, shit...he was fucking with me. The little bitch. And I swallowed it all. Shit, Hunter, you're an idiot.

I almost smiled as I said, "You're a crazy fuck, Vermin, but you're not a murderer. But back then, the way you were goin', you'd have got us both put in jail."

"I was havin' fun!" he snapped back.

"This is a business, dumbass. Fun is secondary!"

"Shit, you're such a tight-ass."

"If you'd played the game my way, you little shit, we could still be in LA. Don't you miss it?"

He grumbled but nodded. "Russia sucks nine months out of the year."

"Only nine?" I asked as I turned to Pavel and Bear. "As for you two, you knew what was happenin' with those two boys, on that plane. I kept you alive, and this is how you repay me? Not very grateful."

"What you mean?" Pavel asked, scowling.

"Oh, cut it out! You're not that fuckin' dumb. There was no way that jet was takin' off, from Kino. You saw that yourself. What'd you think those bastards were gonna do, give you a lift to Tucson? You and Bear are alive 'cause of me, asshole."

Bear growled, "Maybe was not so good to do."

In answer, I pulled him close and kissed him, holding his head to mine, keeping my lips on his...and feeling the chip at the base of his skull.

He finally managed to push me away, spitting, "I am not like you!"

Considering how he'd been, today, I had to admit, "No, I guess you're not."

I also now had to acknowledge my throat was killing me and pain was screaming through my body; I was having a hell of a time keeping it at bay, and was wishing I'd set negotiations time for next week instead of a couple hours. I took in a couple of deep breaths then made myself go to Tony. Slowly guide him to his feet.

"You'll be okay, now," I told him. My voice was starting to croak, again.

He looked around then finally focused on me, confused and more than a little afraid. *"What is happening?"* he asked.

"It is done," I managed to say.

His voice was so softly I could barely hear it. *"What are you?"*

I smiled at him. *"You named me. Devil. Let's go back to the room. I really need a bath, a gallon of water to drink, and I would kill for a dozen Advil."*

He pulled away from me, still shaky and nervous but able to stand upright. He adjusted his Speedo back into place before he said, *"I can walk."* He looked at the four of them then back at me and saw the blood on my face and body. *"They hurt you?"*

I shrugged. *"They think they did."*

"You let them hurt you...for me..."

I nodded and got a bit dizzy, so I smiled and tried to give a shrug...but oh, that hurt.

He glanced down and seemed to finally notice, *"You...you have no clothes..."*

I vaguely shrugged, again. *"I been naked, before. Let's go to our room. Okay?"*

He began backing to the door, his eyes still locked on mine. *"What will you want from me?"*

I paced him, fighting to keep my focus clear. *"I want you to go home. Ride your horses on your family's ranch. Build yourself a life. Be as good of a man as I think you are. I want you to heal and be okay, as okay as you can be, and when that happens, I will be happy. And you will never have to see me, again. I promise you."*

He gave me the slightest of nods as we reached the door. I grew dizzier so he steadied me, saying, *"Come. There is sand on your back. And more blood. I will clean it."*

He took my arm. Let me use him as support. And I went with him.

And for the first time in my life, I honestly felt proud.

FIVE

Oh, the beauty of Tony washing my back. The wonder of it. The tenderness of it. Never had I been so content or felt so easy. He cleaned the cuts to my lips. Stopped my nose from bleeding. Caressed soap all over me with his gentle hands. And I let him. He did not remove his Speedo as he ministered to me. Nor did I ask him to. There was nothing sexual to it. I just...I loved every moment of him touching me. The kindness and caring. I wept, silently, as its elegance enveloped me, letting the shower's spray hide my tears.

I don't think I fooled him into thinking I was as strong and stoic as I pretended, but he said nothing.

Towels appeared and he dried me in the corner where the vents whispered warm air over us. I couldn't help but lay my head in the crook of his neck and breath in the humanity of him, and he let me.

Bottles of sparkling water appeared on the dressing table, and I drank one of them down, in one go. On the couch was a pair of board shorts and a sleeveless tee-shirt. He nodded to them with a smirk, saying, "They claim to have nothing else in your size."

I chuckled. My voice still croaked as I said, "It's just a game. Posturin' and posin' before we really start playin'. It's silly, and the only way it works is if you let it."

He stepped back to look at me. "I don't understand you."

I shrugged and pulled on the board shorts.

"I'm not complicated," I said. "I'm just a greedy little shit, like most people." I was tying the string when I added, "But you're not..."

He leaned against the dresser. "I no longer know what I am."

I didn't know what to say to that, so I slipped into the flip-flops and asked, "Didn't they bring you anything to wear?"

He shook his head.

I growled. "Then you take the shirt."

He sighed. "That will leave you dressed only in those." He motioned to the shorts.

I smiled. "Half the fun of these games is knowin' how to play. I want you next to me durin' this meeting. I don't trust those bastards, not one bit, and I won't have you hurt, again."

A lopsided smile crossed his face. "So I *am* your property."

My property. What joy those two words built in me.

And shame.

I shook my head. "It's necessary, to finish this up. Help me win."

"Can you win?"

"I already have."

He pulled on the shirt and took the towel. "You should drape this around your neck. Otherwise your chest may distract them."

I grinned and started doing half-pushups using the dresser, even though it hurt like shit. "I know."

Moments later, the Coordinator entered without warning.

I rose and snarled, "Where I come from, it's considered polite to knock before entering a room!"

He just looked at me, cold as ice, and said, "We're ready."

"It hasn't been two hours, yet."

"Hasn't it?" He was daring me to make it an issue.

I shook my head and sighed. "Wait outside."

He frowned then made himself exit, leaving the door open.

I went to Tony, took the towel and wrapped it around his waist, saying, in Spanish, *"I do not want you on display."*

"Too much of a distraction?"

"Temptation. People will normally vote for their best interests, but not always. I want no one to get any ideas or get carried away with anything other than what is at hand."

"You lay too much on me."

"Impossible."

The Coordinator led us to an elevator, which took us up at least a dozen floors before opening into a perfectly appointed office that had a wall of windows overlooking that amazingly beautiful garden. Truly magnificent, even in the dark. The meeting was to be held around a long mahogany table at one end of the room. I deliberately took a seat with my back to the windows so I would not lose even the slightest bit of focus.

Five people took seats across from me, all in black with wide-brim hats and veils to keep me from seeing their faces. They looked so much alike, I couldn't tell which was male and which was female. Their chairs were high-backed and black leather, so they seemed to blend in with them, and to their right was the pastel Coordinator. There were no introductions, so I numbered them One through Five, going left to right.

Tony sat to my left, looking at no one, so as I settled in, I croaked, "Dearly belovéd, we are gathered together on this day, in the sight of God and before all others, to figure out what the fuck you think you were doin' to me."

That caused a little bit of a ripple.

"Such language is unnecessary," said the Coordinator.

"Just settin' the parameters, honey," I shot back.

"Then let's begin," said #3, who seemed to be the tallest and thinnest of the group...maybe. "How were you able to arrange sell orders on three-quarters of a trillion dollars of our associates' shares? With no warning to us and at two minutes prior to closing bell in New York?"

"You said it was in Paris," snapped the Coordinator, and I really think I should call him by another name since he was now acting more like a pissed off pit bull on a short leash, ready to go for the throat.

"Oh, did I?" I asked, batting my eyes at him. "Oopsie." Then I turned back to #3 and said, "Y'know, a smart businessman would have figured I was misdirecting, so done a light check of every Stock exchange that was due to close prior to the party startin'." I then stretched and flexed my pecs, giving them all a good long look.

"I should've had you chipped," snarled the Coordinator.

I pointed at him but kept my eyes on #3, saying, "I want him out of here. Business don't continue till he's gone."

The bastard exploded to his feet, ready to tear into me. "You don't tell us what to — "

"Stop!" It came from #5, who was closest to him. That one then seemed to focus on me as they said, "He's an integral part of our Network, so he must remain."

"Even if it's him who gave me access to your data?" I chirped back.

Another ripple of *What The Fuck*.

"You're lying!" he howled.

I looked at him, calm and cool as cucumber dressing, and said, "Of course you didn't *mean* to. You just got sloppy and arrogant, and somewhat condescending, 'cause you figured I'd never understand what I had. That and you were so focused on Vermin, my partner. Granted, he was on your side...and he is real cute. You must've been rather upset when it was decided he should get handed over to the cops instead of me."

No ripples whatsoever. So...the backstabbing *had* been at their behest. Good to know, for sure...and also added to a suspicion growing in the back of my mind that they'd wanted him charged and locked away so they could spring him for their use, here. He'd mentioned his paperwork said he was still in the nuthouse. Wouldn't take a lot of money spread around to get that all handled, nice and neat. So tread carefully, Hunter; they won't play as sweet and kind, with you.

Of course, no way in hell was I going to let them know I'd gotten the information I needed to arrange everything when the Coordinator had changed accounts for transferring funds for the jobs. Fact is, the bank may have done it, automatically, and he might not even have been aware. But by going from forty-thousand per subject to two-hundred-and-fifty, he'd jumped me into a whole new set of requirements for reporting to the IRS. And having just those two account numbers helped me cross-reference my way into the business of lots and lots of companies, groups and organizations associated with those accounts...well, me...with the assistance of that super-hacker I knew. He was able to backtrack where the money had come from and through which banks, then make a little map to connect them all. If it's done electronically, it can be traced, no matter how good your protection.

Of course, there was a lot more to it than that, and I know I hit a few innocent companies who just happened to be in the area, but that's war, baby. In a bombing campaign you can blow up orphanages as well as munitions factories.

I'd used this information to keep track of what various companies and organizations were doing with their cashflow and managed to avoid investing in a couple that were crashing and burning even as they and the business media swore their bottom lines were great and glorious. Some might think that's a form of insider trading and illegal as hell; I just see it as research. But in doing so, my portfolio became solid as a rock, as *Cazador Investments*, and the hedge funds I ran grew big enough to play with the big boys; just not so big they caught the attention of the monsters.

What they *were* big enough to do was set up a panic if they issued a massive stock dump. An order I'd established when the requisition came in for Thiago. As I said at the time, it did not feel right, and by going with my instincts, I probably saved my life, and Tony's.

I'd set it up for a Friday at two minutes prior to closing, so there wouldn't be time for the panic to get really going till Monday opening. Since I wasn't around to stop it, my guess was the Network's associates had lost about three...maybe four-hundred-billion in actual value. Enough to get their attention.

There were a number of ways they could counter it, but they could do nothing till the markets opened. Considering I worked everything out of New York, which didn't open till after Tokyo closed...and had a secondary sell order arranged for Monday that could wipe out just as much value, if not more...that would do irreparable damage to their brand. The only way they could stop me was by letting me go home and leaving me alone.

As for the Network, itself, I'd also arranged to have information about it to be transferred to Interpol, in Lyon. Evidence regarding human trafficking. The only way that could be delayed was by me at my desktop computer in my condo in Miami. I'd also set that up before I flew down to Rio, and unless I cancelled it by Sunday, midnight, it was done.

Meaning we'd have to head out pretty damned soon.

But no need to bring out the big guns, yet. We were just getting started in the negotiation process.

So first things first. Tony. I held up any discussion till they removed the chip in his neck. They had a little operating room set up on one of the lower floors, and within the hour a doctor, nurse, and anesthesiologist were prepped and ready to go.

I made myself watch, just to make sure they didn't pull some shit and have him *react poorly to the anesthetic*.

Son-of-a-bitch, I hurt for him through every minute of it. They said it was just like removing a cyst. Some nice strong Lidocaine, small incision, flick a switch on it, pull the sucker out with tweezers, some suction, couple sutures and a nice tight bandage.

Jesus, God, that fucking thing...it looked like a spider curling its legs around his spine, and even the thought of that having been in him...in Jerome and Theo and even Bear...it made me ill.

I was shocked at how little blood there was. He wasn't completely out of it, but they still had to monitor him so took him to an upstairs room overlooking that magnificent garden to recuperate. The nurse remained with him, overnight, to make sure he still didn't bleed out.

I let her know I would be very, *very* appreciative if he was well cared for. Anything he wanted in food or drink or videos, he could have. And she'd be really glad if she kept him happy and, most especially, alive. I really didn't need to do that; the way she looked at him, I could tell he'd have been a mass-murdering Nazi bastard and she'd have made sure he was tended to in very loving way possible.

I did not blame her.

I didn't see him till late the next afternoon, because as soon as he was settled in, the Network and I got down to serious negotiations and the writing of my new contract.

Line by fucking line.

Thinking they'd wear me down.

Big mistake. I'd had a nice long sleep coming here, so I was alert and ready to rumble, despite the aches and pains of my...oh, let's call it my *sexual liaison*.

I won't bore you with all the legal crap. Suffice to say, I got set up as a client, at a hefty discount, I still had to do the ten-million dollar bond, but soon as that was set, I put in an order for Theo and Jerome. Full ownership, so I could do as I wanted. Delivery to the Las Vegas compound within two weeks.

"I'll decide on the location of my own place by then," I'd said.

"What about Tony?" #2 had asked.

"He's already mine," I shot back.

Committing to three of the boys seemed to settle a lot of nerves. Big investment, there; no way would a good businessman abandon that.

Once the contract was signed, sealed, notarized and copies handed all around, I was done and could go visiting.

I would swear that between midnight Friday and Saturday afternoon Tony had gained an inch in height and this layer of peace and happiness had begun to infiltrate his being. I'd seen nothing like it in him since that first night, in his own bedroom. What brought me joy was how he no longer looked at me with wariness or confusion or disdain or even hate.

No love or acceptance, either...but one can't have it all.

They had given him pants and a shirt to wear, as well as a neat leather jacket for outside and a pair of espadrilles. Those brought the first real smile to his face.

"Alpargatas," he said, pointing to them. "We have a man on the ranch who makes them from old rope. Torn canvas. To just your size. So comfortable...almost as good as boots."

He was on a balcony overlooking the garden, and oh, my God, how I loved the way he looked, standing there. Tall. Trim. Healthy. Not as haunted or wary or resigned, as he had been. I was seated at a table in his room, my arms propped on the back of a chair as I gazed upon him.

"Were you a gaucho?" I asked, joking.

"Oh, I was never so good," he said as he came back in the room. "My family was not there long enough for me to learn much. I know how to ride, yes; I was on a pony before I could walk. And at ten years, I was in a small *carrera de sortija*, put on by my grandfather. Horses like me, because they know I like them. But when I turn eleven, we move to Los Angeles so my father could represent the family with grocers. I would ride whenever we went home, to visit, but you are not meant to ride the horses in California. Only pet them. Still it impressed many girls that I could go to any horse, no matter how ill-tempered, and soon be stroking its nose. Feeding it carrots. Having it nuzzle me."

"So you're a horse-whisperer, huh?"

He wandered back out on the balcony, saying, "There is no such thing. A horse wants only to trust you, and for you to trust it. If you reach that point with one, they will do anything for you. I think that is why women love horses so much. They sense this. Know this. And it's not something they can be sure of, in a man."

His gaze drifted across the garden, looking a thousand miles away. Unreadable. Heartbreaking.

"How's your head?"

He shrugged.

"You up for traveling?"

He shrugged, again.

"We're goin' home, tomorrow mornin'," I said.

He froze. "Home?"

I nodded and spoke to him in Spanish. *"I have to stop in Miami, first, but it is another private jet so we set our own schedule. After that, I am taking you to Santa Rosa."*

He looked at me. *"Taking?"*

"All the way to your family's ranch. I want to make sure you get there okay."

"But how? I have no passport."

"I am having one made up. US. It will get you down there and you can get an Argentine one..."

"I am American..."

Right, I forgot. *"Did you already have an American passport?"*

He nodded. *"When I became a citizen."* He looked back out over the garden. *"Papá brought me down to the ranch, a few times. Tried to get me to stay...but I was foolish..."*

"Then if you want, we can stay in Miami and get you a new one. A rush job. Say you lost yours..."

"No!" The word snapped from him and his voice grew edgy. *"No, I want to go home. I want to go home. Do not say this to me if you will not do it. Do not promise me..."*

"I swear. We will go."

That calmed him enough to keep looking out at the garden, but noticed a slight tremor in his hands. He noticed I noticed and shoved them in his jacket pockets.

He still did not trust me. Still did not believe me. But he wanted to. I could see it. And I so desperately wanted him to, as well. I wanted to hold him and assure him and fulfill any request from me. Wanted to prove to him I was no longer a beast, but a man, like him...a man who wanted only the best for him.

Instead, I went to my room and refused to let myself think for the rest of the night.

*****

Good to my word, the next morning he and I boarded a private jet in an air field next to a massive office complex outside Moscow. All big and glass and gleaming. We took off without a word from Russian Customs. I guess since we weren't checked into the country they didn't want the hassle of checking us out.

We stopped in Lisbon to refuel then landed in Miami just before eight pm. Ten minutes with some very polite immigration people and we were in a car to my condo.

I had an extra bedroom so gave that to Tony, delayed implementation of the relay to Interpol and the sell order, per my agreement...but only for two weeks, for my safety. Then I crashed until nine am the next morning.

Tony wasn't interested in seeing Miami; he was antsy about getting going, so we cleaned up and had Cuban food delivered for a late lunch. I gave him a pair of slacks that fit him a bit loose but were comfortable, added in a designer tee-shirt and neat sports coat. Once we finished eating on my balcony, we headed on.

I had a meal catered on the plane, served by a pretty flight attendant who paid special attention to Tony. He noticed and was actually shy with her, which only increased her interest.

Since it was to be an overnight flight, we slept...well, he slept. I was awake most of the flight just watching him sleep, stretched out on a comfortable couch, a light blanket covering him, the lights dim and giving him an almost angelic glow.

Yes, I know, I know, I was obsessing.

I'm sure half his beauty was in my own mind, but I didn't care. I was hoping for something impossible. That he would be able to live in peace, now. Would lose this sharp edge of sadness in his eyes. Would look at me with gratitude and acceptance.

That he would forgive me.

That's really all I wanted...for him to forgive me.

So I could forgive myself. Because it hurt me, so deeply, to know how much pain I'd brought him.

The problem with this long, quiet flight was...my brain would not let me rest. There was too much time to lie there and think, and I had to finally acknowledge that something in me had changed. I mean, I didn't feel any real difference. Truth is, if I'd been offered a million-five to take another man like Tony or Thiago, I could see myself doing it.

Sort of.

But I found myself putting little caveats on the possibility. If I bought him from a drug cartel or...or if he'd done something wrong, like raped a woman and got away with it. I thought of that swimmer in California who was caught in the act and punished with a silly three month sentence. He was pretty enough to sell. Or that jock in Missouri who raped a fourteen year old girl and got off with no jail time by making his victim the criminal. He had a nice look and a decent body. Someone like that, I'd have no problem selling on down the line.

But I couldn't take someone innocent, again...someone I didn't know was worthy of punishment. Even the thought of grabbing a man just walking down the street made me cringe with disgust.

So was I still a hunter? Hawks and wolves don't care about what they kill...lambs, calves, kittens, puppies...all that mattered was if it will feed them and their young. Had I gone from being a lion hunting on the veldt to nothing more than an avenging angel? Was I that middle-class?

I had no answer. Whatever had happened, it was not a conscious decision on my part. And lying there, my brain whirring as I gazed upon Tony, no matter how I'd try to stop and think of who I was and why it had happened, my mind would only laugh and wander into superfluity.

Wait, is that even word? I'd have to look...that...up...

Shit, see? I'm still doing it.

Oh, but dear God, how I wanted to hold him. Sleep with him. And it wasn't for sex; it was just to have him by me. Lying next to me. My arms wrapped around him and his around me. I wouldn't care about anything in the world so long as we were together.

And that would never happen. I kept telling myself that, over and over — it would never happen.

Would it?

Could it?

Shit.

*****

We landed in Buenos Aires to go through immigration, and the worked-up US Passport did all right for him. In fact, there were more questions about mine. I hadn't been noted as leaving Brazil, which raised a few issues...until I began spitting my *richer-than-thou* bullshit and complained about my *former* assistant for ten minutes before they finally let me go just to shut me up.

We left the attendant in Buenos Aires, to her serious disappointment, got back on the plane and I gave Tony my phone. He hadn't asked for it, like he was afraid if he spoke to his parents all my assurances would turn out to be lies and he'd wind up in somebody's compound in Africa. But now he knew for sure we were in Argentina, so he couldn't put it off any longer.

"Pilot says we'll be to Santa Rosa's airport in about fifty minutes," I said, "so you might want to phone home."

He froze. I'd never seen him so jumpy, even in that blank room. Even when sitting across from the Network's owners and operators he'd kept steady, not the least bit concerned about where he was or who was seated across from him. But now? He was shaking.

"What? But...what...what do I say?"

"Meet me at the airport?"

"No," he whispered, shaking his head. "No...it is two hours to drive...we should get a car...can we get a car? Then I can call them from the airport."

"I...I guess. Hertz? Avis? Enterprise?"

"Oh, no...last I come, Papá would meet me and...and..."

His voice trailed off and he looked at the phone for a couple minutes, then grimaced and dialed a number. I offered him the earbuds, but he shook his head. Then he tensed.

"Hello," he said, in Spanish, *"may I speak with Mr. Micheri, please? ... I am Antonio Patricio Micheri de Cardoza."* He jolted and continued. *"Yes, Tonio Micheri."* He looked at me, startled and murmured. "Someone is yelling others to come..." He turned back to phone, wary. "Mamá?" He began to breathe heavy. "Mamá! Mamá! Mamá!" And he was unable to say anything else, just "Mamá," over and over and over, his breaths deep and sharp.

I took the phone and said, *"Mrs. Micheri, my name is Hunter..."*

"What is this?" said an older woman's voice. *"Was that my son? Is that Tonio?"*

"Yes. Yes, it is and we are en route to Santa Rosa's airport and..."

"He's coming home? Where has he been?! Is he coming home?"

"Uh, yes...yes, he is coming home."

"Oh, thanks to God...five years and...where was he?!"

"I...I cannot tell you that. We will be at Santa Rosa in forty-five minutes. Is there a place we can hire a car?"

"I will meet you there."

"He told me it is a two hour drive so..."

"I will meet you there. We have a helicopter."

They did? Shit.

She ended the call and I left the phone with Tony. He kept looking at it, shaking and murmuring, "Mamá," over and over.

I couldn't handle seeing him like that, stuck in this loop of uncertainty and disbelief. Unable to advance beyond the moment when he'd heard his mother's voice for the first time in years. I would never feel that way were I to call my mother or father. Never be so caught up in the idea I was going to see them, again, that my mind shut down. When they'd thrown me out of the family, I'd sworn not to even try and contact them until I could come back richer than Solomon...and there would have been no love returning with me. But Tony, even though all he was saying was that one word, over and over, I could hear the love in his voice...hear how he was still fighting to keep from losing himself in the idea of being home, just in case it wasn't true.

Just in case.

And his mother's voice...so excited and relieved and happy and terrified it was all a lie...a voice I would never hear for me...so welcoming and human and real...it cut deep into my soul and mocked me for the loser I truly was. A man with no family. No love. Just money.

I looked out the window to watch the countryside pass far below. Golden fields punctuated by groupings of trees and long narrow roads. Soft rolling hills. We passed over a river with no banks. Wide and open and pure. Wide spaces cut into small farms. A series of shallow lakes. All of it reminding me of Spain...reminding me of the last time I'd been truly happy.

Gazing upon Fernando...before I knew what it all meant...

I finally noticed Tony's voice had grown softer. I turned to see he'd put a hand to the window and was also looking out as he continued to whisper, "Mamá, Mamá..."

Moments later, we glided in for a short, sharp landing at Santa Rosa, and it was as minimal an airport as you can imagine — just two old buildings, maybe one flight a day.

Tony saw a bright red and blue helicopter, by the older of the buildings, and stopped speaking. He dropped the phone and before the jet had finished taxiing was at the door.

"Tony, hold on," I said. "Just a minute."

But before the jet even stopped, he yanked on the emergency handle. The door popped open and he jumped out and skidded to the ground and staggered towards the helicopter as the co-pilot screamed after him, "What the hell have you done?"

I bolted to the door and saw a woman who was strong and nicely rounded, in jeans and a plaid shirt, with a wide-brim hat, quickly approaching him, arms outstretched. Tony slammed up against her and they wrapped their arms around each other and rocked back and forth, joyous.

I jumped out and hurried up to them, and I could just make out Tony was saying, "Mamá, Mamá," again, over and over.

The woman said, *"Tonio, where have you been? We were so afraid. We had all but given up. Where have you been?"*

Then her right hand slipped up Tony's neck to hold his head and she felt the bandage and froze and looked at me in absolute horror.

I quickly put a finger to my lips.

Her expression showed she agreed to keep silent and just kept holding Tony, as he clung to her like a child.

I rode with them to the ranch, in the helicopter. It was going to take a week to get the jet back into flying condition, so I put the pilots up at a decent hotel and rented a car from a dealership, for them.

"Whatever else it costs you," I said, just let me know. It's all on me."

I could already tell one of them was wondering where he might find a good whorehouse to catch a nice venereal disease, while the other would not have minded being the one he caught it from, if I read him right. But neither one interested me so I left them to their own devices and desires.

Flying low and fast over the Pampa...oh, my God, it was even more gorgeous from a few thousand feet up. Wide and open and mostly flat. Good range for cattle and sheep. Clear clean skies. Rain clouds in the not too distant north. The chopper was a four-seater so Tony sat in the back, still holding his mother, his head buried against her shoulder.

I did co-pilot...or can you call it shotgun if you're in a helicopter?

The trip took us fifteen minutes, following a long narrow road that led past farms where god knows what kinds of grains were being harvested to an area of open pastures covered with cattle and no fences. Then we passed over a group of men on horseback racing in the same direction as us. They saw the chopper and waved their hats in the air, and I would swear I almost heard them whooping.

I could see we were approaching a white, amazingly elegant hacienda surrounded by groves of trees. It was attached to the road by a drive that must have been at least a mile long, and had three large lovely pools of tree-shaded water around it. Two massive barns and stables were close by, as was an interlocking series of corrals that had horses of all sizes and hues.

The chopper landed in an open space between the house and the corrals, and some of the horses were not happy about it. Sra. Micheri leaned up to explain, *"We usually land in front of the house, but that is so far from the entrance, and Tonio's father will be coming this way."*

Tony looked at her and said, "Papá?"

"Yes, Tonio," she said, her face kind and loving. *"He was in the far range. He is coming as fast as he can."*

The chopper's rotors stopped and we opened the doors. Tony and his mother got out of the thing and I had barely set foot on the ground when we heard the riders thundering up, and they *were* whooping. A man who looked like Tony would in twenty years dismounted at a near gallop and bound up to grab him in his arms, crying, "Tonio!"

A moment later, a young man in full Gaucho gear, younger than Tony, heavier, not as tall, jumped off his mount and grabbed Tony from the back. I could see their faces shared many of the same features. He was weeping.

"Tonio...it really is Tonio...where have you been?"

I wandered around the helicopter to watch more gauchos arrive and crowd around Tony. He greeted them all while still clinging to his father and brother.

Out of respect, I turned to the corrals. Most of the horses had settled down, but one was still snorting and huffing and prancing about, irritated.

Sra. Micheri turned to the pilot, *"Wait till we have the horses in the stables before you move this thing."*

The pilot nodded and leaned against the chopper to wait. Then Sra. Micheri turned to me.

"You are Mr. Hunter?" I nodded. *"Do you know what happened to my son?"*

"Only a little."

"Was he arrested?"

"In a way."

She eyed me, unsure what I meant. *"We have heard horrible things about ICE in the United States..."*

I hesitated, unsure of what to say.

She continued with, *"Was he tortured?"*

I had to take in a deep breath to give myself a moment to think, but there was only one answer. *"Yes."*

She took a moment to accept that then whispered, *"Why? Do you know why?"*

Her eyes were hard on me, and too damned knowing for my liking. But c'mon, Hunter, man up.

"I know only a little," I said, *"and to reveal even that would be a betrayal to Tony. Please do not ask me to. Please. I do not wish to offend you by refusing to answer. It is better if he tells you. Let him tell you. He will. Just give him time."*

She was going to argue, but she saw I meant it so turned back to watch Tony and his entourage wander towards the corrals. We wandered after them.

"We thought that woman he married had killed him," she said. *"Her weeping that immigration must have taken him rang false. His English is good. He knows who our lawyer is, in Los Angeles. He would not have gone quietly. Nor would he have stayed quiet for five years. How can he have been quiet for five years? Even in prison..."*

I had to give her something to make it understandable, so I put my hand to the nape of my neck. *"You felt this?"*

She glared at me. *"An injury, yes."*

"Not an injury. A device was implanted that controlled him. If he did anything they did not want, it would cause severe pain. Make him black out. He was silent because he had no choice. He stayed alive hoping he could find a way to let you know...find a way to come home."

"Do you have one in you?"

"No."

Her eyes grew dark and dangerous. *"Why not?"*

"I was...I was different from him."

"Different?"

"Yes."

"Tell me, who are these 'they'?"

"I do not know."

"You are lying to me."

Well, it seemed Tony got his bluntness from his mother. *"I...I have suspicions, but I do not really know."*

She nodded. *"Your Spanish is Castilian, but it is not classroom Spanish. Where did you learn?"*

"Spain. My father was in the Air Force."

"Are the people who did this from there?"

"No. They do not know Spanish. Tony and I used it to communicate. To plan."

"To plan? So you stole him away from them."

I looked away. I'd already said way more than I intended.

"I brought him home. I can say no more."

She took in a deep breath, fighting herself. She really wanted answers from me, it was obvious. But she let that breath out and said, *"I will put aside all of my questions, for now, and focus on one thing. You did bring my son back to me. To his father. To his brother and sisters. He is alive and healthy. Physically healthy. For that, I thank you."*

She heard that horse still prancing around, huffy, and noticed Tony, his father and brother were watching, at the corral fence.

Sra. Micheri called over to them, *"Tonio, why do we not go inside for an iced drink? We have food, and we will have a party to welcome you home. Bernardo, take Tico into the stable."*

"That is Tico," Tony said.

Bernardo grinned. *"You remember him? Always so full of himself."*

"He was a yearling when I was here. He is big and strong."

"It has been a few years, brother."

"He has done well," said Sr. Micheri, *"but he has always hated that thing."* He motioned to the chopper.

Tony smiled and patted his father's chest, and I cannot even begin to describe how happy that made me. Then he climbed up to sit on the corral's fence. Bernardo leaned on a post to watch him.

Sra. Micheri told me, *"Tonio was here when Tico was foaled. He remained an extra week, to be sure the pony would be all right. He has been back, twice, and each time, Tico knows him."*

"But it has been years, has it not?"

"Seven years. Tico is soon to be nine."

Tony called, "Tico, Tico, Tico," and clicked his tongue, using every tone, rhythm and inflection you can think of.

The horse stopped in mid-snort and looked at him, as if to say, *Do I know you?*

Tony slipped off the fence, into the corral, and kept saying "Tico, Tico, Tico."

The horse hesitated. Looked closer at him. Snorted.

"Tico, Tico, Tico."

It hesitated then gave off a combination of neighs and whinnies as it started for him, bouncing its head up and down. I would swear the sounds coming from it were cries of joy as it strode up to Tony and wrapped its head around him. He circled its neck with his arms, gripping its mane, whispering, "Tico. Tico. Tico."

Bernardo grinned at me. *"My brother always was good with horses."* He hopped over the fence to help the gauchos herd the other horses into the stable.

I couldn't move. To see my beautiful Tony embracing this amazing stallion and it caressing him with its nose, it was too perfect and I felt tears stream down my face.

Then Tony's voice broke into a soft whimper of, "Tico..."

And suddenly he was sobbing. Deep. Gut-wrenching. Horrifying.

The horse nudged him, gently, as if to comfort him. He held its mane and leaned against it.

Sr. Micheri came over, stroked Tico's nose then put an arm around Tony. He did a clicking sound with his tongue and started walking the horse. Tony stumbled but held onto Tico and walked with them, weeping the whole way into the stables. Bernardo and the gauchos all focused on the other horses, in respect...but I saw more than one cast me a suspicious glance.

I felt like I was going to break in half.

Then I realized Sra. Micheri was glaring at me...and murder was in her eyes. *"Tonio jumped from that plane as if he was escaping. He has yet to look at you, once. I believe you had something to do with hurting my son. It is good you brought him home, where he can be cared for. It is better that you leave, now. I will have a man drive you back to Santa Rosa."*

What could I do? I took her up on the offer.

And never saw Tony, again.

And every day since has been a form of hell.

SIX

That was two years ago, and there hasn't been a day go by that I haven't thought about him. Wondered how he was doing. Hoped he and Tico were ranging over the Pampa. Begged the fates to let me know that he was even alive and well. I have no idea. I've been frozen out of his life.

Now I was headed down the 25, on my way home from Chicago, after a long, long drive down the 80...and oh, my God, there is nothing in Nebraska that even approaches being pretty. But driving is a lot easier to do than flying, for me. Besides, I now had no set destination or plan or goals.

I got off in Colorado Springs hoping to find something for lunch that wasn't MacDonald's or Subway, but of course, there was nothing but Del Taco and Wendy's and Chik-full-of-shit everywhere. Nothing appetizing. The only reason I even contemplated stopping in any of them was all the hot little Air Force cadets chowing down in their nice tight uniforms...at least half of whom were obviously randy enough for anybody's lips to make their dicks happy. I chuckled as I thought about getting some protein, that way. I've been keeping myself up, and I'm only thirty-four, not quite daddy territory, yet...even if some of the brats did look like they were still in grade school.

Shit.

But instead I just did a turn-around and headed back for the freeway, thinking I'd find something better at the next exit. Then I passed a Walmart Center and saw a cowboy type in jeans, boots and the barest of tee-shirts, despite the chill, calmly leaning against an old pickup truck. Mid-twenties, really nice face, dash of freckles, long sandy-colored hair, a nicely pumped chest, tight abs, well-formed legs, and best of all — a tattoo sleeve of a forest on his left arm. He also wore a white woven hat, pushed back on his head, and was smoking a cigarette.

And I would bet it was a clove ciggie.

I hit the brakes on my CRV, nearly got rear-ended, *did* get honked and cussed at, then swung onto the parking lot and roared up to him. I screamed to a halt in the slot diagonal to his and hopped out and yelped for joy and he gaped at me in shock.

"Hunter?" he asked.

"Vermin!"

I grabbed him in a bear hug and he squeezed my ass and we jumped around for joy like a couple of teenage girls who'd just seen their pop idol coming out of the supermarket.

"I thought the motherfuckers killed you," he cried.

"Bitch, I'm indestructible," I howled back.

We went in for a kiss at the same time, and it was fucking awesome. God DAMN, it felt good to be holding him, again.

And yes, that ciggie was clove.

We wound up in a cantina nearby, feasting on greasy tacos, guac, chips, fajitas, the whole friggin' menu, along with more than a few beers. Looked like I'd be stayin' the night in Colorado Springs, 'cause no way in hell was I drivin', even tipsy.

Oh, did we spit the bullshit, back and forth. Been here. Gone there. All new life. No wife. It was glorious. Then we got down to specifics.

"So you live in Denver, now?" he asked.

"Nope," I said. "Just passin' through."

"Where to?"

"Wherever. Got no set address. Are you here?"

"Nah, we wound up back in LA."

"We?"

Vermin got his wicked little grin going, and I thought he really ought to patent it because it was so fucking perfect on him, then he said, "C'mon, Hunter, you're smart enough to figure out who I mean."

Holy shit. "Not all four of you?"

His grin widened like a Cheshire cat's. "We're in business together. OdvetaRR Services." He laughed at my obviously confused expression. "It means *reprisal*, in Czech, and since Lubie and Vac are from there..."

I still had my WTF expression on.

Oh, he was loving this. "Pavel's real name is Lubomír Kruta. The guy you called Bear is Václav Kruta. They're brothers by different mothers, is how they put it. Horace had to change his name, thanks to something you pulled on him, so he's now Gerald Smith, and you have to call him *Gerald*, not *Jerry*. Sounds fake, but it works."

"So you guys stuck together..."

"Shit, yeah. We did the arena thing for another six months. Usually with me as the *victim*. The guys thought they talked me into it, but I could see you were havin' a blast when we raped you — wait, can you even call it rape if you're enjoyin' it?"

"I'd say no, but then you guys pissed on me and that was over the line."

"Yeah, it's their macho bullshit. *Show you who da man.*"

"They wish. So what'd *you* think of Pavel's blowjobs?"

"Lubie. Call him Lubie. And I liked yours more. Not so mechanical."

I laughed. "I thought he was almost as good as you."

"*No*body's as good as me." Then he winked and nodded to a nearby table. I used my phone to sneak a look and saw a couple of hot little cadets seated there trying hard not to seem like they were listening in...and intrigued.

Kitteh rumbled, *And here you are, stayin' the night...*

"So what happened?" I asked, sending Vermin a nod that they might be fun. "Why'd you stop doin' it?"

"Attendance dropped to shit, thanks to somebody fuckin' with a lot of client's bottom lines." And he looked hard into my eyes when he said that.

I just smiled. No need to verify his suspicions.

You see, after leaving Tony I'd flown straight to Miami and shut down everything, there. Sold the condo, had my hacker shift my funds to a Swiss account, the whole nine yards. Then as soon as I was done, I'd flown to the Las Vegas compound. Theo and Jerome had been there a week, and they looked even better than when I'd kidnapped them. I guess it was the Tony effect — work it or you'll wish you had.

Once I'd been given their codes, I'd taken them to LA and had a doctor remove the chips. That's why I'd watched how Tony's was done, so I could see how it was turned off, before removal. Then I'd set them free with money enough to take care of them for a while.

Jerome grudgingly gave me forty-eight hours before he'd call the cops and tell them everything. That's all I needed to vanish.

I'd found out Theo's parents were in Mexico City, with his two younger brothers, so he'd headed straight there. I don't know how he got back into the country, but he did...and his story brought down the mayor.

I'd left each one's chip with him, so those helped back up their claims.

Then I'd met with my hacker and erased myself from the internet.

Hunter no longer existed, and don't tell me it's not possible to ghost yourself; it is.

It wasn't until then that I let Interpol be notified about the Network. They're still finding locations used to hold and abuse other human beings. Hungary, Poland, Romania, Mexico, Venezuela, South Africa, Saudi Arabia, Egypt, Turkey, they all had a compound where the rich could go to have their fun. Russia didn't give a shit about it all, so theirs is still probably viable, and China just refused to even acknowledge the possibility.

Dutch police also found ocean containers remade into torture cells, and cross-referenced the requisition paperwork they found with people reported missing, all in slow steps and stages but building up a mass of very solid information. It was turning into a nice slow-burning scandal, considering all the higher-ups being connected to it.

I hadn't expected much to be done in the US. There were at least two members of Congress up to their eyeballs in it, and they'd stop any detailed investigations. As for Mr. Movie Star, suddenly he went into retirement saying he wanted to write his memoirs and maybe name names and all. Lots and lots of salacious promises that have yet to be fulfilled...and I doubt ever would.

At least I knew that some of the men I'd provided were found and freed.

To my shame, I couldn't say all were.

I'd also let the sell orders go through, collapsing the value of several major companies and investment firms around the globe. Including mine. I'd always felt stocks were nothing but a gamble. If you were dumb enough to rely too heavily on them, as income, you shouldn't be surprised if they gave out. Look at what happened in 2008 — trillions in value vanished overnight, and not a damn thing's been done to prevent it happening, again. Nothing new about that.

The only proactive thing I did was quietly forewarn the Carvalho family about the impending catastrophe. Last I checked, they were weathering the storm. As was Mueller, by default.

Dammit.

Because I'd recently heard Eddie was running for Congress, with daddy's backing, as a fucking Republican. So I'd hopped on up to Chicago, given money to his opponent's PAC and leaked a *bit of info* on the younger Mueller. The media is just beginning to take notice. Hopefully, they will keep noticing. And digging. And kill his political career before it begins.

So now I live a life where no one can find me. Where nobody knows my name. Where few people see me. Hiding in plain sight, as it were. Because they are still looking for me. The police. The Network. Those whose fortunes I crushed and reputations I ruined. Taking someone from a hundred billion in value to a measly little ol' billion is just plain unacceptable.

But seeing Vermin, again...I threw caution to the winds and stopped to let myself be open and free and alive, again. And see if he still wanted to take revenge. It was so nice to watch him grinning at me.

"So..." he said, not a hint of anger in hie eyes, "you fucked me, and I fucked you, and you fucked everybody. Right?"

I chuckled.

"Y'know," he continued, "for a long time I thought you were nothin' but a scared, greedy little shit, but now I see you were provin' how much of a hard-ass you were."

I shrugged. "Business is business."

"Bullshit. So what ever happened to Tony?"

Oh, shit. "You still jonesin' for him?"

"He is the one who got away. Twice."

"You had him — plenty of times."

"Aw, fuck, you know 'bout that, huh?"

I nodded. "Where you stayin'?"

"Why?" But his smirk had replaced his grin.

"They still there?" I tilted my head back at the two cadets.

His smirk went more wicked as he nodded. "And I got condoms."

"What you say we put the past to bed and start a whole new life?"

He chuckled. "I'm at that La Quinta, just over the road. Nice and close to where I need to be, and cheap. We can't charge your rates, yet."

"What do you do?"

"It's in the name, Hunter. OdvetaRR. Three Rs, in English. Reprisal. Retribution. Revenge. All the fun shit." He leaned in to whisper. "A certain cadet raped a girl and got out of jail time by joining the A-F. She got pregnant; he got nominated to the academy by his Republican congressman."

"Wait...I read somethin' about that...jeez, a year ago. Got caught in the act and the girl was trashed for filin' charges?"

Now Vermin nodded. "My source says he likes comin' to a certain pub 'cause they won't card him if he's in uniform."

"That what you were waitin' for when I came up?"

"Nah, he can't come out till after six. I was just enjoyin' the scenery. Mountains capped with snow..."

"You weren't cold?"

He shrugged. "I got a coat in the truck." Then his wicked little grin returned and he leaned in close to whisper. "And a gun. And some rope. And a gag. Wanna have some fun, tonight?" Then he glanced at the cadets. "Or tomorrow night?"

BAM! I felt a roar of happiness behind my heart and had to take his hands in mine. They were freezing, even after being inside for hours. "Are you suggestin' what I think you are?"

"*Show him the meaning of life*. That's why I'm here."

"But in a La Quinta?"

"It's up to you. Have the boys, tonight." He cast a glance at the two cadets then licked his lips and batted his eyes at me. "That cadet, tomorrow."

I could barely breathe. I hadn't realized how much I'd missed that. How much of myself I'd shut down till that moment.

How fucking bored I was, now.

I don't pray. Don't believe in heaven or hell, so I'm not afraid of death. I'd saved the men I wanted to save, so had no trouble sleeping. And now I was being offered something new and fresh...and even justifiable.

"Reprisal, retribution, revenge," I murmured.

"For a price," said Vermin.

The three Rs. Something I'd once almost thought of doing, myself. The mere hint of it sent a jolt straight to my balls. I let a low rumbling purr come from within. Vermin chuckled and gripped my hands as tightly as I gripped his.

Fuck the world...Hunter was back in business.

THE END...?

HUNTER

CODA
The Sheriff's Boys (no more)

ONE

"God damn that little shit," the Sheriff snarled.

Needless to say, he was not in a good mood. He had just received a text from Hunter, his *business associate*, and learned he was on his way with fresh cargo. Which was expected. What was *not* expected was that he would be sneaking not one man across the border but seven.

Six men he wanted to sell to the Network, *plus* the one fucking guy he was actually sent to collect.

What the fuck had gone wrong? Had he figured out this trip was a set up? Did he suspect the Sheriff was out to get rid of him? Or was this a middle finger to the new Coordinator the Network had sent in to handle Arizona and New Mexico? A self-satisfied freak whose way of proving himself was trying to save shit-loads of money, and never mind the mess it could make of things. Or maybe it was Hunter's way of showing the bastard he had no idea who he was dealing with.

But the thing was, he hadn't been in on the meeting where this new guy had suggested his fees were high. Of course, the whiny-assed Coordinator who currently dealt with Hunter had fought against dropping him. The little bastard was known for the quality of men he delivered, so he'd more than proven his worth to the Network. And their district's initial return on the cargo was now well into eight figures, so he knew the Network's final gross take was probably ten times that. Not a profit-maker you want to mess with.

Plus Hunter had been smart enough to do his hunting among the low-lifes who were part of the drug cartels. And those who were working for mining and lumber interests, in Mexico, and were trying to take over people's land or steal their crops. The latter was how his main source for product had become the Mayor of a nice medium-size town up in the Mexican mountain forests. The guys he'd collect from him would be missed by no one...and there had been some damn good-looking ones in there. The Sheriff might not be into male-on-male sex, but he could tell Hunter had the eye and was unwilling to accept anyone who wasn't up to the Network's standards. Twenty to thirty-five years old. Attractive. Tested by the little shit, himself, to make sure they could get it up and could be gotten off, even under arduous circumstances. No, there had been no complaints about the quality.

However, even something high-end can get to be too pricey.

But they had to be careful, here, because Hunter also had other connections and connections within those connections. All secret and careful, on his part, meaning they'd lose them once he was done away with. That would hurt. And then there was him being unwilling to answer even the simplest questions from the new guy? Like...who were these connections? Why don't we know them? How sure was he that the men he was taking weren't going to be missed?

The Coordinator was also unhappy about the two occasions where Hunter actually was tricked into accepting men who were strictly off limits.

"He claims he's always on top of things," the new guy had said, "but he still returned both men to the States, and we lost a huge payment on one."

"Which was made back," snapped the Sheriff. "And since both were American, they had to be snuck in. Leavin' 'em there would've made things worse."

"But they weren't even from his usual sources," the man snarled. "They came from idiots who'd been referred to him by his *other* connections. He should have known they were using him to get rid of men who were merely problematic. Instead, he fell for their lies and could have cost us everything!"

"There's always gonna be people like that, and the little shit worked his way 'round them both. One got dumped near his home and the other left in a place he could be found, both jacked up on drugs so they figured bein' kidnapped and molested was just a bad trip. You got no reason to bitch."

The bastard had huffed and puffed and spit out more concerns, and despite it all, the Sheriff had to admit his points were well-made. Hunter was also getting pretty full of himself. Flat out cocky. Which usually leads to catastrophe. Then had come wanting more money...despite having all his expenses paid! Including the money going to the Mayor for his *help*.

"I'm takin' all the risks," he'd said in his snarky way, "so I'm due much better compensation."

So the Sheriff had finally agreed with the new Coordinator that it was time to have someone else take over the job, at a far more reasonable fee. He made his own connection with the Mayor and asked him to continue providing men of the same quality to a new guy, once they had one hired on. Of course, the son-of-a-bitch had weaseled more money out of them, to agree to it...but without Hunter's full cut, that still put them way ahead.

The thing is, transporting and selling men into sexual slavery was hardly the sort of enterprise one could just fire somebody from. Nor could you merely decide not to renew the contract. No, the little fuck had to be shut down, completely, in a way that no one in the regular world would notice...and would not piss off the Network. The plan they'd come up with was supposed to be foolproof, considering Hunter had a serious prohibition against taking Anglo guys, no matter what.

"They bring on too much trouble," he'd said, over and over. "I know the woman who gets women for the Network won't touch anything blond or light-haired. Too much chance the media'll use their disappearance to work up panic and help their ratings."

Which was why the Sheriff had been working with the Mayor to set up a situation Hunter could not get out of.

They'd had Emilio, the Mayor's assistant, contact a guy in El Paso...a kid, really. Only twenty. But he'd been caught sucking off his commanding officer, in the Army, so he'd been drummed out, nice and quiet. Now he was desperate for money, and he was the kind who wouldn't be missed by anybody. They'd hired him to come to Mexico with the understanding he was to pretend he'd been kidnapped, then he'd be handed over to Hunter as the Mayor's *new offering*.

Of course, Hunter would quickly figure out he was American, but as mentioned...he'd been faced with situations like this, before. So he'd probably plan to junk the guy up on peyote and sneak him across the border, then dump him somewhere to be found while still high.

Except...this time they had arranged for a couple of Federales to catch Hunter...and for one of them to fuck the kid then strangle him...so it would look like Hunter had raped and murdered him. No matter what he said, he'd go down for it, and once that story was out, the Network would cut him off, complete.

But instead...Hunter had gathered *six* young Latino males to bring across the border, along with the slutty fag. SIX! At Douglas, Arizona. Where he had his own contacts to get across. No way could their plan work, now.

What the hell had gone wrong?

The Sheriff found out, seven minutes after Hunter's text. The Mayor called, in near hysterics. He admitted he'd let Emilio also handle the transfer of the kid to Hunter, and the dumb son-of-a-bitch had brought in his cousin, Reuben, to help. That had put Hunter on his guard and he had taken control of the situation in nothing flat.

So...those two little shits were the ones who had fucked it up.

"I tell him to meet Hunter outside the casa and to leave before he sees the boy," the Mayor said in halting English. "And to be alone! But Hunter...he sees Reuben and thinks Reuben has molested the boy, so he captures Emilio and Reuben, both, and calls his connections and it is big disaster. I try to think of how to make this work okay, but I have no time."

"But that's just two guys," said the Sheriff. "Who're the other four?"

"Hunter is angry. He wants more. So I think of a Muslim boy in town. I think to get rid of him, to make his family go away. But Hunter takes three others, with him. One I know, Oscar, a good boy; the other two I do not know. When I realize his plan, I tell him to stop but he does not. And now they are coming to you."

"Shit. Call in the Army!"

"Oh, no, I do not want a situation like in the south. They will make them disappear and I know the mother of Oscar..."

"What d'you want me to do?"

"If he is able to get them across the border, they must be returned."

"And just how the hell do you propose that?!"

"You have the connection in Border Patrol..."

"And Hunter's got his own damn connections. Hell, I hear he's even buddies with a drug lord, down there, and that can be messy if not handled careful."

"I know who this is. He is not involved; he will not care."

"You so sure 'bout that?"

"...Yes."

"Okay...this is gonna cost us a shitload..."

"Hunter keeps the money that was for me. He was angry and refuse to pay for the Anglo boy."

"'Course he wouldn't! That's why nobody was supposed to be around when he saw the kid. The plan was, he gets stopped with a *dead, drugged-up, kidnapped American* in his truck and forty-thousand in cash. It's a one-day story if it happens in Mexico, but this side of the border? It's news for a week. All kinds of investigations and FBI and Border Patrol; too damn much could come out. So I gotta let him come across, get the guys from him and figure out what to do, next. But it's still gonna cost us. I wanna keep one of 'em."

"Theo," said the Mayor. "He is the Muslim boy. His parents purchase the pharmacy in the Davelos District, since six years. Many people like them, but many others fear they front for ISIS. They have two other sons. If Theo is to vanish...I will talk them to sell their pharmacy to me. To take the other sons to Mexico City, where they will be safe. Where there are more of *their kind*. If he is no good, I suggest Reuben, because he has been to an American prison. Oh...but no...no, Emilio will not accept this."

"Little shit's got no say in what he will or won't accept. Now I gotta go. Start gettin' ready for the delivery. Call off your Federales; if Hunter don't make it back to the States, won't nothin' help us with this."

The Sheriff closed the door to his office, locked it, sat back at his desk and pulled out a bottle of Wild Turkey. He needed to think...and after the second shot, he got an idea.

He had another problem that concerned a few of his men. He began to wonder if he might kill two birds with one stone. He also knew a Western was being shot near Old Tucson, so contacted the production manager and learned they were shut down for a few days. Seems the lead actor had gotten drunk and fallen off his horse, breaking his collarbone. They had to wait till he was healed enough to handle the pain before they could resume shooting. So they had a four-room honey wagon available to *borrow* for a day or two.

That would be perfect. After four more phone calls, he had a plan of action laid out. He sent a driver he knew straight over to pick the honey wagon up, then arranged for six of his men to meet him at an RV park near Sierra Vista. That would now be ground zero.

He headed out, but he was only halfway there when Hunter texted him that he was crossing the border.

"Little shit must've hot-rodded that fuckin' van of his," the Sheriff growled.

Like a good officer of the law, he pulled over to the side of the road and texted Hunter a single word. *Indian*. That meant that things weren't cool. So rather than head for the rendezvous, Hunter would now check into his room and wait to hear from the Sheriff, giving him time to finalize things.

He also received a report that the Feds were planning a quickie drug raid at that same hotel, thanks to a Border Patrol officer who'd been caught doing something illegal. He called the officer in charge, and soon had an idea of who Hunter's contact had been, in border patrol...which could prove useful.

By seven in the evening, his men had assembled at the RV park. They were big, butch, buff, and brutal, on both sides of thirty. All were in worn jeans and had numerous tattoos peeking around athletic tee-shirts, almost like it was a uniform, and each with a prison record a mile long that also carried a nasty reputation, thanks to becoming a little clique unto themselves, in prison. That made them perfect for jobs like this.

The honey wagon arrived, moments later, and turned out to have four doors to private rooms and two for the toilets, one male, one female, both with small showers. Each room had a fold-out couch and single chair, dressing table, mini-fridge and a sliding door that opened into a narrow hallway on the other side of the truck, leading from the rooms to the toilets.

"You usin' shit like to transport guys to jail, now?" snarled Elias, a powerful black man with a shaved head and eyes that could kill with a glare.

"Pretty fuckin' fancy," said Kilo, who wasn't quite as black, had a solid if not as built up body, and who carried an aura of gentle danger. He was bouncing on the couch in Room 1, like a kid.

"Cut the shit," the Sheriff snarled. "We gotta keep these rooms neat. Keep things lookin' cool."

"There gonna be *any* fun?" asked Sinder, a sunburned cowboy who looked like he could bring down a steer with one arm tied behind his back.

"Yeah, but not here," said the Sheriff. "I want each of you behind a door, includin' the toilets. When we hit the motel, you come out. And don't say shit to nobody. Just do as I tell you. Got it?"

They all nodded and positioned themselves.

The Sheriff had already contacted his people at Border Patrol, so everything was in order. He joined Elias, in the first room. It had a window slot that opened into the driver's cab, so he could watch as they headed for Douglas...and make a few more phone calls to finalize some details.

Things were looking good.

*****

Hunter drove a white cargo van with a hidden panel under the back floorboard, and he always stopped at this ratty, single-level motel close to a *Dairy Queen*. So as the honey wagon approached the motel, the Sheriff looked through the slot and could see the van parked under the one shaded area...with Hunter walking up the corridor, wrapped in nothing but a towel and carrying a load of laundry.

The Sheriff huffed. He was a hot little shit, and knew it. Well-built, hair on his neat chest, abs and legs, no tattoos, and a non-stop smirk that all but begged to be slapped. It was proving harder than they expected to find someone who could replace him because he also spoke fluent Spanish and knew how to make the men he collected ejaculate, no matter how straight they were. He'd also built a reputation for being trustworthy. The Sheriff was close to thinking it might make more sense to just pay his requested rate than have to rebuild this part of the Network, basically from scratch. But it's always been hard as hell to argue with accountants. All they see is numbers, not reality.

They pulled up behind the van and the Sheriff got out, as did the six Brutal Men...not one of whom even hinted at a smile.

Hunter tossed his clothes into his room and sauntered up to them. Without a word, he unlocked the van and showed its back was covered with empty cardboard boxes and sheets. "If you boys'll get the boxes out, I'll show you what we got," he said.

They removed the cartons to reveal there were seven young men. All bound hand and foot, and gagged. All nicely built. All attractive. Six had dark hair and tanned skin; one was blond and fair.

Hunter pointed to the blond, saying, "Not him."

The Sheriff looked at the guy, sighed. He hadn't realized the kid they chose was so damned obviously *not* Latino. It would've been so much better if he'd had dark hair, too, and Hunter not figured it out till after he'd been molested. Except...somehow he always seemed to know when a guy wasn't Mexican and wouldn't share his trick for determining that. So he just huffed and made himself growl, "Oh, they fuckin' didn't."

Hunter just nodded.

"Son-of-a-bitch, I thought you was just bein' paranoid. You gonna handle this?"

Hunter nodded, again, saying, "But that terminates Mexico."

The Sheriff sighed; that was the last thing they wanted. He turned to his men and noticed they were eyeing the cargo in ways that were anything but sweet and kind...except for a lean, mean muscle machine named Oren; his eyes were on Hunter, and he looked ready to pounce.

The Sheriff smirked, thinking, *I wish I could let you have him.*

He motioned to the bound men and each Brutal Man grabbed one. Two of them were regaining consciousness so struggled a little, but they were handled with no trouble. Each one's bindings were cut off then their clothing was torn away, completely. The Sheriff noticed the near smiles this brought to all his guys, but that was why he'd picked these six — their joy in handling fresh inmates was legendary, to say the least, especially once they'd become a pack, while in Matagorda State Penitentiary.

The Sheriff noticed one young man was phenomenally handsome in a Telenovela way, from perfect face to exquisite body to nice-sized dick. He looked at Hunter, in askance.

"That's Oscar," Hunter said, smiling. "Got him near the university along with those two." He pointed to a couple of muscular young men. "The one that was in shorts is Juan; the one in jeans, Tomás."

The Sheriff nodded and fought back a sigh. So these three were off-limits, which was really unfortunate. Oscar, alone, would have paid for everything, twice over.

Hunter nodded to another trim young man being held by a very possessive Sinder. "That's Emilio."

Ah, the troublemaker.

264

"And that one's Reuben." Hunter pointed to a stockier young man with wavy hair, being held by Walt, who would have fit in perfectly with a Hells Angels biker posse.

And there was the other little shit who'd fucked everything up. Good to know.

Then Jude, a regular-looking gym rat with a way-too-serious tan and sun-bleached spiked hair, motioned the Sheriff over. He was holding a trim, very sweet-looking young man...the only one who was circumcised.

Hunter followed him, saying, "That's Theo. He's Muslim."

So this was the boy they could keep. The Sheriff eyed him, carefully. Inspected every square inch of him, including his surprisingly elegant feet. He was moaning and starting to squirm, but it did him no good.

"How old?" the man finally asked, holding Theo's lovely face in his hand.

"Twenty."

"He been tested?"

Hunter nodded. "He grew to about eight inches."

"Virgin?"

Hunter nodded.

The Sheriff did a careful examination of Theo's lovely ass and agreed the Mayor's suggestion was excellent.

"This one's in room three," he said. "You first in the shower. An' be careful."

Jude frowned at hearing that, but quietly carried Theo to his door in the honey wagon.

The Sheriff pointed to Emilio and said, "Him in number four, shower next. Him in number two, shower last," while pointing to Reuben. "Those three in number one," he told the rest of the Brutal Men. "No showers."

As they did what they were told, the Sheriff escorted Hunter back to his van. "That Theo boy's gonna cover the cost of all this shit, plus a little."

Hunter smiled. "So long as he's not hurt; he's too pretty."

"No need worryin' 'bout that. This client's high-end. He ain't goin' off-roadin' in no Ferrari."

Hunter laughed.

The Sheriff continued, "If you'd just brought him, we'd been happy. Dumb as shit, what you did, an' goddamn lucky you got away with it."

"I had an ace."

"No more. That Border Patrol agent you're buddies with...he turned on you. They're lookin' for drugs."

Hunter had growled and was silent for a moment, then looked around, wary. "But I must be under surveillance, now. Isn't all this suspicious?"

"Yep. But...there's a movie shootin' out in the desert. Honey wagon's headin' out there. Told 'em I'd do a search. If they stop the semi, nothin' in it but car parts. Just a guy got lost, stopped by, and you give him directions to Cochise. GPS sucks out here. The driver...uh...let's just say, dressed like you are, with your history, they can put two an' two together an' make if forty seven, if they want. But as of now, they think your dealer's comin' in through Lordsburg, after midnight."

"Horace is showin' up, at midnight. So he *is* in on bustin' me."

"Horace, huh? He's buyin' his way out of trouble."

Hunter's voice grew sad. "Doesn't work," he said. "They'll fuck him over, anyway."

The Sheriff shrugged. "Leave the van," he continued. "There's a Chevy 'round front. Take that." He gave Hunter a set of keys. "See Phil in Anaheim. He'll set you up fresh docs. Coordinator's got a plan for LA, and you're part of it. We'll handle your boy..."

"No," Hunter said, cold and angry. "Don't."

The Sheriff eyed him. "What you up to?"

Hunter showed the Sheriff a photo he'd taken on his phone. It showed a very well-built, cowboy-like Border Patrol agent, standing at parade rest, hands behind him, everything about him close to perfection, with his well-proportioned dick at full attention as Hunter kissed it.

The Sheriff hesitated. "He's Border Patrol."

"He's in big trouble. He might run."

"Still pretty iffy. Trouble ain't that bad." The Sheriff eyed the image. Once again, Hunter was bringing forth a prime piece of meat worth its weight in gold, and with an excuse for it to vanish, so he had to ask, "How's his ass?"

"Virgin, he says."

That increased the price, nicely. "Mouth?"

"Virgin, he says."

That doubled his value. "Can you verify?"

"I will."

The Sheriff eyed him, almost smiling. Hunter drove him crazy with his *I'm-all-that* attitude, but oh, could he deliver. "When?"

"Give me a week. How much you think he'll bring?"

The Sheriff looked long and hard at the photo, his eyes cold and calculating, his body unmoved.

"Gotta do some checkin'," he said, "but I'd say half a mill, with no strings."

Hunter nodded. "Make it so."

The Anglo kid was starting to come around...the Sheriff couldn't remember his name; some kind of rat or rodent or something...so he just helped Hunter move him into the room and flop him on the bed. Then he left without another word and got in the cab of the honey wagon. They headed for the AZ80, back to Sierra Vista, as the semi aimed for the 191.

They'd have to find a way to take care of that kid, since he knew what'd been planned for Hunter. Maybe hand him off to the Network as well, once Hunter had dropped him off. He had a nice ass on him. Something to think about.

But that could be decided later.

*****

They drove through the Mule Pass tunnel to find a camper-van was stopped on the left side of the road, by a shed. The Sheriff had the honey wagon pull up beside it, the doors facing the camper and away from the main road, and he got out. He knocked on the door for Room 1 and went in.

This room had Juan, Tomas and Oscar in it, all lying on the fold-out couch, atop each other. All unconscious. Limbs crisscrossing each other. Elias had his phone out and was taking photos. It was obvious from the bulge in his jeans he wasn't wearing undies and would love to *alleviate some inner tensions* using one of the young men.

Or all...depending on his reputation for stamina.

The Sheriff stopped and smirked. "That's a pretty picture," he sneered. "Been playin' 'round?"

"Little," said Elias, smacking his erection. It shifted, happily.

"These three gotta go back untouched."

Elias smirked and cooed, "But they been touched, a lot."

The Sheriff snarled. "Have you fucked 'em? I fuckin' told you not to fuckin' fuck any of 'em till I gave the okay!"

Elias's smirk vanished. "No, sir. Just arranged 'em all on the bed. Couple different ways. Felt 'em up as I did it, sure, nothin' more. An' they do feel nice. Solid. Strong. Like this chico I took, day before I made parole."

"Okay," said the Sheriff, calming down. "You give 'em the GBH?"

Elias nodded. "Pretty one caught on and fought me. Had to force it down him. That was fun. Reminded me of this hot-shit trash motherfucker at Matagorda. Thought he was too white to get fucked by a black man. Proved him wrong...several times..."

"Aw, cut that shit out," the Sheriff snarled. "These three're goin' in that camper van. I'll send a guy in to..."

"Don't need no help." And his smirk was back.

"Fine. But you don't do jack shit with a damn thing more than your hands on 'em, got me?"

Elias nodded and shifted Oscar off Juan, his fingers dancing across Oscar's dick in coy little moves.

"This how you fucked men in prison?" the Sheriff asked, wary.

Elias picked Juan up and kissed his left tit, then said, "Didn't have no drugs...no posse, to start...so used a choke hold. Made things lots quieter."

"Any of them die or...or say they can't breathe?"

"Watch it, motherfucker," Elias snarled, sending the Sheriff the coldest glare ever. "An' since when do I give a fuck what a fuckin' white guy says or does?" Then he smiled and added, "In prison."

The Sheriff sighed and exited then held the door open as Elias carried Juan outside and to the back of the camper.

Next came Room 2. That held Rueben, who was naked, bound with his arms behind him and gagged. Oren was watching Walt hold Rueben's dick in his hand as the Sheriff entered. Even a quick glance said it was fair-sized and nicely shaped, with a hint of saliva on it from having been sucked. Its foreskin was just visible. Reuben's eyes held absolute fury.

"Boys..." the Sheriff said, a jokey warning in his voice. Since both guys were fully dressed, he didn't feel the need for more than that.

"You should've seen it two minutes ago," Walt said. "But all I done is edge him. No cum, yet."

The Sheriff checked Reuben over, ignoring the man's angry grunts and squirming attempts to avoid him. Smooth muscles in a nice form on his body. Softer than the others, and rounder, overall. Hair where there should be. And a tattoo on his left hip...one the Sheriff recognized.

"He was in Matagorda," he said. "In the States."

"Elias knew him," said Oren, smirking. "The look he gave this guy..."

"Wouldn't be surprised," said Walt. "He likes what I'm doin'. Wants us to think he don't, but he got hard, damn quick." Then he juggled Reuben's balls, chuckling, to the guy's furious howl.

"Loves gettin' a blow job almost as much as you love givin' 'em." Oren then smirked at the Sheriff, adding, "My bet is, he thought his pretty mouth'd keep his ass safe, but if I know Elias..."

"Nothin' wrong with fuckin'...or suckin'," said Walt. Then he dove in on Reuben's dick, making the guy squirm and groan from the sharp, sudden pleasure of it.

The Sheriff focused on Walt to say, "Y'know, we're gonna want at least two cum shots out of him."

Walt stopped sucking long enough to say, "I ever let you down?" before plunging back onto Reuben.

"You said we've got 'em till Friday, right?" Oren asked, wary.

The Sheriff nodded. "This guy and his buddy fucked everything up, so all you boys get to have your fun."

Oren smiled and said, "We like that."

Walt pulled back, leaving Reuben's dick quivering, and chuckled, adding, "In prison, he'd take 'em when I was done with 'em and show 'em what fuckin's all about. Real tag team shit."

"They were ours, after that." He stepped closer to the Sheriff, eager. "Is the little guy the other one?"

The Sheriff shook his head. "You'll see which."

"Don't really matter. I just like to keep little Jews like him for days. And days..."

"He's Muslim."

"Oh." Oren frowned, suddenly confused. "They got the same kind of dicks as Jews?"

The Sheriff snorted and exited. Man...sometimes he despaired for American education.

In Room 3 he found Theo lying on the bed, wrapped in a towel, bound and gagged and also blindfolded. And conscious. Jude was seated next to him, wrapped in a towel that barely covered him, showing off smooth, solid muscles and hairless arms...and he was reading.

The Sheriff raised an eyebrow. "You think you're foolin' me with that book?"

Jude held it up to reveal it was a cookbook...for crock pots.

"I'm hungry," he said, "so started up a pot in the shower."

"You brought a fuckin' crock pot with you?"

"It was already in the room. As was this volume, and there were veggies in the fridge. Strapped it down. Should be done in an hour. There's even bread to go with it."

"Shit...make a list of what you used and clean the pot, when you're done. I gotta replenish it. What about the boy?"

He did not use that word about Theo lightly. His trim body and smaller stature than the other guys was one reason for the Sheriff to see him like that, as was his young face.

"I washed him," Jude sighed. "Oh-so-slowly. Oh-so-completely. Oh-so-carefully. In ways that caused me extreme pleasure." He ran his fingers over Theo's nipples, making the boy cringe. "Too bad he's not available. He's exactly what I'd have kept when inside. Especially due to this." He lifted Theo's towel to show off his lovely dick. "He grows quite nicely, and his tush is the epitome of the word."

"You want a bonus? He stays a virgin."

"I don't know...I mean, sex is a powerful incentive..." he started, then saw the Sheriff's glowering expression and quickly added, "...but money is so much stronger."

"Keep it that way."

Room 4 had Emilio lying naked on the bed, his hands bound above him, his ankles bound to its foot. He was awake and gagged. Kilo and Sinder were in the room, both in just their briefs and, again, a couple of very obvious erections pressing against their undies. The Sheriff noticed Emilio's nice-looking dick was halfway erect and gleaming, probably from saliva. The horror in his eyes confirmed the Sheriff's suspicions.

"God, you boys're all jumpin' the gun, here," he snarled.

"Jus' primin' the pump," said Kilo as he fondled himself.

"Don't get carried away," the Sheriff chuckled. "Your buddies might not appreciate it."

"So he *is* one we get?" asked Sinder, like a happy puppy.

"So long as you don't get too much too soon."

"Can we at least take the gag out?"

"Mouth don't matter none," added Kilo.

The Sheriff huffed. "If you wanna risk it."

The two men giggled and grabbed at each other, Sinder saying, "Then we can give him another shower."

"Might be hot water, this time."

"That works lots better."

The Sheriff grimaced and exited. This was something he did not need to know about.

He saw the camper van was running and waiting, so he went to the back door, opened it, and looked inside to see Oscar, Juan and Tómas lying on the couches as if they were sleeping. All were covered with light blankets to hide their bindings and nakedness. The Sheriff closed the door, went up to the woman who was driving and said, "Take 'em through Naco. I got it set up, there. You know where to go, after that, nice and easy. AC to the max. These guys didn't do nothin' to warrant this happenin' to 'em. I'll let the Mayor know they're comin'...but I want you to give the bastard another message from me, face-to-face. He got lucky, this time. As for the other two...they'll be brought down, once the boys're done. How he handles it is up to him."

She frowned. "I hear one of 'em's his son-in-law."

The Sheriff snorted. "Well...if he wants us to keep him longer, all he's gotta do is ask. But if he wants him sooner? He can fuck off. It's his own goddamn fault this shit came down. He should've told Hunter no when he started his greedy-assed little dance. Go down for one guy an' come back with seven? That's total bullshit. But I'll handle Hunter. And I can guarantee you one thing...that *son-in-law* and his fuckin' cousin ain't gonna do jack shit like this, again. I'll send him links to the videos."

She smirked. "Can I see 'em?"

The Sheriff laughed. "Crazy ass bitch. I ever said no to you?"

She giggled with delight and they fist-bumped, then she put the camper in gear and drove through the tunnel.

The Sheriff got back into the honey wagon and they continued on up the road.

TWO

By the time they reached the RV park, the Brutal Men had finished the veggie goulash, Jude had washed the crock pot, and Reuben and Emilio had been manhandled in ways they'd never experienced before. The Sheriff had Emilio, Reuben and Theo transferred into his SUV. All three now appeared to be unconscious, but he still had them blindfolded.

"You get some GBH in 'em?" he asked Jude.

The man nodded. "Not much, just enough to make them sleepy. Here's the list of what I used for the goulash."

He offered a slip of paper. The Sheriff gave it to the honey wagon's driver, saying, "Buy these and put 'em in Room 3 before you return this to the film set." He handed the guy a couple of twenties and the honey wagon headed on. Then he told the Brutal Men to follow him to a Home Depot, in their cars.

Elias, Kilo and Jude had come together in Elias' souped-up Impala. Sinder was on his motorbike. Walt was in Oren's car, so off they went in a nice little caravan.

And Oren made sure to be following Sinder, for one very basic reason. "He has got the nicest ass," he said to Walt.

"Who?" asked Walt, feigning innocence.

Oren motioned to Sinder.

Walt nodded. "It's his legs. They're real. So's his dick."

"You had that?"

"Couple times. Nice. Real nice. Uncut."

"And you didn't let me in on it?"

"That's all he wanted, and he knows what you're up for."

Oren snorted. "Like he's a virgin. Maybe I'll make up for it, tonight."

Walt laughed. "Don't think so. Those two beauties'll keep us busy."

"Still think the little Jew was the cutest. Shit — Muslim!"

"Yeah, but I hear he's payin' our fare."

"Oh, well, next few days with those two, I'm happy." He chuckled, long and deep. "This road look familiar, to you?"

Walt glanced around. "It's desert. All looks the same."

"But don't it remind you of another road? Hmm? Few weeks back?"

Walt looked at the white of the land. The black shrubs and cacti. The dark distant hills. The sky filled with stars. Then he laughed, soft and easy. Oren joined in his laughter.

Yeah, it reminded them both of another road.

Oh, did it ever.

Three weeks ago.

Just past midnight.

Oren and Walt had been headed for a weekend of drinking, gambling, and the kind of debauchery only Vegas could offer. Hopefully with some boys from one of the strip shows. They'd just finished taking another dumbass kid up to that penthouse in Phoenix, for the Sheriff. Some kind of deal with the penthouse's owner to supply good-looking guys from the jail for his fun. Now they were off till Sunday evening, when the kid had to be returned to the jail.

What was best? They'd already been paid for this part of the job.

And for keeping their hands off him.

Which was hard to do, dammit. He'd had the sweetest-looking ass and thickest basket they'd ever seen in a white guy. But he had a hood on so maybe his face was butt-ugly. Just to be safe, they'd been good.

Maybe on the way back to the jail they wouldn't be.

So now they were headed up the 93, aiming to hit Vegas by two AM, when the shows ended. Grabbing at each other's crotches as they laughed and drank, first from a bottle of bourbon then a bottle of beer. It was the Sheriff's van and he'd said they could use it, and never mind they hadn't mentioned they'd be heading out of state. He hadn't put any restrictions on it.

They were almost to the 97 when Oren saw the tail lights of a car off the road...hell, completely off the shoulder. Two young men were stumbling around it, one of them cursing at his cell phone. The area was totally deserted that time of night, so it took nothing more than a glance between Oren and Walt to catch what the other was thinking.

Start the debauchery early.

Walt was behind the wheel, so he stopped and backed up as Oren looked out his window to watch the guys and giggle with anticipation. One was about six foot and one-sixty-five, all of it smooth muscle that added form to the jeans and t-shirt he was wearing. Tops sneakers on his feet meant he really was as tall as he seemed, and his blond buzz cut framed a face that was all cheekbones and jaw and cute nose and cupid lips.

His buddy was a bit shorter, darker and nicely built, though not quite as much of a gym rat. He wore tighter jeans that showed off a pair of perfect legs riding up to the kind of ass one can only dream about. His hair was longer, with swirls of it on his arms and peeking over the buttons of his designer shirt. His face gave him more of an Italian feel, with dark eyes and a nose that were truly-upper-class, and he wore boots. He was the one cursing his cell phone.

"I get the brunette, you get the blonde," said Oren.

Walt did not argue, just stopped the van and said, "Bet they're still in college, maybe roomies or frat bro's."

"Makes it even tastier," said Oren as he got out.

"I can't fuckin' find it," the blond was screaming at his buddy. He had that Colorado accent that's a bit flat and touched with country, but only barely. "Why the fuck don't you have a flashlight in the fuckin' car?"

"'Cause I ain't dumbass enough to run off the fuckin' road!" Brunette screamed back at him, then snarled into the phone, "No, I can't fuckin' hear you now!" His voice was East Coast, maybe a Jersey boy.

"Hey, you guys all right?" asked Oren as he approached.

Brunette looked at him, furious. "Does it fuckin' look like we are!?"

Blondie came staggering back to the car. "Dammit, Zack, the guy's offering help. You always gotta be such an ass?"

Walt's eyes locked on him as he came around the van's nose, and he smiled. *Oh, yes...all mine....*

"Sorry," Zack said, still pissed. "But this fucker wrecked my car!"

"Well, it's not like you could fuckin' drive it, condition you were in."

"And you weren't? A fuckin' monkey could drive straighter'n you!"

Walt caught a whiff of whiskey on Brunette and sent Oren a quick signal that the guys had been drinking. He giggled and wandered over to their car, flashlight in hand, just as Blondie scrambled up the embankment.

"I don't know what happened," he said, his words slurred. "I was drivin' fine then suddenly we're off the road and at a dead stop and — "

"You were texting!" snapped the Brunette. "Drunk, drivin' and texting! Shit! How come your phone had bars and mine don't?"

"'Cause I put my money towards equipment and not a car that ain't worth a shit!"

"My dad gave me this car, and if you've fucked it up..."

While they argued, Oren looked under the car and grinned. The front right tire was dug into the dirt. No way to just back it out.

Walt had gone to the back of the van and was opening the doors. Oren quickly joined him, saying, "They're lucky not to've flipped."

"Gives me new respect for Beemers."

"They aren't gettin' it out without a tow..."

"Got ya," said Walt, holding up two rolls of packing tape, to Oren's delight, before turning to the guys to call, "Hey, hey, calm down. Don't look like much damage. I bet if we jack up the front, we can use a chain I got to pull you back on the road. Then we'll see if anything's really messed up."

"I don't have a jack," said Zack. "I've got run-flat tires."

"We got one that should work," said Oren.

"You think?" said Zack, hopeful. "My dad didn't want me to bring the car out here. Said this'd happen, so if I can just..."

"Let's see what we can do," said Walt as he winked at Oren, then he slipped one of the rolls of tape in his pocket and headed back to the BMW. He tossed the flashlight to Blondie. "Why don't you and I keep lookin' for your phone while Zack and my buddy work on the car?"

Blondie nodded and headed off, the flashlight beam sweeping before him, Walt following.

Zack headed to the back of the van. "Really appreciate this," he said. "Can't even get roadside service to respond."

"Middle of nowhere," said Oren. "Middle of the night."

"No shit. First car to pass in ten minutes."

"Excellent."

And Oren whipped a strip of tape around Zack's mouth and pulled tight. He gasped, tried to cry out and instantly began to fight, but Oren had the upper hand. The feel of Zack's nice full body twisting against his own nearly drove him crazy with lust. He wrapped an arm around Zack's neck then quietly

Kyle Michel Sullivan

snarled in his ear, "Be smart, be smart. I could break your neck if you don't stop. I won't hurt you. It's your pretty blond buddy we want. Just put your hands behind you and I'll leave you alone. C'mon. Be smart."

But Zack kept struggling...until he was close to blacking out. He began to go limp, so Oren shoved him onto the floor of the van and whipped tape around his wrists and bound them tight, then yanked a bandana from his pocket and wrapped it around his mouth. Zach tried to fight back but couldn't coordinate as Oren pushed him into the van and wrapped more tape around his ankles. Now he was immobilized.

Oren stepped back to look at him...the curve of his legs bound at the ankles, his hands taped behind him, his ass so inviting...this was so much like heaven, he had to give the guy a smack on his butt before he closed the van's doors. Then he looked around and saw the beam of the flashlight sweeping the ground and caught a glimpse of Walt slipping up behind Blondie.

Oren giggled and jumped to catch up to them.

Blondie heard him coming and glanced back to see Walt right behind him. "I'm not having any luck."

"I am," Walt said, then he grabbed the neck of Blondie's t-shirt and hugged his arms around his chest to immobilize him. Oren bounced up to them, pulled a bandana from Walt's pocket and jammed it into Blondie's mouth just as he started to scream.

He fought harder than Zack had, which only made Oren's dick needier...and Walt's damn near explode from the beauty of it all. But it also made it harder to slap the tape over his mouth to hold the rag in...though he finally did. Oren then looped tape around Blondie's wrists, barely avoiding being kicked as the guy twisted and grunted loud curses. Walt and the guy fell to the dirt, but soon his feet were bound, as well.

Oren lifted Blondie up, revealing his t-shirt had torn open and down one shoulder, showing off a nice pair of pecs and lovely tits surrounded by softy downy hair. It was so beautiful, Oren had to lean in and suck on one.

Blondie howled and squirmed and snarled at him, but Oren grabbed under his arms and Walt took his legs and they carried him to the van, fighting and struggling, and flopped him beside Zack.

"So now what?" asked Oren.

"Get off the road and have some fun?" Walt asked, not even thinking about joking.

Oren sneered, "You wanna get started on 'em both?"

"Not yet. Got a game I wanna play. If you're up for it."

"What's that?"

"You know it." Then he cast Walt a secret wink.

Oren grinned and said, "Oh, right, I like that one."

Walt climbed into the back of the van, then Oren closed the doors and got behind the wheel. He drove up to the 97 crossover and turned around to head back towards Phoenix, the guys fighting and cursing in the back.

There was a rest area about ten miles down the road, all gravel and no facilities but a picnic table or two. If any trucker had stopped there, they'd be sound asleep and the van could park well away from them. They pulled in to find a couple of semis at the far end and no cars. Oren stopped well away from them, put up a sunscreen and climbed into the tail to find Walt lying between the guys, left hand groping Zach, right hand fondling Blondie, despite their cursing and attempts to twist away from him...and damn, they looked pretty that way.

"Smorgasbord," Oren chuckled.

He knelt beside Zach and Walt let him take over massaging the guy's crotch.

Zach tried to squirm away, but Oren straddled him then all but tore open his jeans to show he was wearing a pair of CK briefs...and oh, did he look gorgeous in them.

Walt focused on Blondie, sucking from one exposed tit to the other as he fondled the guy's crotch. He kept muttering, "Pretty...pretty," as he rubbed his own erection against the guy's left leg.

Oren nudged him, asking. "You still wanna play the game?"

Walt cast him a glance and smiled, nodding.

"Okay," said Oren. He forced both guys to look at him as Walt returned to sucking on Blondie's nips. "Here's the deal. One of you is gettin' fucked, and we don't care which."

Both guys jolted and struggled and howled that they were into that sort of thing, but to no effect.

"I'm gonna suck on you," Oren continued, looking at Zach before turning to focus on Blondie. "And my buddy is gonna suck on you. First one to cum gets a pass on gettin' fucked. We'll work you for ten minutes. If neither of you cums, you both get fucked. How's that?"

Both of them shook their heads, horrified. Oren chuckled.

"Good. Ready when you are, buddy," he said to Walt, giving him a swat on the ass.

Walt rose to straddle Blondie's thighs, sighing with a deeply satisfied smile. "Got the timer set?"

Oren prepped his phone and showed them all — ten minutes.

"Starting at first lips," Walt continued, then he tore Blondie's shirt open, all the way, and pinched both of his nips before running his hands down the guy's abs. Nice abs. Covered with blond down. Very picturesque.

Blondie did not agree. Not one bit. He twisted and bucked at Walt, but could not keep the man's fingers from toying with his navel and drawing up his sides and circling his nips, again.

At the same time, Oren unbuttoned Zach's shirt, stopping at the bottom button, then spread the shirt open to reveal a full set of pecs swirling with hair and a treasure trail leading to heaven. Not solid abs, like Blondie, but not fat or sloppy, just male. Beautifully male. He trailed his fingers over Zach's nips, so soft and brown, then down the treasure trail to finally caress the elastic band of the CKs. Pull it lower. Lower. Revealing a thick bush of pubes that surrounded the base of what promised to be an elegant dick.

Walt quickly unzipped Blondie's jeans to find he wore a pair of EA silk briefs.

"Oh, fuck, I want these," he muttered.

Oren looked and chuckled. "Have fun gettin' 'em off. Together?"

Walt looked at him, saw he was toying with the CKs and nodded. He gripped the EAs and, in unison, they pulled the briefs down to reveal both guys' dicks.

Zach's was nice and fat, circumcised and with a glorious helmet. Behind it was a pair of ripe balls in desperate need of milking.

Blondie's was longer and slimmer, but well-formed and uncut. His pubes were sandy-colored and his balls were scrunched up to his scrotum.

Walt and Oren each massaged their guy's dick and balls for a couple minutes, testing them, examining them, playing with them, just to see how they would react. They tickled with their fingers, and pulled and rolled and caressed in ways that would make any man go wild...and to their victims' horror, they began to respond.

Zach's was growing thicker and readier, so Oren had an idea he'd been down blowjob lane, before. His dick flipped from side to side as he tried to wiggle away, but all that did was make it seem like it was begging to be taken.

Blondie's wasn't getting bigger, but Walt's manipulation of his balls had caused them to drop, a little, and his dick would shudder at each touch. Looked like he would be a show-er, not a grow-er.

Oren held up the phone, said, "Three, two, one," then hit the timer and both he and Walt dove in on their respective guy's dick.

Zach reacted to Oren, fast, his dick soon full and fat in its need. Oren knew how to work it, too, sliding up and down its sides with his lips and tongue, sucking over the head, rolling his balls gently with his fingers, diving in halfway down the shaft to whisper over and up then using his free hand to pinch and flick at Zach's nips. He was overwhelming the guy with exquisite moves, taking him into uncontrollable need and desire.

But Walt...he knew how to give blow jobs. Oh, did he ever. Blondie may have started semi-flaccid, but Walt slowly sucking him into his mouth, his tongue caressing the shaft nonstop and toying with his foreskin as he let his fingers curl around his balls, milking them light and easy, it all brought life to that shaft in ways unimaginable to a straight guy. Walt also ran his free hand up Blondie's treasure trail to swirl his fingernails around his nips, first one side then the other, lightly dancing over the down. Almost scratching him but not quite. By the end of the second minute, Blondie had proven he actually was a grower in the dick department, and his now solid erection curled up and back, his head fat and red and tender, his balls shivering from Walt's touch.

Oren chuckled and recorded Walt's work on his phone and shifted to catch himself sucking on Zach, then back to Walt and return.

Within a couple minutes, Zach gasped and groaned and cried out and jolted and shoved his dick deeper into Oren's mouth, making him back off just as a geyser of cum shot out his slit. Thick and creamy, it leapt up a foot before flopping back onto Zach's shirt and belly. Then another and another as Oren laughed and continued stroking the shaft and fondling his balls.

"I win!" he cried. "What will your friend, here, say?"

A second later, Blondie howled and tried to twist away from Walt but it was too late; he also shot a wad out. Not as intense as Zach's, nor as rich-looking, but no question what it was. Most wound up in his pubs and on his jeans, with a little on his belly; Walt kept it from flopping down on the guy's silk undies.

Oren and Walt looked at each other, chuckling deep and growly, then leaned across to kiss, full tongue and hard and sloppy, and pinch each other's nips through their shirts.

"Shit, yours tastes good," Oren murmured when they broke apart.

"It's yours mingled in," Walt whispered back.

"Oh, fuck...fuck...wanna race?"

Walt nodded then turned back to Blondie, pulled out a pocket knife and opened it, then grabbed his EA briefs at the right hip and sliced through them. He did the same to the left hip and yanked them off the guy. He held them up, like a trophy, howling, "Souvenir!" Then he shoved them in a pocket.

Oren laughed and flipped Zach onto his belly. The guy screamed and struggled as Oren then yanked his jeans halfway down his thighs, revealing his CKs.

"Want my knife?" Walt asked.

"Don't need it," Oren laughed as he grabbed the seam of the elastic and tore it open then ripped the CKs off and tossed them into a corner of the van before stopping to gaze upon the guy's amazing ass. Round and perfect. Hair swirling over it, light and elegant. Oren massaged it, over and over and over, loving the feel of it. Not the firmest ass ever but smooth and ripe and lovely...so lovely he dove in and stuck his tongue into Zach's hole, bringing a shriek of horror from the guy.

Walt used the phone to record Oren rimming Zach, who struggled but could not avoid him. He pounded his feet on the van's floor, his boots making sharp knocking sounds, so Walt moved to sit on them. That put him directly behind Oren's ass, so he grabbed it with one hand while still recording over Oren's shoulder, with the other.

Oren jolted up and snarled at Walt, good-natured. "You think you're gonna fuck me?" he growled.

"While you fuck him? Wouldn't mind doin' that, again."

"You got your own bitch; use that."

Then Oren sat back, unzipped his pants, pulled out his already very hard dick and spit on it. Walt recorded it over his shoulder, licking his lips. He loved the look of Oren's dick. How long and straight it was. A head that was the epitome of what a head should look like. He'd been hoping for some fun with it once they were in Vegas, before they went shopping for chorus boys, but watching Oren lube his dick with his spit and line it up with Zach's ass and then push it in damn near made him cum without even touching himself.

Zach cried out in pain and bucked to try and get Oren off him, but his captor wrapped his arms around him and used his legs to keep him in place as he pushed his dick in deeper and deeper, loving how tight he was. In seconds he was shifting himself up and down inside of Zach, ignoring the guy's howls and curses and demands, his gingers digging into the guy's skin.

Walt returned to Blondie, who was watching Zach's rape, in horror. He was breathing fast, from fear, making his chest and nips look very inviting. His dick was flaccid, again, and lying back on his pubes in a way that was so amazingly sexy. Walt liked fucking, fine, but he got more pleasure from being face to face with a man...and being serviced by him. Especially since he'd noticed that Blondie had a really nice mouth.

He straddled Blondie's hips. Looked hard at him.

The guy looked back, wary.

Zach's cries of pain had become soft grunts, by this point, as Oren pumped into him with a steady rhythm.

Walt undid his jeans and released his dick from his briefs. He was proud of it, even though it wasn't as lovely as Oren's. Or as large. But it was ready to go.

"You got two choices," Walt murmured. "This goes in your mouth, or in your ass. That's how I got shown what it's all about. When I was in jail. I saw what happened to pretty guys, like you, who got butt-fucked. Bleeding. Trouble shitting. AIDs. But your mouth? You suck it off, use some Listerine and you're done. Nice and easy. So what's it gonna be? Ass?" He held up his right hand, which had the phone. "Or mouth." He held up his left hand, which had the knife.

Blondie looked at him, horrified. His eyes darted between Walt's hands. Then he looked at Oren, who was still fucking Zach, grunting and growling like an animal. He looked back to Walt and indicated the left hand.

Mouth.

"Okay," said Walt, leaning down to nearly on top of Blondie. "But get this — if you say one word or bite me, I'll cut your throat and your buddy's, too. Got me?"

Blondie nodded.

Walt carefully removed the tape around Blondie's mouth, and his lips looked even nicer than he'd remembered.

"Please, just let us go," Blondie said, barely a whisper. "Please. We won't tell anybody. Just let us go."

Walt smiled and said, "We will." Then he flipped Blondie onto his stomach and rammed his dick into him. No way did he trust those teeth.

Blondie screamed but Walt wrapped his arms around the guy's neck, held the blade next to his carotid artery and fucked him, hard, snarling, "This is another life lesson. Don't trust somebody who's already proven he can't be trusted. You came second; you're supposed to be gettin' fucked."

It took Walt no time to work himself up to sensations of the greatest beauty. He loved the feel of Blondie's ass around his dick as he rubbed in and out of it. So tight...like it was grabbing at him. Sending screaming lightning through every part of his body. He looked at Oren to see he was pumping faster and faster, about ready to explode.

Oren looked back at Walt, with a lewd smile, then suddenly rammed hard against Zach and almost howled.

That jolted Walt and he let himself swirl into a climax that was worthy of drowning in, and he came inside of Blondie. Over and over and over as Oren did the same to Zach.

And they clasped hands near the end, like lovers.

Walt smiled at the memory of how perfect that orgasm had been. The tingling from the top of his head to the tips of his toes. How much he pumped into Blondie, whose name he never did find out. How when Oren had pulled back, his dick still hard and dripping, and had used Zach's briefs to wipe off, they'd both found they were still ready to go so had swapped guys and done some more fucking, again, just like in prison. Then cut the guys' bindings and dumped them out of the van and driven away, secure in the knowledge they would never tell anyone they'd been raped by a couple of passing strangers.

What made it even better was how the weekend had been perfect, too. Lots of kissing and groping and fucking and sucking with overbuilt chorus boys...and they'd even made use of the guy they were taking back to the jail, for the Sheriff. That had satisfied them for weeks...hell, right up till now.

They'd checked the news for the next few days, but the only story about the boys was they're been carjacked and beaten and the car wrecked. No one knew who the guys in the van were. They'd gotten away with it.

Now they were headed out to have some more fun. And while the two Mexicans were pretty, deep down Walt had to agree with Oren and hope Sinder would be the one they could have the most fun with, tonight. Or sometime over the next couple of days.

His legs, ass and dick all but cried for their tender misuse.

*****

It was nearly midnight when they arrived in a wide parking lot to find a minivan with tinted windows waiting for them.

"Leave your cars here," said the Sheriff. "Get in the van and put on the hoods. Do not try to peek."

"Been there," said Oren.

"Done that," laughed Walt.

"Usual shit," said Elias.

"Might wanna pee, little boys," the Sheriff said. "It's another hour's drive."

The Brutal Men shrugged and stood in a line to piss against a dumpster. The Sheriff snuck a couple of shots of them as they did it, and had to admit they had been a well-matched crew. They'd worked together so much. Knew each other so damn well.

They got into the minivan, slipped on the hoods, and Elias made certain Oren and Walt sat next to each other and not near Sinder; he'd noticed the looks they were casting him, and didn't wany any trouble, not now. Then off they went.

Fifty-five minutes later, they arrived at a massive ranch-style compound in the middle of the desert. Electrified fences ran its entire perimeter, and the extensive house was three-quarters of a mile from the main road. It was surrounded by a six-foot wall painted in the color of the sand, and inside was a cool, elegant, tree-shaded courtyard with green lawns, sheltered gardens, a huge swimming pool, orange trees bearing fruit, a flowing brook and a house of stone walls and solarized triple-pane glass. Solar panels on the roof provided the energy needed, and complete silence surrounded them. They drove into the courtyard, the gate opening automatically, and were met by two extremely well-built male caretakers in tight shirts, tight pants and boat shoes, wearing balaclavas with openings for the eyes.

Only when the driveway's gate was closed did the Sheriff let the Brutal Men remove their hoods. As they got out of the mini-van, he told them, "Okay, have at it. Just sign these releases."

The caretakers handed each of them a clipboard with sheets of paper that basically said, *Anything recorded here belongs to us.*

The Sheriff already knew they would all sign. They'd been here, before, more than once. Each of them. Sometimes together. Always for the same basic instructions for instances like this.

Do what you want. What happens here is in the strictest confidence. No marks on the merchandise.

They signed, then Kilo asked, "What's the real limit?"

Jude said, "What you askin' for? It's on the paper."

"Actually, there is one," said the Sheriff as he opened the back of his SUV. He pointed to Theo. "You cannot have him, but the other two...well, I gotta return 'em to Mexico...just without noticeable marks. Understood?"

They all nodded, grinning.

"Any food you want," the Sheriff continued, "ask. Same for booze. No drugs. Don't want no performance issues."

Sinder grabbed Emilio's feet and yanked him halfway out of the SUV, saying, "Never had a prob with that."

Emilio tried to kick him but only made Sinder laugh as he fondled the guy's dick and balls. "Neither will you, motherfucker."

Oren draped an arm over Sinder's shoulders. "Does that make you a fatherfucker?"

"What the fuck...you think I got kids?"

"In today's world?" said Elias. "Shit, that's child abuse."

"Almost had," said Kilo. "But when I got sent in, bitch got rid of it."

"Knew all about your fucked-up genes," said Walt.

"Not half as fucked up as yours," he snarled back.

"Now guess who's gonna get fucked-up, again," said Oren as he flipped Reuben onto his belly and gave him a solid swat on the ass. The guy howled in fury, not fear, making Elias smile.

So Oren also remembered Reuben, from four years back, when the dumb fuck was just another eighteen year old punk caught sneaking some X across the border. Of course, he'd sworn up and down it wasn't his, that it had been planted in his car, but he'd still got three years, then paroled and deported after nine months.

Elias had just finished pulling his pack together and was already known as the motherfucker in control of his block, with Kilo, Sinder and Jude to back him up. They'd been getting first dibs on the fresh meat, so when cocky-assed Reuben came rolling in, he was theirs...and they took him in the showers. That was the first time Elias had invited Oren and Walt to join their company...and oh, had they proven their worth. Especially Walt and his amazing fucking tongue. That had come in very handy on days when the guards were being bastards and they couldn't go hunting...and really needed some relief. He'd known white guys who loved dick, but not like Walt.

What was funny? Elias actually believed Reuben *had* been set up. He'd been on his way to a party in Yuma, with his girlfriend, and let slip the name of the guy who told him about it. That same white-ass motherfucker was the reason Elias was inside. He and Kilo had been camping down in Playa Blanca, where they didn't have to worry about being black and could just enjoy each other's company. They had struck up a chatty acquaintance with the guy, on the beach. Nothing asked. Nothing suggested. Except...*why cross back into the States at Mexicali when San Luis was so much easier and closer to home?* That kind of shit.

Kilo hadn't cared one way or the other; he just liked being with Elias...and vice-versa. But like a dumbass, Elias had decided a San Luis crossing would save them a couple hours, on the drive. Instead, they'd been caught with five bags of coke in the trunk of his car. The bastard must've snuck it in when they were running around in the surf. Both he and Kilo had been handed ten year terms. After all, who's going to believe a couple of black guys over a nice white man's claim of innocence?

Elias sighed at the memory. It wasn't as if they hadn't been in prison before. When you're black and white men run the system of justice, it's like your home away from home. So they hadn't argued or blamed anyone but the asshole who set them up. And they had watched each other's back. Built up their crew. And when Kilo made parole six months before Elias, he'd restarted a *working acquaintance* with the Sheriff...something both of them had done with him, many times, before...and their new boss had been kind enough to make sure that white-assed bastard suddenly wound up overdosing on his own shit. And now? Now they were doing fine.

Just fine.

He smiled as he watched Sinder and Walt carry a struggling Emilio into the house, led by one of the caretakers. That guy was way prettier than Reuben, if a bit older. But he was also a virgin, if he caught the Sheriff's drift right. That sent a tingle straight to his balls. He loved initiating virgins into the real world.

He chuckled and took Reuben's arms as Kilo grabbed his legs, then they carried the guy after the others. Oren and Jude trailed behind, yammering and jostling each other the whole way like a couple of frat boys.

Yeah, Elias thought, *tonight was gonna be a good night.*

*****

The Sheriff sighed as he watched the men enter the house. Everything was ready for them, and he knew they'd come through. No pun intended. Well, maybe a little. He motioned the other caretaker over and nodded to Theo.

"I'll be back for him, in the mornin'. 'Bout ten. Needs to be ready. Better keep him in the guest house, out of reach for them." He looked at Theo, almost tenderly. "Gonna be a long trip, son. But worth it, in the end. Better'n what your buddies're gonna go through. But them's the breaks."

Theo shook his head and tried to say something, but the blindfold and gag shut him down. The caretaker picked him up as if he weighed nothing, despite his struggles. His towel slipped off. The Sheriff grabbed it and lay it over his groin then headed over to the minivan.

The driver was standing next to it, watching the caretaker carry Theo into a side building, shaking his head. He fired up a cigarette.

"Much chatter on the way?" the Sheriff asked him.

"Glad that kid's not goin' in the house," the driver said. "The things they wanted to do to him...shit..."

"Bunch o' pissant pups still thinkin' they're alpha dogs."

"Am I still back, tomorrow?"

The Sheriff nodded. "Two. Two-thirty. In the 350, high-top. You know that air field at Salome?"

The driver nodded.

"I'll be there, waitin'."

"Not here for the pickup?"

"Don't need to be," he said, almost sad. "They'll have 'em ready."

"Then I better get some sleep," the driver said as he crushed his cigarette. He got in the minivan and drove away.

The Sheriff returned to his SUV, pulled out his phone and sent a text. To the new Coordinator.

At set at compound. 1 for 10 am, virgin; 2 for Mexico, punished; 6 for the arena, no virgins.

The response: *Well done.*

The Sheriff sent a *thumbs-up* and followed the minivan out of the compound.

THREE

To say the desert compound was massive would be a massive understatement. The first time Elias dropped off a human play-toy for a client, he'd estimated the grounds were at least a mile square and the house about eight-thousand square feet. Built from stone mined in the area, its windows a dusky shade to help it blend in, with terra-cotta tiles for the roof and thick canvas shielding half the pool, the other half being inside the main building, it was impressive beyond belief and damn near invisible, even from above. The Master Bedroom, where he usually delivered those he brought in, was a five minute walk from the main door, past a massive living room, massive dining room, massive game room stocked with a screen large enough for a small multiplex theater, massive bathrooms with showers that could hold a dozen men his same size, and several bedrooms that were not all that much smaller than the Master one. He liked coming here. Liked being allowed to stay a few nights, even if he had to be a client's toy for a while. He'd learned long ago, sex is just sex, whether it's with a man or a woman...and he'd serviced both.

He knew Kilo and Sinder felt pretty much the same way as him. Jude, almost. That's something you learn about your buddies, in prison. That's why they all had the same tattoo that Reuben carried, a crude design hand-carved into their skin; they had put it on each other, like a brand. That was why he and Kilo were carrying Reuben into the bedroom. They wanted to start their fun with someone who had no idea what was coming and would fight them to the fullest extent...and that would be Emilio.

Elias had to admit, it was the struggle that excited him, the most. Kilo just enjoyed fucking. Sinder would happily participate, but it wasn't the most important thing to him; he loved forcing the new guys to suck him off.

Of course, considering how Walt and Oren had looked at Sinder, that could wind up being fun, too. Watch those two try to take him down, again. See who wound up fuckin' who. This'd be a wild and crazy couple of days.

They entered the Master Bedroom and had to walk another hundred feet to a bed that was big enough for all eight men. They tossed Reuben on it, then Elias straddled his torso to hold him in place as Kilo knelt beside them and removed Reuben's gag and blindfold, slowly, carefully.

Reuben coughed and choked and gasped and hacked, so Elias ran his hands up over guy's chest and flicked his nips, saying, "We know what you tried to do, so your buddy gets it, first."

He heard someone approaching and looked around to watch the second caretaker enter with a folded bundle of clothing.

"Cool," said Kilo when he saw the man. "We're gonna play a game with this one."

Elias maneuvered himself off Reuben and took the clothes from the caretaker, giving him a nod of thanks. He dropped them on the bed and picked up a pair of cargo pants. He chuckled.

"So what you think? Sneakin' in to have some sin? Or? Guy walkin' by, gets taken to try and then he's shown why he's all ours, no lie." He tossed the pants on the bed and smiled at Reuben. "Shower. Dress yourself up. Get some sleep. Play along if you wanna leave here on your own two feet. You know how it goes."

Then he grabbed Reuben's wrists and tore the tape off, without a bit of trouble.

Reuben finally said something in Spanish, but Elias slapped him and smacked his tattoo. "Don't pull that shit. You remember me."

"No...I...I..." Reuben choked out. "I don't do that, no more."

"Then you shouldn't of fucked up," said Kilo.

Then Elias and Kilo left the room. The door closed behind them; no handle on the inside so Reuben could not get out.

They met Jude in the corridor. "They're waitin' for you. In the gym."

"They wanna work him out?" Kilo asked.

Jude shrugged. "Just wound up there."

"Bullshit," said Elias. "Sinder's up to somethin'."

The three strolled back towards the living room then took a turn to where the indoor part of the pool was. Next to that was an open space holding two massive total body workout machines, side by side, with additional benches, rows of dumbbells and stationary bikes. Two walls joined at a corner were nothing but windows reflecting the room, thanks to the darkness outside.

Sinder and Walt were holding Emilio upright, and he was still struggling. Elias had to acknowledge the guy had a lot more stamina than he expected. Oren was leaning against one of the machines, his eyes hard on Sinder's ass.

"What's the plan?" Sinder asked.

"Why me?" Elias asked. "You brought him here."

"Gym seemed like a good startin' point."

"And you're lead dog," said Walt, licking his lips.

"Watch yourself, bitch," Sinder shot back, then he gave Emilio a good looking-over. They guy was nicely built but not from a gym. More like a runner and aerobics or cardio moves. He could've built up like them if he wanted. He felt up Emilio's dick and balls. Nice size. Uncut like his own. Decent spread of pubes up his abs and swirling down onto his legs. Not the biggest ass, but he was still going to be a lot of fun.

Elias went to a closet door, saying, "First, cut that shit off him and get rid of the gag and blindfold. He can holler much as he wants." He looked in the closet to find workout clothes, board shorts...and a black Speedo. "Oh, look at this. I bet you'd be real pretty in it, chico. Gives me lots of ideas."

He took the Speedo back to Emilio. The gag and blindfold had been removed and his hands were being cut free, now.

"You speak English?" Elias asked.

Emilio looked at him then looked around. He rubbed his mouth and worked his jaw then said, "What you do? Why I am here? What you do with me?"

"Somethin' to wear," Elias said, then he tossed the Speedo at Emilio. "Don't want you just...oh, hangin' 'round."

The guys laughed.

Emilio caught the Speedo, then once his feet were free, slowly pulled it on, working it up his legs and over his slim ass to cover himself, shaking and glancing between the men, saying, "Please, I...I have wife. Children. I am not to be here...this is mistake..."

He showed them his wedding ring.

Oren grabbed him from behind, wrapping his arms around him in a tight grip, saying, "Says who?"

At the same time, Walt groped Emilio's crotch. "Got a lot to offer."

Emilio cried out. "No, please stop...I do not do this..."

"Not from what I hear," said Jude, toying with one of the man's tits.

"You know how to swim?" Sinder asked Emilio.

"No, please...I...si...yes...I...I..."

Sinder laughed and shoved both him and Oren into the pool.

It was the shallow end, so Oren kept hold of him, plunging all the way to the bottom then standing up and swinging Emilio around before letting go. By the time Emilio was back on his feet and wiping water from his face, the rest of the men had stripped off and were jumping in to join them. Oren laughed and pulled his soaked clothes off, as well.

The Brutal Men surrounded Emilio. Shoved him against each other. Pulled at his arms and legs. Grabbed him. Pinched his nips. Groped his crotch, fondling his dick and his balls...and his ass. Howled for joy when he staggered back into one of them. Lifted him up and threw him across to each other, like a pool toy. Spun him around to kiss him, deep and hard. Full tongue. Kicked his feet out from under him, making him plunge underwater.

Emilio howled in terror as they kept on and on and on. Sometimes losing his balance and falling. Other times being pushed underwater, with his mouth held open, and forced to accept one of their raging hard dicks. Choking when he came back up for air. His cries echoed around the pool as the water sloshed around them.

Elias found himself lost in how lovely Emilio looked, soaking wet. The black Speedo tight around his hips. His trim body fitting it perfectly. He looked like a diver off one of those cliffs in Mexico. He'd always thought that was one of the wildest, sexiest things he'd ever seen, and now he had a guy like that here to own and be owned. It was like a dream come true.

He motioned for Sinder to hold Emilio's left arm and for Jude to take his right, then he kicked Walt, saying, "I know how much you love dick."

With no more need of encouragement, Walt dove between Emilio's legs and yanked the Speedo down from his crotch to reveal his flaccid penis. Then he got to work, doing everything he could to make him hard. The guy twisted away, cursing, so Kilo wrapped his arms around the man's right thigh. Elias grabbed the other as he kicked Oren, next. "And you eat ass, right bitch?"

He and Kilo held Emilio prone in the water, Walt still sucking on him hard and heavy. Oren laughed and dove under to tear the Speedo at one of its seams, leaving it caught around Emilio's other leg, then he grabbed the guy's ass cheeks and rammed his tongue into his hole.

Emilio screamed bloody murder, thrashing and splashing and cursing as best he could, but he was unable to stop the assault. Their hands pinched his tits. Mouths kissed him. Teeth bit him. No matter what he tried to stop the onslaught, it continued and continued. And to his horror, the magic of Walt's lips and his fingers milking his balls almost as hard as his shaft got his dick to growing...and growing...

Oren popped up for air then dove back down to continued digging his tongue into Emilio's ass.

The others laughed and howled like wild dogs, joining Emilio's cries. Sinder and Jude now sucked on his tits, using their tongues and teeth. Elias and Kilo mauled his thighs. Soon, Emilio lost all control of his body as it responded to the exquisite sensations shooting through him...and he drew close to firing.

Elias noticed and kicked Walt, saying, "Don't get him off, yet. Take his leg."

Elias handed Emilio's leg over to Walt, saw Oren was having way too much fun, and shoved him away.

He broke the surface to Emilio's right.

Elias positioned himself between his legs, his fat dick raging hard.

"C'mon, bitch," he said to Oren, "eat a man." Then he smacked his own ass in the water.

Oren smirked and dove back in as Elias shifted closer to Emilio. He grabbed Walt by the hair and pulled him close, saying, "Now, you suck every last drop from this motherfucker."

Then he positioned his thick massive head against Emilio's hole and pushed in.

Emilio shrieked and fought him. "No! Stop! You tear me in half!"

But Elias gripped his hips as he kept pushing into him, Kilo holding tight to his leg and waist, Walt holding his other leg as he sucked on him.

"Oh, you really are a virgin," Elias all but purred, now pushing in and pulling out, not too heavy or too hard. He liked how Oren's tongue kept working him. Then he leaned in to bite Walt's ear, saying, "I want him to cum while I'm in him."

Walt chuckled. Elias began rubbing deeper, into Emilio, loving every second of it as he groped his ass to hold him in place and pumped and shifted and pushed back against Oren's tongue.

"Just like takin' a new bitch in prison," Elias growled as he went faster and faster. "You know how many I done? Can't count that high."

Emilio howled and wept and struggled. Blood stained the water. He finally stopped fighting, just grunted and whimpered in pain. His dick got harder and harder and harder under Walt's insistent lips. He began to clench around Elias' shaft, pulling tight, making the man nearly scream for joy as he pumped faster and faster. Sinder and Jude pinched Emilio's nips and Walt sucked more and more intensely as Kilo caressed his belly and thighs. Oren reamed Elias like a madman, making him go even crazier with his anal assault on the guy until suddenly Emilio gasped and tensed and jolted and cried out and Walt moved back and held his dick straight...and he fired a long, hard stream of cum up and up, until it slowly, slowly fell back onto his face. Another shot up to fall on his chest and more onto his abs and into Elias' hair.

Sinder and Jude laughed for joy at seeing his explosions...until Elias felt a wave of euphoria come screaming up from every part of his body, tripled in intensity by Oren's tongue, and he slammed harder into Emilio and fired his load, grunting and growling like a wild animal, sloshing water everywhere, tinted even more red with blood as he pumped deeper and deeper into him, not stopping until he could take no more. Then slowly, slowly, slowly he let his arms encircle Emilio's torso and draw him up completely from the water and away from Sinder and Jude and Kilo and Walt to embrace him like a lover, kissing his nips and his abs and his navel and his neck as his own dick slipped out of the guy's ass, and finally, finally, he forced a kiss on him.

Emilio let him do as he wanted. Let his hands go where they wanted. Let Elias' mouth stay on his mouth, rough and hungry, still. He was numb and blank. When Elias finally released him...he silently slid back into the water. Would have gone under, but Sinder took hold of him. Kept him afloat. Drew him close to caress him and kiss him. Then guided him to the pool's ladder, draped him face down over it and ran his hands over the man's rear, tenderly.

"Yeah, ain't much there," he said, "but damn, it's pretty."

He kissed each cheek. Took a little nibble of the skin. Sighed, deep down.

"Been a long time since I had one like this," he murmured. "Smooth and soft and almost a virgin."

His dick was raging, so he positioned it between Emilio's legs and slowly pressed deep into him...and slowly pumped in and out of him.

Emilio whimpered but did not even try to squirm away. Instead, his hands gripped the bannisters to the ladder, tight and shaking, and he tried to hide his face behind one of the bars as he wept.

Walt and Kilo slipped over to join them, caressing Sinder's ass and legs and back and nips and neck and head, kissing and pinching and fondling and groping.

Oren now used his tongue on Sinder's anus, stroking himself as he toyed with the man's balls, getting him ready...trying to time it to the just the right moment where he could take the next step and enter Sinder with his dick.

But suddenly the guy jolted and came inside Emilio and he pulled out and shoved Oren away. Then he grabbed Walt and forced him to suck the rest of his cum out of him. He laughed then grabbed Oren by the hair and shoved him to Walt's other end, snarling, "Fuck him, bitch."

By this point, Oren was too hard and ready to go, so he shrugged and shoved himself into Walt, and they did him up like a spit roast, keeping Walt underwater, only letting him pop up on occasion to gasp for air. Then Sinder came, again, as Oren fired into Walt.

While they enjoyed themselves, Jude took a turn inside Emilio, with more tenderness but still a near animalistic need to him, growling into his ear, "You love it, you love it, you love it, you know you do," while fondling him and letting short sharp yelps of pleasure explode from him until he came.

Emilio said nothing. Just continued to weep.

Kilo was last. He rammed himself into Emilio, making him cry out, and clawed at his sides and around at his nips and bit his neck and back and shoulders and rammed him harder and harder and harder, finally pulling him off the ladder to hold him around his waist and float back, still pumping into him as he mauled him...until he shoved him off and shot his cum into the air like a geyser, howling for joy. Then he plunged back and underwater and swam to the other end of the pool and returned, like an Olympic champion.

When they finally dragged Emilio from the water, he was in shock. Barely responsive. They carried him into the adjoining shower, cut the remains of the Speedo off, and Sinder held him bent over...and forced him to take him in his mouth as the other guys washed him without an ounce of tenderness.

Elias stood back to watch, and had to smile, remembering all the times they'd taken a cute cocky white boy or full of shit Latin lover in the showers, in Matagorda. Newbies were the best. Virgins. usually. They never knew what to expect till it was all over and Walt had done his thing on them, as had Sinder. Then the pack had owned them. Like now. As Sinder came, again, and cum trailed down Emilio's chin. Ah, the good times.

They finished washing Emilio then dried him, just as rough and hard. Elias finally pushed them aside and took him from them and caressed his whole body before tenderly picking him up, like he would a lover. The guy let the man carry him all the way into the Master Bedroom without a sound.

In there, they found Reuben crouched on the farthest corner of the bed. Still naked. Elias snorted and tossed Emilio next to him. He bounced against the headboard, still out of it, and wound up face down. Reuben just watched, shaking and unable to move.

Walt leaned against Elias' chest, batting his eyes and doing a fake whine of, "Don't I get somebody to fuck?"

Elias laughed and looked at Reuben, then shrugged a nod as he said, "Should've got dressed, bitch. Might've saved you till the mornin'."

Walt whooped and jumped onto the bed to grab Reuben. The others joined him. Reuben tried to scramble away, then fight them, but six against one was overpowering. They yanked him to the foot of the bed, face up, and held his arms above him and spread his legs apart and let Walt suck on him until he was moaning from pleasure, despite himself...and finally let his cum spurt up and all over his belly and chest.

Then they yanked him back and flipped him face down onto the bed, beside Emilio, and held him there, spread eagle, as Walt slammed into him.

Reuben still struggled, but in a way that was vague and silent, as if he'd surrendered to the inevitability of his rape.

It didn't take Walt long to unload. He growled and hissed and shoved into him as deep as he could, over and over and over. When he finally stopped, breathless, and pulled out, he muttered, "I been primed so hard for this since this mornin'. Oh, but there ain't nothin' like it. Nothin'."

Then each of the others took their turn in Reuben, who continued to accept it, silently. By the time they were done, dawn had just begun to break.

Elias found handcuffs in a dresser drawer so chained both Emilio and Reuben to the headboard, lying facing each other, then he and the guys collapsed all over the bed and fell into a deep sleep.

No need to plan for tomorrow; they had a couple more days to play with these two.

But Elias had to admit, this had been a damn good start.

*****

The Sheriff arrived just after nine AM and peeked into the Master Bedroom. He saw eight naked men lying about, next to and on top of each other, a panoply of beautiful arms, legs, backs, torsos, asses, dicks and tattoos. He was actually glad they had enjoyed themselves.

The two caretakers came up and he asked, "Sleepin' gas?"

Both caretakers nodded.

"The two that're handcuffed, they need to be cleaned up, dressed an' fed. They're goin' home, an' I want 'em awake when they go. I'll give 'em the low-down 'fore their ride leaves. The rest...keep 'em under; they're goin', as is. Driver'll be here about two...two-thirty. Make sure they're shackled."

The caretakers nodded.

"The boy ready?"

The caretakers led him to the guest house, into a smaller version of the Master Bedroom. Theo was lying on the bed, unconscious, dressed in neat tan slacks, a burgundy silk shirt, funky socks and loafers, looking like nothing more than an adorable college kid taking a nap between classes.

"I heard from the airport," the Sheriff said. "His flight's ahead of schedule. He wasn't touched, right?"

The caretakers shook their heads, no.

"Good. He should make our client real happy. Finish him up. I'll take him with me."

The first caretaker picked Theo up. The other opened an oblong box that looked like a coffin. It was cushioned and had a headrest. He was laid into it, tenderly, and the lid was latched on. They carried it to the Sheriff's SUV and slipped it in the back. It just fit, with the rear seats down.

Then the Sheriff headed back into the house and allowed himself one last look into the Master Bedroom. He sighed. He really was sorry to see these boys go. They'd been good to work with, and he'd once actually considered using Walt to replace Hunter. But when he and Oren had raped those two boys, three weeks back, they'd jeopardized the whole Network. Would've been better if they'd killed them and buried them, in the desert. Or at least worn condoms and masks or balaclavas. But taking the son of a state senator and letting him see your face the whole time? When you have a goddamn record? DNA on file? And leaving his torn briefs in the back of a county van? That had GPS tracking?! That was too goddamned stupid to be allowed.

Now the FBI was searching for Oren and Walt. The Sheriff had been able to deflect it for a bit till they worked out how to handle the situation, but the only way to truly end it was to get rid of anyone they'd been associated with. Work it so it looked like they'd run off to Mexico. Because once shit like this gets caught in the flowing shit-stream of justice, it wouldn't stop till it reached the Network...and that could not be allowed.

So now the Sheriff had to break in some new guys, and he hated the trouble it would take. The care in selection. A real pain in the ass.

He'd also have to figure out another way to get rid of Hunter without pissing anybody in the Network off. They liked his work. The merchandise he offered. He had good taste.

And didn't he fucking know it?

Well...there was plenty of time for that, now that he was off to LA. Dealing with that whiny-ass Coordinator. Who didn't like Hunter, either, but who did like the money he was helping them make...and who said he could keep an eye on him, in that town.

Yeah, good luck on that.

The Sheriff sighed. That's the problem with this business. Once the cash gets good, you don't wanna mess with it. You get lost in maintaining how good things are instead of planning for the future.

But maintenance was for losers, and the Sheriff was no fucking loser. He knew change was inevitable, and it was best to prepare for it. That's what had kept him ahead of the game.

He let himself take one last look at the group of beautiful men slopped across the bed. The idea of what these men had done, last night, and knowing how much they had enjoyed themselves...and that it was all on video from a hundred different angles...he could almost understand being gay. Because there was something truly erotic about how these young vibrant bodies were so casually nestled against and on top of each other. Almost prurient...and at the same time, innocent. He actually felt sorry for having to send them to the arena.

But it was what it was, so the Sheriff headed on to his SUV.

"Ain't like they're my men, no more," he thought. "They're the Network's."

And that was just too damn bad.

THE END

ABOUT THE AUTHOR

Kyle Michel Sullivan is a writer and self-involved artist out to change the world until it changes him...as has already happened in far too many ways. He has lived in London, Los Angeles, San Antonio, El Paso, Kansas City, Honolulu, Austin, Houston, and now resides in Kenmore, NY.

He has won multiple awards for his screenplays and has all sorts of books available — from sunshine and light (*David Martin*) to cold and dark (*How To Rape A Straight Guy*, which has been banned a couple of times) to flat out crazy (*The Lyons' Den*) to mainstream (*The Alice '65*). *Underground Guy* was a return to his cold, dark roots, followed by his first SF-Horror novel, *The Beast in the Nothing Room.*

He uses Tolstoy as his guide and tries to build characters as vivid and real as possible. He has a lot of fun doing it mixed with angst, anger, and amazement ... but that's the lot of a writer.